I0761938

PARADOX

LUCY ROY

Paradox

Tessa Avery Book Two

ISBN (hardcover): 978-1-7353385-3-8

ISBN (paperback): 978-1-7353385-7-6

ISBN (ebook): 978-1080246908

Cover art: Denise Worisch

Edited by: Jenifer Knox

Formatting: The Swamp Goddess, Book Formatting and Design

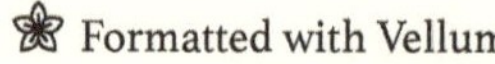

To my daughters.
Sorry, kids, but these mermaids aren't sparkly.

ALSO BY LUCY ROY

Tessa Avery Series

Chaos

Paradox

Entropy

Half-Blood Rising

The Valkyrie's Bond

The Valkyrie's Calling

The Valkyrie's Triumph

Stay up to date!

Instagram: @lucyroywrites

TikTok: @LucyRoyWrites

Lucy Roy's Facebook Page: https://www.facebook.com/AuthorLucyRoy/

Newsletter: http://bit.ly/lucyroynewsletter

Lucy Roy – A Reader Group: https://www.facebook.com/groups/LucyRoyReaders/

Twitter: @LucyRoyAuthor

Major Greek Gods

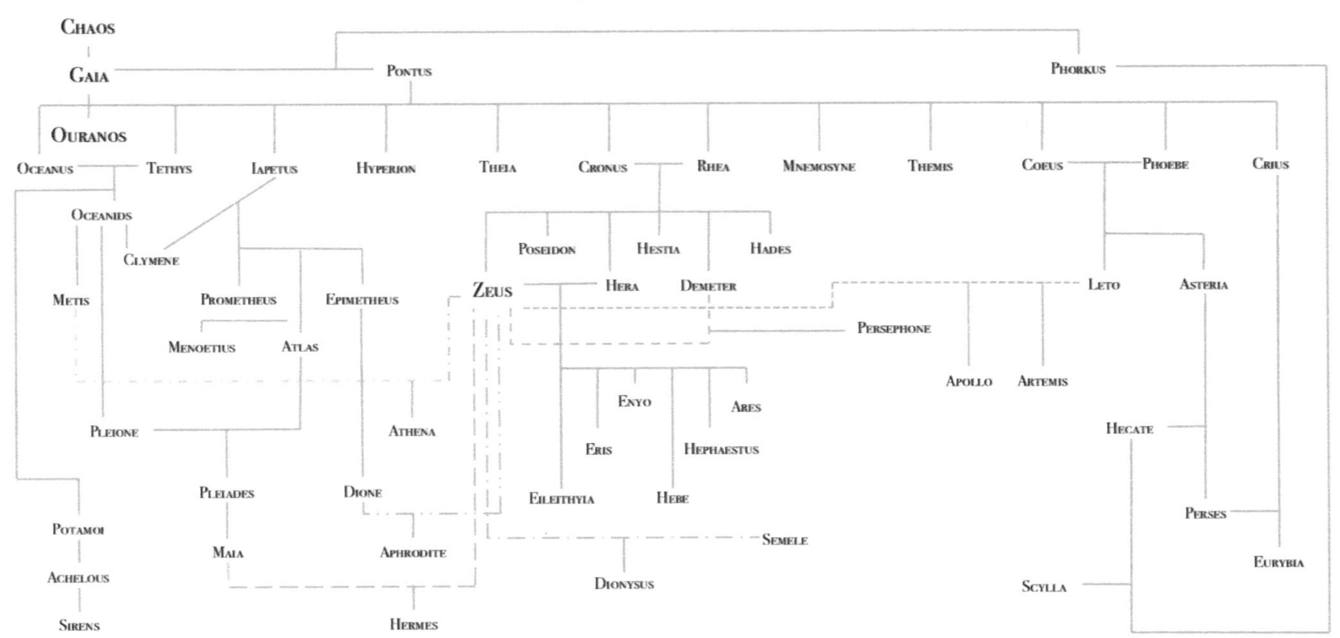

1

TESSA

When I was about ten, a blizzard came through my little hometown of Renville, Pennsylvania. After going through all the DVDs we'd stockpiled over the years, John and Analise had insisted we watch the *Lord of the Rings* trilogy. I grumbled and complained because I was ten and annoying, but I finally gave in when Analise promised to make blueberry pancakes for dinner.

I had rolled my eyes when John complained about the discrepancies between the books and the movies while Analise gushed over how handsome Aragorn was. And of course, Legolas, the beautiful blond elf, quickly became my first movie crush.

I mean, who doesn't love a guy who can sling arrows like that?

Even at ten, the gravity of Frodo's journey resonated with me. I was in awe of his bravery as he made his way to Mordor, where he would likely meet certain death. Yet despite being surrounded by trained warriors and faced with impossible circumstances, he had succeeded. He'd destroyed the ring, saved the world, and lived to tell his tale.

And in the end, he went home, hoping to return to his old life.

Yet who could endure what Frodo did and just pick up right where he left off?

No one, that's who.

Now, sitting in Zeus' living room, taking in the faces of my family and friends and recalling vague memories of both my old life and new, I was beginning to feel a bit like Frodo when he'd sat as his desk, penning the words to his book as he tried to figure out how to move forward after so much had changed.

The strands of my life as a Titaness were scattered about like bits of thread on a sewing room floor, trying desperately to force themselves into the tapestry of my life as an Ischyra, a human gifted with immortality and the powers of the gods of Olympus. I had been irrevocably changed, and not a single person in my life—god, Ischyra, or otherwise—could help put things back in their place. I couldn't simply go back to being Tessa, Titaness of Olympus, twin sister to Atlas and daughter of Iapetus and Clymene any more than I could go back to being Tessa Lynn Avery of Renville, Pennsylvania.

Somehow, I had to be both.

But first, I had to rescue my brother, and it was starting to look like that might not be an easy feat.

Propping my elbows on my knees, I pressed my fingers to my eyes. After a moment, I let my hands drop to my lap and stared at Zeus, aghast at the information he'd just shared with me.

"You're telling me my brother has been wasting away in a cave in *Morocco* for nearly three thousand years?" I asked.

Our leader cleared his throat and shifted in his seat, then looked around the room at the others who were present. I followed his gaze and noticed everyone seemed equally as uncomfortable as he did.

Turning accusing eyes on my brothers, twins Prometheus and Epimetheus, I frowned. "You two could've teleported in and taken him ages ago! Why wouldn't you have gone to him?"

"When we told you he was inaccessible, it wasn't because we couldn't find him," Prometheus explained. "He refuses to see reason. He's been punishing himself for your death, and for our mother's."

"But it wasn't his fault," I protested. "Iapetus and Cronus are the ones responsible."

Epimetheus walked around the sofa and knelt in front of me, pulling my hands into his. Green eyes—the same as mine and our brothers'—bore into mine. "We all know that, Tessa. That's never been a question. Please believe that."

"I just don't understand why he's punishing himself so harshly," I whispered.

"He's your twin," Apollo said. He tapped a long, pale finger on the crystal wine glass in his hand. "Your other half, born of the same energy. Did you truly think the loss of your energy wouldn't affect him profoundly? As a twin myself, I can say it would certainly affect me."

"You and Artemis are hardly the poster children for strong sibling relationships, so I find that hard to believe," Prometheus said.

"Be that as it may, the point remains the same. Were my twin to die, her soul destroyed, my psyche would be affected. That's just the way it is."

"But I wasn't really dead," I argued. "My soul wasn't destroyed, it was just hidden away. I'd expect grief, not insanity."

"Chaos is another dimension, Tessa," Hestia explained, her blue eyes soft. She tucked a lock of fiery red hair behind her ear and matched my position. "That connection would have been damaged, at the very *least*, the moment Hecate sent your soul there."

"Fine, but once I was reborn a human, shouldn't that have fixed things?" My heart ached at the thought of my brother—strong, unshakeable Atlas—deteriorating in a cave all these years due to my absence.

"It's possible," Nate said, running a thumb along the back of my neck. "The likelihood is, he was too far gone by then to know what was real from what wasn't."

"Have any of you attempted to speak to him?" I asked.

"We have," Prometheus confirmed. "He won't see us. The first time we went, not long after Zeus lifted his sentence, he said we were too painful a reminder of the sister he'd let die. We've gone back many times over the centuries to no avail. The most recent attempt, about two years ago, ended with Epimetheus nearly losing an arm."

My eyes widened as I turned back toward Epimetheus. "He attacked you?"

"He's become unstable over the years," Athena explained, her tone gentle. "At first, he was simply reclusive. Content to live in solitude. Now, though...well, he hasn't actually spoken to anyone in centuries, that we know of."

I shook my head. "That still doesn't explain why you all didn't just go into that cave and take him."

Apollo sighed and sent a look toward Zeus.

I looked back and forth between the two of them, brow furrowed. "What?"

"We—" Zeus cut himself off when Hestia cleared her throat. "I felt it...unwise to bring him back here in such a state. His instability on the mountain would have likely caused more trouble than—"

My eyebrows shot up.

"Than he's worth?" I snorted. "Unbelievable."

Hera let out an annoyed huff, her dark, exotic eyes flashing. "Oh, for the love of us all. He's one of the strongest warriors to ever come off this mountain. It doesn't matter why he's there or how much of a lunatic he's become; his place is *here*. Tessa, go to Morocco and bring your damned brother home." She sniffed and adjusted her deep-green skirts. "I don't see why you're all making this so complicated."

"She wanted details, Hera," Athena said. "With what she's been through, she's entitled to that, at least."

Hera waved a hand dismissively, and the gold bracelets on her slender wrist made a musical tinkling sound. "Deal with the details later. Just go and get this thing done already. He'll be much easier to handle now that his twin has returned."

Apollo set his glass on the coffee table and looked at me. "I have to say that I agree with Hera on this. You're almost certainly the only person that will get him out of that mountain without further harm to himself or anyone else. Sitting here talking about it won't make it any more, or less, true."

I let out a heavy breath and stared down at Epimetheus. He was my older brother by a good hundred years, and even though my memories had barely begun to filter in, I knew, without question, he would tell me what I needed to hear.

His eyes searched mine, then he smiled softly. "You're his twin. If anything can bring him home to us, it's you."

I struggled with his confidence in me. At best, I felt like I was half of who I used to be. Confusion as to who I was still swirled in my mind, and I had no idea how long it would take for the rest of my memories to sort themselves out. I loved my brothers and wanted us all to be together again, but Atlas had been in isolation for almost three thousand years.

What if he was damaged beyond repair?

The ache I'd felt moments earlier started working its way through my chest as I realized just how possible it was that I would never get my twin back. I'd barely had time to remember the man I'd shared a childhood with, and now I was being faced with the task of saving him myself or risk losing him for good.

I closed my eyes against the pain. Quietly, the words he'd whispered to me flowed through the chaos in my mind.

Never doubt your greatness, Tessa. You will move mountains.

I'd heard those words since the moment I stepped through the portal into Olympia, and if ever there was a time I needed Atlas' faith in me, it was now. Yet here, thousands of miles from where he'd holed himself up in a mountain, that faith felt nearly nonexistent.

'Don't think like that.'

A smile flickered across my face as Nate picked up on my thoughts. As a Coercer, his ability to communicate telepathically was far stronger than the other gods, so my mental walls, the walls that kept everyone else out, barely had to falter for him to get a sense of where my mind had gone.

"Okay." I rubbed my hands on my legs nervously. "It looks like we're going to Morocco. When do we leave?"

No one spoke for a moment, and I saw Epimetheus slide a glance toward his twin.

"What?" My eyes darted between them. "You just said—"

Epimetheus gave me a sympathetic smile. "Tessa, we want to go as soon as possible, but don't you think you should take a bit of time to acclimate? You've only just gotten your memories back."

"She barely *has* her memories back, you mean," Apollo muttered.

"So?" I frowned at the twins, ignoring Apollo's usual snark. "Our brother needs our help. I don't need my memories to know that."

Nate slid a hand down my arm and twined his fingers through mine. "He's right. Give yourself a few days, at least, before making plans like this. See if more of your memories come back first."

"I have to agree with Nathaniel," Zeus said, sounding reluctant as he drummed his fingers on the arm of his chair. There was a shrewd look in his eye that made me shift uncomfortably in my seat.

"We've been trying to get Atlas to come out of that hole for years," Hera argued. "Why wait any longer?"

"Because there's a better chance of success if she's got her damn wits about her," Zeus snapped.

"Tessa, dear, a few days won't make a difference," Hestia said. "You've barely woken up. Why not see if your mind clears a bit more? Train up a little, just to make sure you'll be able to defend yourself, should something go wrong."

I looked at Athena, the beautiful brunette sitting beside me, and one of my oldest friends. I arched a brow in question.

She smirked. "You wouldn't have to ask me twice, you know that."

"At least I've got one ally," I grumbled.

"Two impetuous goddesses going hunting for an unstable Titan is the last thing we need," Prometheus said.

"Oh, but what about your friend, that Mary girl? We could bring her," Athena suggested, her eyes twinkling. "If she and I are to be friends, this would be a wonderful bonding experience."

"That's a great idea." I grinned. "She'd be so upset if she missed out on this. Eric, too, probably."

"Lovely, it's settled then."

"That's just what we need," Nate muttered.

"Enough!" Zeus snapped.

I pressed my lips together, trying to contain my laughter, and Athena's gray eyes sparkled as she looked at her father.

"Tessa, I understand that you are still becoming accustomed to your true self, but I would encourage you to try to leave some of your human proclivities behind. You cannot include recruits in a mission like this," Zeus said.

I arched a brow. "I can't change who I was the last eighteen years, Zeus. I won't just write them out of my life."

"Then take them out to dinner. Get roaring drunk, for all I care. It doesn't change the fact that recruits have no business coming on this trip."

"But why not?" Hera challenged him. "This—what's her name?"

"Mary," Epimetheus said.

"Yes, thank you," Hera said before continuing. "This Mary girl will be going off to battle soon enough. Surely a trip to some dusty mountain won't kill her."

Zeus let out a sound of frustration. "For once, can you not challenge me?"

"Can we get back to the matter at hand?" Apollo interrupted.

"I thought this was the matter at hand?" Athena frowned up at him. "Weren't we discussing who will be joining us on the mission to retrieve Atlas?"

"No," Apollo said slowly. "We were discussing when Tessa would be *able* to make that trip. She and I seem to be the only ones who think she's capable now, despite her... limitations."

"I think she's capable!" Athena countered.

"No, you just want to be contrary. There's a difference."

"Alright, let me put an end to this," I said, holding up a hand to quiet the bickering siblings. "Although I'd like to leave immediately, I acknowledge that some of you have made valid points. I need to take time to get my bearings. I'll give you three days; four, at most, but then I'm going to get Atlas, whether I have your support or not. In the meantime, I'll brush up on whatever it is you all think I need to brush up on."

"That sounds fair," Nate said, squeezing my hand. "No need to rush."

I looked at Zeus. "You said Hades will be here tomorrow to talk about the security of Tartarus?"

Once again, the strange rippling feeling went through my mind as the last time Hades had been brought up. This time it was accompanied by the brief flash of memory, too quick to latch on to.

"Yes, he should be here midday," Zeus replied. "He's currently speaking with his guards and inspecting the security of the walls and wards that surround the realm. We need to be certain your father and Cronus have no means of escape."

Tensing, I tried to control the panic that set in as I thought of them escaping. "Has he said anything about whether my father and Cronus are still secure?"

"As of yesterday, they were still locked in. We'll get more details from him tomorrow, though."

Something in Zeus' tone sent unease through me. "Okay," I said, brushing off the odd sensation. "Until then, I have a few things I need to address."

"And you should probably get some rest, as well," Hestia said.

"She just slept for two days," Prometheus pointed out.

"My mind is also trying to bombard me with almost a thousand years' worth of memories," I told him. "My body isn't tired, my brain is."

"Alright," he said with a sigh, then rubbed his hand across his face. "I was just hoping—"

"She needs to rest if she's to find herself, Prometheus," Hestia interrupted. "Let's not push too hard today."

I smiled at her appreciatively as Epimetheus stood and held out a hand. I let him pull me to my feet, then he wrapped his muscular arms around me in a crushing hug.

"I can't tell you how happy I am that you're here, Tessa," he whispered, his voice raspy with emotion. "Take all the time you need. I'm not going anywhere."

I hugged him back, then pulled away and pressed a hand to his cheek. "Neither am I."

He grinned, then handed me off to Prometheus, who took me from his twin and placed a hand on each shoulder and looked me in the eyes. "Don't feel pressured to do things faster than you're able. As much as I want our family back together, I need you to be ready for that to happen."

"Thank you." I wrapped my arms around his waist and let him envelop me in a hug. "I promise, we'll all be together soon."

"I know," he whispered. "Now, go do what you need to do. We'll speak in the morning."

TEN MINUTES LATER, Nate and I stood outside of the dorms, listening to the voices of recruits in the courtyard.

Turning to face him, I shook my head. "I can't go in there. Who knows what they've been saying about me?"

Nate eyed the entryway warily, then raked a hand through his sandy-brown hair.

"I'm not crazy about you being thrown into the midst of that group, myself," he admitted.

Just then, Eric Anderson, one of my oldest friends, came rushing through the gate. His shaggy blond hair, blue eyes, and lean, muscular build gave him a classic surfer look, but the wide, relieved smile he wore as he jogged toward me was almost boyish.

"Tessa! I thought that was you." He gave Nate a tight-lipped smile in greeting. "You don't want to go in there. Come on, I'll take you guys around the back."

"Why?" I looked past him toward the courtyard, where voices still chattered loudly.

He put his hand on the small of my back and started leading me toward the side of the building. "So far, only Mary, Yana, and I know what actually happened to you," he explained quietly as he took us down the narrow alleyway between the dorms and the apartments next door. "Everyone in there is waiting for you to make an appearance."

"Who's in there? What are they saying?" Nate demanded as we came out on the lawn that spread out from the back of the building.

Eric rolled his eyes and let out a sound of annoyance. "About a dozen recruits with nothing better to do than wait around in the courtyard gossiping any time we're not at training. So far, I've heard you've tried to kill Charlise and Zeus, stolen Zeus' power, you're pregnant with Zeus' baby, you're trying to overthrow Olympus, are in cahoots with the rebels, and probably a few other things that I haven't heard yet."

My eyes widened. "What the—are you serious?"

Nate chuckled. "That's far less creative than I would've expected."

"Yeah. The three of us have been taking shifts when we're not at training, waiting to catch you before you came in."

"How come?" I asked.

He cocked his head in the direction we'd just come from. "Because those dicks in there are annoying."

A sense of relief washed over me at his words. The last time Eric and I had spoken, he'd asked me out and I'd turned him down. At the time, I wasn't sure if our friendship would be able to recover. Despite Mary's earlier reassurance that my friends were still my friends, a small part of me had worried the rift between me and Eric—the result of my rejection of him—would increase, once he realized I wasn't the girl he'd grown up with.

Overcome with emotion, I threw my arms around his waist and hugged him. "You don't know how happy it makes me to hear you say that," I whispered.

He tightened the embrace and rested his chin on my head. "I know, Mary told us," he murmured. Pulling back, he smiled down at me. "You don't have to worry about us bailing on you, Tess. That'll never happen."

Quietly, Nate knocked on the window. A few seconds later, Yana's face was pressed to the glass. When she saw us, she flung open the window.

"Tessa! Thank the gods! Come, get in here quickly."

Nate grabbed me by the waist and boosted me up. I pulled myself through, falling to the floor between Yana's bed and my own, grunting as my elbow smacked into the hardwood.

"Isn't your kind supposed to be a bit more graceful than that?"

I looked up and saw Mary leaning over me. Her light brown hair was wet and hanging over her shoulder, dripping onto the floor. She'd changed into ripped, black jeans and a white sweater with patches of pink lace sewn on in random places.

I scowled at her. "Yes, well, apparently, I haven't figured that part out yet, so leave me alone. You're dripping on me."

She reached down and helped me stand, then went about wrapping her hair up into a bun as Eric and Nate hoisted themselves through the tiny window.

Yana stood at the foot of her bed, still in her uniform, with her hands on her hips and her wide blue eyes narrowed in my direction. Her black hair was still up in the tight braid she always wore for training.

"This window gets far more use as a doorway than I anticipated," she observed, pursing her lips. She met my eyes and gave me a hesitant smile.

There was an awkward silence as my friends and I looked at each other. Finally, I sat down on my bed and pulled Nate down next to me. The others perched on Yana's bed, facing us.

"So...how are you feeling?" Yana asked after a moment.

"I'm alright. Still a little weird in the head."

"I still cannot believe it," she said, shaking her head slowly. "How does this kind of thing happen?"

"Scheming between Titans and witches, apparently," I replied before diving into the full story. Nate and Mary supplied a few details they'd learned while I was still asleep.

"You remember it all, then?" Yana asked when we finished our tale, her eyes wide. "Your life before?"

"Hardly anything yet. The more recent stuff is the clearest, but I'm hoping it'll all come back quickly."

Eric cleared his throat. "So...how old are you, anyway?"

Mary smacked his chest with the back of her hand. "Rude!"

He winced and pulled back. "What? You were both wondering, too."

"I certainly was," Yana said in her deadpan voice.

"About four thousand years," I replied, laughing. "A little less."

"That's her chronological age," Nate added. "Technically, she's only been alive for about seven hundred years.

"Geez. Here I thought Nate was the cradle robber," Mary muttered, then shifted curious eyes to Nate. "How old are you, anyway?"

"I'm just over three thousand," he said, his lips wobbling with humor.

Mary narrowed her eyes. "How much over?"

He winced. "About thirty-two hundred. I honestly couldn't tell you the exact number."

"So, this is life now," Yana said, her expression amused. "Friends who are so old they do not know how old they are."

"Where will you be staying now?" Mary asked. "I'm assuming you aren't going to be coming back here."

I thought I detected a note of sadness in her voice.

"I can't. It's just not safe," I said. "Titaness or not, Menoetius might still be able to dream walk into my head, and Nate has the best chance of waking me if that happens."

"Gods, you would think being a Titaness would give you some immunities to that bastard," Eric grumbled.

"He's a Titan, too, and I'm still not one hundred percent yet. Not even close." I looked back and forth between them. "You guys are really okay with all of this? I honestly expected you to run for the hills."

"It is weird, I will grant you that," Yana admitted. "I certainly had some conflicting feelings at first. Mary has told us that you are still you, though."

I nodded. "She's right, more or less. There's just a little bit more of 'me' to deal with now."

"That's part of why we had Mary stay with you when you were asleep," Nate explained gently. "Hestia and Apollo were able to give her the entire story."

Mary grinned. "Apollo was super grumbly about it, too. He's kind of a dick, isn't he?" She raised her eyebrows at Nate.

A smile twitched at the corners of his mouth. "As he is my brother and an Elder, I'm going to refrain from answering that."

She nodded knowingly. "Uh huh." She turned her smiling eyes back to me. "Besides, how many recruits can say one of their best friends is a Titaness? Oh, and can I have your bed? It's way more comfortable than mine."

"Nice to see your priorities are in order," I said dryly.

"I wouldn't be me if they weren't."

2

TESSA

When Nate and I left the dorms a short while later, I felt like a weight had been lifted from my chest. At some point between saying goodbye to Mary at the palace and arriving at the dorms, I'd convinced myself that my friends would want nothing to do with me. Hearing confirmation that they were still the same loving and loyal people they'd been a few days earlier brought me a huge sense of relief.

"I think I need to start training," I said to Nate once we'd arrived back at his cabin.

He toed off his shoes and fell back onto his overstuffed leather sectional. I dropped the suitcase of belongings that I'd packed from my room, then sat down next to him and rested my head against his chest.

He began twirling the end of my braid around his fingers. "So soon?"

I shrugged. "No time like the present, right?"

I looked down at my wrist and brushed a thumb over the three wavy purple lines on the inside of my wrist; the mark of an Ischyra. I'd had it since birth—my human birth, that is—and now they represented a part of me that I desperately wanted to cling to.

"I don't think going back to training with the Ischyra is the best way to go about that," he said cautiously.

"No, of course not. And stop reading my mind," I said, looking up at him teasingly.

"I'm not," he said, pulling me back against him. "I'm just pretty sure I know where your thoughts are right now."

"I just feel useless." Absently, I drew circles on his chest, focusing on the way my finger moved so I could force myself not to focus on what I was actually feeling. "Everyone else has their power and knows how to use it, and here I am with this awesome gift that I've barely scratched the surface of."

"Who did you train with before you were an Ischyra?"

"My brothers, I guess." I sat up and scrubbed my hands over my face in annoyance. "I don't remember."

He gave me a sympathetic smile. "You will, just give yourself time. Until then, I'll help however I can, and I'm sure your friends will do the same."

I snorted. "A Titaness being trained by Ischyra. Who'd have thought that's where my life would be?"

"You can learn from anyone, love. Rank doesn't matter here."

"I know. It's just...a few days ago, the thought of training with two Titans was both thrilling and terrifying. Now I'm the Titan, and the last thing I want is to be terrifying."

He cupped my cheek in his hand and gave me a soft kiss. "Your friends will never see you as terrifying, Tessa. Deep down, you know that."

I tapped my thumbs together on my knees as I considered the idea. "I don't know, we'll see. They have their own training to do; they don't need to be wasting time with me."

"That's entirely your call, but I can assure you, they won't consider it a waste of time." He stood, then took my hand and pulled me to my feet. "Come on, let's go get some rest."

The last thing I felt like doing just then was going back to sleep, but I knew he was probably right. Like I'd told the twins, my brain was tired. I felt better now that I'd spoken to my friends, but my mind still felt a bit like mush.

When we got into his bedroom, I dug through my suitcase and pulled out my pajamas and bag of toiletries, then went into the bathroom, closing the door behind me.

Away from the distraction of conversation with friends and family, my mind began to resume its own little civil war, causing a dull ache to bloom in my head. Flashes of color and light danced through my thoughts, old and new memories asking for recollection.

I let out a heavy sigh, then turned on the shower, letting the water heat up as I stared at my reflection in the mirror above the sink.

Thanks to Hecate's spell, my appearance was the same now as it had been in my previous life. My blonde hair, green eyes, and golden tan skin looked just as they had when I was a Titaness. I was unsure why she'd crafted it that way, but I was beyond thankful that she did. I didn't know what I would've done if my face didn't match my twin's.

An array of emotions flitted through my mind and across my features.

Curiosity. Hope. Wonder.

Happiness at having been given the opportunity to meet John and Analise, Mary, Eric, Nate, and all the other people I'd lived through the last eighteen years with.

Anger that my Titan family had been torn apart because of my mother's decision to put my protection over her own life.

I understood why Clymene had done it; I might have even done the same for my own child, had I been in her shoes. But it didn't change the fact that our family had been destroyed as a result.

My brothers had been beaten down psychologically, and I'd missed out on thousands of years of life, only to return just in time to fight a war against the same monster who'd wanted to suck me dry of my power so long ago.

Gritting my teeth, I thought of everyone who'd been party to the recent events of my life. Cronus, Menoetius, and Iapetus for wanting to use me; my mother for choosing to end her life and letting the world think I was dead; Hecate for going along with her plan; Apollo and Hestia for agreeing to guard the truth.

The list went on, and the more I added to it, the angrier I got.

Calm yourself, Tessa.

I flinched, startled by the whispered words in my mind. The voice was familiar and…irritated.

Yet another memory of another time, no doubt.

Regardless of who'd spoken to me and when, I heeded their advice. Anger wouldn't get me anywhere.

I closed my eyes and took a deep breath, willing my swirling emotions to settle, grabbing onto the positive emotions and squashing down the bad.

After a few seconds, I straightened my back, then stared at the girl in the mirror once more, unsure which version of me was staring back. Fear was written all over her face. I dared that fear to challenge my determination, to tell me not to be angry, not to scream or cry or break things and people and gods, until I got all of my fury, grief, and sadness out.

My life had been taken from me, and I had every damn right to be pissed about it.

Taking a deep breath, I forced myself to focus on the good things. I'd been reunited with my brothers. My friends from both lives still stood by me, and there was a man waiting for me in the next room who cared for me deeply. Maybe even loved me.

Despite the changing nature of my life, their support didn't seem to be wavering.

I clung to that, hoping to all the gods that it wouldn't change.

When I emerged from the bathroom a short while later, showered and in my pajamas, Nate was lying on the bed, one arm thrown over his face.

He lifted his arm and smiled when he heard me walk in, then

held out a hand, beckoning me over. I slid in next to him and let him wrap a strong arm around me.

"Hi," he murmured, kissing my temple. "How are you feeling?"

I sighed, breathing in his clean, woodsy scent, and closed my eyes. "I don't know. All over the place."

"How so?"

I shifted so I was looking up at him before speaking. "I'm just so... angry, with all of them. I wouldn't trade the last eighteen years for the world, but gods, I'm so fucking angry."

His eyes searched mine as he brushed my wet hair off my forehead. "Would you like to leave for a while, digest all of this somewhere that isn't here?"

I smiled ruefully. "Only if you come with me."

He put one finger under my chin, tilting my mouth toward his, and brushed his lips gently across mine. When he pulled back, his midnight eyes bore into mine. "Just say the word and we're gone," he whispered.

"Okay." I swallowed back the lump in my throat. "For now... Can you just kiss me again?"

Shifting so we were laying face-to-face, he cupped my face in his hand and drew my lips to his. His kiss was gentle at first, testing, then deepened when my fingers curled in the material of his shirt.

Parting my lips for his, I slid my fingers into his hair and arched my back, pulling his body against mine.

Tears pricked the corners of my eyes as I realized just how happy I was to have him here, and how content he was being here. I needed to feel him close to me, to feel happiness so I could beat back everything that was threatening to unravel inside me. Everything in me ached as I tried to reconcile the unfamiliar feelings of the past with the comfortable, familiar ones of the present. Pushing it all back, I let myself get lost in Nate's arms.

After a few moments, he pulled back and met my eyes, taking in my tears. Gently, he brushed one away, then another, before kissing my forehead. "Get some rest. We can talk more tomorrow."

I nodded, then let him pull me closer to him, tucking my head in under his chin.

"Hey, Nate?"

"Hmm?"

"Thank you."

My dreams started out hazy, as though memories were trying to work their way to the surface while I slept.

I was in the process of trying to coax a memory through, when the dream shifted focus and I found myself standing in the clearing Menoetius had brought me to in our last dream walk. Cheery sunlight filtered through the trees, belying the feeling of doom that permeated this place. Whatever memories had yet to resurface, I knew none of them reflected this small bit of forest in a positive light.

A cloudy sensation of immobility rippled through me as screams of pain echoed in my mind, but just like last time, the thought slipped away before I could grab hold.

Dread washed through me when I realized why I was back here.

"Hello there, Tessa." Menoetius' voice was smooth, and an evil smirk twisted his lips as he took in my expression. He held the same silver knife that he'd tortured me with, less than a week ago, in his hand. It made a soft thudding sound as he tapped it lightly against his dark pants. "Something bothering you?"

"Not a thing," I said, trying to keep my voice from shaking.

"That's good to hear." He took a slow step forward. "Tell me, have you figured it all out yet?"

"Can't you just read my mind and find out?"

His jaw clenched and he eyed me shrewdly. "Mind reading is not an affinity. It's an innate part of an immortal's being. I can't disable your ability to prevent my reading your thoughts any more than I can disable your ability to walk." Realization flashed in his eyes, and he laughed cruelly. "You haven't gotten your memories back yet, have you?"

I narrowed my eyes. "I don't know what you're talking about. And how are you able to do a dream walk if you can't read my mind?"

He laughed, then pointed the knife in my direction. "You've always been terrible at keeping your walls up while asleep, so it's easy to get past the barriers meant to keep me out. I can disable your power in here—" he pointed at the ground with his dagger "—because your mind is weak out there."

I shrugged, trying not to let him see how much his words terrified me.

"So? Have your memories returned yet?" He twirled the dagger around in his hand and smirked. "I'm quite anxious to know how you're handling some of my favorites."

"Of course they have." I didn't bother keeping up the 'I'm just an Ischyra' farce. He knew the truth.

"Ah, wonderful. Then I'm sure you remember my fondness for this place, yes?" He looked around, staring disdainfully at the sky. "It's much lovelier at night, don't you agree?"

My heart slammed against my ribs as Menoetius snapped his fingers and the clearing was suddenly bathed in moonlight. A battle warred in my mind, one half trying to reclaim the memory, while the other half rebelled, scrambling to force it back. Something awful had happened here, something I wasn't entirely sure I wanted to remember.

He took another step toward me, and I felt a sudden sting on my wrists. I glanced down but saw nothing there.

"Your ignorance truly does amuse me."

Nate. Where was Nate?

'Nate!'

Slowly, my oldest brother began to stalk closer. I cast a quick glance over my shoulder and saw the massive tree looming barely a foot behind me.

I tried to shift to the side, hoping to avoid having my back against anything solid, but he was too quick. He leapt forward and grabbed my shoulders, slamming me against the trunk. I hissed as the rough bark tore through the fabric of my shirt. Pain, razor-sharp, wrapped around my wrists and ankles.

"Tell me, Tessa," he whispered, his breath hot as his lips pressed to my ear. "Do you remember your final days? I have to say, of all of the memories I have of you, those are some of my favorite."

I swallowed hard, not wanting to give him any more confirmation that I had absolutely no idea what he was talking about.

"You need to let me go," I said, my voice barely above a whisper.

He leaned back and ran his eyes over my face. I tried to look away from his hate-filled stare, but he gripped my chin in his massive hand and jerked my face toward his. "Tell me...has Zeus told you what he thinks he has in store for me?"

He pressed the tip of his blade to my neck. I sucked in a breath and tried to pull away, then forced myself to remember that the godsbane-infused blade couldn't kill me.

Pain, I could deal with. Maybe not easily, but deep down, something in my mind told me I could do it if I had to.

I gritted my teeth as he turned the flat side of the blade against my throat, pressing it into the flesh. "I don't know what you're talking about. He doesn't tell me anything."

He dragged the blade lightly across my skin. I tensed in anticipation of the pain I knew the poisonous blade would deliver.

"And that son of his? What has he told you? Or have you been too busy being a whore for him to learn anything useful?"

"I don't know anything," I said through gritted teeth, struggling uselessly against his power.

"Don't lie to me, little girl. I know all about you. Zeus thinks he'll use you as a weapon against me, doesn't he? He thinks you can stop me from bringing my father home?"

He pressed the cool blade harder against my neck, just barely breaking the skin.

I struggled against his grip as the godsbane trickled into my blood.

"Even if Zeus did think that," I hissed out, "I wouldn't be much use against you, would I?"

A cruel laugh rumbled through his chest. "You don't know him well at all, do you?"

He turned the blade, letting the sharp tip slice through the thin flesh that covered my collarbone. I was unable to hold back a cry of pain as I felt the knife brushing against bone as more poison entered my body.

A maniacal gleam sparked in his eyes as he dragged the knife across my shoulder and slowly started to dig it into my upper arm. The more I screamed, the brighter his eyes became, full of enjoyment at my agony.

"I bet if I pushed this in just a little further, every single memory of yours would return," he said, a grin slowly spreading across his face. He put more pressure on the blade, and I felt blood slowly begin to trickle down my arm. "Would you like me to do that for you? Wouldn't you rather just get it over with?"

Black dots danced across my vision as the blade continued to pierce my flesh, tearing through my shirt as if it were paper. I pressed my lips together as waves of nausea began to roar through me, and my body rapidly began losing strength. I wanted to scream, cry, try to fight back, but the godsbane was making me weak. Soon, I'd be unconscious. That thought terrified me more than anything.

"I'd step away from her," a menacing voice said.

Menoetius froze, and his smile grew wider. "Hello, little brothers," he said, pressing the blade farther into my shoulder, the pain sending a torrent of tears down my cheeks. It was nearly halfway through my shoulder now. "How nice of you to join us."

I struggled uselessly as my vision began to go red and my breaths started to come in heaving gasps. Again, I wanted to cry out, beg my brothers to help me, but I couldn't muster the strength for more than a whimper.

Without warning, Menoetius yanked the blade out. I screamed at the sudden absence of pressure, and he shoved me to the ground. My chest heaved as I tried to see through the fire that was tearing through my body. Slowly, my vision began to clear, and the pain began to dull to a burning ache.

"She's going to wake up now, and you're going to leave her be," Epimetheus growled.

"My, my." Menoetius wiped the tip of the blade on his pants, smearing my blood across the fabric, then slid the weapon back into its leather sheath. "Is baby brother finally growing a backbone?"

I cast a glance toward Epimetheus and just barely saw his eyes flick toward Menoetius' midsection.

I lowered my eyes and saw that his sheath was less than a foot away from me, the handle of the knife tilted slightly back. Willing myself not to vomit, I pulled my body into a crouch.

"I was hoping you might finally tell us why you insist on tormenting her," Prometheus replied, his tone almost conversational.

Before Menoetius could respond, I jerked forward and grabbed the knife, using what strength I had to shove it into his side, jamming it to the hilt.

He roared in pain as the godsbane flowed into his body.

I felt a rough shaking sensation and a hard pressure in my mind. The scenery around me began to waver, and Prometheus and Epimetheus disappeared from view.

Just as Menoetius pulled the knife from his side and spun toward me, I woke up.

3

TESSA

Back in Nate's room, I groaned as I touched my hand to my shoulder. When I pulled it away, my palm was coated with blood. The nausea had subsided for the most part, but my blood still prickled as the last of the godsbane burned itself out of my system. Memories beat at my mind, but I shoved them away with enough force to make me wince. With the pain and fear of Menoetius' attack still coursing through me, whatever memories he'd been hoping I'd recall were the last thing I needed to be dealing with.

Nate's face was grim as he walked out of the bathroom, holding a wet rag. He crouched in front of me, then gently pressed it to the deep, slowly healing wound on my shoulder.

I hissed as the cool water touched the fading injuries but stayed still as he continued to wipe the blood from my skin.

Nate met my eyes, his own filled with fear and worry. He opened his mouth, but bit back whatever he was going to say, then looked to my brothers who were standing in the doorway. "He's going to keep doing this, isn't he?"

Prometheus raked a hand through his short, dirty-blond hair and sighed. Both he and Epimetheus were still dressed for bed, hair mussed from sleep. "Yes, I think he will."

"Why, though?" I asked. I took the rag from Nate and held it against my shoulder. The wound had mostly closed, but the cool water helped ease the residual sting of poison.

Epimetheus sat down next to me and took my hand. "What did he say to you before we intruded on the dream?"

"Not much. He asked about my memories and wanted to know what I knew. He seems very concerned with what Zeus plans for him." I looked up at Nate. "He knows about you, Nate. Somehow, he knows we're in a relationship."

"What?" Nate looked at my brothers, confused. "How is that possible?"

"How does he know about *her*, would be the better question," Prometheus stated, folding his arms across his chest. "He may not have known who she was during that first dream walk back in her dorm room, but he clearly knew of the existence of a Mimic for at least a week. We've known her true identity for two days, and before that, I assumed only a handful of others knew what her powers as an Ischyra were."

"No, he knew about me longer before that," I said, staring down at the floor. "I didn't realize it until the dream walk last week, but he's been in my dreams for a while. He definitely knew who I was."

Nate sat down on my other side. "How do you know?"

"I caught flashes of someone there, in the periphery. The dream where I was sparring with Atlas, he was there in the woods."

"Are you sure that wasn't just part of the memory itself?" he asked.

I thought for a moment, recalling the dreams I'd had before I'd shattered Hecate's spell, then shook my head. "No, definitely not."

"How do you know?" Prometheus asked.

"I just know. The rest of the dream felt natural, the way any memory would. When I noticed someone else was there, it didn't feel right. Kind of like something had been superimposed onto it."

A silence hung over the room as they processed my words.

"Come with me," Nate said, his tone resigned.

He reached down and took my hand, and the four of us teleported onto Apollo's front lawn.

Nate didn't bother knocking before opening the wide double doors into Apollo's stark white home. He led the way down the hallway toward the French doors that opened into the living room.

"Apollo!"

A door opened next to us and Apollo stepped out, still wearing his pale gray suit from earlier.

His eyebrows shot up when he saw us. "She's back less than a day and you already need my help?"

"Menoetius was in her mind again," Nate said.

Apollo stared at me for a moment, then shook his head as he opened the doors to the living room. I thought I heard him mumble something about a "fledgling goddess" as he walked past.

Once we were all seated, he looked at me. "Does Menoetius know you've learned your true identity?"

"Without a doubt," I replied.

"Nathaniel managed to stop the dream, then?"

"After the twins infiltrated it," Nate confirmed. "It took a moment, but we managed."

"Any injuries?" Apollo asked me. "You don't seem nearly as distraught as last time."

"Last time, I thought he was going to kill me. Now that I know he can't do more than wound me, my head's a bit clearer. And yes, there were injuries." I shoved the sleeve of my shirt up so he would see the red mark that remained on my shoulder. "They're nearly healed, though."

Apollo pursed his lips and eyed the fading wound on my shoulder. When he looked back at me, I thought I saw a brief flash of pity.

"I would imagine the problem is that your mental walls are still weak. If they were stronger, you'd be able to control who is able to walk into or remain in your dreams."

"What are you talking about? I could block all of you out before I had my Titaness strength back. Wouldn't I be stronger now?"

"Yes, when you're conscious, it isn't an issue," Apollo explained.

"Keeping your mental walls up while asleep is an entirely separate skill. You'd likely be able to throttle the bastard within an inch of his life in the waking world, but if your walls falter while you're asleep, he wouldn't have any trouble sneaking in and disabling your power."

Prometheus shook his head. "No, she should be able to do that instinctively."

"Could you, when you were a boy?" Apollo asked him, arching a brow.

"She's nearly four thousand years old!"

"Her soul spent three thousand years in Chaos. Any skills she learned back then will be rusty at best, if she even remembers them at all. She's an infant, Prometheus."

"Listen, we're all going on very little information here," I said, trying not to be insulted that he'd just called me an infant. "Some more than others. A little understanding would be appreciated."

"Fine." Apollo leaned forward and rested his elbows on his knees. "Can you recall from your previous life whether you were able to block others from dream walks?"

Pursing my lips, I tried to think back to my life before, but nothing came to me.

I blew out a heavy breath. "I don't know."

"Even for a Titaness, there are certain things that take time to perfect," Apollo explained. "Just as it takes time for Ischyra to become one with their abilities, so, too, does it take time for deities to perfect their powers."

"Atlas was teaching you," Epimetheus said, snapping his fingers. "I remember now. He used to have us do dream walks with you regularly, to practice. Once he abandoned Cronus, he'd worked with you almost every night, right until that last time."

"That's right," I said, nodding slowly as the murky memory swam to the surface. "He'd mastered the ability to block his mind almost immediately, so he was trying to teach me."

"And then you were killed, so your lessons came to an end," Apollo said quietly.

I leaned my head back on the sofa as I recalled my first visit from Menoetius.

"In the first dream walk, Menoetius said I'd always had trouble with mental abilities. It made no sense at the time, because I was doing so well with my training, but that's probably what he was talking about."

"So it would seem," Apollo muttered.

"What I want to know is who told him a Mimic had been awakened," Epimetheus said, "and how he recognized her when all of us were in the dark."

Apollo tapped a finger on the arm of the sofa. "The only ones who knew of her true identity before her demonstration were Hestia, Hecate, and myself."

Prometheus raised his eyebrows and crossed his arms over his chest, his expression asking the question for him.

Apollo sent him a level gaze. "In case you've forgotten, Hestia and I were under an interdiction. We couldn't have told anyone, even if we wanted to."

"And Hecate?" Epimetheus spoke quietly. "She could have told anyone she chose."

"Considering the lengths she went to hide Tessa in the first place, don't you think that's a bit ridiculous?" Apollo countered.

"No, I don't suppose I do," Epimetheus replied.

"Hecate's spell..." I said slowly. "She said putting a spell on someone who can disable powers is 'tricky,' so the memory spell she put on everyone else may not have worked as well on our brother. He could've recognized me immediately, even if no one had told him who I was."

"Oh, well that's just lovely," Apollo snapped. "You could have mentioned that sooner, you know."

My eyebrows shot up. "I've had a lot going on the last few days. Sorry to have inconvenienced you. And how was I supposed to know you didn't know that?"

He rolled his eyes. "So nice to see your snark has returned along with your memory."

"Excuse me?" I sat up in my seat and glared at him, the anger I'd managed to tamp down earlier rearing up. "Where do you get off—"

"Moving on," Nate said, cutting off my retort. He took my hand and gave me a reassuring squeeze. "If it wasn't one of you three, who could it have been?"

Prometheus turned to face me. "Before your demonstration for Zeus, who knew of your powers?"

I sighed and tried to smother my irritation with Apollo. "That I know of? All of you, Zeus, Hera, Chiron, Yana, Mary, and Eric." I ticked off each name on my fingers. "Anette was there the night Menoetius did his first dream walk, so I'm not sure how much she knew. Oh, and the mentors who helped train me once I started working with Ares and Athena. Genevieve, Olivette, and several others."

"That's nearly twenty people who knew a Mimic had come into being," Epimetheus said, scrubbing his hands over his face as he leaned back on the sofa.

"At minimum, *and* assuming they didn't tell anyone. If Menoetius' memories weren't gone, he would've recognized her the moment he saw her." Apollo gaze became unfocused for a few seconds, then he blinked and looked back at us.

"What are you—"

"I called Hecate," he explained. "She should be here—"

Before he could finish his statement, there was a knock at the door. A moment later, Hecate walked in, wearing a long black night-gown and matching robe, her curly dark hair pulled back in a loose braid.

"Thank you for coming," Apollo said.

"You barely gave me a choice, Apollo," she said, adjusting her robe as she took a seat next to him. "Your bellow in my mind didn't leave much room to argue."

Her gaze flitted around the room as she took us all in, lingering on Prometheus and Epimetheus, who were glowering at her, before turning her stormy gray eyes to me. "What seems to be the problem?"

"Tessa appears to be unable to keep her mental walls up while asleep," Apollo explained. "Menoetius attacked her again. I'd like you to do something about it so they don't keep coming to me each time that lunatic enters her mind."

Hecate arched a perfect black brow at him before facing me. "Another dream walk?"

"Yes, just a little while ago," I confirmed. "Nate and my brothers helped get me out of it."

Quietly, she studied me, her gaze roaming across my face and around my head.

After a few moments, I shifted uncomfortably.

"I'm sorry," she said, smiling. "I'm checking the strength of your mental walls, now that you're awake. They're very strong, but Apollo is right. They're not quite strong enough to hold while you're asleep." She gave me a curious look. "You never learned this skill in your earlier life?"

"No." I tried to keep the annoyance out of my tone. "Atlas was trying to teach me, but by then he didn't really have much time."

"No, I suppose he wouldn't have," she murmured. "Well, despite your chronological age, your deific skills are insufficient due to lack of training and a millennia of disuse. They will get stronger over time, but for now, I can do a cloaking spell that will block your mind against those who would wish you harm."

"Another spell?" My mind immediately rebelled against the idea. Her first spell had essentially ruined my life, and I was only just beginning to pick up the pieces.

"You said a spell won't work on him, though," Prometheus said.

"The spell isn't for him," Hecate explained, inclining her head toward me. "It's for her."

I rested my head on the back of the sofa as I considered my choices.

The only option I could see, aside from her spell, was to have Nate and my brothers continue to keep an eye on me while I slept. Even though I knew they would do it, I could never ask that of them. We all had lives, and I would likely crack under that level of monitoring.

"Alright," I said, sitting up straight. "I'll do it."

The corner of Hecate's mouth lifted in a smile. "That's good to hear, but if you don't mind, I would like to get out from under your brothers' glares first."

I glanced up at the twins and saw that they were still shooting daggers at her.

She stood and reached out a hand. "Have you remembered how to teleport on your own since your return?"

I felt my face redden as she pulled me to my feet. "No, not yet."

"Ah, not to worry. It will all come in time."

Nate stood to follow us, but Hecate waved him off.

"I'll send her back to you in just a little while, Nathaniel. She's safe with me, I promise."

He clenched his jaw, looking as though he wanted to argue.

"It's fine," I whispered, despite my own hesitance at being alone with her. "I'll be back in a bit."

"Alright." He touched my hip and brushed a kiss across my forehead. "I'll be back at the house."

"And here I thought you'd stick around so we could bond some more," Apollo deadpanned.

I rolled my eyes and faced Hecate. "Let's go."

She gave me a small smile, then teleported us away.

Hecate's home was a gorgeous Victorian, set back on a wide, sweeping lawn, with gingerbread trim and a wraparound porch. With its high, arched windows, sharply pitched roof, and rounded corners topped with inverted cones, it looked a lot like a doll house one would find in an antique store.

"So, Tessa, how have you been adjusting?"

Night blooming flowers rioted along the front, lining a short, stone path to the front porch. I broke from my ogling and glanced up at Hecate as we ascended the wide stone steps.

"I think I'm doing alright. I still feel more Ischyra than Titaness, at least in my head."

Hecate gave me an apologetic smile as she held the heavy wood-and-glass door open for me. "I'm sorry. I know that must be frustrating."

My eyes widened when I stepped through the door and took in the interior.

"Gods, this is beautiful," I breathed, momentarily forgetting my frustrations. The entire home was reminiscent of the early twentieth century. The ceiling in the foyer stretched all the way to the roof. A wide double staircase extended up to the second floor, and a similar one went from there to the third. A chandelier made of vibrant stained glass hung above us, glinting in the moonlight that shone through the giant round window that overlooked the front yard. Dark hardwood floors matched the rich crown molding in the foyer and sitting room. Straight-backed velvet couches, richly upholstered chairs, and shiny, wooden end tables adorned a sitting area that was papered in a beige and white Art Deco design.

Hecate laughed at the expression on my face. "Thank you. I spent many years on it. Art Deco is one of my favorites, in terms of architecture and design. It's got just the right blend of Victorian and modern."

"I knew Apollo's home was lacking something," I said.

"Yes, he goes for simple yet extravagant." Touching my shoulder, she gestured toward the living room. "Let's do this, shall we? I'm sure Nathaniel is eager to have you home."

The smile slowly faded from my face.

A few days ago, I didn't question where home was. It was and would always be back in Renville, where I grew up with loving guardians and amazing friends, both human and Ischyra. I nearly laughed out loud at the thought of what Josh and Leila would say if they saw me now.

Hecate's words made me realize just how relative the term 'home' had become.

Hecate stepped forward and placed her hands on my shoulders.

"Tessa, you will be alright. I know this is hard, and there are many things you're going to have to work through in the days and weeks to come, but if I didn't think I could save you, I never would've agreed to Clymene's terms."

"Thank you." I forced a smile onto my face and willed my eyes to meet hers. "I appreciate you helping my mother, really, but I'm a little nervous about what it means for me. I've missed out on so much."

She put an arm around my shoulder and led me toward one of the long, green velvet sofas. "I am truly sorry for my part in that, Tessa. I want you to know that."

"Why did you help her?" I asked as I sat down. "Why not just protect me from Cronus some other way?"

She tightened her robe around her thin frame and sat down next to me. "At that point in time, the only way to ensure he would stop hunting you was if he thought you no longer existed."

"And that's it? You faked my death so he would stop hunting me?" I shook my head. "That seems a bit excessive."

She was quiet for a few seconds as she stared out the large living room window. "I'll be honest with you, Tessa. I agreed with your mother because I felt it was the best way to protect you, yes, but also because I knew what it would mean for Olympus—and Earth—if Cronus managed to get ahold of your power. The ability to mimic the gifts of others is a power that was made for you. It suits you. Putting it in the hands of someone for whom it wasn't meant would equal disaster."

I leaned forward and rested my elbows on my legs, then rubbed at my eyes as I processed what she'd said. While something deep inside had told me that was the case, it still struck a chord knowing, in some sense, I'd been seen as an object, not a deity.

"So, Cronus wasn't the only one who saw me as nothing more than a weapon," I said quietly, keeping my gaze averted so she wouldn't see how much that hurt.

Hecate dropped to her knees in front of me and put a hand on either side of my face, forcing me to meet her eyes. "You are no one's weapon, Tessa. Do you hear me? I knew what he intended to do if he found you, and I did what I felt was right, what I *still* feel was right, to prevent that from happening. To protect you and your future."

"And my family? My brothers?" I jerked my face from her hands, swallowing the lump in my throat. "Did you know that Epimetheus grieved for us so badly that he married Pandora, the first woman who showed him love, only to watch her die on their wedding night? That Atlas has been torturing himself for millennia because he couldn't save me?" I wiped at the tears on my face, angry that I hadn't been able to control them. "Did you even try to prevent those things from happening?"

Hecate was silent as she stared at me with an unfathomable expression. Her eyes brimmed with tears as she took in my words. Quickly, she knuckled them away and moved back to her seat next to me.

"No." She cleared hear throat and smoothed out her robe. "No, I didn't realize that was the catalyst for those things. And I'm sorry for that."

"Why?"

For the first time, she looked frustrated.

"What would you have had me do, Tessa? I couldn't have erased their memories of you back then. Do you know what it would have done to their minds if they'd had three thousand years to forget you? The outcome today would have been far different, had that been the case."

"But once you realized what Zeus intended to do, that he didn't plan on destroying Cronus, why not tell them the truth?"

"Because they would've started another damn war just to get you back," she snapped. "And I was not going to do that to them, to you, or to the people in the realms who would've fallen into the crossfire."

"You could've just let me live my life as an Ischyra, none the wiser. I was happy, and now you've changed all of that." I glared at her, furiously trying to push down the anger that was rearing up inside me, clawing to be let out. For a moment I thought I saw a flicker of fear in her eyes before she took on a concerned expression.

"You don't think you can be happy in your new life, Tessa?"

I stared down at my hands, clenching and unclenching my fists as I considered her words. Happiness seemed to have become just as relative as home. I had my friends, my brothers, and Nate, but it was difficult to be happy with one without feeling as though I was slighting another.

"Tessa, you still have all of the things you had three days ago," Hecate said quietly. "More, even. You've got a family."

"I had family," I whispered. "Do my guardians even know what's happened?"

When she didn't answer, I turned to look at her, and the expression on her face told me all I needed to know.

My heart sank. "They knew, didn't they?"

"They did," she said, nodding. "On the off chance someone discovered your true identity prior to your transformation, I cloaked your home and told them everything. They needed to know the truth if they were to be able to fully protect you."

"And you put an interdiction on them to keep them from talking, right?" I couldn't hide the disgust in my voice, despite knowing full well they'd likely requested it themselves. Hecate's words confirmed my thoughts.

"I did, at their behest. As soon as I explained your situation, John asked me to place interdictions on them both."

"That certainly sounds like John." I couldn't find it in me to be angry with him or Analise, knowing the risk they'd put themselves at when they took me in. "Did you tell them my name?"

"I did. It's your name, Tessa. It's what was given to you as a Titaness and is what suits the deity you are."

"And my appearance? Why did you make me look the same as I did back then?" So many questions were flooding my mind about how I'd gotten here. "If I was reborn a human, shouldn't I look different?"

"Again, your appearance is part of who you are. You're Atlas' twin. Your energy and his are shared. To change things that are, in essence, you, would affect that energy in a negative way. I crafted my spell to bring *you* back, both inside and out."

"I suppose I should thank you for that, then." It almost pained me to say the words, but I truly was thankful. I already felt split in two; being able to look in the mirror and still see myself helped ease that feeling a bit.

"I know you're angry with me," Hecate said hesitantly. "I would be, too. Yet I can't help but feel as though there's something else going on."

I arched a brow. "Such as...?"

"Have any of your memories returned?"

"Some. I can tell that they're there, but it just feels very crowded up here," I said, tapping my temple. "Everything hurts, like my whole body is trying to deal with all of these changes but it doesn't know how."

She smiled sympathetically. "You still feel like two people in one mind, don't you?"

"I do," I said, a bit annoyed that she was better able to put my feelings into words than I was.

She took my hands, ignoring the way my body tensed at her touch. "I won't lie; this is going to be difficult for you and those who care for you. The most important thing is to know when to lean on your loved ones. Allow them to help you through this. Do not try to recover your true self alone, because you'll only isolate yourself."

"My true self?" I let out a harsh laugh. "I wouldn't know where to begin trying to recover my 'true self.' I don't even know who she is."

"Well, for starters, she's not one or the other. You don't need to make a choice between deity and Ischyra. You *are* a Titaness, but being an Ischyra, living in the human world, has changed that part of you. Eventually, those two parts will come to coexist, but for right now, they're fighting against one another. Conquering that may take time." She smiled and cupped my cheek with a cool hand. "There is a great deal of love for you in this world, Tessa, more than you can comprehend. Have faith in that, and I'm certain that will happen quicker than you think."

I exhaled a long breath as I tried to hear the truth in her words.

Even though I was angry with her, I knew deep down she was right. This wasn't something I could do alone.

"Thank you." I scrubbed a hand over my face as exhaustion slowly began to creep into my mind. "Can we do this spell now? I'd like to try and get some sleep."

"Of course." She slid forward, then paused, her bronze fingers inches from my chin. "I have to ask...would you like me to restore your memories? It's up to you if you'd prefer they return on their own, but I would still like to give you the option. If you'd rather someone else do it, there are others who'd be willing to help."

"No, but thank you. I'm hoping it won't be much longer, and I'd rather avoid anyone digging around in my brain if possible."

"I understand. I just thought I'd offer." She scooted a bit closer, then cradled my face in her hands. Her gray eyes bore into mine as she began murmuring words below her breath. I felt a strange *prick* in my mind, then she let her hands drop to her lap.

"That should do it," she said, smiling. "Now no one who wishes you harm can enter your mind."

I felt an immediate sense of relief wash over me.

"Thank you," I said.

"It's the least I can do. Now, let's see if we can get you to teleport yourself back home, shall we?"

About twenty tries later, after managing to teleport myself to various rooms in her home, Hecate finally managed to help get me back to Nate's. By the time I stepped onto his lawn, the sky was tinged purple, as the sun approached the horizon.

As I made my way across the grass, I tried to clear my mind of all my Ischyra memories. I was becoming increasingly frustrated at my inability to recall things that were second nature to all of the other gods and goddesses, and I knew sooner or later, they were going to get tired of helping me relearn old skills, skills I should've conquered eons ago.

Apollo had called me an infant, and I was beginning to think he was right.

Feeling a sense of resolve, I stopped just before going inside and sat down on one of the white Adirondack chairs on the porch. Closing my eyes, I tried focusing on an older memory.

The first one that came to me was murky, but after a few moments, I managed to grab ahold of it and pull it forward.

It was of a day I'd spent exploring Earth with my brothers. Atlas and the twins had gone to Earth several times, always leaving me behind because they felt it was "too dangerous." Not long after Atlas began helping me learn how to hone my physical fighting skills, only a few decades prior to my death, I'd insisted they take me with them.

We ended up in Egypt, about twelve hundred years after Khufu's pyramid had been constructed at Giza. The memory was fuzzy, so I pushed harder, willing it to come to the surface.

I remembered how I had been mesmerized at the sight of the structure. It was beautiful, nearly blinding, with its smooth white limestone shell not yet shattered by the earthquake that would come two thousand years later. Even as Titans, we could recognize the beauty in such a human creation.

When I pressed my hand to the silken surface, I could feel the thoughts and emotions of the people who'd spent years toiling away as they built the massive structure—the slaves who'd suffered in the desert heat, the architect who felt pleasure at seeing his creation realized, and the pharaoh who'd watched with pride and trepidation as his final resting place was constructed.

I'd run off, hoping to escape my brothers' watchful eyes so I could explore on my own.

Then a new memory came, of a hand clamped over my mouth and a smooth, slender arm wrapped around my torso. Stringy brown hair fell across my shoulders, and the smell of sea water flooded my nostrils. My assailant jerked me against her body and hissed in my ear.

"You should've stayed with your brothers, you stupid girl."

4

NATHANIEL

I hated watching Tessa go off with the witch alone. I trusted Hecate; I knew she wouldn't hurt Tessa, but a dull ache had begun to form in my chest over the last few days any time she was out of my sight. I didn't need to psychoanalyze myself to know that feeling was dread.

I'd thought she had died. When she used my father's lightning, the scream that had ripped through the arena was one of pain so fierce I wouldn't have expected anyone to survive. She'd laid there, crumpled on the ground, unmoving, for what felt like an eternity. It was only a few minutes, but it had given me a minuscule glimpse into what her brothers must have felt when they thought they'd lost her for good.

I sat down on my sofa and rubbed my hands over my face, trying to forget the image of lightning dancing across her body, but it felt permanently seared into my mind.

The sofa shifted, and when I opened my eyes, I saw that Prometheus had taken a seat. His eyes were weary when he looked at me.

"She'll be alright, Nathaniel."

"I just want her back here, that's all."

He gave me an understanding smile. "I'm sure it won't take long."

"Nathaniel, how much of Tessa's memory has returned?" Epimetheus asked. He'd worn a perplexed expression ever since Hecate and Tessa had left, as though trying to puzzle something out in his mind.

"Not much, from what I can tell. Why?"

"There's something that's bothering me, and I'm not quite sure how we should address it." He glanced at his twin. "Or if it even should be addressed."

"What's on your mind?" Prometheus asked.

Epimetheus stared at him, his eyes hard and expression tense. "Don't you remember what Menoetius did to her?"

Prometheus' jaw tightened. "How could I forget?"

"Exactly my point. I would think those memories would have been some of the first to return for her, but the fact that they haven't concerns me."

Confused, I looked between the two of them. "What did he do?"

The brothers exchanged a glance, then Epimetheus turned and gazed out the large window that looked out over my lawn.

His lack of response sent a new sense of dread washing over me.

"What he did in those dream walks...did he do that to her in her previous life? Torture her?" I asked.

Prometheus leaned forward in his seat and rested his elbows on his knees. He stared at the floor for a moment before raising his eyes to mine.

"Torture would be putting it mildly."

I swallowed back the bile I felt rising in my throat and forced my mind to stop conjuring up pictures of things I knew Menoetius had done in the past.

"Is it possible she's moved on?" I asked.

Epimetheus snorted quietly. "Tell me, what are you picturing in your mind right now? Are you imagining all the tales you've heard of Menoetius' cruelty? The physical and mental torture he loves to inflict on his victims?"

"More or less."

"Imagine being the victim in those stories and recalling all of those things at once. Would you be catching up with friends and snuggling with your lover, or would you be rocking in a corner somewhere?"

"Shit." I exhaled a breath as the gravity of his words sunk in.

"Exactly," Epimetheus said, turning to stare out the window once more.

Prometheus sat with his head in his hands, still as stone.

"Then what do we do?"

"We either let them return in their own time, or force them out of her subconscious and get it over with," Prometheus said, looking pointedly at me.

I stared at him incredulously. "Absolutely not!"

"Who else would she trust enough to enter her mind in such a way?" He sat up a bit straighter and faced me more fully. "You can stop the flow of memories before they get to be too much; allow her mind to rest."

"Even if that were true and she wanted me to do that, it's been nearly impossible for me to enter her mind since her transformation, unless her mental walls slip."

"I believe she's more in control of her power now," Prometheus added. "Her mind isn't divided into two beings fighting against one another anymore. She could easily let you in. You could even do it while she was asleep."

I sighed and shook my head. "I still don't think it's the best course of action. Even if it were, I wouldn't be willing to do anything until we convince Atlas to come home. I have a feeling she'd need her twin in order to get through something like that."

"When do we plan to do that?" Epimetheus asked.

"She needs a few days before making that trip," I replied. "Preferably longer, but knowing her, that won't happen. She's angry, and she wants her brother back."

"As do we," Prometheus said with a sigh. He stood and stretched his arms above his head. "It's late. I need to get some sleep. We'll discuss the logistics of retrieving Atlas tomorrow."

"I'll be there shortly," Epimetheus murmured. "I'd like to wait until she returns."

"Alright, then. I'll see you both in the morning."

I waited until Prometheus had teleported away before discussing the topic of Tessa's memories with Epimetheus any further.

"You can't expect me to pull those memories from her mind," I told him. "I won't do that to her."

He ran a hand down his face and let out a frustrated sigh. "And what if they damage her when they return?"

"She's strong, Epimetheus. I think she'd prefer to let these things happen on their own."

"It's not always about what she'd prefer, Nathaniel!" His voice cracked with emotion as his expression turned pained. "I was there! I know what he did to her. It took months for us to realize something was wrong."

"Months?" I stared at him, incredulity quickly turning to anger that they could've been so drastically unaware their brother had be tormenting her for that long. "How is that possible?"

"A witch who was especially gifted at memory spells had wiped her memory. And please, don't ask me to discuss those memories with you. They're hers to disclose if she chooses to."

I rubbed my hand over my chin, trying to expel the sudden desire to shake him. It had been clear to me since the moment she'd shattered Hecate's spell that her relationship with Epimetheus had been different than what she'd had with her other brothers. He'd been her best friend, yet he'd been oblivious to what was happening to her. That knowledge probably hurt him more than anyone, though, so I forced myself to stay cognizant of that.

"Alright. Then let me ask this. How did she react once she had her memories back?"

"With fear first, then anger." A smile ghosted across his lips. "She was very angry."

I raised my eyebrows. "Then why would this time be any different?"

He dropped down onto the couch and put his head in his hands.

"You're right. I know you are. I just don't want her to hurt anymore." He lifted his head, then wiped his eyes, remaining quiet for a moment as he collected himself.

"I understand that, and trust me when I say I would do anything to keep her from experiencing any more pain." I leaned forward and propped my elbows on my knees. "Epimetheus, what you need to understand is that eighteen years as a human has made Tessa a different person. I know that may not make sense to you, but mentally, emotionally, she's strong. I've got no doubt she can handle whatever is thrown at her."

"I think you put too much faith in a human's ability to cope with major trauma," he grumbled.

"And I think you put too little," I countered. "I've lived among humans for nearly two thousand years. I've seen what they've survived, what horrible actions and events have allowed them to thrive."

"That's not the case for all of them, though. How can you be sure that she'll come through?"

I sighed wearily. "I was the one responsible for her remembering her own death. I pulled the memory of her being forced into Chaos out of her mind. Or have you forgotten that?"

He was quiet for a moment as he considered this. "How did she respond to that?"

"Just as you'd expect. She panicked, cried, dropped to the ground, and contemplated punching me." I couldn't help but smile at the memory of how badly she'd wanted to hit me that morning. It was one of the first things that told me she would be different. "Once she got that out, she got back up and moved on. Just as she did when Menoetius attacked her last week."

"You told us she was nearly catatonic when you arrived in her room," he reminded me.

"You don't need to remind me what she looked like. I saw those burns, I saw the fear in her eyes, but I also saw her defiance. I saw her refusal to let it destroy her. She is not weak, Epimetheus. You let your love for her blind you to that."

"I just want her safe," he whispered through clenched teeth.

"And she will be," I said, trying to be reassuring. "But you need to let her find her own way, and that means not sheltering her from everything that could hurt her."

He was silent for a moment as he looked at me appraisingly. "You really do care for my sister, don't you?"

"More than you know. And believe me, if I could hide her away until we have Menoetius and this rebellion dealt with, I would. I won't do that to her, though."

A smile lifted the corner of his mouth. "She did stab him with his own blade. I suppose that's something."

"It certainly is."

A noise on the front porch drew my attention. I walked over and flicked the curtain aside and saw Tessa sitting in one of the large wooden chairs.

"She's back," I said as I opened the door and stepped outside. Epimetheus came out just behind me.

"Hi," she murmured absently, staring off into the woods.

I took a seat in the chair next to her, while Epimetheus sat down on the floor and leaned his back against the railing.

"Where's Prometheus?" she asked.

"He went back to the palace to get some rest. I told him I'd wait here until you got home," Epimetheus said. "What are you doing outside?"

She sighed and rested her head on the back of the chair. "Trying to sort through my memories."

I held out my hand and she laced her fingers through mine. "Have you remembered something new?"

"Yeah." She smiled wryly, then looked at her brother. "Our trip to Egypt."

"You went to Egypt?" I asked.

"Yep." She shifted her gaze to me. "I was attacked there."

Epimetheus grunted. "A Siren," he said, shaking his head. "Vile creatures."

I frowned, not expecting that. "What was she doing that far from the sea?"

"Cronus and Menoetius had a witch working with them," Epimetheus explained, giving me a pointed look. "One of the primordials. He got them to lift the Sirens' curse for a short period of time, allowing them to leave their shoals so they could find her. Cronus told the one who came after Tessa he'd free them from the curse permanently if she brought her back to him."

I nodded. "I suppose having their abilities at his disposal would prove beneficial, although I'm surprised they bought into it."

"They were desperate," Tessa said. "They didn't want their lives to be dependent on whether or not a human could survive their song, and they didn't want to live out eternity living on sandbars and tiny bumps of rock in the ocean. Helping him, at least in their eyes, ensured they would be free once the war was over, if he won." She flicked a glance at me. "In a way, I felt bad for them. I know you probably think that's crazy, but they just wanted their freedom."

"So, they'd believe anything," Epimetheus said. Slowly, a smile formed on his lips.

I raised my eyebrows. "What about this could possibly make you smile?"

He looked at Tessa with eyes full of pride. "You beat that information out of her, with her own weapon. It was the first time we realized you actually had it in you to fight."

The corners of her lips twitched up. "A long, wooden stick."

I couldn't help but smile at the thought of a Siren attempting to use such a rudimentary weapon. They'd been terrible fighters in their day, always relying on their song to disable prey.

"You took us all by surprise with that stunt. Atlas hadn't gotten past basic staff training with you yet."

"Psychometry comes in very handy when it comes to weapons training," Tessa replied, a frown flickering across her face.

A brief look of confusion furrowed Epimetheus' brow, so quickly Tessa missed it entirely.

"What happened to her?" I asked, eyeing him curiously. "To the Siren?"

Tessa answered instead. "I'd broken her wings and beaten her bloody by the time my brothers found me. Epimetheus broke her legs and Atlas beheaded her." Tessa made a slicing motion with her hand. "Then Prometheus threw her body in the Nile."

"Well at least some good came from it," I muttered.

"Yes, but unfortunately, there's a whole new slew of them," Epimetheus said, sighing.

"The original Sirens have been killed off, right?" Tessa asked.

"They have, but their descendants number in the hundreds at this point," I replied.

Epimetheus tilted his head back against the rail and closed his eyes. "I'm sure we'll be dealing with them soon enough, especially if our brother succeeds in freeing Cronus and our father."

"Let's hope not," Tessa said with a sigh. "For now, I wouldn't mind a few hours rest. I'd like to see if this spell of Hecate's works."

Epimetheus stood, then leaned down and kissed her cheek. "I'll see you in the morning. Let me know if any more memories resurface."

Tessa smiled up at him. "Will do."

Once he was gone, she climbed over the arm of her chair and into my lap. I wrapped my arms around her and rested my cheek on her hair as she snuggled against me.

"You okay?"

"Yeah," she murmured. "I just needed a hug, and you make me feel better."

I smiled. "I can do you one better, if you'd like." I brushed my lips across her cheek. "Close your eyes," I whispered.

Once they were shut, I stood, then teleported us to the summit.

She opened her eyes when the cold air bit at her skin, and for the second time, I was treated to the look of wonder on her face as she took in the moonlit view of the Olympic mountain range.

Biting her lip, she smiled up at me. "You really know the way to a girl's heart, don't you?"

"I do what I can," I replied. I carried her into the wooden shelter and sat down on the bench, letting her curl up in my lap again. "Now, what were we talking about?"

She grinned and snuggled against me. "Probably about how wonderfully amazing you are," she teased.

I chuckled. "I just pay attention, that's all. You loved it here last time."

"Because it's beautiful." She sighed. "So peaceful."

Absently, I began rubbing slow circles on her back, letting the silence stretch around us, The only sound was the whipping of the cold wind as it gusted against the side of the shelter.

We sat like that for a few moments, and I debated whether to tell her about her brothers' concerns that she was repressing memories. I didn't want to involve myself in their family business, but I also didn't think keeping secrets was helpful to anyone at this point.

"Tessa, I want to tell you something."

"Hmm?"

"In the interest of full disclosure, you should know about a conversation I had with your brothers while you were gone."

"That sounds ominous." She shifted and looked up at me with a questioning look. "What is it?"

"They're concerned you're repressing some of the more unpleasant memories of your earlier life. They didn't tell me what those memories were, specifically, but it was suggested that I try to retrieve them for you, help you remember in a more controlled manner so as to not overwhelm you."

She sat up and raised her eyebrows. "Is that so? And why do they feel that way?"

"Epimetheus seems to think you're handling this transition too well."

She relaxed a little, then put a hand on my cheek. "While I think it's wonderful that you're all so concerned, you need to let me work these things out on my own. I know there are unpleasant things in my past, but if I handled them once, I can do it again."

"That's more or less what I told him."

"Well that's good to hear. My brothers can be smothering. I don't think I could handle an overprotective boyfriend, as well."

I smiled and ran my thumb along her jaw. "As much as I'd love to protect you from the evils of the realms, I won't stifle you in that way." I rested my hands on her hip. "Tessa, I've seen your strength, felt it, when I was in your mind. I have no doubts—none—when it comes to what you're capable of. I know you'll be able to handle whatever gets thrown your way."

Her bright green eyes brimmed with tears as they drifted over my face. "Thank you," she whispered. "I didn't realize how much I needed to hear someone say that until just now."

"I will always be in your corner, no matter what. I need you to know that."

She gnawed at her lip, and I waited patiently as she worked out what it was she needed to say.

"Can I ask a favor?"

"Of course."

"If you ever think I'm in too deep or am biting off more than I can chew, I need you to tell me." She gripped my chin in her hand and met my eyes. "Seriously, Nate. I need you to tell me."

I smiled up at her. "Tessa, have you met yourself? Once you've decided on something, there's no talking you out of it. Your brothers have been trying to for days."

She rolled her eyes. "That's because they're being stupid and overbearing. I meant what I said, Nate. I trust you to be my partner in all of this, to back me up and not just try to keep me safe."

I took her hand and brought it to my lips as I considered her words.

I had advocated for the woman I'd loved two thousand years ago. I'd loved Karis so much that I couldn't bear the thought of her being in danger. As great a fighter as she was, I'd sheltered her, kept her close, convinced her to always choose to safest option when I should have encouraged her to become stronger. Instead of helping her overcome her weakness, I taught her to tolerate it, to allow her to let me compensate for it.

For nearly two thousand years, I'd placed most of the blame for her death on Apollo. He'd sent her into danger, a Siren disabled her, and a human shot an arrow laced with godsbane right through her heart. Not once had he shown any guilt or remorse over sending her away, something I always hated him for, despite having moved on from her death.

Tessa's words made me wonder if I was more complicit in Karis' death than I wanted to admit. Had I taken more time to help her, she might've been better equipped to defend herself. It was possible she'd still be alive today.

Breaking from my reverie, I tightened my arms around her. "Alright. If I think you're in over your head, I'll pull you out."

"And if my brothers try to stop me from doing something crazy?"

I arched a brow. "I will stand by your side... within reason."

"Fine, within reason," she said, rolling her eyes. "Seriously, though, that means a lot to me. I don't need an advocate; I need a partner, and I know—or at least hope—that's what you'll be for me." She took a deep breath. "It's one of the reasons I think...I might be falling in love with you.

I smiled, hesitant to show how much her words meant me. "Is that so?"

She shifted so she was straddling my hips, then put her hands on my shoulders. "I think I might be. Is that okay?" She let her forehead drop to her hands. "Gods, I suck at this."

"It's completely okay," I said as I nudged her hands away from her face. "Do you know why it's okay?"

She leaned back and stared down at me. "Why?"

"Because I'm pretty sure I'm in love with you, too."

Her eyes grew wide and her lips curved into a smile. "Well that's *quite* fantastic to hear." She took my face in her hands and put her lips to mine in a soft kiss. When she pulled back, she grinned. "I thought I'd just majorly embarrassed myself."

"Don't ever feel like you can't tell me how you feel, Tessa. Please."

She nodded, then kissed me again, this time with more intensity, slowly working her lips over mine.

I gripped her waist and pulled her toward me, then forced back a groan as she rolled her hips against mine. She let out a quiet sigh as I moved my lips down to her neck and slid my hand up the back of her shirt.

Not here.

I wasn't sure if the thought was hers, mine, or both, but regardless, I slowly shifted her back.

She rested her forehead against mine and bit her lip. "Does this mean you don't want our first time to be on a bench at the top of a mountain?"

"No, I most certainly do not. Nor do I want it to be right after you've just woken up from a three-thousand-year nap with no memory of your previous life." I brushed her hair from her face. "I want your head to be perfectly clear."

"I suppose I can appreciate the logic."

I kissed her neck, letting my lips trail softly against her skin. "Although I wouldn't be opposed to giving it a shot in the future," I murmured.

She tightened her arms around my neck, shivering as my fingers danced up her spine. "That can definitely be arranged."

By the time Tessa and I had woken up, curled up in bed together, it was nearly midday. I was relieved to find that she hadn't had any more intrusions while she'd been sleeping.

As she stood at the bathroom sink brushing her teeth, dressed in soft black pants and a thin pink sweater, I leaned against the door frame with my hands stuffed into my pockets, taking in the sight of her. When she caught me staring in the mirror, she grinned.

"I think Hecate's mind block spell is working," she said through a mouthful of toothpaste.

"Maybe. Or it means your brother chose not to return for a second time in one night." I walked up behind her and slid my arm around her waist, then kissed her temple. "You did stab him, after all. I doubt he was expecting you to fight back."

She paused in her brushing. "Way to be optimistic."

"All I'm saying is, I think we should give it a bit more time before declaring success. In the meantime, we need to try to work on getting your mental walls up."

She wiped her face on a towel and turned to me. "I know, and I agree, but can we please just have a day where I don't have to do a ton of mental gymnastics? My brain and body are tired, Nate, and I have a feeling this meeting is going to be taxing enough." Wrapping her arms around my waist, she rested her chin against my chest. "Please?"

Any resolve I might've had dissolved at the sight of her bright eyes staring up at me. "I suppose that's fair."

"Thank you," she said, then pulled back. "Besides, I have an idea on that."

"What's that?"

"Well, before Hecate sent me away, Atlas was working with me to hone those mental powers, at least the dream walk aspect. I kind of remember his lessons, but I don't think we'd gotten terribly far. I'm thinking he might be able to help me, once we get him back here."

I raised my eyebrows. "I—Tessa, I don't know if you should be putting too much hope into Atlas's ability to help so soon. He's been living in solitude for three thousand years. He's not likely to be the same brother you once had."

She shook her head, and a look of determination crossed her face. "No, I won't believe that. He's my twin. It might take some time, but I'll get him back."

"I hope that's the case, but I don't want you to get your hopes up. In any event, it'll likely take quite a while for him to get back to normal. You need to work on your powers now."

"I know. And trust me. I'm optimistic, not unrealistic. It'll be hard, but it'll happen"

The corner of my mouth quirked up and I laced my fingers through hers.

She looked at me curiously. "What is it?"

"You're stubborn. It's kind of cute."

"Cute?" She rolled her eyes, then slid her arms around my neck. "I'm nearly four thousand years old, Nate. Please don't call me 'cute.'"

"Ah, that's right. I forgot I was the jailbait in this relationship."

"You're so very funny," she said dryly. "Now, kiss me so we can get on with this."

Grinning, I obliged.

Last night, I'd felt desperation in the way she'd kissed me; her need for happiness, for something other than the tumult of emotions that resided in her mind, struggling to fight against the memories of her old life. Her mental walls had been a mess and did very little to keep me from seeing her thoughts. She'd been filled with anger, sadness, grief, and a whole host of emotions that refused to settle or give her peace.

Now, as she stood on her toes kissing me, pressing her body against mine in my dimly lit bathroom, I wanted nothing more than to skip that meeting and take her to bed, to give her the happiness that she needed. I wanted to touch and explore every damn inch of her until there wasn't a drop of sadness or anger left.

After a few moments, I pulled back and looked into her wide eyes as they stared into mine.

A slow smile spread across her face. "You want to skip this meeting, don't you?"

"Very much," I whispered, touching my forehead to hers.

"Hmm. I like that idea."

I chuckled, then tucked her hair behind her ears. "Unfortunately, we can't. This is important, and the first time I make love to you, it will not be a quickie before we go to my parents' house, any more than it will be on top of a mountain." I kissed her again, gently, then touched her chin. "I'm going to take my time with you, Tessa," I whispered.

She made a small sound of contentment and tightened her arms around me. "I'll take that as a promise for later, then."

I laughed, then took her hand in mine and teleported us away.

That was one promise I'd be happy to keep.

5

TESSA

My mind was still buzzing from Nate's promise when we appeared on the palace lawn. As we made our way up the sloping, rocky lawn toward the wide marble terrace, I took a few seconds to enjoy some vivid flashbacks of our day at the springs, *before* we'd been interrupted by Dionysus and Hermes.

We had just reached the large French doors, when Athena stepped out, jolting me from my memories.

"It's about time!" She shook her head, then hitched up the hem of her long cornflower blue dress and descended the stairs. "I was about to come looking for you."

Nate raised his eyebrows. "What for?"

"Not you, Nathaniel. Tessa." She waved a hand dismissively at him. "Go inside, Apollo wants to speak with you."

I bit my lip and tried not to laugh at the stunned look on Nate's face. Apparently, his oldest sister shooing him off wasn't a normal occurrence.

"Why does he need to speak to me?" he asked.

Athena huffed, then turned her face up toward her youngest sibling. The fact that she was a good foot shorter than him would've made her stare down nearly comical, if I didn't know she could lay him out with half a breath.

"I don't know, Nathaniel. He just told me to direct you to him when you arrived. Now shoo, I need to speak with Tessa."

Nate arched a brow at me, and I shrugged in response.

"Alright, I'll see you inside, then." He gave me a quick kiss, then jogged up the marble steps and disappeared through the giant palace doors.

Athena waited until he was well out of earshot before narrowing her eyes at me. "Tessa, are you going to be alright to attend this meeting?"

Confused, I shook my head. "Why wouldn't I be?"

She arched a brow, staring at me expectantly.

"What is it, Athena?"

Her eyes widened and she covered her mouth with one hand, smothering a giggle. "Oh dear, your memories still haven't returned, have they?"

"Well...no, but it's only been a day." Wariness replaced my confusion as I took in her perplexed expression. "Athena...what is it?"

"It's just...well, Hades is in there..."

"Yes, I'm aware." I arched a brow, even as I felt something slowly try to dredge itself from the depths of my memory, tickling the back of my mind like an annoying stray hair. I had the immediate urge to slap it back.

She gnawed at her lip. "And...you two have a, um, history."

"What are you—oh, gods!" I clapped my hands over my face as the fog lifted and I was hit with a deluge of memories.

Vivid memories.

She winced. "There it is. I'm surprised you'd forgotten about him. You two were quite smitten."

"Shit. Shit shit shit." I ran a hand through my hair as pain started to blossom in my forehead. "Dammit!"

"It's alright," Athena cooed, taking my shaking hands in hers. "I'm sure Nathaniel won't find it at all awkward that you had a... relationship with the ruler of the Underworld. I mean, he *is* quite handsome. For a raging narcissist," she added, muttering the last bit.

My whole body began to tingle, so I sat down on the ground to avoid falling over. I pressed my fingers to my forehead, trying to ease away the drilling pain and nausea that accompanied the flow of new memories. "I feel like I'm going to be sick."

Athena dropped down in front of me. "Do you need to leave, go lie down? I just thought it would be better if I checked with you before you go in and see him for the first time in front of...everyone."

I rested my head on my knees in an attempt to block out the sun that had suddenly become far too bright. My mind was forced open as each and every memory from our tumultuous and unstable relationship came rushing back.

A flood of anger coursed through me as I recalled our fights, our all-out battles that always ended in one or both of us bruised, bloody, and full of rage.

Fiery passion quickly followed as I recalled a time or two he'd taken me against a wall, furiously dousing the flames of anger. Another time in my own bed, my moans muffled in my bedding so no one would hear—

"Dear gods, Tessa, close your walls!" Athena exclaimed.

"Fuck off, this is your fault," I snapped, the pain of the memories nearly putting me in tears.

Atlas, locking me in my room to keep me from seeing him.

'He's too dangerous, Tessa. He's no good for you.'

Epimetheus helping me sneak through my window so I could go meet Hades in secret, because Hades was the only one at the time who was willing to train me to defend myself.

The only one who believed in me enough to teach me how to wield my power.

What was probably only moments later, the shaking started to slow. I felt Athena run a cool hand across the back of my neck, then she took my hands in hers.

"I'm sorry," she whispered. "I didn't realize—when you woke up, it seemed like you were accepting things just fine. I knew your memories were coming back piecemeal, but I hadn't realized how...slowly it was happening."

I inhaled deeply through my nose as I tried to settle my nerves, which had suddenly found themselves on fire. Recalling Nate's words from the night before, I began to contemplate letting him dig out my more unpleasant memories just so I could get it all over with at once. The memories of Hades weren't exactly unpleasant, per se, but considering my reaction to their return, I could only imagine what the response would be to less savory things in my past.

"It's fine." I cleared my throat and fanned my flaming cheeks. "We don't exactly have a handbook for navigating all of this. I just need a minute, that's all."

Her concerned expression told me she didn't buy it.

"Tessa, how are you doing? Really, I mean. You seemed alright when you first woke, but now I can't help but think you're struggling a bit more than you'd like us to know."

I looked out over the mountains and sighed, then took a few seconds to sort out the newfound memories and push back the emotional baggage attached to them. Hades had clearly been a big part of my life, at least toward the end, but I couldn't deal with those memories now.

If I was being honest with myself, I didn't care to deal with them ever.

"I'm angry," I finally said. I shook my head and kicked at a stone on the ground in front of me. "I can't help it."

"I understand." She wrapped her arms around me and rested her head on my shoulder. "I would be burning things to the ground if I were in your shoes."

She went silent, and when I looked at her, I realized she was crying.

"Athena, what is it?" I asked.

She choked back a laugh as her granite eyes met mine. "I promised I wouldn't cry when I saw you today, and now here I am, blubbering like a fool." She wiped her cheeks with the back of her hand and smiled at me. "Gods, Tessa. I just missed you so much."

I exhaled, then leaned my head against hers. "Well I'm here now. I can't promise it won't be slow going at first, but I'm here."

We sat like that for a few more minutes until we'd both settled ourselves. My memories of our friendship were murky, but my feelings toward her weren't. Despite not having known her for long in my previous life, she'd become like a sister to me. We'd bonded from the moment we met, and it hurt knowing how she must've felt when she'd thought I was gone.

"Alright, we should head in." I said reluctantly, not wanting to look away from the view of the mountains and the valley below. It was the same home I'd known for nearly seven hundred years before I'd died, but everything was different now.

"Yes, Prometheus has been glowering at Hades for the last twenty minutes, so we should probably go lighten the mood. I think Epimetheus finds this all quite funny, which is a relief, considering his recent bout of stoicism." Athena stood, then reached out a hand and pulled me to my feet.

My legs wobbled a bit upon standing, but I managed to steady myself. "He always did find my embarrassment amusing."

"And, ah, there's something else you should know," she said, wincing. "Persephone is in there."

I stopped in my tracks at the mention of Hades' wife. "Well that's just peachy, isn't it? Could this get anymore awkward?"

"She's quite reasonable and incredibly sweet," Athena said. "If anyone makes it awkward, I'd put money on one of your brothers."

I gave her a dubious look. "Or yours. But...if you say so..." I started walking toward the stairs, then stopped. "Wait, what about Nate? I should probably—"

She bit her bottom lip and shook her head. "Knowing Apollo, he's already told him."

"Gods," I groaned. "He's such a pain. What do I say to him?"

"Just do what I do and ignore them both," she suggested.

"Easy for you to say. You're not going home with one of them."

She looped her arm through mine and led me up the steps to the front door. "Not to worry. Nathaniel is no fool, Tessa. I can't imagine he assumes you to be a virgin after all these years."

I felt my face flush. "No, he knows I'm not, but I'm sure he also didn't assume I had a love affair with the ruler of the damn Underworld, either," I hissed as we entered the hall.

She winced.

"What?" I followed her gaze down the hall and saw Nate standing in front of the door with Apollo. "Shit."

"That meddlesome ass," Athena said, glaring at Apollo.

Apollo smirked when he saw us. Nate cast a glance in my direction and raised his eyebrows as a disbelieving smile formed on his lips. Without a word, they both disappeared into the sitting room.

"Did he just...smile?" I asked.

"He did," Athena said, looking confused. "That's disconcerting."

"I'll say. I'm starting to think I should probably leave."

She tightened her grip on my arm and continued to drag me toward the ornate French doors that led into the sitting room.

"Absolutely not. We're on the verge of war, Tessa, a war which is being led by *your* brother. Like it or not, you're just as much a part of this as the rest of us." She pushed open the doors and nudged me inside, closing them quietly behind us.

Zeus' sitting room felt more crowded today than it had yesterday, despite the similar number of occupants. Zeus and Hera sat in the two armchairs that faced the fireplace, while my brothers, Nate, and Apollo sat on the sofas that flanked them. Standing in front of the fireplace were Hades and Persephone, the petite, dark-haired, russet-skinned harvest goddess and daughter of Demeter. Her clothing—dark leather that all but dared someone to mess with her—and jewel-handled daggers at her hips completely belied her delicate, heart-shaped face, which was currently impassive.

I had to stop myself from sucking in a breath as Hades stepped forward to greet us. As I took in the sight of him, more memories of our time together came rushing back, and I felt my cheeks burn red once again. Frantically, I scrambled to make sure my walls were rock solid.

Tall and slender, he had a boyish face with a long, regal nose, full lips, high cheekbones, and black hair that fell across his forehead is short waves. His clothing was dark—a black button down, with dark gray pants paired with shiny, black wingtip shoes.

"Tessa," he said, his voice soft and far from the harshness I remembered. He crossed the room, then pulled me into a hug and let out a long, shaky breath as he pressed his cheek to my hair. "It truly is wonderful to see you."

"Likewise," I said as the familiar smell of smoke invaded my nostrils.

Trying not to be too obvious, I gently put my hands on his waist and nudged him back.

"I was surprised when I heard of your return," he said as he pulled back, keeping his hands on my arms.

I cleared my throat as I slowly extricated myself from his grip.

"Yes, well, weren't we all?" I smiled, trying to keep my tone light.

Just then, Persephone stepped forward and extended a hand, nudging her husband out of the way. "Tessa, it's so lovely to finally meet you," she said, her voice as sweet as honey. "I've heard so much about you."

'I promise this won't be as awkward as it seems,' she added.

I blinked, then stared for a second, hoping she wasn't just saying that. If I were in Persephone's position, and Nate's ex had come back from the dead, I wouldn't be nearly as comfortable as she seemed.

Then again, she'd spent the last two thousand years with Hades, so I suppose that was more than enough time to gain confidence in their relationship.

Taking her hand, I smiled at her, feeling awkwardly tall next to her petite frame. "It's nice to meet you, too."

Hades put a hand on the small of my back and gestured toward the sofas. "Come, sit. We've much to discuss."

I took a seat on the sofa next to Nate, with Athena on my other side. I slid my hand into Nate's and gave it a gentle squeeze.

'I'm sorry—'

'No need,' he replied. He smiled, but the hard set of his jaw told me he was anything but fine.

"Alright, we're all here," Athena said. "What do we know?"

"Right." Zeus clapped his large hands, dispelling a bit of the awkwardness in the room. "Hades and Persephone have news from the Underworld."

Everyone's attention turned to the Underworld rulers who were standing in front of the fireplace. I saw Hades' eyes drift toward me again, so I pretended to pick at the fuzz on my sweater.

Hades cleared his throat. "We've just been from the border of Tartarus, and the news we received from the giants who guard the realm is quite disturbing. Crius and Cottus claim that in the last few days, a number of their soldiers have located several weak spots on the outer walls of Tartarus."

"Crius?" I shot a look at Zeus when Hades mentioned Cronus' brother. "He's still alive?"

"He has no interest in the goings on of our feud with Cronus, so long as he has work to do in the Underworld," Persephone added with a bite. The sweetness of just a few moments ago had melted into something harder.

"I see." I frowned, now quite convinced.

"What about these weak spots?" Zeus asked.

Hades nodded. "Crius isn't sure how, but according to him, there are now at least three areas where the walls that protect the realm are noticeably weaker."

"Have you confirmed this?" Zeus asked.

"We have," Persephone replied. "We've called for Hecate and a few of her witches to come examine the walls to work out the best way to repair them."

"And the prisoners?"

"All remain inside for now, and it doesn't appear any have regained their corporeal forms," Hades said.

"What about my father and Cronus? Are the wards strong enough to hold them?" I asked.

Hades looked down at me and his dark eyes softened. "Just barely."

Epimetheus spoke up, his voice quiet. "How much more would the walls need to weaken?"

"A fraction more and they would have a way through. We're working on another method to strengthen them again, but something seems to be preventing any measure from working fully."

"What other method?" Nate asked.

"Additional wards around the walls," Hades explained. "They'll act as a failsafe should the magic in the physical walls fail."

"The wards would keep the prisoners non-corporeal, then?" Nate confirmed.

"Correct."

"And we've no idea how this has happened?" Zeus asked.

"None." Hades shook his head. "No one has left Tartarus since the end of the war, so it would seem this is happening from outside the realm."

Prometheus, who'd been sitting sullenly in the corner, raised his eyes to Hades. "None enter or leave the Underworld without your knowledge, or so you say. Is it possible you've missed something?"

"It is not something I *say*, and I'm quite certain you know that," Hades said softly, not sparing my glowering brother a glance. "And no, I have not missed anything."

"Well, the Centimanes certainly don't have the power for something like this," Hera said. "Unless you know something we don't about your guards."

"No, they would have to be receiving help from someone," Hades agreed. "But I've seen no evidence that my men are the ones responsible. I plan to interrogate them fully, though."

"What about Menoetius?" I asked. "If he can disable powers, is it possible he's messing with the power that keeps Tartarus sealed?"

"Possible, but unlikely," Hades replied. "He'd still need help."

I rubbed a hand across my forehead as something pricked at the back of my mind, just out of reach.

"Tessa?" Nate ran a hand up my back. "Have you thought of something?"

"I'm not sure." I squeezed my eyes shut and started drumming my fingers on my knees, trying to latch on to what my mind was trying to show me. Gently, I prodded at the memory, hoping to avoid another onslaught.

Finally, it struck me. I looked up at Hades.

"The Phlegethon."

Everyone looked at me, but I ignored them and kept my eyes on Hades and Persephone.

Persephone gave me a curious look. "The river?"

"Yes. Its fire is what keeps prisoners inside Tartarus, so if someone managed to weaken it, couldn't it weaken the entire realm?"

"Theoretically, yes," she replied slowly. "If they had access to the right kind of power."

Hades folded his arms across his chest and pursed his lips. "What are you thinking?"

"I think...Yes, I remember my mother teaching me that there were certain magics that could allow someone to handle—manipulate—Phlegethonic fire."

'Phlegethonic?'

I almost smiled at Nate's amused tone.

Hades drummed his fingers against his arm as he contemplated what I was saying. "While that's true, none of our guards have knowledge like what Clymene passed to you. The only interactions they have are with each other, and even if that weren't the case, none possess the type of magic required for such a feat. That's primordial magic, Tessa. Not many beings have access to that."

I nodded, feeling a little deflated.

"We'll look into it, though," he said quickly. "It's possible Menoetius has found a primordial witch to ally himself with. If that's the case, then yes, it's possible."

"It wouldn't be the first time," Prometheus grumbled from the corner. I gave him a curious look, but he seemed to be avoiding my gaze.

"It's not as though we've got any other leads," Apollo said with a sigh. "Although I would hope a witch with that kind of power would know better by now."

"As would I," Hades agreed, casting a glance toward me. "Considering Menoetius' past associations, I won't discount anything at this point, though."

"I'll be heading to Earth to track down and interrogate a few leads," Persephone said. "If I find anything of use, I'll report back immediately."

'Track down?' I asked Nate. *'What exactly does she do?'*

'I'd have to let her explain it better, but essentially, she uses Earth magic to track down certain targets. They're usually creatures who need to be either questioned or punished. Criminals, that kind of thing. A bit like what your humans call a bounty hunter.'

I pursed my lips as I reassessed the tiny goddess in front of me. I'd thought her tough exterior was just that. I was surprised to learn what her role as queen of the Underworld actually entailed.

"Alright, well, let us know if you find out anything else, and we'll all keep our ears to the ground topside," Zeus said, standing to see Hades out.

"Of course," Hades replied. Ignoring his brother, he turned his attention to me, raising his eyebrows expectantly. "Tessa, a word before I go?"

"I—sure."

He gave a quick nod, then turned and strode toward the door.

I cast a quick glance at Nate, not sure what to say to him.

'Tessa, Stop worrying about what I think. Go see what he needs.'

Giving him a small smile, I stood to follow Hades into the hall. Before I could get far, Persephone stepped in front of me.

"It was nice to meet you, Tessa." She cast a glance toward the door. "I look forward to getting to know you better."

The way she spoke made it seem as though she actually meant it, which dispelled some of the remaining awkwardness leftover from our initial introduction.

"Likewise," I replied, forcing as much sincerity into my tone as possible.

I made my way out into the hall, letting the door click shut behind me before I turned to face my former lover. His lean, muscled form was resting against a narrow mahogany accent table, and his hands gripped the edge so tightly his knuckles were white. He stared at the ground, fierce anger marring his smooth, porcelain skin.

I leaned against the wall opposite him, and we stood in silence for a few moments.

"Were you aware...while you were gone?" he finally said, his voice tight and quiet.

"No."

He nodded and kept his gaze locked to the travertine floor. "I should have searched for your soul," he murmured, his voice laced with guilt. "Once I gained control of the Underworld, I should've looked for it. I just assumed it was sent to Elysium."

"What would that have accomplished?"

He raised his dark eyes to mine. "A soul that does not make passage into the Underworld knows only desolation. If I'd known yours wasn't there—"

"Please, Hades." I pressed my fingers to my eyes and sighed before looking at him. "I can't take another person blaming themselves for not knowing something was wrong."

He cocked his head to the side and frowned. "What do you mean?"

"Prometheus and Epimetheus are killing themselves over not recognizing me as an Ischyra. Nate's upset because he wasn't there to wake me when Menoetius was in my head, and—"

"Menoetius was in your mind?" Hades pushed himself off the table, his tone abruptly becoming forceful. "When?"

"In a dream walk. Twice now. Last week, before...everything, then again last night."

His eyes went cold, and I saw a flash of the angry, volatile god I'd known when I was younger. "What did he do to you?"

I crossed my arms over my chest and averted my eyes, annoyed with his demanding tone. A memory started to push at my mind, one that had started to return during Menoetius' dream walk. I closed my eyes and forced it off before responding.

"It's fine." I looked up at him. "Done and over with. It's really not something I care to rehash."

He took a few steps forward and gripped my chin, then tilted my face toward his as his eyes searched mine. "There are blank spots in your memory." Releasing me, he eyed me curiously. "Your memories still haven't returned?"

I glared at him, rubbing my chin where his grip had felt bruising. "There are a lot of things I still haven't remembered. It's coming back, just slowly."

"Nathaniel can give you those memories back quite easily. Why hasn't he?"

"I don't want him to. I want them to come on their own. I'm a bit tired of people meddling in my head."

He let out a low growl. "Gods, Tessa, will you never learn? That's idiotic and dangerous. Here."

"Hades, no—"

Without waiting for my permission, he clamped his hand on my shoulder, cementing me in place, then touched a cool finger to my temple.

Before I could react, I felt my body go limp in his arms as the first memory slammed into me.

I STRUGGLED USELESSLY against the bonds that held me to the tree deep in the woods. My arms strained against the ropes that had been woven from godsbane fiber, each move leaving me weaker than the last. Tears streamed silently down my cheeks as a feeling of desolation worked its way through me.

"Why are you doing this?" I cried. "Give me my powers back!"

Menoetius gave me an evil smirk, then gently tucked a vibrant purple blossom behind my ear. The pain of the godsbane flower against my skin made me whimper. "Soon enough, little sister."

He pulled out a crude wooden cup and the new dagger our father had just forged for him, the shiny, engraved silver glittering in the moonlight.

A breathy voice spoke from just behind me. "How do you plan to keep her quiet?"

"That is what you *are here for," Menoetius snapped, slowly dipping the blade into the cup. When he pulled it back out, it was dripping with a pearlescent blue liquid.*

Someone snapped their fingers, and I felt something pinch in my throat.

I opened my mouth to speak, but no words came out.

Panic set in.

"CALM YOURSELF, TESSA," Hades whispered, brushing a hand gently over my hair. "They're just memories. It will all be over soon."

My entire body heaved as I clung to him, my fingers clutching the stiff fabric of his shirt as I buried my face in his shoulder, unable to stop the flow of emotions that were battering into me as my memories returned. Before I could latch on to any of the comfort he offered and drag myself to the surface, I was pulled back in.

"TELL ME. In all her lessons, has Mother explained the different ways godsbane can be weaponized?" Menoetius smirked as he pointed the dagger toward me.

My eyes flicked back down, and dread washed through me when I realized what coated his blade.

I shook my head violently, trying desperately to scream as he stepped closer, but his witch had taken my voice.

"You see, this—" he held the dagger inches from my face "—is godsbane serum. It can coat most anything, turning it into a weapon instantly. My poisoners just created it for me."

His eyes were wild, full of insanity, as he touched the glittering blade to my cheek.

"It hurts, doesn't it?" he whispered.

My breathing picked up as he dragged the blade across my face, then in a single path down my neck, arms, and to the tips of my fingers, leaving thin red slices in my flesh. Pain tore through me, clouding my vision with black spots. I felt my body sag against the ropes as unconsciousness began to take me.

"Oh no, that will not do." He turned to the witch standing next to him. "How long until she heals?"

"Not long," the soft voice responded. "I can heal her now, if you'd like."

"Do it. And when will my brothers return?"

"Zeus has called them to his home, so not for several hours."

My brother eyed me like a predator stalking its prey. "Perfect. Heal her."

Cold hands wrapped around my wrists, and I jerked out of my semiconscious state. The pain of my injuries instantly evaporated, the blood that had streaked across my skin, gone.

Menoetius reached down and lifted two thin swords off the wet grass, then slowly dried the dew off the blades on his pant leg before dipping the ends into the serum. Without hesitating, he drove one through each of my shoulders, tearing through flesh and sinew, blinding me with pain as he pinned me to the tree. I screamed soundlessly, struggling against the ropes and poisoned metal with a ferocity I didn't know I possessed, but to no avail. Silent sobs of pain and helplessness began to wrack my body.

Desperately, I prayed for darkness, but whatever the witch had done was forcing my mind to remain alert. They wanted me to feel every burn, every slice of his knives.

Menoetius slapped my cheek, then took my chin in his painful grip.

"Do not fall asleep on me now, little sister. I have a few more things I'd like to try."

6

NATHANIEL

"You're not at all curious as to what they're speaking about?"

I slid a glance at Hera, whose face was incredulous. Hades and Tessa had been out in the hall for about five minutes, and I was honestly surprised it had taken her this long to start eavesdropping.

"No, mother, I'm not. If she wants to share their conversation with me, she will. Let it go."

"It sounds as though they're arguing." She clicked her tongue. "He never was good for her."

"I think you're the only one who would be surprised by that, Hera," Apollo said with a sigh.

She pursed her lips, then cocked her head to the side, tilting her ear toward the door.

"For the love of us all, woman, give them some privacy," Zeus said, dropping into his normal chair opposite the fireplace. "If you can't trust your son's judgment when it comes to women, then clearly you didn't raise him right."

"Me?" she scoffed. "As though you had no part in his upbringing!"

"Yes, and I raised him to trust his instincts."

I leaned back and rested my head on the back of the sofa, trying to drown out the sound of my parents' bickering.

Epimetheus mimicked my pose and turned his head to face me. "Are you truly alright with her speaking with him alone?"

I snorted. "No, but it's not something I care to argue about, either."

"That's quite noble of you."

"I'm saving myself the hassle of fighting with her unless it's absolutely necessary. That's not noble, that's self-preservation."

"Self-sacrificing is more like it," Apollo muttered. "You'd likely feel differently if you'd been around to witness the fiasco they called a relationship." He took a sip of wine and raised his eyebrows. "One of the benefits of being the youngest, I suppose."

"I still haven't thanked you for forcing your vivid memories on me when I walked in," I said, glaring at him.

"I just thought you should have fair warning, that's all."

"Yes, and your memories of walking in on the two of them tangled up in bed were truly necessary to convey that warning."

"I apologize. That one must've slipped through my walls."

"That's bullshit and you know it."

"Ignore him, Nathaniel," Athena said. "He's just—"

Whatever she'd been about to say was cut off by a pained cry from the hall.

I was on my feet and bursting through the door within seconds. When I got into the hall, Tessa was on the ground. Hades was holding her up, whispering in her ear. Her hands gripped his arm as her entire body heaved. Fear pulsed off her and into me with ferocity.

I dropped to the floor in front of her, shoving Hades out of the way,

"Tessa, look at me." I gripped both sides of her face and forced her to meet my eyes. Hers were wild with fear and overflowing with tears.

"N-N-Nate...h-h-he—" Her words were cut off as another memory took her, causing her entire body to retch.

I slapped her cheek lightly. "Look at me! What happened?"

"You son of a bitch!" Prometheus roared, advancing on Hades. "What did you do to her?"

"She's fine, Prometheus," Hades murmured, folding his arms across his chest and staring down at her shrewdly. "She just needs a bit of time."

"A bit of time? Look at her!"

She closed her eyes as she gripped my arms and tried to steady herself. "I r-r-remember—" Her words cut off as she sucked in a deep breath and buried her face in my shoulder.

"What did you do, Hades?" Apollo asked, his tone careful.

"Something you all should've done the moment she woke," he snapped, his calm demeanor from just a few moments ago evaporating.

"He gave her back her memories," I bit out. "All of them."

There were a few seconds of stunned silence.

"You did what?" Athena whispered.

Persephone shook her head and stared at Hades incredulously. "You fool. What were you thinking?"

Epimetheus took a menacing step toward Hades. "Did she ask you to do that for her?"

"No, she did not." I brushed my hand over Tessa's hair, smoothing it off her face where her tears had caused it to stick. Her breathing began to steady. *'Are you alright?'*

She took a deep breath then gave a quick nod, keeping her eyes on mine. *'I need to get up.'*

Standing, I reached out a hand and pulled her to her feet. With shaking hands, she wiped at her tears, then rested her forehead on my shoulder as she took a few more deep breaths. I ran my hand up and down her spine, trying to soothe her.

"Stow the kid gloves, Nathaniel," Hades said. "I didn't hurt her."

My gaze shot to where he stood on the other side of the twins. "You have no clue what you might've done."

"You're being over-dramatic."

Persephone smacked the back of his head and shushed him.

Tessa's entire body stilled, and something in her gaze shifted. The look of fury that formed in her eyes at his words was nothing short of terrifying. All other emotion fled from her expression as she turned to face him.

"You had no right to do that, Hades," she said, her tone even.

Persephone's entire body stiffened, her demeanor changing as she moved to stand in front of her husband, a hand on the dagger at her hip.

Hades' eyebrows shot up. "You'd prefer your memories come back at a more convenient time, then? Maybe when you're in the midst of attempting to rescue your brother? Considering his current lack of sanity, I can't imagine that would end well."

"It's not your place to make that choice for me," she snapped, taking a step toward him. "And stop talking to me like I'm a child!"

I put a hand on her shoulder before she could go any further.

"You're weak without those memories, Tessa," he said, ignoring Persephone's hissed warning as he stepped out from behind her. "You know it as well as I. It's not my fault you're choosing to bury your pain instead of facing it!"

"Is that what this is about? There aren't enough miserable souls in the Underworld to torment, so you thought you'd pay me a visit, help me 'face my pain'?" Tessa ran her hands through her hair and let out a disbelieving laugh. "You sadistic piece of shit!"

I barely had time to throw myself in front of her before she lunged at him. "Tessa, stop!"

"Let me go, Nate!" She beat against my chest, struggling against my hold. Coercion flew off her as she tried to get around me, hitting me so forcefully I almost faltered.

Slamming my mental walls up tighter, I gripped both of her arms and used my full weight to keep her in place. "Absolutely not."

"Hades, go wait outside," Zeus ordered, stepping in front of his brother. "Now is not the time—"

"Oh, just let her get it out of her system," Hades replied. He jerked his chin toward Tessa. "Look at her. She's been holding her emotions in since the moment she awakened. Here I thought she was struggling to handle her past, and it turns out you fools were helping her ignore it."

"I bet you really fucking love this, don't you?" Tears thickened Tessa's words as she continued to strain against me. "Was that enough pain and hurt for you for today? Have you met your fucking *quota*?"

"You'll thank me when you manage to save your brother without getting yourself killed in the process!"

"Hades!" Zeus roared, stepping in front of him. "Wait. Out. Side."

"Easy, my love," Persephone purred, putting one hand on his chest in a soothing gesture. "This isn't helping anyone."

Hades shook his head, then tsked before sliding his hands in his pockets and turning to stride down the hall.

"Still as ungrateful as always, I see," Hades called back.

She broke free from my hold, managing two steps past me before I latched onto her arm again.

"Tessa!" I jerked her toward me. "Enough!"

She glared at me but stopped her struggling.

"Bring her back in the living room," Zeus ordered. "Prometheus, Epimetheus, let's finish this discussion outside."

"A discussion about me?" Tessa demanded.

"That's none of your concern. Now go settle yourself down before you hurt someone."

Seething, she jerked away from me and stormed into the living room, slamming the door open with a resounding crash.

Zeus turned his glare on me and my siblings.

"You three get her calmed down. I won't tolerate these outbursts."

"Then maybe you should put a leash on that damn brute," Hera snapped. "He's the one that caused this."

Ignoring Hera's rebuke, Zeus looked at Prometheus and Epimetheus, who wore identical masks of anger. "Come, let's go wrap up. They'll deal with her."

"I'm staying with my sister," Epimetheus said, his tone leaving no room for argument.

Zeus' lip curled in annoyance, but he didn't argue. Without a word, he turned and stormed down the hall, Hera trailing after him.

"Make sure she's alright. I'll deal with Hades," Prometheus said to his twin, before following Zeus out.

Before following them, Persephone hesitated. "Please apologize to Tessa for my husband's behavior," she said with a sigh. "Well-intentioned or not, I know he can be a bastard at times."

I nodded, but otherwise gave her no guarantee I'd pass along the message.

Once she was gone, Athena exhaled an angry breath. "Father should've known that would happen the moment Hades got here."

I raised my eyebrows and looked down at her. "I'm assuming that wasn't an unusual occurrence?"

Apollo snorted quietly from beside me. "That's putting it mildly." He sighed, then gave me a tight smile. "Come, let's go check on her."

When we entered the living room, Tessa was crouched in front of the fireplace, her arms wrapped around her head as she rocked on her heels. Her emotions swirled around her; fury, anger, grief, love, joy, pain, pleasure, and everything in between, all tearing through her mental walls and into mine like shrapnel.

Trying to ignore the discomfort they were causing me, I stooped down beside her and rubbed a hand up her back, stilling her movements. Epimetheus crouched down and pulled one of her hands into his.

"What can I do?" I asked.

Her whole body tensed, then she let out a deep, slow breath.

"Take me home." She sniffed and lifted her head. Her eyes were red with tears that ran in rivulets down her cheeks. "Please. I just want to go home."

Keeping her hand around her brother's, she leaned forward and pressed her face into my chest. I slid my arms around her and pulled her tight against me.

I met Epimetheus' eyes and raised my brows in question. *'Is it alright if I take her back?'*

His features were tense as he stared down at her. *'Whatever she needs.'*

'Do you want to come with us?'

'No, I don't think it's me she wants right now,' he replied, his tone tinged with sadness. *'Just take care of her, please.'*

"Please, Nate," Tessa said, her voice barely a whimper. "Please, just take me home."

"Why don't you let Apollo calm you down a bit first?" Athena suggested gently.

Epimetheus glanced up at her, then back down at Tessa. "That might be a good idea," he said quietly.

Tessa shuddered in my arms, not lifting her head from where it was pressed against my chest.

I tightened my arms around her, then glanced over at my brother. He was standing behind Athena with his arms folded, staring at Tessa with a look of concern.

'What is it?' I asked him.

He pressed his lips together and flicked a glance at me. *'Convince her to let me use my magic to calm her. I know what memories she's dealing with, Nathaniel. This won't be easy, for either of you.'*

I frowned, then eased Tessa back a few inches until she was looking up at me.

'I feel everything that's coming off you,' I told her. *'Let Apollo calm you down a bit, then I'll take you home.'*

'And you'll stay with me?' Even in her thoughts, her voice sounded small, fearful.

I brushed a hand over her hair and kissed her forehead. *'Where else would I be?'*

She pushed a vision of me punching Hades into my mind, and I couldn't help the laugh that escaped.

'As much as I would love to, I don't think now is the time.'

She lifted her face and gave me a rueful, tear-filled smile, then allowed me to help her to her feet. Taking a deep breath, she turned and faced Apollo. "Would you mind?"

He offered her the same tense smile he'd given me in the hall.

"Of course not." He held out a hand to her, his tone surprisingly gentle. "Come here."

She put her shaking hand in his, and immediately, the pale,

yellow light of his healing magic flowed between them. It was brief, only lasting a few seconds, but the effect was instantaneous as both her body and mind began to relax.

When he was done, he let go of her hand, then placed both of his on her shoulders.

"Look at me, Tessa." He waited until her eyes were on his before continuing. "Do not let the memory of your brother's viciousness succeed where his actions did not. He does not deserve the satisfaction of breaking you."

Her lower lip trembled as she stared at him, then she nodded. "Thank you," she whispered.

He gave her a pained smile, then nudged her toward me.

"Go home. Get some rest. We'll regroup later." He gave me a pointed look. *'Stay with her. See if you can get those friends of hers up to spend some time with her.'*

I gave him a sharp nod, then took Tessa's hand. I met her eyes and was relieved to see they seemed clear. "You ready to go?"

"Yeah." She gave me an unsteady nod. "Let's go."

7

TESSA

As soon as we returned to Nate's, I made a beeline for the bathroom. Apollo's magic had subdued the physical and mental reaction to the return of my memories, but it did nothing to erase the filthy feeling that enveloped my entire body.

I hesitated, towel in hand, before turning on the water, and looked back at the door. Nate was standing there, legs crossed at the ankles and leaning against the frame. He hadn't done his hair today, so it fell in an adorable mess across his forehead. One hand was in his pocket and the other rubbed the back of his neck. The expression in his midnight blue eyes made me think he was afraid I'd become breakable.

As much as I didn't want to admit it, I was beginning to feel that way. Having all my memories returned had left me feeling...damaged. All the wonderful memories of my life as both a Titaness and an Ischyra kept getting beaten back by the very clear memories of the times my oldest brother had taken me into the woods and tortured me. Menoetius had hurt me in ways no living being should ever experience, and for the second time in my life, it was pulling me apart, piece by piece.

"Will you sit with me?" I asked, struggling to get my voice above a whisper. "I don't want to be alone," I added when I saw his confused expression.

He crossed the room and took my face in his hands, then laid his lips on mine, kissing me in a way that left me breathless. Heat and love pulsed through my body, stubbornly pushing back the pain brought on by my newfound memories. Knowing him, he was likely being bombarded with my emotions, but he knew exactly what I needed.

He pulled back and looked at me tenderly, then ran his thumb along my jaw. "Go on. I'll be back once you're in the shower."

Once I'd stripped out of my clothes and climbed in the shower, Nate came in and sat on the bathroom floor, leaning against the glass wall.

"Talk to me," I said, closing my eyes against the hot water as it ran over my face. "Distract me. I know you've got questions."

"Don't you think there are more important things to discuss than what I'm curious about?"

"Yes, but that's not what I want to talk about right now."

He was quiet, and I knew he was trying to talk himself out of asking the things he wanted to ask. After a few moments, he broke down. "So...you and Hades?"

"Me and Hades," I muttered, reaching for the shampoo. "Consider him the highlight of my rebellious youth."

He let out a harsh laugh. "Yes, I could see why he'd be perfect for that. I take it your parents didn't approve?"

"My father was gone by then, and my mother...she didn't really seem to care who I consorted with, as long as they fought for the right side." I rinsed the shampoo out and started working a few drops of sweet-smelling oil into my hair. "My brothers, though...they hated him. They were all so damn overprotective of me from the day I was born; even more so once my powers emerged." I set the bottle down with a thud. "I'm a Titaness and they treated me like nothing more than a human. I met Hades one day when he and Zeus came to meet with Prometheus and Epimetheus, and he took an interest in me. Or maybe in my lack of training, I don't really know."

"And you started...a relationship?"

"I wouldn't call it that, exactly." I shut off the water and pulled my towel off the hook on the wall inside the shower, then started drying myself off. "I liked him because he didn't define me by my power. He was the only one who didn't seem to give a shit one way or another what kind of power I had. He saw my potential and helped me... accept it, I suppose. Tried to help me harness it."

Tightening the towel around my chest, I opened the shower door and stepped out, then slid to the floor next to him, tucking myself against him.

Absently, I drew my fingers up and down his arm. "Plus, he was the first person to acknowledge how badly I needed to be properly trained. My brothers insisted on protecting me, but Hades insisted on helping me become a fighter. Atlas helped eventually, but I don't know what would've happened had Hades not pulled me out from under their thumbs." I shrugged. "In spite of everything, no matter how much I hate him sometimes, I'll always be thankful for the things he helped me achieve. Any confidence I gained in my past life was largely thanks to him."

"I can appreciate that." His arm tightened around my shoulders, so I snuggled in closer. "Why didn't it work out?"

"We were together, more or less, right up until the end, but what you saw today was typical of pretty much every fight we had, and they happened often. We cared for each other, don't get me wrong, but it never went beyond that. Deep down, I knew he wasn't the one for me. We damaged each other far too much for that."

"In other words, I don't need to worry about you itching to rekindle a lost love?"

My head jerked up. "Nate!"

He smirked, and I smacked his chest when I saw the teasing look in his eyes.

"Jerk," I murmured, gripping his chin and kissing him.

He chuckled, then stood and pulled me to my feet. "Get dressed, then we'll talk."

Once I brushed out my hair and pulled on a pair of soft leggings and a long-sleeved shirt, I found Nate in the living room on the couch. His head rested against the back, and he was drumming his fingers rhythmically on the arm.

"You okay?" I asked as I sat down next to him.

He tapped his head and smiled, then pulled me into his side. "Yeah. Athena was just checking in."

"She's worried about me."

"She and Apollo both are. She told your brothers you were safe and to leave you be for now."

I let out a sigh of relief. "Is it awful that the last thing I want right now is to deal with them?" I felt terrible even thinking it, but the idea of the twins' concern, their suffocating need to make sure I was safe being forced on me right now was nauseating.

"No, of course not," Nate said. "You're all going to have to adapt to this new life you have, Tessa. Although, I'd like to think they have better perspective now than they did back then."

I twisted so I was laying with my head against the opposite arm of the sofa, my feet in his lap.

"So, I had another question," he said hesitantly, slowly rubbing a hand up and down my calf.

I arched a brow. "Something not involving my love life?"

"No. Well, I don't know, actually." He cleared his throat and shifted uncomfortably. "You and Apollo...you seemed very comfortable with him back there. Did you—"

My eyes widened, and I sat straight up, stunned. "Absolutely not! Why would you think that?"

"You two looked close when he was giving you his magic, and he willingly had an interdiction placed on him to help keep you safe." He sighed and rubbed his hands across his face and groaned. "I sound like a jealous boyfriend."

Relaxing, I settled back against the sofa. "I knew Apollo at a time in his life when he was too young to be so uptight and...curmudgeonly. He was still an overconfident prick back then, but to a much lesser degree. He knew what Menoetius had done to me. We were never any more than acquaintances before..."

I trailed off, struggling to finish the sentence.

Before I died.

Yesterday, that had been a simple fact. Hecate performed a spell that had essentially killed me. I had died, been killed to protect both myself and Olympus, then I was reborn. Period.

Today, it weighed on me differently. There were emotions, thoughts, and knowledge tied to it all that hadn't been there before. When I'd recalled the events surrounding my death when I was an Ischyra, I'd felt fear, but it was combined with confusion and curiosity because I was detached from them. I didn't know who those feelings belonged to at the time, but I knew I needed to find out.

So much had happened in the days and weeks leading up to my death. Painful, traumatic, life-changing things I couldn't bear to think about. Just the what-ifs of that day itself caused shivers of panic to slide through me.

What if Iapetus had finished off Clymene and gotten to Hecate before she'd had a chance to do her spell? He and Cronus most certainly would've taken me, forced my power from me by whatever means necessary and used their own witch's spell to wield it themselves. If they didn't kill me, they likely would've given Menoetius a run for his money in the pain and suffering department. Taking a god's life force, destroying them completely, was painful—as far as deaths went. Draining a god of their power was another thing entirely.

Nausea began to swirl in my stomach as I contemplated what they might've done.

They would've taken my power, drained it from me bit by bit, and used it to tear down all of Olympus. They would've used it to mimic every power they could, taking over Earth and enslaving the humans that lived there. That pure and utter destruction would've been able to exist because of me, because of my ability to mimic any power I came across.

"It would've been my fault," I murmured.

"No." Nate said the word with finality, not needing to ask where my thoughts had gone. He shifted closer and pulled me into his lap.

"Seconds, Nate." I forced myself to meet his gaze. "If Atlas hadn't been there with me that day, if he hadn't been able to hold off Cronus for those few seconds, they would've used my power to destroy everything." I closed my eyes against the memory of Menoetius demonstrating the spell he and his witch had been working on. It had been meant to siphon out a deity's power, only it hadn't been perfected, so I had become their test subject. My hands started to shake as the first of Apollo's healing magic began to wear off. "Do you know how much it hurts to have your power taken from you, pulled from your body?"

"Gods, Tessa," he murmured, pressing his lips to my hair and holding me tighter. My mental walls were wide open, so he could see every flash of memory in my mind.

"Apollo's magic is fading," I said through gritted teeth. "It hurts."

"I can try a bit of Coercion," he offered half-heartedly. "That might help."

I shook my head, the movement quick and jerky.

"No. No, I can't medicate this away." I gripped his shirt and pressed my face into his chest. "Just don't leave me, okay?"

He let out a deep, shuddering breath.

"Never."

In that one fervently whispered word, I knew he meant it.

Sobs began to wrack my body as the memories slowly began to tear down the magic Apollo had used to help settle me. Bit by bit, his light was extinguished by fear, helplessness, loss, and unrelenting pain. As I lay there crying, I wished desperately for it to all to end.

In the back of my mind, I knew this was likely just the beginning.

8

NATHANIEL

I wasn't sure how long I'd been asleep before I was woken by my sister's voice in my mind.

'I'm out on the porch. Come outside.'

Careful not to jostle Tessa, I slowly eased myself out from under her, then pulled a blanket off the back of the sofa and covered her.

When I opened the door, Athena stood on the other side.

"I've come to relieve you," she said with a soft smile. "Father would like to see you, and I assumed you wouldn't want Tessa left alone just yet."

I rubbed the back of my neck and glanced back at Tessa. Her crying jag had lasted nearly an hour before she'd finally fallen asleep. I was hesitant to wake her any time soon.

I sighed and looked back at my eldest sister. "What does he need to see me for? I'd rather not leave her just yet."

"Rumblings Earthside that require our attention. I'll let him explain it all." She eyed me warily. "You look dreadful, Nathaniel. How is she?"

I stepped onto the porch and quietly closed the door behind me, then sat down in one of the wooden chairs. Athena sat down next to me.

"I don't know. We talked some, then once Apollo's magic wore off, the floodgates opened." I pinched the bridge of my nose and closed my eyes, wishing I could forget everything I'd seen in her mind. "Those things Menoetius did to her..."

"She was his little lab rat." Athena stared down at her hands, her lips pressed into a thin line. "When we discovered what he was doing—"

"Why didn't he just take her power then? Why go through the process of all of that torture, when Cronus just wanted her power?"

She leaned back in her seat and turned her face toward me. "There were two reasons, as far as I could tell. The first was that the spell to fully remove her powers without killing her had yet to be perfected. Cronus wouldn't have been able to wield the full power of two Titans at once, so he needed to be able to take on small portions of her power at a time, replenishing day by day. She would've been a well spring of power solely under his control."

I nodded, acknowledging the logic. "And the other?"

She raised her eyebrows and leaned back in the chair. "The other reason is conjecture on my part, but I see no reason for it to be inaccurate. Menoetius enjoys torture. He finds it fun. He likes belittling and humiliating others. Tessa had a power that he could've only wished for, so he did what he could to ensure she knew she was beneath him, despite what her abilities might've been."

"I would've thought being able to simply disable her powers would've gotten that message across," I muttered, rubbing my hands over my face as I tried to erase from my mind what I'd seen in Tessa's thoughts.

Repeatedly, he'd tied her to a tree and taken her power, using every manner of torture available to torment her. He'd used her as his pin cushion to test his newest godsbane infused weapons—whips, knives, arrows, among others—and as his test subject for painful spells, the most agonizing of which were attempts to siphon her power.

Fortunately for her, it seemed his witch didn't get that one quite right before she and her brothers figured out what was happening.

"Disabling powers is a parlor trick for him," Athena said bitterly. "Inflicting physical and psychological pain when a being is at their weakest is where his true gift lies."

I squeezed my eyes shut, hating the question I was about to ask. "There's something I have to know. I don't know if I've seen all there is to see when it comes to Menoetius, but—" I swallowed, then faced my sister. "Was she ever—"

"No." Athena leaned forward and took my hand. "She was never assaulted in that way, Nathaniel, I can promise you that. Menoetius only dealt out pain he could inflict himself, and raping his own sister was not his style."

"Menoetius had friends," I bit out. "Plenty who would have been more than willing."

"We would've seen it when Hecate restored her memories, but also...Hades would've known."

I frowned. "How?"

She gave me a sad smile. "Hades' greatest gift is locating the most epic source of pain within a person, conscious or subconscious, and exploiting it. After we discovered what had been happening to her, he insisted on examining her, despite Hecate's claims that her memories of those events had all been restored."

My eyebrows shot up. "He did *what*?"

Athena squeezed my hand in hers. "He had Tessa's permission, and he did it while she was unconscious. She wanted to know, Nathaniel, and despite what you saw today and what you know of Hades, he did care for her. Their relationship was volatile, but even he hated to see her in such pain." She tilted her head to the gave me a knowing look. "You're worried about him, aren't you?"

"Maybe. Yes." I smiled at her ruefully. "It's a lot to take in. One week ago, would you have pegged Tessa as the type to have a relationship with someone like him?"

Athena laughed, then shook her head. "Gods, no. I can see why that might throw you for a bit of a loop."

"I guess that just drove home how little I truly know about her now," I said with a sigh.

"I disagree. Those two have a strange chemistry, I won't lie, but at your cores, you and she are entirely in sync. I've never seen a more perfect pair."

"It does feel that way." A smile ghosted across my lips as I thought back to the day we had met. Tessa hadn't cowered under whatever power or influence she assumed I'd had. She'd been open with her thoughts and feelings, not once attempting to hide her disdain or annoyance with the things we'd discussed.

"It *is* that way. Why do you think you've been one of her clearest memories? It's not your roguish good looks, trust me," she teased. "It's because she loves you, baby brother. I don't know that she's said it outright, but it's true. She's your other half, a perfect match."

"And you didn't think that about Hades?"

"Truthfully? I did. Then I saw him with Persephone. They're nearly as well-suited for one another as you and Tessa. Persephone is the light to his dark, a balance Tessa could never have given him. If anything, Tessa fed into his darkness."

"How—?" Then it dawned on me. "He's an empath."

Athena nodded. "Yes. And she's a Mimic. Take a violent empathic god who lives in a bubble of negative emotions and put him with a very powerful Mimic, and you've got...well, to be blunt, their entire relationship was essentially one long bout of make-up sex."

I choked out a laugh. "Gods, I did not need to hear that." *Or picture that.*

"Lighten up, Nathaniel," she said, patting my arm. "Her lack of virginity shouldn't come as a surprise."

"And this conversation is done." I squeezed her hand and stood. "Keep an eye on her. I'm hoping she'll sleep a bit longer."

Athena smiled up at me. "Of course. I'll let you know when she wakes."

"Thank you." I gave her a quick kiss on the top of her head.

"Actually, wait." She gnawed at her lip, then sat up a bit straighter. "I wanted to ask you about Apollo."

I let out a suffering sigh. "What about him?"

"It seems as though you two have been getting on a bit better these days."

"And?"

"He's your brother, Nathaniel." She tilted her chin in a slightly challenging gesture. "I think you should try to mend fences with him. I know he wants to."

"I tolerate him, just as he does me. What more do you want?"

"Progress. Tessa's family is fractured, her twin has gone mad, yet here you are wasting your relationship with Apollo because you're too damn stubborn to find common ground."

"That's not fair. Tessa's circumstances are nothing like mine."

"No, they're worse," she said. "She would kill to have her brother here with her. You've got yours, yet all you two do is glare and snark at one another. And for what? Disagreements from millennia ago?"

I dragged a hand through my hair and looked out over my front lawn. "I'm working on it, Athena. In my own way, I am."

"That's all I ask." She smiled sweetly. "Now go. You don't want to keep the Overlord waiting."

I snorted at her use of the nickname we'd given Zeus when we were younger.

"No, I certainly wouldn't want that."

9

TESSA

My dreams began as mundane visions of my life as a Titaness, mixed with memories of my life as an Ischyra, then slowly became interspersed with terrifying memories of my oldest brother's attacks.

As the frequency of those memories increased, other painful memories resurfaced.

Hecate and Hades drawing the memories of Menoetius' cruelty to the forefront of my mind. Panicking as I hid from Cronus because I hadn't been taught to defend myself. Fighting with my mother and brothers when I wanted to begin training to fight. Sneaking off with Hades so he could teach me the things my brothers wouldn't. Sobbing at my father's feet, begging him to abandon our tyrannical leader and return to our family.

Crushing hurt when Father looked down at me with disdain and shoved me off like an annoying pet when I spoke against our ruler.

The terror in my mother's eyes when she realized who and what was coming for me. For her.

Even in my dreams, I could feel fear seeping through every part of me. I struggled within my own mind as I tried to drag myself back to the waking world so I could stop suffocating under the weight of my past. I called out to Nate but couldn't seem to get through my own pain.

Just as I began to think I would be stuck in this dream world permanently, I heard a voice, measured, yet forceful.

"You can make it stop, Tessa."

Frowning, I watched as a scene unfolded in front of me. My father and mother were fighting as I cowered in a corner, hiding from his wrath. I couldn't hear the words they were shouting at one another, but Iapetus was furious, and Clymene looked... broken. Distraught.

"I can't."

"Of course you can," the voice continued. "You've done it before. This should be child's play for you."

My parents continued to fight. Iapetus raised his hand to my mother. She flinched, and I nearly launched myself forward. I was the reason they were fighting, after all. I'd just informed my father I wouldn't be supportive of Cronus' cause, that I would be standing against him in the war, alongside my brothers. He blamed Clymene, told her she was too soft on me, had taken advantage of all his time away to poison me against him.

It wasn't so long after that when he decided a daughter who wouldn't fight with him wasn't a daughter worth saving, so he agreed to help Cronus take me, drain my power so he could use it for himself.

"It won't do any good if you continue," the voice told me. "Accept that and remove yourself from this place that no longer exists."

"I'm trying," I whispered, unable to tear my eyes from the scene before me. "I can't make it stop."

After a few more seconds, everything around me faded, and I was left standing in an expanse of black emptiness. My heart began to pound as I was reminded of the emptiness of the Void, the nothingness that was Chaos that I'd recalled that day in front of school.

"Well that was quite depressing," a sardonic voice said from behind me. "I expected more from you, Tessa. You should have been able to remove yourself from that nightmare with barely a thought."

Turning around, I found myself facing my former lover. The fear that had been coursing through me turned immediately to anger.

"Get out of my head, Hades," I growled.

He arched a brow and folded his arms across his chest. "Why? It looks to me as though you could use a bit of help with those dreams of yours. I would think you'd be grateful I ended that one before it became any more miserable than it already was."

"Fuck off." I turned from him and started to walk away, unsure where—or if—this vast, empty space began or ended.

Hades' slow footsteps followed behind, moving closer despite the rapid movement of my own feet. The loud echo of my steps increased in tempo as I tried to outpace him.

"You know, I don't understand why you're so upset with me," he said, his tone conversational. "The way I see it, I did you a favor."

"You would see it that way." I suddenly wished Hecate had banned everyone from my mind and not just those who meant me harm. A mental doorbell would've been great right about now.

"I don't see it that way." He appeared in front of me, and I jumped, closing my eyes, annoyed that I'd let him startle me.

"It *is* that way," he continued. "You, as usual, are just being stubborn."

"Get out of my head," I repeated, stepping around him.

Once again, he appeared in front of me. "Tessa, stop."

I put my hands on my hips and took a step back. "Why? After what you pulled earlier, *why* should I even entertain a conversation with you?"

"Because deep down, you know you needed those memories back. You must know that it was stupid to try to wait until they came back on their own. You know I was *right.*"

"Even if I did agree, and I'm not saying I do, it doesn't change the fact that you just did whatever you wanted with absolutely no regard for what *my* wishes were."

He shrugged. "I'm not going to apologize for that. You never would've agreed to it if I'd asked."

"You're right. I wouldn't have." I shook my head in disgust. "You know, for a few seconds back there, I actually thought you'd gotten nicer since the last time I saw you."

"It's not my fault you mistook my concern for weakness." He snapped his fingers and two high-backed, red velvet armchairs appeared. He gestured toward them before taking a seat. "Sit."

"No."

He rolled his eyes. "*Please* sit."

"I said—"

"Then kick me out." A sly smile spread across his face. "If you don't want me here, kick me out, wake yourself up, and I'll never bother you again."

I snorted. "Unlikely."

He sat down and propped an ankle on his knee, then spread his hands in front of him in an "I'm waiting" gesture.

I opened my mouth, but no witty retort came to me. My lip curled in aggravation. He knew what he was doing. Worse, he knew that *I* knew what he was doing.

I dropped into the chair that faced him and raised my eyebrows expectantly.

"You need help, Tessa."

"I have help. Two brothers, a boyfriend, and a slew of gods and goddesses."

"Not one of whom has a damn clue what you're capable of. You need *my* help."

"Oh, so now you want to be helpful?" I shook my head in disbelief. "Where was that benevolence a few hours ago?"

He chuckled. "I've already given my answer, so I don't care to repeat myself. Admit it. They don't get it. They never have."

"Oh? And you're just the guy, right?" I arched a brow. "Tell me, does Persephone know you're here?"

He smirked at my attempt to bait him. "Believe it or not, she's half the reason I came."

I frowned. "What are you talking about?"

"Persephone knows I would be less than thrilled if your life ended for a second time, so she thought I should try to help you." He shrugged. "She's a bit of a bleeding heart that way."

"Huh. Imagine that." I sighed, then looked at him. "Alright, say I let you help me. What do you propose?"

"Aside from resuming our prior training? Right now, you've got a band-aid holding your mental walls shut and a lover who will wake you if you're attacked in a dream. Neither of those are sustainable solutions, so I'm going to teach you how to keep yourself safe within your own mind while you sleep." He cocked a brow. "It's something you should've let me teach you sooner."

"Atlas was—"

"Spare me. Atlas was a dreadful teacher."

"He was not!"

He waved off my protest. "I'm better suited for this task."

"Says you," I scoffed.

"Says any person with a lick of sense," he shot back. "Have you forgotten the things you accomplished, once you finally allowed me to draw out your power? Once you finally allowed *yourself* to draw out your power?"

I huffed, not wanting to think about those darker, final days of my life. "Of course not. I'll ask again. What are you proposing?"

His feline smile told me he knew I was giving in. "So often my powers as an empath are used for punishment, but in your case, I believe they can be used for a far more beneficial purpose."

"Like what?"

"Survival. Even sparring together, Atlas went easy on you, made it fun. We both know I was the only teacher you had who was willing to push you to your breaking point, willing to hurt you. It was the only way you ever showed sign of success. You learned more in those last few years of your life than in the centuries prior."

"Nate—"

He held up a hand to cut me off. "Will be a huge help in this process, I'm certain."

I paused, momentarily surprised. I had no doubts, of course, but I didn't expect him to have the same confidence in Nate that I did.

One corner of his mouth pulled up in an amused smile when

he saw my expression. "Nathaniel has been a Coercer for Olympus for three millennia and alive nearly two hundred years before that. Do you really think his only duties involved transitioning and training recruits? Liaising with those wretched humans?"

"I guess...I hadn't really thought about it."

Based on the gleam in Hades' eyes, I had a feeling it was probably something I should've thought to ask sooner.

"Don't bother asking," he said, reading the question in my eyes. "I'll let you prod him for those details. Your Mentalist powers are weakened now, so those will have to be your main focus while you can get back up to your former strength." He cocked his head to the side in question. "How did you do with those while training as an Ischyra?"

"Okay, for the most part."

Eyes narrowed, he tapped his fingers against his lips. "It took you some time to truly grasp those powers before. What made it easier this time around?"

"I'm not sure, exactly. It might have been because those were the first powers I was exposed to."

"How so?"

"Nate used Coercion on me back when I was still human."

His eyebrows shot up in amusement. "And you say I have boundary issues?"

I shifted in my seat. "It was necessary, sort of. He and Chiron think his was the first power I absorbed, and since it happened when I was still human, it may have left more of an impression than the others."

He was nodding before I'd even finished speaking. "Yes, making the transition from human to Ischyra with a touch of a true god's magic already active in your system would've been a benefit, certainly. Had you gotten into any mental combat training prior to your awakening?"

"A little, but Athena and Ares were more focused on my elemental abilities."

"Alright. We'll focus on that and sealing up those mental walls of yours."

"And how exactly are you planning on doing that?"

His expression turned gleeful. "As you said, I'm a sadistic piece of shit. Use your imagination."

"Tessa, wake up!"

I was ripped from my dream walk and dragged back to Nate's living room in a startling jolt. Frantically, I reached out for Nate, only to find the spot he'd occupied earlier empty.

"Tessa!" Athena's sharp voice brought my focus to her. She was kneeling in front of me.

"Where's Nate?" I demanded, my eyes darting around the room.

She gave me a sympathetic look and rose to sit on the couch next to me. "Zeus called him up to the palace, so I offered to swap places." Her gray eyes ran over my face. "What were you dreaming about? You seemed distressed."

I scrubbed my hands over my face and sighed. "Everything. It's like my mind won't shut down now that it has all this new information to process." I cast her a glance. "Then Hades showed up."

She groaned. "What did he want now? To apologize, I hope?"

"Hardly. He wants to go back to teaching me."

She opened her mouth, then pursed her lips, tilting her head in consideration. "You know, that might not be the worst idea."

My eyes widened. "You actually agree with him?"

She shrugged. "Despite his shortcomings, he was quite a good teacher, from what I recall."

I slumped back against the couch. "I guess."

"Would you like to go back to sleep?" she asked quietly.

"No. I'm trying very, very hard not to lose my shit right now, so I need some time before I face those nightmares again." As annoying as my conversation with him might've been, I wasn't going to complain about the reprieve Hades had given me from my dreams, considering where they'd been going. Already, I was dreading going back to sleep tonight, knowing what I would likely be facing.

"Alright." She tucked her feet under her and rested her arm on the back of the sofa. "What should we do, then? I think a distraction might be a good idea."

"Okay." I nodded. "Tell me why Zeus called Nate away."

"Ares has been in Athens the last few days. There's been a significant uptick in empousa attacks, globally, along with widespread crop failures throughout the Western Hemisphere over the last week."

"What do you think is causing them to fail?" Empousa attacks weren't abnormal, especially considering Menoetius had been gathering forces to his side. The vampiric women likely would've been the first faction to side with him, considering his disdain for the human race. Knowing him, he'd offer them free reign to feast on humans and Ischyra once the war was won.

There were very few creatures who could cause widespread crop failures, though.

"It would appear the Telchines have been reemerging. Or, at least, their descendants."

"The poisoners? I thought they'd fallen into the weaponry trade." The group of alchemists had started out as artists and metal workers and were once staunch allies of Zeus' mother, Rhea. After a falling out with Zeus and his siblings, the Telchines had turned to poisons, tainting the Earth and causing a great number of human deaths, before turning toward weaponizing their creations. Zeus and Poseidon had destroyed the original eighteen, but not before several of the females had given birth and scattered their children around the globe, hidden from deities who might hunt them down.

"Back when you were still alive, they did," Athena explained. "Now, it seems they're going back to their roots; poisoning food and water sources just to torment the humans, anger the gods, and have the Ischyra chasing their tails, investigating." She gave me an apprehensive look. "There's something else. Cornelius, our lead Ischyra in Athens, has reported rumors of Sirens on the mainland."

My eyes widened and my heart began to pound as I thought back to my encounter in Egypt. "Does he think the rumors are true?"

"Good question. As you well know, a spell like that requires incredibly powerful magic. Which brings me to our other concern. Poseidon popped in as I was leaving. Apparently, Scylla is missing a few witches."

I shook my head, momentarily sidetracked. "Wait…Hecate put Scylla in charge of the witches?"

"She did. It's been about two thousand years now." She shrugged. "She's surprisingly good at leading them, considering her temperament."

"You mean bossy and bitchy are good qualities in a leader?"

Athena arched a brow. "The witches are a bunch of cliquey fools. She's exactly what they need, if you ask me. I'll be heading out to speak with her later, if you'd like to come. Visiting an old friend might be a nice way to pass the time."

"We'll see." The sea witch and I had been friends in my previous life, but her temperament was often more volatile than Hades'. I wasn't sure if that was what I needed to be around right now.

"Well, I'm assuming Nathaniel will be sent to Athens to look into things there, so you might as well find something to do. With everything that's going on, Father has opted to have an actual Ischyra take on Nathaniel's liaison and training duties so he can return to Olympus permanently."

I frowned. "What for?" Based on conversations he and I have had, Nate didn't seem to have much inclination to get involved in dealings on the upper half of the mountain.

Athena gave me a small smile. "He needs to be a god again, Tessa. He's shirked those responsibilities for far too long. Besides, I don't see him fancying leaving you for extended periods any time soon."

I let a shaky breath as relief washed through me. "I realize this probably makes me sound weak and needy, but I'm *really* happy to hear that."

"I'm sure you are." She smirked.

"Who will be taking over for him?"

"Rudolfo. You know him, correct? From your hometown?"

"Yeah, he was good friends with Eric's guardians back in Renville. I've always liked him."

"He was the first Coercer, after Nathaniel, so he's the logical replacement."

"Huh. I didn't realize he was that old." Frowning, I drummed my fingers on my lap for a moment. "Hey, can I ask you something?"

"Of course. What is it?"

"What *were* Nate's responsibilities? Back before he became a liaison?"

She bit her lip, her expression becoming perplexed as she formulated her answer. "That's a bit complicated," she said finally. "I think Nathaniel is better suited—"

"Athena..."

"Really, Tessa, it's not my place. He had his reasons for distancing himself from us all back then. That's his story to tell."

I gave her a curious look. "I thought that had to do with Karis? Or at least, partly to do with her."

"That was part of it, certainly, although that affected his relationship with Apollo more than the rest of us." She gave me an apologetic smile and squeezed my hand. "I'm sorry, Tessa. I just really think this is something you should talk to him about."

I let out a breath, seeing no sense in arguing. "Fine."

We sat in awkward silence for a few moments before Athena changed the subject.

"So, if you don't want to go visit Scylla, what kind of distraction are you looking for? Would you like me to go get your friends?"

I considered that for a moment. Sitting here, talking with Athena about simple things, was helping keep my mind focused elsewhere as my memories slowly separated into individual pieces. My head didn't feel clouded so much as it felt full, which I hoped meant I'd be able to deal with it all in smaller doses. Seeing my other friends might be just what I needed.

"Yeah, that actually might be a great idea," I told her. I looked at the clock above the fireplace. It was three in the afternoon. "Aren't they at training, though?"

"Tessa, I'm in charge of the Ischyra. Do you think anyone will question me if I snag a few recruits off the training field?" She shook her head and laughed. "I'll be right back."

She teleported away, and sure enough, returned a minute later with Eric and Mary in tow, both wearing identical shocked expressions.

"Hey, guys." I gave them a small, hesitant smile. "How's it going?"

Ignoring my question, Mary frowned. "What's wrong? You look like shit."

Athena snorted, then gathered up her skirt and sat down next to me, tucking her legs beneath her. "That's quite a story, isn't it?"

Slowly, Mary and Eric both sat down on Nate's sectional, Mary dropping herself right next to me.

"Ah, wait!" Athena jumped up and walked to the cabinet behind the couch, emerging with a bottle of wine and four glasses. "I have a feeling wine will be a necessity here."

Mary's eyebrows rose as she accepted a glass from Athena. "That sounds ominous."

Eric's eyes darted toward Athena then back to me as he hesitantly took his glass. "So, um, how are you feeling? Mary's right, though... you don't look so great."

I ran a hand through my hair and sighed. "I got my memories back."

"What?" Mary's eyes widened as they darted toward Athena, then back to me. "How? Gods, Tess, are you alright?"

I hesitated, unsure how they would react once I told them about Hades. "I...well, I had a bit of help."

Eric eyed me curiously. "What kind of help?"

I took a deep breath. "Hades, actually. He gave them all back a few hours ago." I took a large gulp of wine.

Eric's hand froze, the glass he was holding a few inches from his lips.

Mary set hers down with a *thunk*. "Hades...as in the ruler of the Underworld?"

I pursed my lips and nodded. "That's the one."

She and Eric sat in stunned silence. Hesitantly, I poked into their minds, trying to gauge where their thoughts were. I sighed when I saw what the issue was.

"You don't need to be afraid of Athena," I said. "She doesn't bite."

Athena's eyes widened as she looked back and forth between my friends. "Oh, goodness, no! I might be an Elder, but I'm also Tessa's friend, just like you."

Mary gave her a "if you say so" look before turning back to me. "Okay, then. Tessa, why the fuck would *Hades* be the one to give you your memories back? Why not Nate? He can do that kind of thing, right?"

I exchanged a quick glance with Athena.

'Just get it over with. They're your friends; they should know who you are.'

"Hades and I used to have a...relationship, of sorts." I winced when Eric's eyes nearly bugged out of his head. "He's an inappropriate ass with no sense of personal boundaries, so he decided to force my memories back to the surface without asking first."

There was a moment of silence, then Mary laughed.

"And here I thought it was crazy that you went swimming with Hermes and Dionysus." She took a large sip of wine, then shook her head. "It turns out you were boinking the ruler of the Underworld."

"I guess life is full of surprises," Eric muttered, his eyes a bit wary as he looked at me. "And now you remember everything?"

"Yes. It's all there. I'm just trying to deal with it all." I glanced back and forth between them, trying to decipher their expressions without reading their thoughts. Eric looked as though he'd been punched in the gut, the shock evident on his face. Mary just looked curious, a little speculative.

"That's, what, seven hundred years' worth of memories all at once?" She let out a low whistle. "I'm surprised you're not catatonic."

"Tessa was never the type to bury her emotions," Athena said, brushing a hand over my hair. "And even if she was, that's what we're all here for, right?"

"Of course," Eric said quickly. "It's just a bit of a shock, that's all. I mean...Hades."

I looked at Mary, who'd gone quiet. "Mare?"

Her brow was furrowed when she looked at me, then she nodded. "Yep. I told you I'd be here for you no matter what, so I am."

I gave her a tight smile, not quite believing her. "Thank you. That means a lot."

Eric did a quick, cursory glance of Nate's living room. "So, where is Nate, anyway? I didn't expect him to unglue himself from you any time soon."

"Zeus needed to see him, so Athena took over babysitting duty," I explained.

"It was either me or my other idiot brother," Athena said, rolling her eyes. "I figured I was the preferable option."

"What are you talking about?" I asked.

"Apollo's been griping at everyone since you left. For once in his life, I think he actually feels guilty about something."

"Apollo? Guilty? I didn't think he knew what that emotion felt like," I said dryly.

"Well, he *did* know who you were and didn't say anything," Mary muttered. Eric's answering snort told me he felt the same.

Athena gave her a shrewd look. "He couldn't, due to the interdiction. According to Nathaniel, Apollo allowed it because he felt it was in Tessa's best interest." Then she turned to me. "When your memories came back, he didn't expect your reaction to be quite so...visceral, I suppose would be the best term."

"I don't know what he expected," I said, unable to hide my annoyance.

"What did he do, exactly?" Eric asked, his expression curious.

I took a slow sip of wine as I figured out the best way to explain how Hades worked. "Hades is an empath, so he feeds off the emotions of others. He's got a specific taste for negative emotions, which is one of the reasons he ended up ruling the Underworld. One of his favorite forms of torture, because it elicits the most visceral response, is dragging rotten memories from someone's mind and using them to drive a person insane. He's quite good at it." I shrugged. "In my case, he likely thought he was helping me, but because of his need for negative emotions, the worst of my memories were returned first and were the most vivid."

"I'm confused," Eric said, frowning. "He did that without your permission?"

I nodded. "He can be a tad controlling."

"It's par for the course with him, really," Athena added.

"So, let me get this straight. You had a relationship with a controlling, sadistic empathic dick who's clearly got no sense of personal boundaries?" Mary's expression turned perplexed. "How the fuck did you end up with Nate after that?"

Athena laughed. "That's quite an apt description of Hades, I must say."

"I didn't remember being with Hades when Nate and I got together," I said. "Although I don't really think it would've made a difference. Nate fits me better than Hades ever did."

"Uh huh. So, what were these memories that he gave you? The ones that let him get his empathic rocks off or whatever?"

I shifted in my seat and averted my eyes. "That's not something I really want to get into now. Tell me what's new with you guys. How's training going?"

"It's going, I guess," Mary said, settling back in her seat. "Things got kind of thrown off once you and Nate disappeared."

"We're hoping the rumors will start dying down soon," Eric said.

"That's good to hear," I muttered. Even though my time with the Ischyra was essentially over, I didn't want to think about what they all thought of me.

"I moved in with Yana," Mary said, looking hesitant.

I gave her a surprised look. "Why? What about Anette? I thought you two were getting closer."

Mary picked at one of her fingernails, avoiding my eyes. "After that night when Menoetius attacked you in your dreams, she got really freaked out. Once your transition happened, she told me she didn't 'feel safe being near such instability.' So...I offered to move out and she agreed. Lucky bitch has herself a single room now." She tried to make her tone light, but it was beyond obvious that Anette's actions had hurt her.

"I'm so sorry, Mare." I gave her a sympathetic smile. "That's real sucky of her."

She shrugged. "I guess I can't really blame her. The leader of a rebellion attacked her roommate's best friend. I'd probably be freaked, too."

"She could've handled it better, though," Eric said. He sounded irritated, and I had a feeling he'd been on the receiving end of a lot of Mary's griping the last few days.

"Definitely," I agreed. "I'm sorry. I feel like this is all my fault."

"No, Tess, it's not," Mary said. "I mean, yeah, some of it might be *because* of you, but it's not your fault."

I frowned, trying to figure out how to take that. "Thank you for the reassurance...I think?"

She winced. "Yeah that didn't really come out quite right. Sorry."

'I think I need a bigger distraction,' I said to Athena.

She nodded. *'Done.'*

"So, you two...how'd you like to go on a fact-finding mission?"

Immediately, they both perked up.

"Definitely!" Mary said, looking giddy. "Where to?"

Athena grinned. "Tessa and I need to go visit an old friend."

10

NATHANIEL

Despite how much I wanted to be by Tessa's side when she woke up, I was somewhat thankful for the distraction. I was at a loss as to how to help her, and I hoped this time away—even if it only lasted an hour—would help me wrap my mind around exactly what she needed.

When I arrived at the palace, Apollo was standing against one of the columns that flanked the front door, waiting. When he saw me, he pushed off from it and walked forward, his brow furrowed in concern. "How is she?"

I stopped at the top of the marble steps and slid my hands in my pockets. "As well as can be expected. Your magic wore off not long after we got home, so it was rough." I sighed, remembering my conversation with Athena. "Thank you again for doing that for her. We both appreciate it."

He nodded. "Of course. Athena is with her now?"

"Yes, but she was still sleeping when I left. I'm not sure how long she'll be out."

"Well, hopefully this meeting will be quick. Hecate and Poseidon are here, and Ares is up from Athens with some news."

My eyebrows shot up at the mention of Poseidon's name. Aside from the recruits' welcome feast and transition ceremony, I couldn't recall the last time the sea god had visited Olympus.

"He's got news from Scylla that he felt warranted a visit with our father," he continued. "Hecate felt she should be here, since both her daughter and her witches are being discussed."

"Are they being civil, at least?" It was no secret their relationship was a contentious one due to Hecate's dislike for Poseidon, although an argument could be made that no man would ever be good enough for her daughter.

"She loves Scylla, so she does her best to be amicable." He shrugged as if it were that simple. "Some family bonds run deeper than others, it would seem."

Without another word, he walked into the palace, leaving me to follow.

We'd been called to my father's war room, a large, high-ceilinged chamber toward the back of the palace that looked out over the sprawling, cliffside gardens. Three tables, each roughly the size of a small car, took up most of the space, the tops of which were each a full relief map of one of the three realms: Earth, Olympus, and the Underworld. Smaller maps were mounted on the walls, and cabinets full of books and other documents bordered the room.

My father, Hecate, Ares, and Poseidon were gathered around the map of Earth, speaking in hushed tones. Zeus barely spared us a glance when Apollo and I approached, but Poseidon, a dark-skinned male who towered over everyone in the room, turned when he saw us.

"Nathaniel," he greeted me. "I heard Tessa has returned. How is she?"

"Sleeping for now," I replied, trying to hide my surprise that he spoke of her so casually. "So, we'll see. What news is there?"

"Scylla has been having trouble controlling her witches," Zeus grumbled, not giving Poseidon a chance to respond. He turned his glare to Ares who stood across from him. "And according to Ares, empousa are terrorizing remote villages in the South Pacific, and pockets of crop failures have been popping up around the world, most notably in the US." He shifted his gaze to me before continuing. "Sirens have been seen quite a ways inland in our Athenian region as well."

My eyes snapped to Ares. "Who told you this?"

"Cornelius, just yesterday." Ares folded his arms across his chest. "From what I can tell, the reports of the Sirens started as rumors, but one of his most trusted soldiers encountered one a few days back, walking on her own two feet."

I rubbed the back of my neck and exhaled. "If someone has spelled the Sirens to allow them on land, is it possible the witches were taken for their powers?"

"That's what I was about to suggest," Poseidon said, cocking a brow at Zeus before facing me and Apollo. "Scylla has lost track of three of her most powerful witches."

"She likely ate them in a fit of rage," Zeus groused, putting his hands behind his back and staring out one of the large windows.

"I'd appreciate it if you refrained from insulting my daughter," Hecate snapped. "You know she wouldn't harm her own kind."

"You also thought you'd be able to keep the empousa under your control, and yet here they are, attacking human villages," Zeus snapped. "I'm not quite certain your character judgment is as on par as it should be."

Hecate's lip curled in disgust. "*You* took away my control of the empousa when you handed Pandora to Epimetheus and gave them free rein to procreate as they pleased! Their mutiny was *your* doing, not mine."

Waving off Hecate's barb, he folded his arms over his chest and looked at Poseidon. "When was the last time you saw Scylla?"

"Not two days ago. A ship of prisoners came through her strait a few days before, and another is set to come through today. She and her beasts are well fed, believe me," Poseidon said dryly. "The likelihood of her snacking on her own witches is quite slim."

"When did she realize they were gone?" Apollo asked.

"The day before I arrived," Poseidon replied. "She sent word to me and Hecate a few hours after she was unable to locate them on her own."

"Who was taken?" I asked.

Hecate tore her glare from Zeus and gave me a long look before responding. "Taygete, Alcyone, and Celaeno."

"Dammit." I pinched the bridge of my nose and blew out a breath as she rattled off the names of three of the seven Pleiades sisters.

"I'm assuming by your reaction you don't see it as a coincidence that the three missing witches happen to be Atlas' daughters," Poseidon said, his tone grim.

"No, I don't," I said with a sigh. I didn't know what Tessa—or Atlas'—relationships with the sisters had been like before Tessa was killed and Atlas had been locked away, but something told me neither would take kindly to the news. "What have you done with the rest?"

"Maia, Sterope, and Electra are staying with Demeter, Hyperion, and Theia in the farming valley for now," Apollo said. "Ischyra have been sent to guard Merope and her family on Earth. They should be able to keep them safe for the time being."

I cast Hecate a reluctant look. "Do you think they've defected?"

"That would never happen," she said firmly.

"I have to agree with Hecate on this one." Poseidon cast a glare at Zeus, daring him to challenge. "You don't know them as I do. They would never support Menoetius."

Zeus dismissed him with a huff. "Fine, let's assume the witches haven't switched sides." He turned his gaze to Hecate. "How does this spell of Menoetius' work? The one that takes power from another being?"

"It works in two parts," Hecate began. "First, Menoetius siphons a portion of a witch's ability to cast—similar to draining a deity of their life force. Second, he would use that ability to cast a spell that would drain a creature of their powers, their affinity, leaving their life force in tact. It's a tenuous process, and incredibly dangerous for the witch whose power is being borrowed." She shook her head. "I'm still quite stunned that Menoetius found one who allowed him such access in the past."

"I don't understand," I said, frowning. "If he can drain a witch's casting abilities, why does he need help draining power from other deities?"

"Because a witch's ability to cast is tied to their existence. It's much different than for other immortals, who could, theoretically, survive without their power. Witches *are* their power; we exist because of it. Removing it would equate to removing a god's life force."

"Does the witch have to be willing?" I asked.

"No, not necessarily, but the one who helped Menoetius previously was. Now that he knows how it works, he wouldn't need the guidance of another witch, only their power, although I'm not entirely certain this spell was ever perfected."

I frowned. "What happened to the witch who helped him before?"

"Destroyed," Hecate replied. "Scylla and her beasts tore him to bits as soon as we hunted him down."

"You actually saw this happen?"

She pressed her lips into a thin line and nodded. "Yes."

"I was there, as well," Zeus said, an unsettling smile playing at the corners of his lips. "Scylla was quite fond of Tessa, so it was one of her more vicious executions."

I grunted in response. Scylla's six wolves never held back when tasked with an execution, and with her own anger to fuel their power, I could only imagine the outcome.

Pushing aside my surprise that Tessa had been friends with the sea witch, I faced Hecate again. "Tessa told me she was attacked in Egypt by a Siren who'd been given the ability to come inland by a witch who was loyal to Cronus. Was that the same witch who lent his magic to Menoetius?"

"It was," Hecate confirmed. "His name was Xander."

"Any known associates?" I asked.

"Xander was a bit of a lone wolf," she explained. "The other witches never much cared for him."

I nodded. "Did he have any children he could've passed his knowledge to?"

"Not that we're aware of, but it's not outside the realm of possibility, so we are looking into it. Regardless, Scylla and I wiped all knowledge of the incantation from existence when Xander was killed." Hecate frowned, then turned to Zeus. "Who have you met with, regarding alliances?"

"Poseidon and I are planning a visit to the Gulf of Volos to meet with Oceanus so we can discuss how his people will participate this time around. We're hoping we can get the water gods to our side, but considering their neutrality in the last war, that may take some convincing. While we're gone, I'm going to need you to round up all the witches, get a feel for who we can trust."

"You can trust them all," she replied firmly.

"Do it, anyway. We can't afford any assumptions."

"I still think it would be wise to take Prometheus and Epimetheus to meet with the Oceanids," Ares said, sounding irritated, clearly revisiting a prior argument. "Clymene was one of them, after all. The twins may be able to convince Oceanus to avenge his daughter's death."

"What about the Potamoi?" I asked, referring to the three thousand river gods controlled by Oceanus. "Do you really think they'll join us?"

Poseidon sighed. "Ideally, yes, although they still harbor a bit of anger over their forced neutrality from before. They're much more volatile than the Oceanids. I've sent Prometheus and Epimetheus to meet with their commander, but I won't be holding my breath."

"However," Ares cut in, "considering that volatility, I'm quite certain seeking their alliance is a fool's errand."

"Maybe, maybe not," Poseidon replied with a shrug. "It's worth the trip, even if it isn't fruitful."

"You're the ruler of the sea realm," Zeus said, glaring at his brother. "You should not be asking for their support. They'll either give it or be punished."

Poseidon gave Zeus a cool smile. "I'm quite sure that's the attitude that lost our father the last war, dear brother."

"Who else have you contacted?" I asked, trying to steer my father away from a tantrum.

"I had hoped to reach out to the Telchines, but it would appear they've already made their choice," Apollo said. "Hades will provide half of his forces, but the rest of his giants will need to remain in the Underworld to guard Tartarus.

"Polyphemus has said the Cyclopes will assist Hephaestus with the forging of any weapons we might require," Poseidon added.

I frowned at Apollo. "Why don't you think we'll be able to get the Tels on board?"

He and Zeus exchanged a glance. Zeus huffed and went back to examining his map, and Apollo faced me.

"We don't know for certain, but we believe they're the ones who provided Menoetius with the weaponized godsbane. No one else can create poisons like they do, and the ways in which he used it during the last war—"

"You mean on Tessa?"

Apollo's expression turned apologetic. "Yes, although there were others, too, and once the war was done, there was still quite the market for godsbane serum, especially with the empousa."

"We also believe they're responsible for the crop failures," Ares added. "According to Cornelius, there have been nearly a dozen reports of unknown diseases ravaging farms, most in eastern Asia and the Americas."

"How can you be sure Cornelius is being truthful with his reports?" I asked.

Ares arched a brow. "He's the one who alerted us to the rebel threat initially, so I'd like to think we can consider him trustworthy."

I nodded, not necessarily agreeing with his logic, but not prepared to argue it, either.

"Considering how news of a Mimic awakening made its way to

Menoetius, we can make no assumptions about who's trustworthy and who is not," Zeus said. "It's entirely possible Cornelius is lying in an attempt to direct our attention elsewhere."

"Even if he is the one passing information to Menoetius, he would've had to come by the information about Tessa somehow, considering he didn't witness her powers or our relationship first-hand," I pointed out. "So, either way, someone on this mountain is sharing information on Earth."

"Then you'll need to scan all of the recruits," Zeus told me. "If any in this generation are at all wavering in their loyalty, I want to know about it."

"Mentors, too," Ares said. "The threat of war can cause changes in loyalties if one thinks the other side is stronger."

Zeus grunted.

"Alright, mentors, as well," I said with a sigh. The thought of mentors being involved in helping the rebellion was a painful one. "I'll head down to the arena tomorrow." I'd already scanned the recruits and mentors several times since their arrival on Olympus; it was standard practice for each generation. The thought of having to dig further irked me, but I pushed it aside to be dealt with later.

"That can be put off for a day or two," Zeus said. "While we're meeting with Oceanus, I need you and Tessa to go to Athens and meet with Cornelius so you can examine the site where the Sirens were reportedly seen. There isn't a trained Psychometric on hand there, and I don't care to hunt one down, so I want Tessa to see if she can get a read on the area. If Sirens were there, I want them hunted down and questioned. We need to know what they're up to. Do a little digging in his mind while you're there...see if you can find out where Cornelius' loyalties lie."

My eyebrows shot up. "You want me to take Tessa into the field now?"

He gave me a surprised look. "She tapped into psychometry before she got her memories back, so she shouldn't have any trouble."

"No," I said flatly. "There's a Psychometric in the current batch of recruits. I'll take her."

Beside me, Apollo let out a resigned sigh.

Zeus' eyes narrowed in annoyance. "I will not send a recruit who has just come into her powers to gather information regarding a missing Ischyra."

"I don't think sending a Titaness who only just regained her memories is the best choice, either," Apollo said.

"I didn't ask your opinion," Zeus snapped. He turned his eyes to me. "You will take Tessa and that's the end of it."

"You expect her to just fall in line two days after being awakened?" I shook my head in disbelief. "That's ludicrous."

He ground his teeth together as he stared me down. "Think what you want, but she is your lover. She'll do what you tell her to, just as you will do what I tell *you* to do."

"You think I'll command her to do your bidding? You think she'd *obey* if I tried?" I let out a sardonic laugh. "No. If you want her to risk herself hours after getting her full memory back, you can ask her yourself."

There was a knock at the door.

Zeus continued to stare at me, his gaze turning from angry to cunning as he called for them to enter. "Ah, Rudolfo!" Pasting on a jovial smile, Zeus turned as the Coercer was led into the room by a servant. "Thank you for coming."

The small, bearded Ischyra gave him a small nod. "Of course. When my leader calls, I answer." He turned his smile on me. "Nathaniel, how are you?"

"I'm doing well, thank you." I felt my jaw tense with annoyance as my father's plan unfolded in front of me.

Zeus chuckled, drawing my attention back to him, then patted Rudolfo's back and turned to me. "Nathaniel, Rudolfo will be taking over your duties with the Ischyra from here on out, so I'll need you to fill him on anything pertaining to the new Mentalist recruits."

Jaw tense, I looked again at the dark-haired man at my father's side. I'd trained Rudolfo more than two thousand years ago, and he was the most powerful of all Ischyra who possessed the ability to

Coerce. If I was going to be replaced as a mentor, it made sense for him to be the one to take over.

His smile turned wary under my scrutiny.

I dragged my gaze back to my father and arched a brow. "Why?"

"Your services are needed elsewhere." Father smiled, barely hiding his challenge to my restraint. "He's more than capable of mentoring the recruits."

'Ease back, Nathaniel.'

Ignoring Apollo's warning, I folded my arms across my chest and raised my eyebrows. "You didn't think to discuss a change in position with me first?"

"I'm not required to do anything of the sort," Father said evenly.

I exhaled a sigh. "Alright. Do whatever you want, but I'm not bringing Tessa into the field before she's ready."

"Perhaps this isn't the best time—" Rudolfo began, eyes darting nervously between us.

"Quiet." Zeus took a menacing step toward me, dispensing all pretense of civility. "You listen to me, Nathaniel. Either you want to be a part of this family or not. If you want to go back to acting as a liaison on Earth, no better than a common Ischyra, feel free, but when you're on this mountain, which you have *chosen* to be, you are a god. You will do what is necessary to protect the realms, which includes getting that girl on board with whatever it is we need her to do."

"And if she refuses?"

"I'm quite certain your persuasive abilities are just as strong now as they were three thousand years ago. Use them."

"You're insane if you think I'm going to Coerce her into complying."

"You're more than strong enough—"

"No."

His face turned red with anger, causing Rudolfo to take several small steps back.

Just as Zeus opened his mouth to respond, Apollo cut him off.

"Father, let's not forget that viewing Tessa as no more than a weapon is what got her soul sent into Chaos in the first place." Apollo gave me a silencing look, then continued, "Perhaps it's best if we reevaluate the manner in which we attempt to gain her assistance."

"She's a Titaness, not some weak human, Apollo," Zeus seethed. "She already said she would do what she could to help protect Olympus and Earth. This is what I am telling her to do."

"She offered her help before Hades returned all of her memories," I argued. "You need to give her some breathing room."

"Nathaniel will go speak with Tessa," Apollo interjected. "But I think you should be forewarned that forcing all of that on her at once was quite damaging to her psyche. She may not be so willing to enter the field just yet."

"It's not my fault she's having difficulty dealing with the return of her memories," Zeus said. "It was going to happen sooner or later, and she should've been prepared for that." He shrugged. "If anything, Hades did her a favor."

I narrowed my eyes at him, taking in the gleam in his eye, the forced casualness of his shrug. "You say that as if you expected this."

He scoffed. "Of course I didn't! How was I to know what he intended to do?"

Poseidon surprised us all by laughing.

"Really, Zeus, what did you expect to happen when those two were reunited? Rainbows and butterflies?" Poseidon shook his head. "As controlling as Hades is, do you truly believe he would just leave Tessa's memories to resurface on their own? He's a ruler and a warrior, just like you. He knows how powerful she is, better than the rest of us, I'd wager. The thought that he'd allow us to rest on our laurels while Tessa remained in the dark about her past and her power is comical."

Zeus rounded on his brother. "Don't you *dare* blame me for his actions. I thought they were just as ill-advised as everyone else."

Poseidon's dark eyebrows shot up. "Did you? Your cunning knows no limits, brother. I find it hard to believe you didn't consider the possibility."

Zeus clenched his jaw and raised his chin defiantly. "I will not be questioned like this in my own home."

"That's just wonderful," I said, lacing my voice with disgust. "You expect Tessa to trust you enough to work with you, yet you're already manipulating her."

Rudolfo began to back toward the door, wisely attempting to avoid my father's rising fury. "Perhaps I should leave—"

Hecate put a hand on his back and gave a small shake of her head.

"We are at *war*!" Zeus roared, slamming his fist down on the table, causing it to shudder. "I will use whatever means necessary to protect this goddamn mountain!"

Furious, I took several steps toward him. "You rotten—"

"Nathaniel, enough," Apollo said, stepping in front of me and placing a hand on my chest.

Glaring, I slapped his hand away, keeping my eyes locked on my father.

"You should go speak to Tessa," Apollo murmured. "See what her thoughts are before going down this path."

"She's not ready for this."

"It's not your decision to make, brother."

I jerked my chin toward Zeus, who was glowering at me from behind Apollo. "It's not his, either."

"No, it is not," Apollo agreed. "Arguing about it any further won't help anyone, though, so just go home. Talk to her, see where her head is." Apollo arched a brow, then switched to telepathy. *'She is strong enough for this. You need to let her choose to prove that.'*

'You don't need to tell me that,' I shot back.

Giving my father one last look of disgust, I teleported back to my front porch, fully prepared to take Tessa and leave this damn mountain if it meant keeping her from Zeus' grasp.

My annoyance grew exponentially when I found Hades lounging in one of my porch chairs.

"Ah, Nathaniel. I was hoping you'd return soon."

I raised my eyes skyward and took a deep breath. "What are you doing here?"

He folded his arms across his chest and smiled. "We need to discuss Tessa's training."

"Her—what are you talking about?"

"Of course, you haven't spoken to her yet." He gave me an easy smile. "I've decided to resume my role as mentor for Tessa."

I closed my eyes and pinched the bridge of my nose. "And why have you decided to do that?"

"Because she needs me to." He looked me up and down, taking in my aggravation. "Is my loving brother the reason for your current foul mood, or do you just dislike me that much?"

"It's nothing," I snapped. "She's got plenty of people willing to train her. Why in all the realms would she accept help from you, after what you did to her this morning?"

"Did *for* her, and because in this case, she knows I'm right. You didn't know her before. She needs someone who can match her strength and balance her weaknesses."

"And I can't?"

"I would never ask you to step aside, Nathaniel, but I will ask you to acknowledge that, when it comes to her education, I am willing to do things for her that you aren't."

"Such as?"

"Hurt her. Break her, if need be."

I made a noise of disgust. "She doesn't need to be broken to be strong."

"Doesn't she?"

"No. Nor does she need you meddling with her life when she's only just gotten it back."

He let out a frustrated groan. "Let me be very clear on something. You've got nothing to worry about when it comes to my feelings toward her. I can't help that I will always care for her, but I also want what's best for her. She and I put each other at an imbalance. You fit her far better than I ever did, just as my Persephone fits me. I would never ask you to step aside, but I will ask that you be supportive in her decision to let me help her."

"You won't ask me to step aside because you want what's best for her? Or because you no longer love her?"

The truth was plain as day on his face, just as it had been this morning when she came into my parents' sitting room and he'd laid eyes on her for the first time in three millennia. I watched him drink her in as though she was the first breath of fresh air he'd had in years. He hadn't simply cared for her, he had loved her, quite possibly more than he did Persephone.

A muscle twitched in his jaw as he stared at me. When he spoke, his voice was quiet and controlled. "I have my queen, Nathaniel, just as you now have yours."

Unsure how to answer, I kept my mouth shut, not wanting him to see how much his lack of denial got to me.

Shaking his head, he let out a quiet breath before continuing. "I want to help her, and I was doing a damn good job of it before that witch shoved her soul into the Void. The things she's capable of..." His voice turned irritated. "Tessa is full of light, Nathaniel, with just the right amount of darkness to balance that out. Just enough to give her the potential to be formidable, although that potential has yet to be realized in this lifetime. I, and I'm quite certain *she*, would be happy if her training wasn't hampered by a bunch of overprotective fools once again."

I took a deep breath and tried to rein in my annoyance and, as much as I hated to admit it, my jealousy. "I'm not saying you weren't effective. She's told me quite the opposite, actually, and I tend to trust her judgment. I just don't think your methods will be best for her, considering her current state of mind. She's not the same person she was back then."

"On the contrary," he countered. "She's exactly the same person she was back then. Hecate may have locked her away, but she didn't change who Tessa is." He made a sound of annoyance and scrubbed his hands over his face before looking at me. "You love her, I can see that, but if you expect her to be able to defend herself adequately against someone who can incapacitate her the way Menoetius can or the monsters that will hunt her down, you'll need my help."

"What do you suggest?" I asked.

"That's to be determined. Tessa and I had quite a conversation earlier, so I'll let you two discuss all of this when she returns."

I stiffened. "What do you mean, 'when she returns'? Where is she?"

"Not a clue. I came to check on her after our dream walk and found your home empty." He eyed me curiously. "Who did you leave her with?"

"Athena."

"Ah." He smirked. "Well, I'm sure she's perfectly safe, then."

Seconds later, I received a mental call from Chiron that told me just the opposite.

11

TESSA

As my ability to teleport myself—much less, multiple people —long distances was still a bit lacking, Athena took the liberty of transporting all four of us to the darkened beach near Scylla's cave. Slow waves made a soft whooshing sound as they lapped the moonlit shore, and twenty-foot dunes carpeted in soft grass towered over us in the darkness opposite the water, stopping a few hundred yards down the beach at a long jetty that extended out into the ocean.

"Your boyfriend is totally going to kill us," Mary muttered. "Where are we, anyway?"

"The Yucatan Peninsula, and Tessa and I are more than capable of handling my brother," Athena said absently.

"The *what?*" Eric's voice was a whispered shriek. "Why are we here? Are we going to get in trouble for leaving Olympus?"

"Athena's an Elder, and I'm a Titaness who just came back from the dead," I replied, hoping I sounded more sure of that then I felt. "So, no."

"What are we doing?" Mary asked, not bothering to hide her annoyance as I started to lead them down the beach.

I glanced back at her. "Some witches have gone missing, and there's trouble in the Underworld. We're here to try to get some information."

'Don't get into too much detail,' Athena warned.

I gave her a questioning look, but she avoided my gaze.

She leaned down and pulled off her shoes, then gestured toward the rest of us. "You may want to take your shoes off. We're going to get wet from here on out."

Mary arched a brow at me and put her hands on her hips, watching me as I tugged off my sneakers and rolled my leggings up a few inches. "Look, Tess, I know you're a Titaness now and all—"

"Technically she's always been one," Athena interrupted.

Mary gritted her teeth before continuing. "But you're still my best friend, according to you. So, can you please tell me why we're here?"

I wrinkled my nose and scratched my head, then let my hand drop to my side. "Okay, listen. You guys need to understand that the person I was as a Titaness...she's, well she's different than the girl you knew as an Ischyra."

"I kind of gathered that when you told me you used to sleep with Hades," Mary said dryly. Eric gave a quiet snort of agreement. "What does that have to do with where we are now? Who's here that can tell us anything about missing witches?"

"Some of the friends I had back then were what you might consider...out of character for me." I gestured down the beach toward a large cliff face. "Right now, we're going to see one of them." I took a deep breath. "It's Scylla."

My words were met with dead silence. Mary and Eric exchanged a wary look, then Mary turned her shocked stare back on me.

"The fucking *sea witch*? Are you kidding me?" She shook her head and turned away, then laughed. "Gods, Tessa. She's one of the most unstable witches there is! Are you insane?"

"No! I just...look, you have to trust me, okay? Scylla's a bit eccentric...maybe a bit volatile, I'll grant you, but she's not a bad person."

Mary turned back toward me, a stunned look on her face. "You're aware that she regularly devours human beings, correct? As in, something you were, not three months ago?"

"Prisoners on death row for incredibly grievous crimes," Athena said. "They're hardly innocent."

"A job she really freaking enjoys, from what I've heard," Mary replied, her tone acidic.

"Look, if you want me to send you back, I'll send you back," I offered.

"No, no," Eric said, elbowing Mary. "We want to be here. Just, maybe next time you could, you know, give us a heads up?"

"Of course." I huffed out a breath, annoyed that I hadn't taken more than thirty seconds to put aside my own emotional baggage to consider how they might feel about all of this.

"Wonderful. Now, shoes off," Athena instructed. The other two complied, rolling their pants up a few inches at the ankles, then we continued making our way down the beach. About fifty feet from the tall jetty, a dark opening started to come into view. Athena and I slowed as we got closer and stared silently into the dark interior.

'Do you think she knows we're here?' I asked Athena.

She wrinkled her nose as she peered into the cave.

'Probably, although I don't know why she wouldn't have come out already.'

"So...are we going in?" Mary asked.

I held up a hand.

'Quiet for a sec, okay?'

Mary jumped at the sudden sound of my voice in her head. *'Dammit, Tessa, warn me next time!'*

I winced. *'Sorry!'*

I was about to try to reach out to Scylla mentally, when footsteps sounded from inside the cave, echoing toward us. A moment later, a tall, curvy woman with chestnut skin strode into view. Wide eyes, a slightly upturned nose, and full, bow-shaped lips adorned her oval face, and thick black hair tumbled down her back. Twin silver clasps in the shape of howling wolves pinned the glossy waves back, revealing high cheekbones. A halter top and matching floor-length skirt that looked like they were made of liquid gold were draped over her statuesque form.

Scylla arched a brow and crossed her arms over her chest. "Back from the dead, Tessa?"

I hesitated for a moment before smiling at her. "If you can believe it."

Flicking a glance at Mary and Eric, she put a hand on her hip. "Who are your friends?"

"This is Mary and Eric. We grew up—well, I've known them almost as long as I was an Ischyra."

"Lovely to meet you both. I'm Scylla."

Mary and Eric were silent, and when I glanced back to see why they hadn't responded, I nearly laughed. Mary's face was scrunched in confusion, and Eric simply looked awestruck.

Scylla's smile turned into an amused smirk. "Expecting a six headed monster?"

Mary cleared her throat as she tried to collect herself. "Yeah, pretty much."

Scylla let out a loud, throaty laugh. "Don't fret, dear. My wolves answer to me, not the other way around." She gestured toward the dark space behind her. "Come on in."

I slipped my hand into Mary's and smiled. "Come on, let's go."

We followed Scylla down a long, winding tunnel that led to a living area. The walls of her cave were an ochre color, and the floor was made of narrow planks of bamboo, dotted and streaked in shades of brown. A large, oval rope rug took up most of the floor space, and furniture made from bleached driftwood was strewn about.

Two archways that stretched from floor to ceiling were cut into the rear walls. Instead of the moonlit beach we'd just left, I saw a bustling coastal village through one, the sun sparkling off crystal blue waters in the background. The second archway was sealed shut with a thick, wooden door that boasted heavy metal deadbolts.

'How is this possible?' Mary asked, looking at the windows and doors that clearly led to places some distance away.

'They're portals, she just always leaves them open. The glass door leads to her home in Greece, and the other—' I pointed toward the wooden door *'—leads to the cliffside where the prisoners come through.'*

After we crossed the threshold, we all stopped and wiped our sandy feet on a mat just before stepping into the living room.

"Explain to me why we couldn't have just teleported right inside?" Eric sounded annoyed as he rubbed the sand from between his toes.

"You can't teleport directly into someone's home," I explained. "It's just a safety precaution the gods built into the teleportation system."

"We were half a mile down the beach," Mary pointed out, shaking off the last bits of sand onto the mat.

"I've spelled the entire area to act as my living space," Scylla told them, moving to a small liquor cabinet and pulling out a slender green bottle filled with dark liquid. "It gives me plenty of time to decide whether I want to invite someone inside."

After pouring us each a glass of dark red ambrosia wine, Scylla kicked off her leather sandals and sat down in a wide cushioned chair. She lifted a brow and looked me up and down.

"So, tell me, how is it you aren't bawling your eyes out somewhere? And do your brothers know you're here?"

"No one knows we're here, and I've done my fair share of crying already. I needed a break."

Athena tossed back her own drink and held it toward Scylla for a refill. "What Tessa is trying to say is that she isn't letting memories of her past overshadow the present."

"Does that include all that Menoetius did to you?" Scylla asked.

"Yes, that includes my memories of Menoetius' attacks."

"Torture, Tessa." Scylla took a slow sip of wine and arched a brow. "Call it what it was."

I inhaled a deep breath and let it out slowly, squeezing my eyes shut against the memories. "Yes," I finally said. "That includes my memories of Menoetius' torture."

"Torture?" Eric turned his wide blue eyes on me. "What's she talking about?"

I waved his question off. "Later. That's not why we're here."

'Tess...'

I could feel Mary's shock and hurt as she realized the gravity of what I hadn't told her back at Nate's, and I couldn't help but feel a little guilty.

'Not now. Later, though, Mare. I promise.'

Scylla cocked her head to the side and gave a sly smile. "Tell me, who were you with when you recalled these memories? I'm assuming they didn't return naturally."

"Three guesses," I muttered, taking a sip of my wine.

Scylla snorted. "Thought so. Well, I'm glad he was there. It was probably best to get that messiness out of the way quickly."

"Yeah, well, he didn't really give me much of a choice," I said bitterly.

Athena cleared her throat. "We can discuss Tessa's memories later. For now, let's get to why we've come."

Scylla nodded and set down her glass. "Yes, my witches. Taygete, Alcyone, and Celaeno have been missing now for nearly three days."

"Atlas' daughters are the one who've gone missing?" My shocked gaze snapped to Athena. "Why didn't you tell me this earlier?"

"We're telling you now."

I shook my head in disbelief at her cavalier attitude. "What about the rest? Where are the other four? What are you doing to get them back?"

Scylla sighed and took a sip of her wine. "I've sent them to stay with Demeter, Hyperion, and Theia in the farming valley for the time being. They'll be well-protected there. As for getting the others back, well, we're working on that. All of my and my mother's tracking spells seem to be failing us in that pursuit, though."

I nodded my agreement. I'd never really known the daughters Pleione and Atlas had together—neither had he, for that matter—but I knew my twin would want them under the strictest protection possible. Two peaceful Titans and an Elder would certainly provide that. I tried to settle myself down, knowing this wasn't the fault of anyone here. "Any idea who might've taken them or where?"

"Most likely Menoetius, although I'm not sure where or why, which worries me a great deal. We've been having a good deal of trouble tracking him down."

"I have some thoughts, actually." I flicked a glance toward Athena, who nodded. "Not about the where, but why. Someone is tampering with the walls of Tartarus. Hades and Persephone are looking into river fire as a possible cause, but since no one can actually manipulate that without magic..."

"Without primordial magic, you mean." Scylla arched a delicate brow. "Do you truly believe any of the sisters—your twin's own daughters—would allow their magic to be used in such a way?"

I shrugged. "I don't know. Quite frankly, I don't know them at all. Even if they wouldn't, if Menoetius knows how to take a witch's magic, he could just be sucking their power, right?"

"Most certainly, especially considering he's got three of them this time around. I can assure you, though, they wouldn't willingly aide Menoetius or Cronus in any way. The Oceanids, including Pleione, have remained steadfastly loyal to Zeus, and the Pleiades follow their mother's lead. Assisting Zeus' nemeses in their escape from Tartarus is the last thing you'd need to worry about them doing."

"And your other witches?" Athena asked. "Are there any you can think of who might be willing to switch sides?"

"The rest recall quite clearly how I handled the last witch who helped Menoetius. Trust me, only a fool would choose to replicate Xander's missteps."

I tried to suppress a shudder at the predatory smirk on Scylla's face as she recalled whatever punishment she'd doled out on the witch who'd helped Menoetius torture me. Knowing her and her love for violence, it had undoubtedly involved a good deal of torture and blood, and both her hands and the jaws of her beasts.

"How would he be able to steal a witch's power, though?" Mary asked, frowning. "Wouldn't he need a witch to perform the power-stealing spell or whatever?"

Scylla nodded slowly. "Yes and no." She gestured toward me. "As was evidenced by Tessa's torture, a witch does not need to be the one to cast it. Xander manufactured it so a deity—Menoetius—could borrow, in Xander's case, a witch's magic to do the casting himself. My mother and I did our best to scour the realms of any mention or knowledge of that spell once he'd been destroyed, but considering how difficult it can be to wipe the memories of one with power like Menoetius, it's possible he retains the necessary knowledge to perform the spell. He'd still need a witch to kick start the process, though, which would explain why mine are going missing."

"Alright, one more question." I set down my glass. "Do any of the witches have the ability to lift a Siren's curse? There have been reports of sightings of them inland recently."

She shrugged, and her eyes darted toward the door that led to the cliffside. "Of course," she said absently. "That's simply a curse. While we witches try to avoid stepping on one another's toes, at one time or another, one has been convinced to break a curse placed by someone else. It's incredibly difficult and would drain him or her of their power for a significant amount of time, but it is possible. It helps a good deal if the person who requested the curse is amenable to having it lifted, as well." Arching a brow, she asked, "Any thoughts on whether Demeter would be open to something like that?"

"Unlikely," Athena replied. "She still holds a bit of a grudge that the Sirens weren't able to return Persephone once she took up with Hades in the Underworld."

"What does Demeter have to do with the Sirens?" Mary asked, looking confused.

"Demeter is the reason they're forbidden from land unless a human manages to survive their song," Athena explained.

I shook my head. "No, that doesn't make sense. Cronus gave them the ability to come on land at least once before, so that ability wouldn't be dependent on Demeter. He used that as a means of enticing them to join his cause."

"What Cronus did was offer them humanity," Scylla said. "A full human form. Demeter cursed them to be miserable, in whatever form they might take. Now, if someone, say Menoetius, used a spell to allow them on land, it would only have a fraction of the appeal it once did. They'd have legs, but they'd be weak. They'd be able to live among us, but they'd still retain their hideous appearance, repulsing any who came near."

"So, if that's the case, Menoetius would need more than one witch in his arsenal if he wanted to remove the curse," I murmured. "The power of one witch likely wouldn't be enough."

"Most definitely." Scylla held up a hand and tilted her head to the side, as though listening for something. Her back stiffened and her eyes flicked again toward the dark door that led to the cliffside.

When she spoke, her voice was tight. "Ah. You all should probably leave now. There's a ship coming through."

She gave a brief smile to Mary and Eric, and her eyes began to darken. "It was lovely to meet you both. Hopefully next time, we'll be able to become better acquainted with one another." Scylla's nose twitched, and she turned her head back toward the door.

"What's going on?" Mary asked.

The words were barely out of her mouth when claws emerged from the tips of Scylla's long fingers, and two tentacles slithered silently out from under her dress, curving up to hover in midair. She stood and began wrapping her long hair up into a bun, revealing a black tattoo that took up most of her back. The six dogs that were inked into her dark skin began to shimmer into three dimensions.

"Scylla?" I stepped forward hesitantly.

Her head whipped around, and her eyes, black as pitch, bore into mine as she let out a hiss.

Suddenly, a small brown dog materialized from her back, leaping to the floor and immediately growing to the size of a large wolf. The moment it caught our scent, it crouched low and growled. One of her tentacles shifted and shot across the floor, causing Mary to let out a yelp as she danced back, nearly stumbling over the sofa as Scylla's tentacle narrowly missed latching onto her ankle.

"Shit." I shot a panicked look at Athena. "Athena, take us back to Olympia."

She nodded and had just put her hands on Mary and Eric's shoulders when a second wolf emerged. Its lips were curled into a snarl, and acidic venom dripped from its snout, hissing as it hit the floor.

Both lowered into a crouch just as Athena teleported us away.

AS SOON AS we stepped onto Main Street in Olympia, Mary spun to face me, her eyes glittering with fury.

"What the fuck was that, Tessa?"

"I'm sor—" I began, but Mary plowed ahead, cutting me off.

"No! What logic made you think you could just say, 'hey, let me take my friends to visit a goddamn fucking man-eating sea witch without checking to see if she might need to *feed* first'? How are you even *friends* with her? Next you're going to tell me you're BFFs with one of the Hydras, too!"

"No! Of course not!"

"Well, why not? You apparently had a massive screw fest with their master!"

"The Hydras never leave the Underworld, Mary. You should know that," Athena said, either ignoring, or oblivious to, the level of Mary's anger.

Mary shot her a scathing glare. "No. Shit. My point—"

"Mary, back off," Eric said, stepping between us. "She gets it. Tessa should have told us what we were going into. There's no need—"

"Oh, fuck off, Eric," Mary snapped. "You would take her side. That thing tried to attack me!"

"Hey, don't take this out on me!" Eric jerked back. "I just don't—"

"Yeah, I really don't give a shit." Mary turned her glare on me.

"I'm sorry!" I held up my hands in a gesture of defeat. "Really. I didn't think—"

"Obviously."

I took a deep breath and tried to steady myself. "I'm trying here, Mare. Please, I need you to understand that."

"Oh, I do, trust me. I'm working my way through this shit show just like you, Tessa, don't you forget that. We've been practically sisters our—well *my*—entire life. Most of our memories have been with each other, and now it turns out you've got an entirely different goddamn life that we're all just supposed to be okay with?" She glared at me, her chest heaving with anger.

Fury and hurt sparked within me. "I have to be okay with it, too! *I'm* the one that has to deal with two childhoods, with two sets of parents, with one brother who's gone insane and another who loves to torture me. So cut me some goddamn slack already!"

She threw her hands up and took a few steps back. "Whatever. Next time you need a distraction from dealing with your shit, count me out. Come get me when you get a fucking grip."

She turned and stalked up the street toward the dorms.

I stared after her, stunned, then looked at Eric and Athena. Both were looking around, clearly uncomfortable.

"What—"

"Tessa, stop," Eric said quietly, his eyes full of sympathy. "I get it. I really do, but Mary's right. You might trust Scylla, but she's a lot more dangerous to us than she is to you." His gaze drifted toward Athena, then back to me. "You should have warned us."

Tears began to spill from my eyes, and I frantically began wiping at my cheeks. I took a deep breath before speaking. "I'm sorry. I don't know what else to say."

"There's nothing to say. You just need to remember that you're a lot less breakable than we are."

"Scylla wouldn't have—"

"Maybe, maybe not. That's the point. Mare and I don't know anything about her aside from her reputation." He sighed and scratched his head. "Look, I know you're having a tough time dealing with all this, but so are we."

"She seemed fine, though," I whispered stubbornly.

"Come on, Tess. You know Mary's not going to spell out her doubts about you, about your new life. She likes to pretend she's tough as nails, but we both know that's not the case."

I gave a watery laugh. "Fine, but how am I supposed to fix things if she won't talk to me?"

"I'll talk to her, you just need to give her some time."

I nodded. "I can do that."

He opened his arms, and I let him pull me into a tight hug.

"We'll always be your friends, Tessa," he whispered. "Don't ever doubt that. We'll never abandon you."

I sniffed. "Thanks, Eric. I really appreciate that."

He kissed the top of my head. "Anytime."

"We should probably get back, too," Athena said quietly. She looked at Eric. "I'm sorry if today was too much for you. It was just as much my doing as Tessa's. She needed a distraction, and I wanted to get to know her friends. I guess that backfired a bit."

Eric shrugged. "It's all good. Mary'll get over it, don't worry." He gave me one last smile. "We'll talk soon?"

"Yep." I nodded. "For sure."

As Eric turned and began walking away, I sighed and gazed up at the sky which was slowly beginning to darken, then looked back to Athena. "Well that sucked."

A sympathetic smile ghosted across her face. "Tessa, you should know that I understand how Mary feels. If you pulled me into one of your adventures with her, I might have felt equally as put out. I should've considered that when we discussed bringing them along."

I dragged a hand through my hair, pulling the tie out and slipping it onto my wrist. "It's fine. I was too wrapped up in trying to distract myself from dealing with my own stuff to look at things clearly, I guess."

She squeezed my arm and smiled. "Go home, spend some time with Nathaniel. Just relax."

My eyes widened as a realization hit. "Shit. He's going to be so freaking mad at me." I covered my face with my hands and groaned. "Gods, I'm ruining everything today."

"He's more forgiving than you give him credit for." She rubbed a hand up my arm. "And considering the events of this morning, I'd say you've got at least one pass. Just go, get it over with. We'll speak tomorrow."

She teleported away, and I quickly followed, setting my thoughts toward Nate's cabin and was happy when I managed to arrive where I wanted and in one piece.

When I stepped onto the lawn, I found him sitting on the porch steps, his arms resting on his knees as he stared at the ground.

As I approached, I saw his jaw clench.

"Hi," I said, my voice uncertain.

He lifted his head and glared at me.

Shit.

12

NATHANIEL

"Hi. *Really?*"

I tried to keep my tone even, but it was a struggle. I'd spent nearly an hour trying to find her after Hades had left, but neither she nor my sister had given anyone any indication where they were going. Athena had teleported Eric and Mary away from training before anyone could ask questions, and I'd gotten no response when I attempted to contact them mentally.

"Listen, I know you're mad—"

"Mad?" I stood and stormed down the steps. "I'm not mad, Tessa, I'm fucking furious! I come back here only to have your *ex* tell me you and Athena vanished not long after he'd done a dream walk with you. Then I find out from Chiron that she stole Eric and Mary away from training without so much as a word."

Her eyes widened. "I'm sorry, Nate, I just—"

"Do you know how worried I've been? Is this how it's going to be from now on? If so, tell me now, so I can figure out how to deal with it."

She chewed on her lower lip and tears filled her eyes. "I'm sorry," she whispered.

I took a deep breath, trying to rein in my anger and annoyance. "Do I even want to know where you've been?"

She turned to stare into the darkening forest and wrinkled her nose. "Probably not."

I narrowed my eyes. She'd been crying, which had weakened her walls enough for them to falter slightly.

"Scylla? Are you fucking *insane*?"

She flinched, and I realized I was shouting. Her apprehension immediately gave way to anger.

"No, I'm not insane, and I don't appreciate you insinuating that!"

"You took two unseasoned recruits with you to visit a sea witch who *eats people* for a living, and you didn't see a problem? My goddamn *sister* didn't see that as a problem?"

"Scylla is my friend," Tessa snapped. "A very old friend. I needed a distraction, and Athena and I thought she might be able to give us some information on the missing witches, which she did, by the way. We decided to bring my friends with us."

"I can't believe I'm even asking this, but did she need to feed while you were there?"

Her mouth opened, then snapped shut.

I arched a brow. "Well?"

"Yes, but as soon as we realized what was happening, Athena and I got us all out of there."

I pressed my fingers to my eyes and took a few deep breaths as I tried not to imagine the dozens of ways that could have backfired. Finally, I dropped my hands and met her eyes.

"I'm going to walk away now before I say something I'll regret. Go inside and just do...whatever. But please, stay there. No more trips down memory lane."

She pressed her lips together, and I saw the lower one tremble slightly.

Dammit.

"Do what you need to do," she whispered, her voice shaky. "I'll be here when you get back."

I teleported away, not trusting myself to say anything else.

~

"HOLD ON—WAIT—LET me get this straight." Dionysus picked up his bottle of wine and took a swig, then wiped his mouth with the back of his hand before continuing. "You're telling me, not only is your girlfriend a four-thousand-year-old Titaness, she had a 'relationship' with Hades, is friends with Scylla, and she kidnapped two recruits to go on an information gathering mission at a sea witch's cave?"

"Yes, that is what I'm telling you," I replied wearily, instantly regretting meeting him and Hermes at his house. I picked up my own bottle of wine and took a large swallow as I stared out over the railing of his rooftop deck.

He started laughing hysterically, nearly rolling off the chaise he was lying on and stopping only when Hermes punched his shoulder.

"Ow! What the—"

"Between his goddamn melancholy and your stupidity, it's a wonder either of you have lovers at all," Hermes said.

"Oh, come on!" Dionysus laughed. "You can't tell me this isn't at least a little bit funny!"

Hermes cast a sidelong glance at me, then took a large pull from his own bottle. "It might be mildly amusing," he admitted.

"She could have gotten them killed," I said.

"Do you know how hard it is to kill an Ischyra?" Hermes asked.

I gave him a pointed glare.

"Right, of course you do," Hermes said, wincing. "My point is, they're hard to kill to begin with, and they were protected by a Titaness—" Dionysus let out a laugh at the word, earning him another hit from Hermes "—and an Elder. Even if Scylla did shift—"

"She did." My eyes narrowed. "A ship came through. That was why they had to leave."

"Oh. Well, that just proves my point. Tessa and Athena got them out of there before anyone could be maimed or killed. It all worked out."

"Yes, fortunately for them it all worked out. The fact remains still remains that it could have very easily gone the other way."

"You're going to have to cut her some slack, brother," Dionysus said, setting his empty bottle on the railing. "She's a Titaness. She doesn't need you to protect her anymore."

"She didn't need me to do that to begin with. That's not the problem."

"Then what is?" Hermes cracked open another bottle of wine and handed it to Dionysus.

I tapped my finger on the rim of my bottle and mulled his question over for a moment.

"She's barely been back two days," I finally said. "Her brother is out of his mind and hiding in a cave, Menoetius seems intent on tormenting her, her mental walls are complete shit, and we've got no clue what the extent of her control over her powers is. Not to mention Hades just bombarded her with nearly seven hundred years' worth of memories without her consent, and now she's forced to figure out how to balance two lives. There is absolutely no certainty surrounding her anymore."

"Okay so let me ask you this." Dionysus rolled to his side and propped his head on his fist. "While all of those things are incredibly valid concerns, does any of this annoyance have to do with her reunion with Hades today?"

I gazed out over the mountain, not meeting his eyes. "Not particularly," I mumbled, taking another sip of wine.

"You've got no issue at all with the fact that she was apparently fuck buddies with the ruler of the goddamn Underworld, and now she's back, and he's digging around in her brain?"

Glaring, I threw my near-empty bottle at him, hitting him on his shoulder.

"Ow!"

"Real nice, D," Hermes said, rolling his eyes.

"What?" Dionysus said, rubbing his shoulder where the bottle had struck him. "I don't know a single person, Titan, god, or human, who would be comfortable with someone like him doing a dream walk with their lover. Do you even know what they talked about?"

"Hades said he wants to resume training her. Apparently, he'd been a fairly decent mentor in her past life, and he doesn't believe I'm willing to put her through enough torment to truly strengthen her." I didn't bother trying to hide the bitterness in my tone.

Hermes snorted. "Of course he doesn't, the sadistic shit. None of us would be willing to do that."

"What else?" Dionysus asked. "Was that really all they talked about?"

I shrugged. "I guess. We didn't really get into it once he told me she'd left."

"So, he basically could have begged her to get back together, then she jetted off to avoid having that awkward conversation with you?"

"Idiot," Hermes muttered.

I shook my head. "You're really not helping." Despite Hades' words to the contrary, I didn't want to acknowledge how much Dionysus' question aligned with my own concerns.

"Okay, so look at it logically," Hermes said before Dionysus could respond. "Has she ever given you reason to think she'd stray?"

"No, but we'd only just gotten our relationship sorted out before she found out who she was, and she'd been awake for about twenty-four hours when she remembered her relationship with him. We know each other well, but our actual romantic relationship has been short."

"Fine, so let's say, for the sake of argument, that she's an unknown here. Persephone isn't. Hades has been over the moon for Persephone for centuries."

"Fair point," Dionysus said. "He also thought Tessa had died nearly two thousand years before he met Persephone, though."

Hermes rolled his eyes. "You're a real dick, you know that?"

"I'm just saying, if it took him that long to move on, then maybe he never got over her. What being goes *that* long without settling down with someone at least once?"

I stood and ran a hand through my hair. "I'm going to head back and talk to her."

Hermes stood and gave me a one-armed hug, then patted me on the back with a grin.

"Don't listen to him," he whispered. "He's jealous. No matter how hard he tries, he doesn't know how to keep a lover."

"Like you do," Dionysus grumbled.

"Let us know how it goes," Hermes said.

I sighed. "Will do."

THE HOUSE WAS dark when I arrived on my front lawn, giving no indication whether Tessa was still up. Slowly, I ascended the steps and walked inside, closing the door quietly behind me.

She was asleep when I entered the bedroom, lying on the bed with a blanket covering her legs and wearing one of my T-shirts. The sight of her in my clothes, claiming something as mundane as a T-shirt as hers, had the doubts I'd been wrestling with earlier melting just a little.

Pushing off my shoes, I climbed into bed next to her, then wrapped my arm around her waist and laid my head on her chest. I took a deep breath, inhaling the floral scent of her shampoo, and felt her body tense, then relax almost immediately.

"Hi," she said, her voice groggy as she woke.

"Hi," I murmured.

She pulled her arm out from under me and began stroking my hair. "Are you okay?"

"Yes," I mumbled against her shirt. "I'm sorry I stormed off like that."

"It's okay." She let her hand come to rest on my back, then kissed my forehead. "I understand. I'm sorry, too."

I closed my eyes and tightened my arm around her waist, content to just lay there, breathing her in.

"Do you want to talk about it?" she asked after a moment.

I sighed. "Yes and no. Hades told me you spoke about your training, so I'm certainly curious what your thoughts are on that."

"And you want to know what else we talked about, right?"

I could hear the smile in her voice.

"Does it make me sound like a jealous boyfriend if I say yes?"

She laughed. "No, of course not. I'd be dying of curiosity if I were you." She extricated herself from my arms and rolled so that we were face to face. "We only discussed him teaching me again. While I still think he's a narcissistic prick, I also think he may have had some valid points."

I arched a brow. "Such as?"

"I need to learn to use my power—or not use my power—under the harshest circumstances there are. In person, I think I'd be able to defend myself well enough against Menoetius, because he wouldn't be able to get through my mental walls to block my power. I'm confident of that. I need to learn how to remove him from my mind and wake myself up if he slips through while I'm sleeping, though. I need to know how to keep my walls up instinctively, without trying, so no one can get in. Even if I'm unconscious."

"And Hades is willing to hurt you in the name of teaching."

"Yes." There was a touch of defiance, a bit of stubbornness in her tone when she answered. "As much as I don't want to admit it, I think that may be what I need. I need to learn under real-life circumstances. Apollo said something back when I was still an Ischyra that was along the same lines and I think he was right."

I frowned, then recalled his words. "He said 'there are no fatigue breaks in war.'"

"Exactly. Athena had just sliced me up with her arrows and you wanted him to give me a break." She put a hand on my cheek and smiled. "He wasn't wrong when he told you I didn't need to be coddled. Menoetius will take advantage of any weakness he sees in me. I need teachers who will help me learn to fight in my dreams, who can teach me to take on anything Menoetius might throw at me. You aren't willing to put me through that kind of anguish, and I don't see that as a bad thing, trust me. You'll have to be okay with him doing it, though. Can you do that for me?"

I pressed my forehead to hers and nodded. "I won't be okay with Hades hurting you, but I *can* acknowledge that his methods might be better suited for this than mine are. I honestly don't even know what mine would be." A thought that pained me, because it forced me to face the fact that Hades likely knew more about Tessa's needs than I did.

"Thank you," she whispered. "Because I'm going to need you there with me."

"Of course. Whatever you need." I tilted her face toward mine and kissed her softly. "Now, tell me what happened with Scylla."

"Athena told me about the missing witches and Ischyra. She wanted to go check in with Scylla, and I needed a distraction." She blew out a breath. "I think it's safe to say that bringing Mary and Eric along with us was probably not the best idea."

"Probably not. What did Scylla have to say?"

"She doesn't think any of her witches have turned against us. She's more concerned that Menoetius still has knowledge of the spell he used to drain my power way back when. She said she and Hecate did an info wipe, kind of like what Hecate did when she erased all knowledge of me." She shrugged. "But that didn't work so well on him in the case of his memories of me, so it's possible that one didn't work, either."

"Yes, Hecate seems to feel the same way. Although, considering the witches all went missing right around the time memories of you returned, I'd say he's only recently gotten that particular memory back."

She pursed her lips and nodded. "Maybe."

"So...speaking of our many problems, Zeus had an assignment for you, but only if you're up for it."

"What kind of assignment?"

I explained Zeus' request that she visit Athens and use her psychometry to try and determine if there was any truth to the rumors about the Sirens. I left out the part about the argument he and I had gotten into.

She thought for a moment, then nodded. "Sure. I can't promise I'll be terribly effective, but I'll do my best. When should we go?"

"In the morning. If you'd like, we can see if your friends want to come. This will be a slightly tamer mission than a visit to a sea witch —" I smiled wryly "—but I think it could be beneficial."

She smiled ruefully. "I suppose a do-over wouldn't be the worst idea."

"Agreed." I kissed her again, letting my lips linger on hers for a few moments before pulling back. "So...you seem better than when I left."

"I'm okay. Having something to do really helped get my mind off of things. My memories are settling in, so it's easier to focus on the things that don't involve me being tormented by my brother. I'm starting to remember the good things more clearly, too."

I smiled and brushed her hair off her forehead. "I'm happy to hear your distraction helped."

One corner of her mouth curved up in a smile. "You want to distract me some more? I seem to remember you making me a promise earlier."

I couldn't help but laugh. "You're incorrigible."

"Uh huh. So, is that a yes?"

Pushing her hair aside, I trailed my lips down her neck. "No. I'm still mad at you."

She shifted closer and hitched a leg over my hips, then lowered her lips to my ear. "Liar."

My hand settled on her bare thigh, and I let out a low laugh as I pulled her close. "Where are your pants?"

Leaning back, her eyes widened with mock innocence. "No clue."

I grinned and ran my hand further up her leg, then lowered my lips to hers. "I'm not sleeping with you tonight," I murmured against her mouth.

She pushed me onto my back and straddled my waist, letting her long blond hair form a curtain around us. A look of determination filled her face and her lips curved into a smile.

"That's fine." She ran her hands under my shirt, then pulled it over my head. "There are plenty of other things we can do."

"You're killing me, love."

She giggled—an unbelievably sexy sound, coming from her. "That's the plan."

13

TESSA

I woke the next morning with a clear head and redemption on my mind. My thoughts felt clear, and as I looked back on my actions from the previous day, I cringed as I realized how they'd affected the people I loved most.

I'd just made the decision to go find Mary and hash things out, pull her out of the arena, if necessary, when Nate woke and spoiled my plans

"Athena did a dream walk last night," he mumbled into the pillow. "I'm under strict instructions to keep you here today. We'll go to Athens tomorrow."

"Okay." Smiling, I rolled toward him and slid my arm around his waist. "In bed here, or just in the house?"

He opened one eye and gave me a playful glare. "You're not allowed to wear my shirts anymore. Especially with no pants."

"Hmm. That almost sounds like a challenge."

"Stop trying to entice me," he murmured, sliding an arm around my waist and nuzzling my neck.

"Is it working?"

"Not at all."

Suddenly, he cocked his ear toward the door. A moment later, I heard footsteps thumping through the house, then Hermes and Dionysus burst in.

"Why?" Nate groaned as they dove into bed on either side of us. "Why do you insist on being here at—" he lifted his head to look at his clock "—six o'clock in the morning?"

"You two really need to practice your timing," I muttered.

Dionysus shifted so he was resting his head on the pillow next to me, letting his brown hair spill across his forehead.

"You two can get frisky later. We wanted to come and see Tessa," he said, grinning at me. "She's so much more interesting now."

My mouth popped open in mock outrage, and I gave him a hard shove. "Jerk!"

He winced, rubbing the spot on his shoulder where I'd pushed him. "A lot stronger, too," he muttered.

"She's a Titaness, you idiot," Hermes said, laughing. "What did you expect?"

"Not to get punched, perhaps?"

"Maybe you should leave, then," Nate suggested.

"No can do, baby brother," Hermes said. "Athena sent us. We are here to occupy and entertain our newly-returned deity."

My eyebrows shot up. "What are you talking about? Why?"

"Because she hates you, clearly," Nate muttered, once again burying his face in my neck. "You all really do have the worst timing."

Dionysus snorted. "Her recruit friends can't miss another day of training, and based on yesterday's activities, Athena feels it's probably best Tessa does something productive today that doesn't involve leaving the house, so you'll have to get your ya-yas out some other time."

Nate propped himself up on his elbows and frowned at Dionysus, his eyes still blurred with sleep. "What did she have in mind?"

"Father still wants Tessa to visit Athens, but he's agreed with Athena that it can wait," Hermes said. He met my eyes, and I thought I saw a flicker of sympathy. "Today, he wants her to attempt a dream walk with Atlas."

"He wants me to *what?*" I shoved Nate off me and sat up, stunned. "My brothers already said that didn't work!"

Hermes shrugged. "As his twin, Father thinks you'll be more successful, and if it works, it will increase our odds of success when we move to extract him from that filthy cave."

I looked at Nate, who met my panic-filled gaze with his own reassuring one.

'I'll help you,' he said. *'And as far as my father's ideas go, this one isn't terrible.'*

I took a deep breath. "Alright, I can try, but I could barely manage to perform a dream walk in my past life. I don't see myself being terribly successful this time around."

Dionysus patted my arm. "Not to worry, doll. That's why we're here. Hermes will help direct you, and I'll keep you happy."

I arched a brow. "Athena sent you to keep me happy while I try to dream walk into my insane brother's mind?"

He frowned. "Who else would you suggest?"

"I don't know. Apollo? His magic calmed me right down yesterday."

Dionysus shook his head. "His magic doesn't change your negative emotions, it just dampens them. I'm an empath, so you'll be absorbing and feeling my positive emotions as though they're your own, kind of like what happens with Hades, only better. Besides, Apollo is a grump. We don't need his negative energy."

"Considering how you react when you absorb Hades' emotions, I'd say it's probably worth a shot," Nate said.

I looked between the three of them, struggling to find a point to argue. Finding none, I sighed. "Alright, but can I at least get dressed first? And brush my teeth?" *And have a nice, private panic attack?*

"Oh, is that what that smell is?" Dionysus said teasingly.

Scowling, I shoved him again, this time depositing him on the hard floor.

"Ow! Tessa!"

"You deserved that one," Hermes said, laughing. He hopped out of bed in a single lithe movement, then grinned. "Go on, get dressed and we'll meet you both in the living room."

Once they were gone, I rolled to my side and leaned over the edge of the bed, grabbing a pair of gray pajama pants I'd left there the night before. As I stood to tug them on, Nate arched a brow and stared up at me.

"I thought you said you didn't know where your pants were?"

"I guess my memory was still fuzzy," I said as I walked into the bathroom, trying to force nonchalance into my voice.

He followed me in, then came up behind me and wrapped his arms around my waist.

"You don't have to do this if you don't want to," he murmured, kissing a spot just below my ear before resting his chin on my shoulder. "I think it's a good idea, but if you're not ready, that's fine, too."

I met his eyes in the mirror and shrugged. "I know, but I think Zeus might be right. Even though it's been ages, I still know Atlas' mind better than anyone else."

He gave me a tense smile and nodded. "I think you're right."

I leaned back into his chest and closed my eyes. "You'll go in with me?"

He tightened his arms around my waist and kissed my shoulder. "If that's what you want."

"Thanks," I whispered, picking up my toothbrush.

A few minutes later, the four of us were gathered in the living room.

"So, what do you recall about dream walks from your past life?" Hermes asked once I was settled on the sofa.

"Not too much. I never really had much cause to initiate them." My eyes flicked to Nate, then back to Hermes. "It was the main way Hades and I communicated back then, though, since my brothers disapproved of our relationship."

Hermes frowned thoughtfully. "Can I ask why you waited so long to practice them back then?"

I rolled my eyes. "My comings, goings, and communications were always being monitored by my parents and brothers. They didn't feel a need to teach me much about my power, and they also didn't want to make it widely known what I could do. Once my abilities manifested when I was a child, they all knew someone would eventually try to take advantage of my power because it was so singular. My parents kept me under lock and key, then once my father abandoned us, my brothers took over. Someone was always with me, no matter where I went."

Dionysus shook his head, confused. "Then how in all the realms were you able to manage a relationship with someone your siblings hated?"

I couldn't help but smile at that. "Athena, mainly. She was one of very few people my brothers trusted with my safety." I looked at Nate. "If you think sneaking off to visit Scylla was bad, we'd have driven you all batty back then."

Dionysus screwed up his face and looked at his brothers. "Isn't our sister supposed to be wise? Isn't that her thing?"

"Something like that," Nate muttered.

"Did Hades teach you how to dream walk, then?" Hermes asked.

"No, Atlas did, but only because I begged him. We never practiced much once I learned, though. Hades and Athena helped me, and sometimes Epimetheus, although that was pretty rare. He was always afraid of getting in trouble with Prometheus."

"Then why did he help at all?"

"He had a thing for Athena, and he was much more of a risk-taker back then." I smiled wistfully. "Trickster god and all that."

Dionysus barked out a laugh. "Oh, gods. Okay, wait, I have to know—did they ever...you know?"

I rolled my eyes and tossed a pillow at him. "Not that I'm aware of, and can we focus, please?"

"Yes, please," Hermes said, casting his younger brother a disparaging look. "Do you recall how you would connect to their minds?"

I shrugged. "Kind of. I learned how to form a mind link with someone when I was training as an Ischyra, and I think it was kind of like that."

"A bit, although it would fall somewhere between that and astral projection. Basically, you'll be projecting your consciousness into your brother's mind. If you're able to astral project, you should be able to enter the dream realm fairly easily. For our purposes, I'm going to make the veil between the waking world and dream realm visible. Typically, one only has to visualize it, but since you're still learning, it'll be easier if you can see what you're reaching for."

I wracked my brain as I tried to remember how I'd done with astral projecting as an Ischyra. I'd managed it, but it had never been a big focus because it wasn't something that would've helped much in my demonstration for Zeus. "Just tell me what to do."

Hermes waved his hand, and a few seconds later, a pale, shimmering wall appeared before us. "Now, all you have to do is picture yourself touching the veil, then reach out for Atlas' consciousness."

I took a deep breath and nodded, then held out a hand for Nate.

"I'll be right there with you," he whispered, lacing his fingers through mine. He looked at Dionysus. "You ready?"

"Absolutely." Dionysus sat down next to me, and almost immediately, I began to feel happiness and positivity radiating from him.

My eyes widened as it slammed into me. "Wow, Dionysus, that's..." I shook my head to clear my thoughts. "Wow."

He wiggled his eyebrows. "Now you know why I'm such a hit at parties."

I laughed. "I'll say. What if Atlas isn't sleeping?"

"Morocco is a couple of hours behind us. Assuming he's sleeping at night—which I'll acknowledge, could be a stretch—it'll still be very early morning there," Hermes said.

"Ok, then. Let's do this." I laced my fingers with Dionysus', finding his hand warm and comforting. I let his power pulse through me, then dropped my mental walls. "Nate?"

He leaned forward and kissed me, then smiled as his consciousness settled into my own.

Shrugging off the discomfort of sharing my mind, I stared at the shimmering gold veil for a moment as I contemplated how best to approach. I knew, without question, that I could do this.

I thought back to the lessons I'd had with Charlise when I'd practiced my telekinesis and astral projection. In both cases, she'd taught me to picture where I wanted my mind to be or what I wanted it to do. This time, I imagined my power as long tendrils, reaching out to mingle with the magic that separated the waking world from the dream realm. It was a strange sensation, almost like I was forcing my hair to stand on end.

After a few seconds, it worked. The moment I felt my power brush against the shimmering fabric of the veil, I pictured my brother's face. It came to me, wavering like he was underwater. Bright green eyes looked out from a strong, angular face. His skin was tan, just like mine, and his hair fell in soft blond waves to his chin. I pictured him smiling, holding my hand as he pulled me through the forest to our favorite sparring spot.

There was a slight tug that told me I'd found his mind, then everything shifted.

I was standing in the clearing we'd always sparred in. Our clearing. It was about half the size of a football field and oval shaped, not dark and overgrown like the one Menoetius had taken me to. My mother had told me it had been a mountain lake once that had dried up over the centuries. Now it was just a smooth carpet of grass that angled slightly with the curve of the mountain.

Despite the peaceful appearance of the dream setting, the state of his mind caused me to recoil. All the pain, grief, and desperation that had built up over millennia pressed in around me, and I had to force myself not to dive back into the safety of my own body.

Now I understood why the twins hadn't pushed further when they did their own dream walks.

'You're going to have to search for him,' Nate said, his voice grim. *'Are you able to push through this?'*

I steeled myself against the horrid emotions that were beating down on me, coating my skin like oil. With each step, an image flashed across my mind. Most of the emotions I expected; grief over the loss of me and our mother, anger toward Cronus and Iapetus, and the desperate desire to cease to exist.

Others, though, didn't fit.

Atlas with one large hand wrapped around my neck as he pulled my life force out with another.

A dagger, coated in iridescent godsbane, plunging into Clymene.

Atlas' laughter mixed with Cronus' as they watched our mother fall.

'This isn't right. Those aren't his memories.' I said.

'You need to find him. Where do you think he'd be?'

Pausing, I turned in a slow circle to examine the full expanse of the clearing, searching. Then, off in the distance between the trees, I found what I was looking for. I began to move toward it, pushing aside the memories and emotions that tried to force their way into my head as I ran for the clear space up ahead. I felt Dionysus helping me, pushing them back, giving me time to reach my destination.

I slowed when I reached the cliff side that overlooked the foothills below. Before me stood a long, single-story stone house. The roof was made of heavy thatch, and windows were cut into the stone every few feet. A dark wooden door stood closed at the front, facing the cliff fifty feet away.

My home.

'He's here.' I whispered.

'Please, be careful.'

I walked toward the entrance and pushed the heavy door open, then looked around the large room.

I couldn't help the gasp that escaped as I took it all in. Everything about it—from the neatly swept floors to the long wooden table that sat across from a large fireplace—was the same. A wall, the same pale brown as the floors, separated the living space from the sleeping quarters that were down the hallway that stretched to the other end of the house. There were five bedrooms in total.

'Menoetius didn't live here?'

'He left before Atlas and I were born,' I told Nate absently. *'He was barely fifty.'*

There was no sign of my twin in the main living area, so I began to make my way toward the bedrooms.

Mine was the first one on the right. Slowly, I nudged open the door, then let out a quiet breath and leaned against the frame as I took in the familiar space.

The bed was made of heavy oak, the tall posts carved with intricately designed flowers and vines. My father had painted it with limewash when I was young, giving it a textured white appearance. Combined with the soft white bedding my mother had made, it looked like a cloud resting in the center of the room.

A dark wood-and-gold chest sat at the foot of my bed, locked tight. I knew if I opened it, I would find mementos of my past life. Drawings of the flora in the surrounding forest that Atlas had scrawled onto rough parchment. The pale blue dress I wore as a girl the first time I met Cronus. The layers of skirts and the cut of the neckline had given me a perfect hourglass figure. There would be gold jewelry, purchased from merchants in Thessaly as gifts from the twins, who always felt the color of the metal brought out my eyes. A necklace made of onyx and rubies that had been a gift from Hades after our first fight. Beautiful books that my father had brought back from Mesopotamia that told stories of far-off places, and others that had been written right here on Olympus, books my mother had used to teach me about the realms and deities.

I had memories here. Good memories, of loving parents and three brothers who I loved with all my heart.

Then Zeus and his siblings had escaped their imprisonment, and Cronus was exposed for the tyrant he was. My family disintegrated, splitting into something I barely recognized. I was left with a traitorous father, an emotionally beaten mother, a brother who'd taken pleasure in hurting me, and three others who protected me so fiercely I could hardly breathe.

Tears dripped onto my cheeks, and I slowly wiped them away with the back of my hand.

Not now. I could fall apart later, when I wasn't trying to reach my twin.

I felt a light pressure on my hands. Dionysus and Nate, lending me their strength and power, offering wordless support.

"I can move mountains," I murmured, letting the door click shut behind me. Hesitantly, I turned and faced the door that stood directly across from mine.

Atlas' room.

Steeling myself, I stepped across the hall and put my hand on the knob. It stuck at first, but finally released. With a deep breath, I slowly pushed the door open. The sound of creaking hinges broke the silence around me, causing my entire body to go on alert.

I gasped as the light behind me filtered into the room.

Where the rest of the house was immaculate, perfectly preserved in his mind, his room was dark and miserable. The sun outside didn't filter in through the two windows in the east wall. No fresh air filled the room, despite the open panes. The walls and floor were black with grime, and the air was cold and stagnant, smelling as though the room had been closed up for too long.

In the corner, still as stone, was my brother. His knees were pulled up, held tight against his body by thick, muscular arms. His skin and clothes, nothing more than rags, were filthy. Hair that was once soft and blond hung in limp locks.

He flinched as I stepped closer, his head turning a fraction toward me.

Nate squeezed my hand, a warning to be careful.

"Atlas?" I kept my voice at a whisper, but in this still, dark room, it seemed as loud as a scream.

He began to rock, the wood floor making a soft creak beneath him.

I took a few steps closer, bringing me within a few feet of him. "Atlas, can you hear me?"

"Of course, I can hear you," he said quietly. "I can always hear you." His voice was rough, grating through my ears like sandpaper, but the sound of it, after so long, nearly broke me.

"Atlas, I need you to look at me. It's Tessa."

"They sent you, didn't they?" He pressed his forehead to his knees, muffling his raspy voice. "He never stops. Nothing but a trick."

"No one sent me."

I took a few steps closer, putting myself well within striking distance.

"Please," I whispered.

Slowly, he lifted his head and faced me, and what I saw nearly caused me to whimper.

His eyes, normally a bright, vibrant green, were muted to the color of moss. A once happy mouth was turned down in disgust, and his teeth, white against his dirty skin, flashed menacingly.

"Tessa is dead," he spat. "You're nothing but a fake. You thought I forgot, but I didn't. Now get out of my head."

"That's not true, Atlas. Look in my eyes."

I reached out to touch his shoulder, ignoring sharp protests from Nate.

The moment I touched him, he sprang to his feet and grabbed me by the neck. With a snarl, he tossed me across the room, sending me painfully into the wall. The whole room spun, and I struggled to get my bearings.

I can do this I can do this I can do this.

Forcing away the ringing in my head, I jumped up and faced him.

"I am your sister, Atlas." I pushed conviction and reassurance into my tone, lacing it with a touch of Coercion. "Your twin. Look at me."

He took a menacing step forward, his eyes slits of fury. "Get out of my head!" he hissed.

"No!" I stood my ground, refusing to back down no matter how much he terrified me. "I'm not leaving until you listen to me!"

He ground his teeth, and I felt a nudge as he tried to force me from his mind.

I pushed back. "I'm trying to help you, Atlas. Don't send me away, please."

"I said get out of my head!" he roared. He advanced on me, and I felt the hard, unmistakable push of his power.

I tried to fight against it, but within seconds, I was back in Nate's living room, shaking.

Nate slipped his hands up my arms and onto my face, tilting my chin so he could look at me.

"Are you alright?"

I cleared my throat and wiped at my eyes, then looked at Hermes and Dionysus before meeting Nate's concerned stare. "We need to go find the twins. That wasn't my brother. Something's in his head."

14

NATHANIEL

"Prometheus, I'm telling you, something isn't right!"

"We already know he's lost his mind, Tessa. That's no surprise to any of us."

"It's more than that. He said, 'they sent you.' Something is messing with him, I know it."

"You're not seeing what's right in front of you! Nothing has gotten to him other than his own grief and guilt."

I leaned against the wall in the living room of the guest wing at Zeus' palace and listened as Tessa and Prometheus argued. The argument had been going on for close to twenty minutes at this point, and Tessa had made little headway with convincing Prometheus of what she'd seen in Atlas' dream.

Epimetheus stood beside me, his brow furrowed as he watched their exchange.

"What are your thoughts on this?" he asked quietly.

"I don't know," I admitted. "I know nothing about him, save for Tessa's memories and what I've been told. He didn't look like himself, though, I will say that."

"In what sense?"

"His eyes, mainly. The color was off. It was a...putrid green, far darker than Tessa's. I would've expected it to be the same."

"That could be the insanity, I suppose. The loss of Tessa's energy could have caused his own energy to dim."

"If her soul hadn't returned, I might agree. His energy should have balanced back out by now, even if his mental state didn't." I raked a hand through my hair as I watched Tessa's lips press into a thin line. "Gods, she's going to cry. I need to stop this."

I stepped forward, putting myself between the arguing siblings.

Prometheus stepped back and glared at me. "Nathaniel, you can't possibly agree with this!"

"You weren't there, Prometheus. I think she might be right," I told him.

"Is that so? Tell me, how is it you suddenly know my brother so well?"

I arched a brow in challenge. "Did you even look at her memory? See what she saw?"

"I don't need to," Prometheus countered. "I've already seen the extent of my brother's lunacy."

Tessa let out a frustrated groan. "Why are you being so goddamn stubborn?"

"It's worth taking a look," Epimetheus said. "Just let her show you."

Prometheus clenched his jaw as he glared at his twin. "Fine," he snapped, shifting his gaze to Tessa.

She exhaled and nodded. "Let your walls down a little so I can send you the memory."

We all stood silent for a few seconds as Prometheus watched Tessa's recollection of the dream walk. His entire body gave a jerk when he saw Atlas toss her across the room. After a moment, he closed his eyes and sighed.

"I'm not saying you're right," he said quietly when he opened his eyes. "Even if you are, what good does that do us? We still can't do anything for him until we see him."

"I know that," she replied. "But now we know that we aren't just dealing with his disconnect from reality."

"We *might* know that," Prometheus countered. "Nothing is certain here."

"Fine. Whatever. I want to leave tomorrow."

"No," the twins and I responded in unison.

She arched her brow and looked at the three of us. "Seriously? I don't need permission from any of you to go rescue my brother."

"No, you don't, but you do need backup," Prometheus shot back. "Which none of us are comfortable giving you just yet, considering you only just got your memories back."

"You have no idea—" She paused and took a deep breath. "Trust me when I say that this is something I can do."

Epimetheus dropped down on the couch, then looked up at her with sadness in his eyes. "You're not ready, Tessa."

She turned her gaze on me, her eyes brimming with tears.

I pinched the bridge of my nose and closed my eyes, trying to figure out the most diplomatic way to phrase my response. "I think you should give it a couple more days," I said, letting my hand drop. "Just so we can at least do a run through with your powers."

"Oh, come on!" Hurt flashed in her eyes. "Way to be 'in my corner,' Nate. Thanks a lot."

I tried to tamp down the irritation this conversation was causing. "Really? That's where you're taking this?"

She put her hands on her hips and glared at me. "Yes. I expect these two to want to keep me under lock and key, but not you."

"I don't want to keep you under lock and key," I said, trying to keep my voice even. "I want you to be reasonable. You have no clue what you are or are not capable of right now. You haven't worked on your powers since your demonstration, Tessa. There is absolutely no sense *whatsoever* in going into a potentially life or death situation without knowing whether or not you'll be able to defend yourself!"

"He's my brother! He's not going to hurt me!"

"I'm sorry, did you miss the part where he threw you across the room like a damn rag doll?"

"I just need time to convince him that I'm alive." Her expression turned pleading. "Please, Nate. You said you wouldn't stifle me. I *need* to do this."

I stepped forward and took her face in my hands. "I also said I would tell you if I thought you were in over your head," I whispered. "I just want to be sure that you'll be able to defend yourself in every way possible should the need arise."

"He's not going to hurt me," she repeated. "I know he won't."

"And what if Menoetius shows up? What if whatever's got control of his mind—assuming we're right—takes control and locks you in? Don't you want to be confident in your own abilities to escape before going into a situation like that?" I brushed my thumb along her jaw, trying to calm her. "Do you think he would ever forgive himself if he hurt you?"

Her eyes searched mine, then she closed her eyes.

"I can do this, Nate." She opened her eyes and looked up at me. "I promise you, this is something I can do."

Epimetheus stood and began to protest. "Tessa—"

"No." She held up a hand to stop him. "We're not doing this. I love you, but this isn't your decision."

"Then let's take it to Zeus."

Tessa's eyes widened at Prometheus' suggestion. "I don't need his permission, either!"

"Alright, let's just stop for a second," I said. "Tessa, you don't need Zeus' permission to do this, but he should be made aware of what we saw in that dream walk. If there's some unknown entity that's taken Atlas as a host, he should know. It doesn't benefit anyone to hold back information right now."

"Okay, fair enough." She huffed out a deep breath. "You go do that. I need to go get some air or something. Just come find me when you're done talking with him."

I eyed her suspiciously. "Where are you going?"

"Don't worry, I'm not going to endanger the lives of myself or others. I got my fill of that yesterday." She leaned up on her toes and kissed me. "I'll see you in a bit."

As we watched her leave the room, Epimetheus turned to me.

"Do you think it's wise to leave her alone right now?"

I looked back and forth between him and his twin. "She needs space. You both need to allow her that."

"You don't get to tell us what to do—" Prometheus began.

"No, I don't." I sighed. "But I would hope that you'd respect your sister's wishes enough to let her be. Now, let's go find Zeus."

Hermes and Dionysus had left from my house to go directly to the palace, so by the time we'd gotten there, Zeus had already been briefed on the situation.

"This is incredibly troubling," he said after listening to my more detailed account.

"I'll say," Dionysus said. "Any thoughts on what could've gotten into his head?"

"If Menoetius is drawing on the power of those witches, he could've possessed Atlas with any number of demons." Zeus frowned. "And where is Tessa? Why isn't she here telling me this?"

"She needed some space," I said. "She's not happy that we aren't leaving to rescue Atlas immediately."

"You all need to stop letting that girl escape you," he grumbled.

"She's a Titaness, Father, not a girl, and she's not escaping anyone."

"Yes, well, perhaps a discussion about the detriments of impetuous behavior should be had."

"That's not the point," Prometheus said. "I'm not entirely certain that her assertions are accurate, but they're worth consideration."

"Alright. Say there is some volatile force affecting your brother's mind." Zeus folded his arms and leaned back in his chair. "How do you propose we remove that presence?"

"Let's go with the assumption that Menoetius is the one manipulating Atlas' mind. If that's the case, Tessa might be able to use his own powers against him," I said.

"How? Unless he's in the room with us, she can't affect him," Prometheus replied. "And I still don't like the idea of her going in there at all. We should try to handle this ourselves."

I shot him an annoyed look but didn't bother arguing.

"That might not be entirely true," Hermes said, sitting forward in his chair. "How did she fare with mind-linking as an Ischyra?"

I raised a brow. "I'm not sure. Why?"

"Atlas' mind is already weakened. Tessa may be able to perform a link and enter his mind."

I looked at him curiously. "For what purpose?"

"If she can take control of his mind and body from here, she could potentially see what's gotten ahold of him. Once we have that information, we'll be better equipped to deal with whatever it is. If it is Menoetius, she may be able to disable his powers enough to either challenge him or scare him off. If it's not, we'll have an ide—"

"Scare him off?" Epimetheus, interrupted, shaking his head. "Unlikely."

"Menoetius has only gone after her when she was asleep," Hermes countered. "When he attacked her in the past, he weakened her first. I don't think he's too keen on the idea of facing her when she's at full power."

"Which she isn't." Prometheus said, shaking his head. "It's too dangerous."

"Enough, Prometheus," Zeus snapped, then leaned back in his chair, stroking his beard absently. After a few seconds, he nodded. "Alright, go find her, have her practice infiltrating minds. Has she done any training at all since she's returned?"

"None, aside from the dream walk and some attempts at teleportation with Hecate."

"Have her work on her mind-linking and astral projection. Her coercive powers might come in handy, as well, especially if she'll have you there as back-up. I won't have her going in there without a little practice."

"How exactly do you expect her to practice? No offense," I said to the twins, "but I don't know that you two will be the best options. She already knows your weaknesses."

Zeus arched a brow and folded his arms across his chest, and I knew I wasn't going to like whatever came out of his mouth next.

"Go find Hades. He'll put up a good fight."

15

TESSA

I teleported down to the arena, not entirely sure what my plan was. I just wanted to be as far away from the god-half of the mountain as I could reasonably get. Already, I was beginning to feel as though my thoughts, my opinions, the things I wanted, were all being pushed aside by the twins' need to be in charge, to protect me. It felt as though what I had to say wasn't worth anything, that they knew best and I just needed to sit back and let the grown-ups handle things.

Yes, getting away from them was exactly what I needed right now.

When I reached the wide marble archway that led onto the arena floor, I hesitated, remembering all the bizarre rumors that were floating around about me now. Pursing my lips, I tried to peek in discretely. Almost immediately, my eyes met those of Fletcher, one of my former mentors, where he was working with a recruit who was throwing knives at a target several yards in front of him.

He eyed me curiously when he saw me. *'What's wrong, Tessa?'*

'Do you think I'd be able to steal Mary for a bit?'

'We're doing weapons today, so I think she's around back with Chiron and the other archers. You can go on back if you want.'

'How many are out there?'

'Two, aside from her. Anette and Damien.'

My lip curled in annoyance at the mention of Damien's name. The last time we'd spoken, we had been sparring. When he'd referred to me as Nate's "pet," I had proceeded to kick his ass. Needless to say, we hadn't left on good terms.

I gave him a tight smile. *'Okay. Thank you.'*

'Of course.'

I backed away from the entryway before anyone else could see me and slowly made my way around the side of the arena, where three targets had been set up. Chiron and another dark-coated centaur were guiding the three recruits, who fired one arrow after another from their bows. Or at least, they were guiding Damien and Anette. Mary's archery skills were better than anyone I knew.

Chiron's eyes lit up when he saw me walking toward them. "Tessa! How are you?"

I tucked a strand of hair behind my ear and tried to avoid the stares of the others. Mary continued to fire her arrows at her target, studiously ignoring me. "I'm good. You?"

"Doing well," he replied. "What can I do for you?"

"I was hoping —" My jaw snapped shut as I got a closer look at Mary's weapon, then turned back to Chiron. "Are those ice arrows?"

He grinned, then gestured for me to move to the side so I wasn't standing directly behind the targets. "Mary's become quite adept at creating weapons from ice. She's been working on these for the last couple of days. There are still some kinks to work out, of course, but they're impressive, to say the least."

"Wow, that's kind of—Ow!" I felt a sting in my side just before there was a quiet *thump* at my feet. I stared down at the ice arrow that lay on the ground, now shattered after coming into contact with my torso. Rubbing my side where it had hit, I glared up at Mary.

"Sorry," she muttered, nocking another arrow and aiming at her target. "Butter fingers."

Any retort I had was cut off by the sound of her next arrow hitting the bullseye. It wobbled, then shattered, leaving only the sharp head and about three inches of shaft embedded in the target.

Scowling, I turned to Chiron, who was smirking. "I was hoping I could steal Mary, if that's alright."

"If it's all the same to you—" *Thwack!* "—I'd rather just stay here," Mary said, still not looking at me as she fired again.

I finally spared a glance toward Damien and Anette, morbidly curious what their reactions were. Damien looked to be pretending to take guidance from the centaur beside him, but his aim looked half-hearted as he fired. Anette seemed as though she was trying to ignore me as she clumsily nocked her own arrow.

"Mary," Chiron said, his voice a mix of admonishment and amusement.

Looking back at him, I waved a hand dismissively. "No, it's fine. I'm sorry I interrupted." I smiled at Chiron. "It's really good to see you."

"You, too, Tessa." He gave me a pat on the arm. "Come back and visit anytime."

With a nod, I turned and started walking back toward the arena's portal door, hurt and not quite sure what to do with myself. Furious whispering ensued behind me, but I didn't bother trying to listen. I heard one final *Thwack*! followed by the sound of a bow clattering to the rocky ground.

I turned around when I heard footsteps and tried not to smile when I saw Mary stalking toward me, an annoyed expression on her face.

"Hey," I said quietly once she reached me.

She huffed and folded her arms across her chest. "Don't go getting all smug. I'm only here because he's my teacher and I have to listen to him."

I blew out a breath, suddenly unsure of what to say. I needed to apologize so badly, but the way she was looking at me right now made me think nothing I could say would be fitting.

"Why are you here, Tess?" she asked after several moments of silence.

I stared down at my hands, absently picking at my thumbnail. "To apologize." I lifted my eyes to meet hers, which were narrowed in annoyance.

"Eric already talked to me, and you said enough last night. There's nothing else to say."

"I'm sorry I dragged you to Scylla's without warning you first. It was really—"

"Stupid?" She cocked an eyebrow. "Reckless? Idiotic?"

"Yes. All of those." I gave her a small smile. "Seriously, though, I'm so sorry."

"I hope you really believe that. You and Athena...you guys can't die unless someone rips your life force out. That's not how it is for us. Eric and I can be killed, Tess. Maybe not easily, but if Scylla or her wolves went batshit and decided to tear our heads off, that would've been it." She shook her head, her eyes running over my face. "What were you thinking, Tessa? I mean, you've done reckless shit in the past, but nothing that put anyone's life in danger."

My eyes flicked toward the front of the arena, where the voices of recruits had gotten louder.

"Come back to Nate's with me. He's up at the palace, so he's not home." I cast another glance toward the archway. "I don't really feel like being gawked at."

"Yeah, fine." Her eyes looked wary as she answered, but she looked at me expectantly. "Aren't you supposed to be able to just blink and get us there?"

My face flushed. "I can take myself, but I can't really carry others with me. My powers are kind of picking and choosing which ones will be useful right now. Come on, we'll take the portal door," I said, gesturing toward the door next to the arena entrance.

She grinned. "You know, that's oddly satisfying."

I snorted. "Whatever. Let's go."

Once we were back at Nate's and settled on his sofa, she repeated her question.

"So? About last night?"

"I was thinking...I wanted my friends to dive into this new life with me. You guys were my world a week ago, and now my world has just exploded into this shitstorm, and I can't imagine doing any of this without you." I swallowed hard, trying to keep the tears that were burning my eyes from falling. "I didn't realize until we were in the moment just how different I am."

"I don't know. You are and you aren't, I guess."

I looked at her skeptically. "You're saying I was stupid, reckless, and idiotic as a human?"

"No. What I mean is...you were kind of goody-goody as a human, sure, but you also did some pretty stupidly reckless things now and then. Obviously, those are relative terms in your case, but it doesn't change anything."

"What's your point?"

"My point is, last night, even if you didn't realize it, you wanted an adventure. The Tessa I know loved adventures. She loved to go skinny dipping and scale silos to watch meteor showers and steal our guardians' cars." She frowned, her eyes darting around the room. "Hang on a sec."

She stood up and went into Nate's bedroom. Curious, I was about to follow her when she returned a moment later with a framed picture in her hand.

"I knew you remembered to bring these," she said, smiling as she handed me the photo. "Do you remember this night?"

Smiling, I took the photo taken before our senior prom. "Prom night. We had so much fun." I traced my fingers over the smiling faces of our human friends, wondering idly how Josh and Leila were faring now that we were gone. I realized with a start that I'd barely thought about them since we'd arrived on Olympus, and I felt a quick twinge of guilt. They'd been such a big part of my life back in Renville, and at some point, I'd let the parts of my human life that didn't pertain to my life as an Ischyra slowly begin to fade into the background of my mind.

"Well, if you remember prom, you'll remember what happened

after prom. We snuck out of our houses so we could go to Josh's party."

I laughed as I recalled the memory. "I almost flipped John's Jeep in the woods on the way to his house."

"Yup. We had to call Eric and Josh to come pull you, me, and Leila out of a massive mud hole when we got a flat so that none of our guardians or parents would find out. You weren't exactly boring as a human, Tessie Bear," she said cheekily, using Leila's old nickname for me. "It's to a different caliber now, so you just need to figure out how to adapt. You need to remember that, even though I loved our little adventures as a human, it's going to take some time for me to adjust to your idea of a good time now."

I set the picture down on the coffee table and gave her a tight smile. "I really messed up last night, didn't I?"

She curled her feet up beneath her and rested her elbow on the back of the couch, propping her head against her fist. "A little. We'll figure it out, though."

I held out my hand, and she squeezed it with her own.

"And, um, I'm sorry I shot an arrow at you," she said, wrinkling her nose.

I laughed. "I'll let it slide, but only because your ice arrows are freaking awesome."

"They are, aren't they?" she said with a smug grin.

"Hey, speaking of ice arrows; you wanna go out back and train some? I feel like everyone's been tiptoeing around me the last couple of days, so I'd kind of like to get some energy out."

She narrowed her eyes. "You're not going to try and get payback for me shooting you, are you?"

I chuckled. "No, I'm just antsy and need some practice."

"Okay, sure. Let's go."

Once we were outside, Mary eyed me warily. "So...what kind of practice, anyway? I'm not fighting you, Tess, sorry."

"Not hand to hand, don't worry. Just elemental stuff. I haven't gotten to do anything since my demonstration."

"Oh. Yeah, let's sit, though. It's easier to focus."

I sat down on the grass beside her, then looked at her expectantly. "Can you show me how you make some of your weapons? I was pretty good at making the fire bullets Eric showed me, but water work was kind of tricky."

"Sure." She straightened her shoulders and held out her hand. "If you're good with fire bullets, I can show you how to make them out of ice. The main thing is drawing on water, which you can do, right?"

I nodded. "Yup."

"Okay, so if you can do that, all you have to do is form the bullet and hold its shape." She stared at her hand where a small bullet, only an inch long, had formed. The water moved, but it looked as though it were encased in plastic.

I bit my lip, then opened my hand. After a few seconds, a blob appeared, the water undulating a bit more than the one Mary had. A moment later, I'd managed to shape it into a bullet.

"Next?"

"Next, you picture how the water changes from liquid to solid and force it to...listen to you or whatever."

"I've frozen water before. Is this much different?"

"It's a little different from what you did in your demonstration. Picture the molecules rearranging into a solid state while also forming the bullet's shape. They stop moving as much, get more orderly, a little more spread out."

I smiled. "I didn't realize there was so much science to this."

She shrugged, then tossed the now frozen bullet in her hand. "I didn't realize it, either, but it helps put it into perspective." She inclined her head toward my hand. "Now you try."

Focusing my attention on the tiny water blob in front of me, I imagined all the molecules moving around, scurrying into a more orderly formation. After a minute or so, I succeeded in making a semi-slushy bullet.

"Not bad," Mary said, dropping hers to the ground and forming another one. "You just have to practice. Mine were slushy at first, too."

"Got it. So is this how you make the arrows, too?"

"Yup. And my knives, but they're trickier, so we'll work on those later."

We worked quietly for a few more minutes as she demonstrated, and I tried to copy her methods.

"You know, you should get Eric and Yana up here to train some, too," she suggested. "It'd be fun."

"Nate and I talked about that. I'll probably ask once we get Atlas dealt with. I don't know."

"Sounds good." She continued to work on her bullets, adding one after another to her pile. "So, can I ask a question?"

"Of course," I replied, scowling as I tried to form another bullet. I cast an annoyed look at Mary's pile, which was slowly melting into the grass.

"What was Scylla talking about last night, about Menoetius torturing you?"

I let out a slow breath and tried to keep my focus on my current task. As much as I didn't want to talk about Menoetius, I knew burying those memories wouldn't help anyone, especially me.

"I'll spare you the details and give you the basic gist." I squeezed my hand into a fist, letting the slushy blob melt back into water, then opened my hand and began again. "My oldest brother is a sadistic monster who liked to try out his new weapons and poisons on me, as well as spells his witch friend would come up with. It lasted for months, as far as we can tell, starting around the time my father told him and Cronus what kind of power I had. One night, Atlas came into my room to say goodnight, and he saw I was missing. While he and the twins were out searching for me, Menoetius had already gotten me back to my room. When they realized I had no clue I'd even been out of my bed, they had Hecate and Hades do a little digging in my mind and finally figured out what happened. That was when Atlas decided to switch sides, although he didn't actually tell anyone for a while."

I glanced up and met Mary's eyes, which were wide as saucers. Her mouth opened and closed, then she huffed out a hard breath.

"Gods, Tess, that must've been awful. Are you alright? Last night wasn't, like, a downward spiral or something, right?"

"No, definitely not. And no, I'm not okay, but I will be. When Hades brought back my memories, those were the ones that came back first. I know he didn't do it that way intentionally, but gods, it was awful."

"Geez. Did he at least apologize?"

I snorted. "No, nor will he. That would mean admitting that he actually did something wrong."

"He seriously doesn't see it that way?"

"Nope." I let another glob of slush melt through my fingers. "He's a lot like Zeus, when it comes to being a ruler. Everything is for the greater good. If Hades' actions will benefit everyone in the long run, then they're justified in his eyes, no matter who they hurt."

"That's obnoxious," she muttered. "And now you're going to train with him?"

"Yeah. I can't stand him half the time, but I won't deny he was a damn good mentor to me back then."

"And Nate's cool with it?"

"According to him, yes, and Hades seems to think Nate will be beneficial, whatever that means. So, we'll see." I frowned, then let my hands fall to my lap. "Hey, can I ask you something?"

"Sure."

"So...when Hades did his dream walk, he mentioned something. He asked if I really thought all Nate did was transition and train new Ischyra."

She dropped another bullet into her pile. "What's that supposed to mean?"

"I don't know, but now I'm really curious. Nate said part of the reason he and Apollo had a falling out was because he'd started to distance himself from the rest of the gods, but I never asked why he did that."

"I thought you said it was because Apollo got his ex killed?"

"That was part of it, but he told me Apollo disagreed with the other choices he was making, too."

"Okay, so what's the big deal? Nate was born a couple hundred years before the Ischyra were created, right? Obviously, he did other stuff."

"No, I know, it's just...Hades made it seem like he had responsibilities that would upset me if I knew about them."

"He's your ex, Tess. He's probably just trying to start trouble."

"No, I really don't think it was that." I pursed my lips as I switched from forming bullets to just small balls of ice. "Rudolfo is basically judge and jury when it comes to Ischyra crimes, right? He has his regular duties, but that's his big one?"

Mary nodded. "Yeah, I think that's what Eric told us. He does inquisitions, gets confessions, that kind of thing. It's why he's so good at hypnosis. Why?"

I shrugged. "Someone would've had to do those things before Rudolfo was born. I just assumed Nate's liaison duties were the bulk of what he did, but now I don't know."

"Huh." She put her hand over mine and lowered it, then gave me a small smile. "Crazy thought, but have you tried asking him?"

"Of course not. That would make too much sense. I also haven't had the chance."

"He seems way too chill to be doing the shit Rudolfo does. I hear those inquisitions can get nasty. Then again, it was a different time back then, and Nate *is* Zeus' son, so what do I know?"

"That's the thing. It was a long time ago." Absently, I watched the small blob of water float in the air in front of me. "Who knows what he was like?"

"Ask him, although I can't imagine he underwent a complete personality transplant. If he was what Rudolfo is now, you'll figure it out." Dropping another bullet onto the ground, she huffed out a breath. "Look at it this way. You never judged Rudolfo for what he does, have you?"

"No, of course not." He'd been friends with Eric's guardians forever, and I'd never known him to be anything but kind, despite what his official duties were.

"Then if that's the case with Nate—which I think we can agree seems likely—it wouldn't really be fair to judge him."

"Even though he kept it from me?"

"I can't believe I'm saying this, but if it were you, is that something you'd come right out and say?" She gave me a sympathetic smile. "He had a hard enough time telling you he was a god, and by the time you'd gotten over that, you only had a few days together before you broke Hecate's spell. Then you were back for, what, a day, once Hades gave you back those memories? I'd honestly think it'd be kind of shitty if he was all, 'by the way, guess what I used to do?' when you were dealing with all of that."

"I guess."

She sighed. "So, how are you and Nate, anyway? What does he think about you taking us to see Scylla?"

I snorted. "He ripped me a new one when I got back here. I've never seen him so angry."

"Yeah? Well I guess it's good to know he won't bite his tongue when you pull some stupid shit." She smirked. "I kind of like him a little more now."

I laughed and shook my head. "I couldn't believe it. He said *fuck* at least once and called me insane."

"All well-deserved."

"Yeah, I know."

"Are you guys okay now, though? Worked it out?"

"Yeah, we're good," I said, shifting so I was looking at her more directly.

"So how come you didn't ask him about what he used to do last night? I know he didn't stay mad at you for long."

My cheeks flushed at her question, and she immediately smacked my arm with the back of her hand. "Tessa! Did you guys—"

"No, no, we didn't sleep together. Just...other stuff."

"Other stuff, huh?" She smirked. "Any thoughts on when 'other stuff' will turn into dirty, sexy stuff?"

I rolled my eyes. "I think we've got bigger things to focus on right now. Life or death things."

"What better time to do it? You could be dead tomorrow. Do you really want to die not knowing what it's like to have sex with him?"

"That's horribly pessimistic and incredibly unlikely." I frowned. "But no, I don't."

"Well, then, get on it. Time's a'wastin'."

I dropped another ice ball to the ground. "We'll get there soon. I just need it to be when my head isn't filled with plans to go save my brother, you know?"

She nodded. "Yeah, I hear that." She took a deep breath, then wiped her damp hands on her pants. "So, about that. What's your plan?"

"I'd love to teleport in there right now and bring him back, but no one seems to think that's a good idea."

"Why not?"

"Atlas is unstable, and Zeus was very clear about not bringing him here if he was a risk to the safety of Olympus."

"Okay..."

"Okay, what?"

"So what are you going to do? You aren't seriously waiting for permission, are you?"

"I—well, no, but I was kind of waiting for some back up. I could probably teleport in with no problem, but I can't guarantee I'd be able to teleport him back *here*, especially if he tries to fight me."

"No one said they'd be willing to go with you?"

"I could probably get Athena to. Hades would, too, but that would just be to piss off Zeus."

Mary snorted. "Whatever. You're a Mimic, Tess. If you don't want to teleport in, fine, but there are other ways to figure out whether he's stable enough to bring home."

"Such as?"

She shrugged. "It's your power. You tell me."

"Helpful," I muttered.

I thought back to the things I'd learned as a Titaness and as an Ischyra, then grinned as an idea popped into my head. "I could probably astral project into the cave. It's not that much different than dream walking, and Hermes helped me with that earlier."

"Do you think you can do it without him?"

"I don't know. Maybe?"

Mary shook her head. "Stop sounding so goddamn unsure of yourself, Tessa. You're a Titaness with a ridiculous amount of power. Call his ass down here and get him to help you."

I chewed on my lip for a moment, rolling her words around in my head. Finally, I pushed all my uncertainties aside and nodded. "Okay, let's do this."

16

TESSA

Needless to say, Nate was a bit confused when I summoned him, Hermes, and Dionysus back with explicit instructions to leave my brothers wherever they were.

'It's just easier if they're not here,' I told him. *'I'll explain when you get here.'*

A few seconds later, the three of them appeared on the lawn, quickly followed by Hades.

Nate smirked when he saw what Mary and I were doing, then dropped down in the grass next to me, leaning in to give me a soft kiss. "Hi."

I grinned at him, then shot a look at Hades. *'Why is he here?'*

'He seems to think you'll need him, for some reason.'

'Doubtful, but whatever.'

"Already rebelling, eh, Tessa?" Dionysus grinned and sat down on the ground next to Mary. He elbowed her, then gestured toward her bullets. "You're not being a bad influence are you, water girl?"

Mary's eyes widened and she looked at me. "Did he just call me—"

"Ignore him," Hermes said, sitting down across from me and

shooting Mary a wink. "He gets his pick up lines from humans, and they tend to be awful."

I raised an eyebrow at Dionysus. "You spend a lot of time around humans?"

He gave me an amused look. "I'm the god of revelry. You couldn't possibly think I get my kicks on this boring rock."

"Um...yeah, kind of."

Nate chuckled. "Dionysus enrolls in college every couple of decades."

"Why?" Mary asked, curiosity coloring her voice.

"Because he's an *empath*," Hades said, rolling his eyes. "He needs debauchery, just like I need suffering. Universities are the best places to find it. They're full of drunken, sex-crazed buffoons. Now, can we get on with why we're here?"

"Okay..." I leaned forward and glared at Dionysus. "And stop hitting on my friends."

"Sure thing, Tessa." He wiggled his eyebrows, causing Mary to blush furiously.

Hades remained standing and aimed a disdainful look at Mary. "Why is there a recruit here?"

I pasted on a sweet grin. "Hades, this is my friend Mary. Mary, Hades. She's been showing me how to make ice weapons."

Mary blinked, shrinking back under his scrutinizing stare.

"Ease up on the creep factor, Hades," Dionysus grumbled.

Hades made a sound of disgust, then looked down at me and arched a brow. "Well?"

"She's here because I want her to be. You guys are here because... well, Mary gave me an idea. About how I could find out what's going on with Atlas."

Dionysus laughed and ruffled her hair. "I knew it! You *are* a bad influence. We should absolutely be friends."

"Shut *up*, Dionysus," Hermes snapped.

Dionysus mimed zipping his lips, then gestured for me to continue.

"I want to astral project into Atlas' cave. It won't require me to waste time training to fight before going in, and it might be able to give us an idea of his state of mind."

"I don't know..." Nate said. "You didn't spend much time on that as an Ischyra."

"Or when you were a Titaness," Hades added, taking a seat next to Hermes. He narrowed his eyes. "Why are you suddenly so certain you can do this?"

"I'm not, but I also didn't think I could do a dream walk, and I managed that fine."

"With help," he amended.

"With help," I agreed. "Which is why you're all here."

"You want me to help you cross onto the astral plane?" Hermes asked, resting his elbows on his knees and propping his chin in his hands.

"Yes. Listen, I know you all have your concerns about what I can and can't do—"

"They do," Hades muttered. "I don't."

I sent him a silencing look before continuing. "But I have to try something. I can't just wait around while I train for whatever it is you guys think I need to train for. My twin is out there, hurting. I can't just sit here."

"That's understandable," Nate said. "I'm just concerned—"

"There's nothing to be concerned about, Nathaniel," Hades said, meeting my gaze.

I closed my eyes, silently thanking him for not arguing.

He gave me a small nod, then faced Nate. "Go in with her, if you're so concerned."

I turned to Nate and laced my fingers through his. "I'd like it if you did. I think I can do this on my own, but having some support and backup isn't the worst idea."

Nate smiled, then tucked a piece of hair behind my ear. "You have my support, love. That's not the problem."

My shoulders slumped. "You don't think I can do it."

"That's not it." He touched a finger to my chin and met my eyes. "I believe you can, I'm just worried it's too soon. Astral projecting is generally safer than going in blind, physically, but if you're not used to being on the astral plane..."

"It's not like doing a dream walk," Hermes explained. "If you can do one, you can generally do the other, but they're different."

"How so?"

"In a dream walk, you're using a direct line from your mind to his, but you're still fully conscious *here*. The astral plane is an entirely different dimension. You'll still be here physically, but you're entire being—what makes you who you are—will be separated from your body. When you did it as an Ischyra, you were only going a few feet, so it was a short trip, making it easier for others to help you return to your body if you needed assistance."

"What are you saying?" I asked.

"He's saying that we can 'wake' you from a dream walk, but we can't call your consciousness back to your body from the astral plane, especially from that far of a distance," Nate said. "Only you can do that, and without practice..."

"If you can connect her to the veil between here and the astral plane, isn't there some way you could anchor her?" Mary asked Hermes.

"Eh. That's not really the way it works," he replied. "That's something that someone who can perform a mind link would be able to do, or even a witch."

Mary gave him a confused look. "Tessa can do mind links, though, can't she?"

Hades tapped his finger on his chin and glanced back and forth between me and Hermes.

"What is it?" I asked. "I know that look, Hades. What are you thinking?"

"The recruit may be on to something. Hermes may not be able to anchor you, per se, but you could anchor yourself to him by linking your mind with his."

Nate considered for a moment, then nodded. "That could work, if you're comfortable with it."

"And Nathaniel would be able to force your mind out of Hermes and back into your own body, if need be," Hades added.

"I don't know," I said, shaking my head. "That would require me to do two very complex things at once. One or the other, I could probably handle...but both?"

"You're quite adept at mind links, from what I recall," Hades said drily.

"That was a long time ago."

He huffed out a breath. "Either you think you can do this, or you can't. Stop wasting time hemming and hawing and just do something already. And stop looking to your lover for permission. You don't need it."

I flipped him off, then turned to Nate. "You'll go in with me?"

"Yes."

"Okay." I nodded, the movement feeling somewhat jerky as I thought about what it meant to form a mental link with someone. I met Hermes' eyes. "Are you okay with this?"

He gave me a lopsided grin. "With you having complete control over my mind and body?" He shrugged. "It might be a bit uncomfortable, but I'm willing."

"Tess, are you sure?" Mary asked. "I didn't think it was going to end up being so complicated."

"I'll be alright," I said.

She smiled, still looking unconvinced. "As long as you're sure."

"I am." I sighed and looked at Hades. "Can you manage to stay calm? I need to be able to focus, and I won't be able to do that if you're pushing your emotions at me."

He nodded slowly. "Just remember what I taught you. Keep control over yourself and you won't have to worry about anyone else."

I swallowed hard, pushing back the lump that was forming in my throat. I held out my hands, linking my fingers with Hermes and Dionysus. Nate placed a hand on my lower back.

Heart pounding, I reached out for Hermes' mind. After a few seconds, I opened my eyes and looked up at him. "I'm not sure what I'm doing wrong."

He smiled and shook his head. "You're overthinking it. Just try to keep your thoughts clear and focus on me."

"What made it easier in your former life?" Nate asked.

"Necessity," I muttered, flicking a glance at Hades and trying not to think about the reasons I had back then.

Nate eyed me curiously but didn't push. "Then what's holding you back?"

"Proper motivation." Hades cocked his head to the side and smirked. "She's too calm. Hermes, Dionysus, let go of her hand."

My eyes widened and my grip tightened on theirs. "No. Don't you dare."

The words were barely out when Hades sent a shock of pain through me, hitting me right in the chest.

I sucked in a breath and jerked my hands from theirs, dropping them on the ground as I tried to force it back.

"Hades!" Nate barked, his grip on my waist tightening.

Hades held up a hand. "Just wait."

"It's...it's okay, Nate." I reached back and squeezed Nate's hand. My breaths were short, but after a few seconds, I'd forced back the pain Hades pushed on me.

"Done?" Hades asked.

I gritted my teeth and glared at him. "Yes."

He pursed his lips and nodded. "Again."

Closing my eyes, I laid my hands on the ground in front of me, curling my fingers in the grass. I braced myself for what he was about to do.

The first emotion he hit me with was panic. He pulled up memory after memory of how it felt to be taken from my room, teleported to the gods knew where, and tied to a tree.

How it felt to be powerless and at the mercy of a monster.

Fear came next—of what Cronus and my father would do to me when they caught me. Fear of the pain that would accompany the slow leeching of my powers, my life force. Fear of what they would do once they were done with me, not knowing whether they'd finished me off or force me to spend the rest of my days in torment.

Nate ran a soothing hand up my back.

Pain.

Knives were dragged across my body, tearing holes in my flesh. Godsbane burned through my blood, charring me bone-deep. A whip tipped in bronze lashing against my bare skin, burning and healing over and over.

I pushed it all back, struggling against the weight of it.

He saved the worst for last.

Despair. Hopelessness. Helplessness.

The realization that the pain might never end.

The knowledge that both my father and brother—my own family—didn't care if I lived or died, as long I served my purpose.

The despair of knowing my mother had killed herself out of guilt, leaving this world feeling as though she'd failed me because she'd loved me too much. She wanted me safe and I hadn't pushed hard enough to learn to protect myself. I'd gone complacent, allowed Clymene and my brothers to shove me in a box, keep me safe.

In the end, it had cost my mother her life.

All because I was weak. A being with near infinite strength, capable of mimicking the powers of the most powerful deities, yet so weak I might as well have been mortal. I'd been selfish and naive and *stupid* to think others would always be there to protect me.

I wasn't worth someone losing their life over.

"That's enough."

Blinking rapidly, I let Nate pull me back to the surface. Disoriented, I stared into his midnight eyes, soft and full of compassion. He cupped my face in his hands and brushed my tears away.

'You are *worth it, Tessa. Don't you ever question that.'*

Closing my eyes, I slid my hands over his and let out a slow, shaking breath.

My mother had died, but she'd done what she set out to do. She'd saved me, but more importantly, she'd saved the people who would've suffered if Cronus, a vicious tyrant with no sense of empathy, who didn't care who lived or died, was able to wield a power like mine.

Mine. This power—my power—belonged only to me.

Clinging to that, I looked up at Hades. The dark eyes that met mine were cold, unyielding, and unapologetic.

"Do you remember now?" he asked.

Without breaking his gaze, I nodded.

"Good. Now, let's try again."

Steeling myself, I latched onto the memories that were attached to those emotions; memories that reminded me just how important it was to do what needed to be done.

Taking Hermes' hand, I waved Dionysus off. "Hades is right. I don't need to be feeling calm right now."

Once again, I focused on Hermes. With a slight push, I was relieved to find myself in the bright openness of his mind.

'You're quite cheery,' I said, feeling a nudge as Nate settled himself in my head.

Hermes laughed. *'Alright. Hopefully this works. All you need to do is access the veil between here and the astral plane, then focus your thoughts on Atlas. Focus on his outward appearance, not the emotions that are connected to him. You don't want to project into his mind, just to his location.'*

'Okay. I'm going to take control now, if that's alright.'

'My mind is yours,' Hermes said, his tone slightly teasing.

'And I'll be there to see what you're doing,' Nate reminded me.

'Just make sure you stay away from his aura,' Hermes warned. *'Touching it is a surefire way to get sucked into his head, and this mind orgy can only go so far.'*

I snorted. *'Got it. Let's do this.'*

Slowly, I pushed Hermes to the back of his mind, making his consciousness smaller until he was just a quiet presence in the background. I turned my thoughts to my twin, gnawing at my lip as I considered how to move forward. Taking a deep breath, I aimed all my energy toward Atlas, specifically the space just in front of the hazy aura that would surround him on the astral plane.

"Please work," I murmured.

There was a slight *whooshing* sensation, and when I opened my eyes, I stood in a darkened chamber.

Turning slowly, I took in my surroundings. Sunlight from a hole in the stone ceiling filtered in, bathing the large cavern in dim light. A small opening, maybe three feet wide and five feet high, led out into the darkness beyond. I couldn't feel Nate or Hermes in my head, so I just prayed they were still there.

Whispering came from behind me, the sudden sound causing me to spin around.

My brother sat hunched on the floor against the wall, arms wrapped around his knees, looking just as ghastly as he had in the dream walk. His clothes were tattered rags, his hair limp and dirty, concealing half his face. He sat on a thin mat, and a crumpled blanket laid at his feet. Tears formed in my eyes at the sight of him.

"Get out get out get out get out." The words were a harsh whisper, so quiet I could barely make them out.

Hesitantly, I took a few steps forward, then crouched down in front of him, careful to avoid the hazy blue aura that undulated around him.

His eyes stared vacantly ahead, as his dry, chapped lips continued to repeat the same words.

"Get out get out get out get out."

I shifted so I was directly in front of him and able to get a better look into his eyes. The moment I was in what would've been his line of sight, he went quiet, causing me to freeze.

"I can feel you." His words were whispered as his eyes darted around the room. "Who's there?"

He froze, then his eyes went dark, slipping from dark green to almost black. They narrowed as he tilted his head to the side in an eerie, feline gesture.

"Hello, there." A smirk formed on his lips as his eyes bore into mine. His voice had lowered to a hiss. "It's been quite some time, Mimic."

I stood, then took a slow step back. In a single lithe movement, my brother leapt to his feet, all signs of weakness gone.

"Who are you?" I asked, scrambling back.

"I'm surprised you don't remember," the thing that spoke through him hissed. "You and that miscreant dispatched one of my sisters all those years ago." The corner of his mouth twitched up in a menacing smile. "Quite a feat for someone like you."

Dread settled in my stomach like a boulder. "I don't know what you're talking about."

"No?" Its expression became amused, full of mocking. "Did you kill so many creatures in your day that you can't remember one from the next? Were you that much of a murderer back then?"

"No, of course not. And how can you see me?"

"Does it matter?" It took a menacing step forward. "All you need to know is that I can, and so can he."

"Who? Atlas or Menoetius?"

When it didn't answer, I took a deep breath, trying to stay focused on its words and not the face it wore. "What are your plans for my twin? Why are you here?"

"My plans aren't the ones that matter, Mimic." Another step forward. "Only his."

"Menoetius?"

It made a disgusted sound, turning my twin's features an evil sort of ugly. "Menoetius is weak."

It took another step forward. I glanced behind me, not wanting to get my back against a wall.

Do I even have physical form here?

This had turned into completely uncharted territory.

"Cronus, then?"

The thing gave a satisfied smile. "The true ruler of Olympus." Its eyes flicked to the floor, then back to me. "Careful, now. It looks like someone else knows you're here. I'd hate to see you get stuck in here with me."

Glancing down, I saw that the aura that hovered around Atlas' body seemed to expand, slowly drifting toward me. I stumbled backward toward the exit. Using my panic as fuel, I shot myself back to my body, and opened my eyes, gasping.

The world spun. I was aware of hands on my face, sharp words being spoken above me, panicked voices calling my name, then a rough shaking sensation.

"Tessa! Get ahold of yourself!"

"Back *off*, Hades!"

"What did you do to my sister?" Prometheus' enraged voice sounded from a few feet away.

'I told you not to bring them!' I said to whoever was listening.

'They just got here. Calm yourself, now,' Hades ordered.

There was a thud, then warm hands slid against my cheeks. "Tessa, look at me."

I forced myself to meet Nate's gaze, my eyes blurry through my tears. Epimetheus' gentle face swam next to his.

"Are you with me?" Nate's voice wavered, but his eyes were steady on mine.

I nodded, swallowing back my shock. I felt Dionysus slide his hand into mine, sending a feeling of calmness through me.

Epimetheus gripped the back of my neck. "Push it back, Tessa. Take it back in."

I nodded, trying to suck back the feelings that were pouring through me and accept the help Dionysus was offering.

Nate leaned forward and kissed me. After a moment, he pulled back so he could look at me. "You're alright. Do you hear me?"

Clearing my throat, I curled my fingers into the sleeves of his shirt. "Yes. That was just...too much." I leaned forward and rested my head against his shoulder, replaying the last few moments in Atlas' cave over and over. Too close.

I'd come too close to being pulled into the darkness Atlas' mind had become.

"What did you see, Tess?" Mary asked. Someone had pulled her back behind Hermes, further away from me.

I sniffed, then wiped my face. "He knew I was there," I whispered. I looked over at Hermes. "That thing...it knew I was there. How?"

"I don't know." Hermes shook his head in confusion. "He shouldn't have been able to sense you like that."

Hades frowned. "How do you know he knew you were there?"

"Whatever is possessing him spoke to her," Hermes said, eyeing me warily. "What was it talking about, Tessa?"

"What did it say?" Hades demanded. He shoved Epimetheus out of the way and crouched in front of me, then gripped my shoulders, giving me a small shake. "What the fuck did it *say*, Tessa?"

Slowly, I met his eyes and spoke numbly. "It said it was surprised I didn't know what it was, that I and 'that miscreant' had killed one of its sisters years ago."

"Sisters? Was it talking about the Siren we met in Egypt?" Prometheus asked.

"No." Fear started to fill me as Hades leaned back on his heels and ran a hand over his chin. "No, Prometheus. It's something else."

17

TESSA

"Let's take this inside," Hades said, standing and brushing off the back of his pants. Without another word, he turned and strode up the steps.

Before I could turn to follow, Prometheus blocked my path. I felt Nate stiffen beside me.

"Astral projection?" he asked, looking furious. "Tessa, are you out of your mind?"

Anger started to push back the tumult of other emotions that had begun to swim through me. "You know, I'm getting really tired of being asked that question."

"Why didn't you come get us?" Epimetheus asked.

I inclined my head toward Prometheus. "That's why."

Hurt flashed across Epimetheus' face, and I immediately felt awful.

'I'm sorry,' I said. *'I know it's not you.'*

'I understand. Just...remember that I want to be there for you, alright? I don't care what Prometheus says.'

'Thank you.'

'I'll still be here, no matter what. Just do what you have to do.'

My throat ached as I heard the certainty in my older brother's tone. It killed me knowing I was about to hurt him worse than he'd been in millennia.

"Tessa?" Hades called from the door.

I slid my hands in my back pockets and slowly followed him into the house. We'd just reached the door when Nate tugged on my hand and pulled me aside.

The twins paused, but I shot them a "leave us alone" look, sending them on their way.

I turned to face Nate, then wrapped my arms around his waist and rested my head on his chest. I let him hold me like that for a few moments, thankful he wasn't pressing me for information.

He kissed my temple, then pulled back. "Do you need to talk before you go in?"

"No, this is something I'd rather tell just once, if that's okay."

He ran his thumb along my bottom lip and smiled reassuringly. "It's your story to tell, whatever it is."

I nodded, then laced my fingers through his and led him into the house. Everyone was seated except Prometheus and Hades, who was studiously ignoring my brother's glare. Prometheus' eyes shot to me when we walked in.

"What did he do?" he demanded, pointing at Hades and taking several steps toward me.

I closed my eyes and gripped the back of my neck. "He didn't do anything. Just...I need you to sit down."

"Not until—"

"Sit *down*, Prometheus," Epimetheus snapped, his eyes not leaving me.

Prometheus went still at his twin's rare show of anger, staring down at him as though he wanted to argue. He cast another glance in my direction, then sat down on the sofa next to Mary.

"So, after projecting into Atlas' cave, it's become very clear that something has taken over his mind," I said, taking a seat on the end of the sofa.

"How can you be sure?" Prometheus asked. "Just because he spoke to you—"

"Not he. She. I'm fairly certain that what's possessing him is an empousa." I took a deep breath. "I need to go in and remove it."

"Absolutely not." Prometheus' tone smacked of authority and finality. "That's out of the question."

"How could you possibly know that, Tessa?" Epimetheus asked. "And why do you think you need to be the one to remove it?"

Staring at the floor, I leaned into Nate when he ran a hand reassuringly up my back. I bit my lip as I tried to come up with the right words, choosing to go with simplicity instead of something that might cushion the blow.

"It's got to be me because...I've done it before."

Heavy silence enveloped the room at my admission, and Nate's hand stilled briefly before resuming its motion up and down my back. Hermes, Dionysus, and Mary looked understandably confused, but my brothers...the shock and hurt at what I'd just revealed was plain on their faces. They'd known I'd kept things from them in the past—Hades was case in point. Exorcising demons was probably something they considered far outside the realm of possibility for me.

After a few moments, Epimetheus broke the silence, his voice rough. "Who?"

"Mother," I replied, ignoring everyone's stares as tears burned the corners of my eyes. "Cronus had a witch separate the demon spirit from the empousa's body and forced it into our mother."

"Why would he do that?" Mary asked, her voice quiet.

I sniffed and wiped my eyes with the back of my hand. "My father was hesitant to kill Clymene at first, but Cronus said it was the only way to prove his loyalty. When he still resisted, Cronus infected her. He told Iapetus that her death would happen 'one way or another,' but if he had to do it, he'd be sure to make it as excruciating as possible. This was his way of proving that." I took a deep breath before continuing. "She came home one night after being gone for two days and went after me. That thing inside her...it used her body to do horrible things, trapping her in her own mind and forcing her to watch."

"How did we not know about this?" Prometheus demanded. "How could you not tell us?"

I raised my eyes to his. "You'd all been gone for weeks, Prometheus. Father was gone, and Mother and I were the only ones left behind. It happened two days before she—we—died."

He stared at me, his expression tense. "You were sparring with Atlas the day she died. The day *you* died. Are you telling me you didn't even tell him—your own twin?"

"No," I said quietly. "I planned to tell him. All of you. I just never got the chance."

"And now? You've been back for days!"

I stared at him, trying to work out an answer. "I don't know," was the best I could come up with.

"You don't—" He sucked in a breath and shook his head, then rested his elbows on his knees and pressed the heels of his hands to his forehead. "I cannot believe you would keep something like this from us."

I squeezed my eyes shut and let out a few unsteady breaths. Nate wrapped his arm around my shoulders and pulled me into him.

"I'm so sorry," he whispered against my hair.

"You question why I have so much faith in her abilities," Hades said quietly, looking at the twins. "This is why. You sit here and act as though you know what she can do when, in reality, you haven't the faintest idea."

"How would we have known?" Epimetheus asked, his pain lancing through me. "How could we have possibly known?"

"Maybe if you'd paid attention for just a single day, you'd have seen what was right in front of you," Hades said, anger coloring his tone.

Prometheus' head shot up. "Don't you dare try to lecture us on family matters."

"Well someone has to," Hades snapped. "I was the *only one* who gave a damn about her abilities three thousand years ago. I was the *only* one to convince her she was capable of mastering her powers, because her own family wouldn't take the time to truly see her. You made her so weak that, by the time she actually believed in herself, it was too late. She was amazing, a true force to be reckoned with, and none of you saw it."

"Easy, Hades," Nate said, glancing down at me.

Ignoring him, Hades continued his rant.

"Do either of you even remember what the last war was like? How many gods and demigods died fighting to save this mountain? Likely not, considering you weren't the ones helping their souls cross into the Underworld once it was done. No, that was left for me to do." He jabbed a finger in the twins' direction. "While you sat up here reveling in *our* success, I was the one who had to deal with crossing the dead. *I* was the one who exacted punishment on those who'd wronged us."

"That's enough," Nate said. "We get your point."

"Do you?" Hades sneered at him. "Do you, really? Aside from Tessa here, you are quite literally the most powerful deity on this mountain, yet you do nothing but sit around up here and mope." He jerked a chin toward Epimetheus. "You're just as bad as him."

I closed my eyes, trying to force back the fury that was pouring off of Hades and into me.

"Hades, you need to stop," I ground out.

"Oh, don't start showing weakness now, Tessa. Your lover went weak, and now all he does is waste his time with those vapid humans."

My head shot up, but Nate squeezed my hand to silence me.

'Go take a walk.'

Shaking, I yanked my hand from his, then stalked toward the door, sending one last scathing look toward Hades.

"Where are you going?" Prometheus demanded.

"Out," I shot back, letting the door slam shut behind me.

I jogged down the steps and sat down on the lawn, closing my eyes as I tried to force myself to calm down. After a few moments, I heard the front door open, followed by the quiet thump of feet coming down the porch steps.

"Go away," I muttered. Hades' emotions were slowly seeping

away, but their residual presence was still making me feel twitchy. My lower lip began to tremble as the grief I'd felt moments before began to creep back in.

"It's just me," a quiet voice said.

I turned and saw Epimetheus walking toward me.

"You didn't have to come after me." I turned back to face the forest, then leaned back on my hands and closed my eyes.

"Yes, I did," he said quietly, his voice pained. "The others are in there ripping into Hades, but I don't have the energy for that." He sat down next to me. We sat in silence for a few minutes before I finally felt calm enough to speak.

"He gets so damn angry," I grumbled, rubbing a fist over my chest where an ache had begun to form. "His temper tantrums are downright painful."

"Should I get Dionysus?"

"No, it'll pass." I watched as wispy clouds, slowly turning a bright orange, drifted overhead before voicing my next thought. "Hades is right, you know."

"I know," Epimetheus said with a sigh. "I know he is. You're far stronger than we give you credit for, and I see now how detrimental that's been. We've held you back. By the time he set you free..."

"I was complacent for a very long time, though. I barely had a century left before I finally pushed to be trained. Before that, I was content with my dresses and my jewelry and my books."

"And we were content to give them to you. Even still, there's not a single deity in all the realms who hasn't been taught to harness their own strength by the time they're a century old." He stared down at his hands, picking at his fingernails. "I can't stand the bastard half the time, but..."

"He was effective." I smiled ruefully. "I know."

"Still is, it seems." He turned his head and gave me a wary look. "You don't still have feelings for him, do you?"

"No, not at all. I don't know that my feelings for him back then were all that real, either. Hades was just the first person to...I don't know..."

"Believe in you?" Epimetheus' voice was sad. "It's alright. You can say it."

"You believed in me." I held out my hand, and he took it in his own. "I know you did."

He swallowed hard, then nodded. "I did. Regardless, I'm sorry I wasn't more on your side back then. I should've stood up for you, not helped you sneak behind our brothers' backs."

I scooted toward him, then rested my head on his shoulder. He pressed his cheek to my hair and sighed.

"You were on my side, Epimetheus. I never doubted that. Maybe if I'd pushed harder, pushed to show you what I could do, instead of keeping it a secret—"

I felt a heavy thump as someone sat down on my other side.

"We would've pushed just as hard to keep you sequestered," Prometheus said, taking my other hand. "I'm so sorry, Tessa. You shouldn't have had to go through that alone."

Tears threatened to overflow at the emotion I heard in his voice, something he always worked hard to keep hidden. "But I did. And I handled it."

"With the help of someone who wasn't family," he replied. "Regardless of what he did for you, Hades wasn't family. We should've been there for you. We should've been there for our mother. Leaving you both alone was idiotic on our part."

"We were in the middle of a war, Prometheus. You couldn't exactly play baby-sitter."

"I could've done more."

"*We* could've done more," Epimetheus amended.

"You're here now, though, and that's all that matters." I sniffled, then wiped tears from my cheeks. "I'm sorry you had to find out about Mother like that. That's not the way I wanted to tell you."

"You've only just gotten your memories back, Tessa. There's so much to sort through, and I should've been more sensitive to that," he said. He looked down at me, concern etched in his features. "Something else is eating you, though. What is it?"

I chewed on my lip, hesitant to voice my thoughts, knowing there was very little logic behind them.

"Once we had the empousa dealt with," I began, "Mother...she just wasn't the same. I don't know what that monster had done to her, but something wasn't right afterward. Now, knowing that she sacrificed herself to save me not two days later, well, part of me wonders if she wasn't in her right mind, or if she did it to alleviate the guilt she felt about the things it made her do."

"You think she let Iapetus kill her out of guilt?" Epimetheus tilted my chin up so that I was looking at him. "Stop that. She was your mother, Tessa. If it were your child, wouldn't you have done the same?"

I closed her eyes and nodded. "I'd like to think so. It's just hard to believe the two aren't related, you know?"

"Tessa, look at me." I turned to face Prometheus then, nearly flinching under his stern gaze. "Despite whatever guilt you may be feeling, you need to remember that our mother did what she did, not just to protect you, but to protect this mountain and all of Earth. She gave her life for Zeus' cause, just like the rest of us would have."

My eyes ran over his face as I processed his words. Finally, I took a deep breath and smiled. "Thank you. I think that might be exactly what I needed to hear."

He gave me a chastising smile. "I think you already knew that, little sister."

"Do you both understand why I have to be the one to deal with Atlas?"

Epimetheus sighed. "I don't like it, but I understand."

"We should still try to find someone else," Prometheus said, shaking his head. "There are other gods—"

I held up a hand to stop him. "If we waste time finding another deity capable of doing this, who knows what that thing will have done to him. The empousa knows that I'm aware of her, and she likely knows what my plan is. I need to get back in there as soon as possible."

"Alright," Prometheus said after a moment. "Fine. Tell us what we need to do."

18

TESSA

"You're out of your minds, every damn one of you!"

"You told me you wouldn't argue, Prometheus," I reminded him. We'd just told him of our plan for Hades and Nate to help me work on my mental combat skills, and it was quite apparent he disagreed with Hades' proposed methods.

He stared at me, dumbfounded. "You're telling me to stand aside while he tortures you! That's not helpful, that's lunacy!"

"You didn't see that thing," Nate said. "She can't—"

"And you!" Prometheus shook his head in disgust as he looked at Nate. "You'd allow this? Contribute to this insanity?"

"I'm not allowing anything," Nate shot back. "This is her choice, and it makes sense."

Prometheus jerked his chin toward Hades. "You're just as bad as he is."

"This is not your call," Hades said evenly.

Epimetheus rolled his eyes and dragged a hand through his hair, then turned toward me as they continued to argue. *'I'm going to take Mary back to the arena. She doesn't need to be here for this.'*

I looked over at Mary, who was standing beside Dionysus, taking in the whole scene with a mix of fascination and fear.

'Alright. Just hurry back.'

He walked over to Mary and whispered something to her. She looked at me, then up at him, and nodded. He put a hand on her back and teleported her away.

"Lay it out for me one more time," I said, holding up a hand to silence the other three. "How exactly will you make this work?"

"You'll do a mind link with Epimetheus, just like you did with Hermes," Nate began. "Once you're inside his head, I'll lock you in, which will force you to actually fight off Hades to get out. It will give you a good idea—or reminder, I guess—of how to fight inside another being's mind."

"And I'll give you your crash refresher in mental combat," Hades finished. "I'm confident it will all come back to you quickly."

Turning my eyes to Prometheus, I arched a brow. "And it's better to refresh my memory here than in Atlas' mind, right?"

"Circumstances are dire, I'll grant you that," Prometheus allowed. "But allowing him—them—to paralyze you, attack you like that? I can't get behind that Tessa, I'm sorry."

"Her soul was just trapped in the Void for three millennia," Hades said, his tone even. "Trapped there because you ignorant wretches made her *weak.* Clymene sacrificed herself because *you made her weak.* It's time you realize you were wrong back then, just as you are now, and let her do what needs to be done."

"How dare you bring my mother into this!" Prometheus growled. "She has nothing—"

"She knew Tessa couldn't adequately defend herself, she knew the lengths Cronus would go to to get her, and she knew the protection of three oafish brothers wasn't sufficient! So, yes, she has everything to do with this."

"That's enough, Hades," I said, cutting him off. "This is not why we're here!"

Hades sent me a scathing look. "No. It's not. And yet, here we are, convincing your brother, once again, that he was a fool." He cocked a brow at Prometheus. "Tell me, if she died for real this time, would you finally admit your faults?"

"You vile son of a bitch!" Prometheus advanced on Hades, his eyes burning with fury. Hades danced back a few steps, his eyes glinting with mirth.

Nate and I jumped between them, then I shoved Prometheus back. Considering his size, I only succeeded in pushing him back a few feet, but it was enough for Nate to get in front of Hades and push him away.

I turned disbelieving eyes on the two of them. "You two have got to be kidding me right now."

Hades jerked his chin toward Prometheus and shrugged. "This is his doing, not mine."

"Really?" I asked, incredulous. "That's your excuse? 'He started it'?"

Dionysus let out a quiet snort of laughter.

Ignoring him, I pinched the bridge of my nose and turned to my big brother. "Listen, if you can't handle this or don't have a better solution, then leave. This is stressful enough as it is."

Prometheus stood in front of me, his jaw clenching and unclenching as he formed his response. His eyes flicked from me to the gods who stood behind me, then back again. Finally, he jabbed a finger toward Hades and glared at me. "If he hurts you, I will throw him off this goddamn mountain."

"So noted," Hades said dryly.

Just then, Epimetheus reappeared.

"Ah, just in time." Hades gave Epimetheus a "come here" gesture, then looked at me. "You understand what we'll be doing?"

"Yes." I took a deep breath, then met Epimetheus' eyes. "You're okay to do a mind link with me?"

"Whatever you need," he said, smiling softly.

"Was Mary okay when you took her back?"

He shrugged. "As okay as she could be, I suppose. It was best to send her home, though."

"Yeah, I know." I rubbed my hand across my forehead, then nodded. "Okay, let's do this."

Hades gave a sharp nod, then folded his arms across his chest.

"Once you're in Epimetheus' head, Nathaniel and I will join you and attempt to simulate how it might be if you're attacked while in Atlas' mind."

"What exactly would you like me to do?" I asked.

"Kick me out, at the very least, but don't be afraid to hurt either of us. Once you've succeeded in removing me, I want you to try and break through Nathaniel's Coercion to get out."

"It's going to hurt, Tessa," Nate said quietly. "Are you sure you want to do this?"

"I am." I sat down on the grass, tugging Epimetheus down to sit in front of me.

"Alright, then." Hades gestured for me to continue. "In you go."

Taking Epimetheus' hands, I closed my eyes, then reached out for his consciousness. After a few seconds, I felt a sharp tug, and I was sucked inside.

The force of his emotions was so sudden, I nearly retreated. Sadness and guilt, harsh and unrelenting, plagued his mind. I expected thoughts and images of Pandora and what the release of her magic had done when she'd died to be attached to the feelings, but instead, they just hung there, taking up space in his head and serving no purpose other than to torment.

Tears immediately began to flow down my cheeks as I stared, paralyzed by the pain that radiated through his mind.

'Can you hear me?' I asked him.

'I can. Try not to worry about me, please. Just do what you need to do.'

I swallowed back my protests, wanting so badly to comfort him, do anything to take away his guilt and heartache. The need to help him was nearly unbearable.

Frustration seeped into my thoughts. If I had this much trouble suffering someone else's emotions, how in all the realms was I going to handle what Hades wanted to throw at me? How was I going to handle being trapped in here, caged up, while Nate barricaded me in?

Before I could dwell on my inadequacies any further, Hades went to work, compounding Epimetheus' guilt with anger, then fear, all pressing down on me. I felt my heart rate accelerate as panic seeped into my veins. No memories accompanied the feelings, thankfully.

On instinct, I tried to throw myself out, but immediately bounced off the steel barrier of Coercion Nate had wrapped my brother's mind in.

It was far stronger than I expected it to be.

Shaking out my arms, I forced back the emotions Hades' was pushing on me. They were relatively mild right now, and I had experience with his methods before, so they quickly became easy to ignore. Closing my eyes, I tried to picture the barrier Nate had constructed around Epimetheus' mind by imagining what it was like to see the veils between realms.

Finally, I saw it. His Coercion didn't shimmer like the pretty auras surrounding Atlas on the astral plane. Instead, it was a thick barrier of magic. When I pressed my own power into it, I felt a forceful shove back. The whole thing rippled but didn't come close to faltering.

"You're a goddamn Titaness, Tessa," I murmured. "You can beat a little Coercion."

'You can do this, Tessa,' Epimetheus said. *'Think back to how it felt when Nathaniel used his power on you before.'*

Blowing out a slow breath, I flashed back to my first day of training as an Ischyra, when Nate had picked through my mind to try and figure out why I was having so much trouble training. His power had poked and prodded with what felt like a thousand hands, searching for what it wanted. Going on that, I pictured my power as tendrils of magic, each reaching out to disassemble Nate's. Keeping my eyes closed, I ran my power over his, pricking at it until I finally made a small hole.

Seconds later, I was sucked back into my body. When I opened my eyes, I saw Epimetheus smiling back at me. Grinning, I met Nate's stare. "How'd I do?"

He smiled back. "You did great."

"For a first try," Hades amended. "You'll need to be quicker than that, though. I hardly attacked you; it can't take you that long."

"Fine, let's go again." I held out my hands to Epimetheus once more.

The second time in Epimetheus' mind, I was able to shove off Hades' emotions and push through Nate's barrier in half the time it took me previously. The third time, I was out within a few seconds, and the fourth, when Hades' really ramped up the negative emotions, I was able to push through almost immediately.

"Alright, let's go a bit harder," Hades said when I'd returned to the physical plane again.

"In what way?" Nate asked.

Hades arched a brow at me. "I'd like to incorporate a small amount of physical pain, in addition to the emotional."

'Are you sure about this?' Nate asked.

'I am. It'll be fine, don't worry. And don't overreact, please.'

'I'll do my best.'

I held my hands out toward Epimetheus. Closing my eyes, I dove into his mind once more.

Hades barely gave me a chance to get my bearings before attacking. Pain coursed through me as he drew on my worst memories, shoving them to the forefront of my mind. My breaths turned to heavy gasps as I began to feel burns form on my wrists and ankles, felt the pain of rope woven from godsbane as it seared my flesh. My stomach roiled as I realized Hades wasn't just making me remember those attacks; he was manipulating my emotions in a way that forced me to relive them.

"I can do this," I muttered, trying to push past the pain and send my tendrils of power at Hades, where he stood before me. I'd felt worse. I'd *experienced* worse.

'Stop second-guessing yourself. I'm right here. We're all right here,' Epimetheus whispered.

I took a deep breath and tried to find strength in my brother's words. I hadn't doubted myself nearly this much in my past life—I couldn't afford to start now.

'You did doubt yourself, though,' Hades said, his voice sardonic. *'Or*

have you forgotten? Your mother nearly died because you doubted yourself so much.'

He recalled the memories of my mother's possession, the horror and hatred I felt when I realized Hades was forcing me to face the demon alone, to feel its claws dig into my flesh as I fought against it.

Suddenly, pain shot through my throat, causing me to gag. A crude, wooden cup was forced to my lips, my mouth forced open as pure godsbane serum was poured down my throat. A stabbing pain through each shoulder, the crack of a whip as it sliced through the air.

It was too much. The more I failed, the more my panic increased.

'Where's the fury I remember so well?' Hades' voice taunted me. *'Reach down, find it, and use it.'*

Gritting my teeth, I reminded myself that this was all in the past. I let the memories come. Each time Menoetius had burned me, cut me, beat me. Each time his witch had taken my voice, my ability to fight back. I let myself remember what it was like to fight the empousa, the pain that creature had inflicted on my mother before coming after me. With each memory, my anger increased, fueled by Hades' enjoyment of my pain.

Then, with a solid shove, I kicked him out of Epimetheus' head, shattering Nate's barrier in the process.

I snapped back into my body, gasping against someone's chest as I clung to the heavy arm wrapped around me.

"Tessa, are you okay?" Epimetheus' quiet voice was just above me, and I realized he was the one who was holding me up.

"Just...give me a sec." I squeezed my eyes shut and tried to remember my breathing.

Silence hung all around as Epimetheus held me, his cheek pressed against my hair.

"You were amazing," he whispered.

Gripping his arm, I kissed the side of his head, then struggled to stand. Nate held out a hand and pulled me up, then cupped my face in his hands.

"I'm so sorry," he said, his midnight eyes wide with concern.

I leaned back and gripped his chin in one hand, leaving my other on his waist. “Do not *ever* apologize for helping me get better at being who I am.”

He pressed his forehead against mine and closed his eyes, seeming to need to get his bearings just as much as I needed mine.

Taking a deep breath, I turned to where Hades was standing, a satisfied smirk on his face. I wasn’t sure whether I wanted to punch him or thank him.

“Again?” I asked.

His brow lifted in surprise. “Do you think you can handle it?”

If I was being truthful, I didn’t think I could. I thought another trip through Epimetheus’ mind, being faced with his pain, guilt, and grief, before being forced to face my own, might send me down a dark road of emotion that I wasn’t prepared to deal with.

For my twin, though, I would do it.

Taking a deep breath, I met Hades’ eyes and nodded. “Yes. I can handle it.”

WE WORKED for several hours before Hades finally determined the day’s lesson to be at an end. Exhausted, I trudged up the steps into the house and flopped down on the sofa, closing my eyes against the pain of the mental beating I’d just taken. Nate sat down beside me, then pulled my legs into his lap and ran a comforting hand up and down my calf.

I opened my eyes as the others came in, trying to decipher the expressions on the twins’ faces. Epimetheus looked nearly as tired as I felt, but I also sensed a certain amount of relief coming from him. Something told me he hadn’t had the opportunity to share his state of mind with anyone, not even his twin. The thought of him suffering in silence all these years made my heart ache.

The tense set of Prometheus’ jaw told me he was still not completely on board with our plan, although based on the appraising look he gave me, it seemed like he might be coming around.

Hands on his hips, Hades faced Prometheus. "Well? Any further arguments?"

My brother looked down at me, then back to Hades. "I still don't want her going in there alone."

"Tough." I said as I struggled to sit up. "Before we finalize plans for the morning, someone should probably go fill Apollo in."

"Why?" Hermes asked.

"If we're doing this, we're probably going to need a healer on hand."

"I'll call him," Nate murmured. His eyes took on a distant look for a few seconds, then he looked at me and nodded. "He'll be here in the morning for the full story, but he's coming with us."

"Fantastic." I let my head fall back onto the sofa and closed my eyes. "Can I go to bed now?"

Apollo was understandably wary when he arrived at Nate's the next morning and we told him our plan.

"Tessa, are you absolutely certain you feel up to this? Going in to get him physically is one thing, but potentially trapping yourself in his mind borders on idiocy." He shook his head. "No, scratch that. It *is* idiocy."

"It doesn't matter if I feel up to it," I replied. "I'm not just going to leave him there. Now, I've gotten a solid night's sleep, so I'm leaving here in about thirty seconds, with or without backup. I'm not letting my brother rot in there any more than he already has." I tried to keep the accusation from my tone, but it wasn't lost on either of my brothers. Hades was there, though, and the negative emotions that hovered around him like a cloud were beating into me with extra force this morning, making it hard to concentrate.

"We haven't left him to rot," Prometheus argued. "We couldn't get near him!"

"He is your *brother!*" I snapped. "You should've known something was wrong the moment he attacked you both!"

"And done what, exactly?"

"I don't know, Prometheus. Something other than leaving him in a cave?"

Hurt flashed across Epimetheus' face at my words, but I couldn't take the time to feel guilty right then.

'Easy, love,' Nate said. *'Fighting with your brothers won't change things.'*

'Stop being so damn reasonable,' I snapped. Then I shot a glare at Hades. "And tone down the dickishness, please. I feel it coming off of you and it's not helping my mood."

"I'm not a television," Hades said. "Tune it out or ignore it. It's time to go."

I slipped my hand into Nate's, then looked at the twins. "Are you coming?"

"Of course we're coming," Prometheus said, shooting an angry look at Hades.

"Then let's go."

We teleported just outside the entrance to Atlas' cave, the same place where he'd attacked Epimetheus. Holes pock-marked the roof, allowing sunlight to stream through and making it more well-lit than the cave I'd seen when I projected in to see Atlas. Despite the sunlight filtering through from above, it still held the damp, miserable feel of an underground cavern. The entrance to Atlas' chamber was dark, appearing smaller on the outside than it had on the inside. The dimly lit area inside was quiet, the murmurings I'd heard earlier gone.

I stared at the dark entrance, debating whether to poke my head in and see if he was awake. If I could just talk to him first, let him know I was there, he might be able to help once I got inside...

'We'll deal with any physical threats,' Nate told me. *'Get in there and do what you have to do. Call out to me if you need help.'*

I gave him a tight nod. *'Thanks. Just try not to hurt him too badly if he attacks you.'*

'Don't do anything stupid,' Apollo added. *'There's only so much I can heal without help from someone who can, oh, mimic my powers.'*

I rolled my eyes. *'I'll do my best not to inconvenience you.'*

Nate took my face in his hands and gave me a long kiss. *'Be really fucking careful, Tessa. Please. We don't know what kind of power Menoetius has given that thing, and I don't want to find out the hard way.'*

'Believe me, I'd like to live to see another day, too.' I took his hands in mine and rested my forehead against his chest. *'Thank you for doing this with me.'*

'Tessa, look at me.' He waited until I'd brought my eyes to his before continuing. *'I love you. I'll be furious if I don't get the chance to show you that.'*

I bit my lip but was unable to hold back the smile his words caused. *'Tell me that again when I'm not about to risk my sanity by exorcising a demon.'* I stood on my tip toes and kissed him again. *'And I love you, too.'*

'Good to know.' He gave me a teasing smirk. *'Now, go save your brother.'*

'Be careful, Tessa,' Prometheus said. *'If it gets to be too much—'*

'It won't,' Epimetheus said, giving me a reluctant smile. *'She can do this.'*

I let out a relieved sigh, then shifted my eyes to Hades. *'If he fights back physically, do whatever you need to do to incapacitate him until I come back to my body.'*

'Get going,' he said with a nod.

I closed my eyes and focused on my twin, then tapped into my Mind Linker abilities. A few seconds later, I was in.

I nearly recoiled at the slimy, dark feel of the presence inside of Atlas.

Hermes had been easy; he was so happy and full of light that there was nothing to fight against when I linked with him. In contrast, the disgusting feel of the monster inside Atlas was bearing down on me, and I felt like I was trying to wade through sludge. A thick blackness coated his thoughts, twisting them into evil and malice, obscuring all that was good about him. I pushed through, forcing myself to dive as deep into his mind as I could go.

I'd done this before; I knew what I had to do now.

Pushing harder against the blackness that was licking at me like flames, I edged toward the deepest parts of his consciousness, until finally, I found him.

"Atlas!"

He was there, bound hand and foot to a wall, his head hanging forward, limp. He looked weak, nothing like the strong mountain of a man who was my twin.

His body twitched at the sound of my voice.

"Who's there?" His voice was feeble, as though weak with disuse. "I can't—"

I pushed forward until I was right in front of him.

"It's Tessa." I reached out with my hand to touch his chin, then lightly slapped his cheek. "Look up, Atlas. You need to see me."

Slowly, he raised his head to look at me, but the movement looked as though it caused him pain.

"Don't believe it..." he whispered, letting his head loll forward again.

"Shit. Atlas, we don't have time for this. It's a really long story, but I'm not dead." I slapped him again, harder this time. "Look at me!"

His head shot up, and when he glared at me, I sagged with relief.

"How do I know you aren't just another trick?" His voice wobbled, and tears formed at the corners of his eyes.

"Because I'm not." I reached up and began untying his binds. "Where's the thing that's trapped you here?"

He stumbled forward as I released his arms, and I caught him just before he fell.

"I don't...know." He pushed me to the side and fell to his knees.

I leaned back on my heels. "Okay, well we need to get it out of your head, so you're going to have to bear with me here."

Just then, a low growl surrounded us, and a smooth, oily voice filled my ears.

"Ah, how I love family reunions."

I felt my lip curl in disgust as I scanned the darkness around me.

Before I could speak, a hard shove sent me flying backward. Just as I hit the ground, the thing latched onto my shoulders and pinned me to the floor. Gashes tore open on arms, ripping a scream from my throat as blood began to trickle across my skin. I struggled to push it off, but I couldn't feel anything more than a gritty black mist.

"You can't touch me in here, little girl," she hissed as she dug the claws of her feet into my calves.

"Fucking watch me," I bit out. I braced myself on my elbows and tried to slide backward, but a hand gripped my neck, forcing me back down with enough force to set my head ringing.

'You have to fight it, Tessa!'

Nate's words were lost as the empousa sank its fangs into my neck, her venom slowly working its way into my system, weakening me nearly as much as Menoetius' godsbane would.

"Tessa!" Atlas' strained voice came from nearby, but the blackness clouding my vision made it impossible to concentrate.

I was failing my brother. I couldn't fight back; this monster was too strong.

'Stop it.' Hades voice reverberated through my mind. *'Put that pathetic nonsense away, now!'*

A whimper escaped my lips, the only thing I had the strength for, as its claws sunk into my biceps, tearing through muscle and flesh, scraping against bone.

'Focus!" Nate snapped. *"This won't kill you, but if you fail, you'll leave your twin alone with that thing. Is that what you want?'*

Atlas. I had to help Atlas.

"And here I thought you would put up a fight," it hissed. "It appears you're just as weak as your brother."

I screamed as the thing dug its fangs into my neck again.

'Get up, Tessa,' Nate said. *'It's too late to start doubting yourself now.'*

I squeezed my eyes shut and took a deep breath, trying to fight through the pain. It was so intense I couldn't even muster the energy to let out another scream.

The demon's laugh turned maniacal, but instead of making me fearful, it stoked a fury deep within me.

"You're still the weak little girl who lived so long ago, aren't you?" Its voice was right next to my ear. "Useless, pathetic, a waste of epic power."

I tried to recoil, but I felt cemented in place.

"He's going to drain you," she whispered. "Over and over again, until all of your power is his and there's nothing left of you but an empty shell."

I took several deep breaths, once again trying to push through the pain. I'd dealt with worse than this. Far worse.

'Calm yourself, Tessa.'

'You've got this, love. Just push through.'

Steeling myself and praying I didn't screw things up in the process, I went still as the empousa continued to tear at my body.

Then I lashed out with the full force of Zeus' lightning, filling Atlas' mind with an explosion of vibrant blue light.

The next instant, I was being propelled backward, coming to a stop as I slammed against the cave floor. Blood continued to flow down my arms and legs as I frantically slapped at my skin, trying to remove the oily black substance that had been left behind when I ejected the thing from Atlas's body.

My strength left me as dots began to cloud my vision. Hands ran over my skin. Pain continued to lance through my body.

There was a blur as I was teleported somewhere, then a blue, cloudless sky above me that was slowly beginning to darken at the edges. I thought back to the day in the arena, when the power of Zeus' lightning had brought me back to my old life.

I'd thought I was dying then, too.

The voices around me slowly began to quiet, then everything around me faded away.

19

NATHANIEL

Apollo and I teleported Tessa back to my house, leaving the twins and Hades to deal with getting Atlas out of the cave. When we landed on my front lawn, I scooped her up in my arms just as her eyelids fluttered shut. The scene from the arena, the last time she'd used my father's lightning, replayed in my mind on a loop. The shockwave of power had been just as intense this time as it had been then, only instead of her screams echoing off the cave walls, there was silence as Hades and I watched her take on that thing alone. We'd watched as it tore at her with claws and teeth, taunted her, used its words to try to break her mentally just as it was trying to break her physically.

Kicking open the front door, I took Tessa straight to the bathroom.

"Take off her clothes," Apollo barked as soon as I'd laid her on the tile floor. "I need to see those wounds."

Biting back the bile that tried to force its way up, I pulled off Tessa's tattered jeans and sweater, trying to ignore the blood and grime that coated her.

A gritty black substance had been left behind on her skin when she and the demon had been blown from Atlas' mind. I rubbed it between my fingers, then lifted it to my nose. "She was right. It was an empousa."

"Of course she was," he replied, not sparing me a glance. "She told you all she'd done this before, didn't she?"

"I really don't need your condescension right now," I snapped. "Why aren't the wounds healing?"

Lifting a hand to his nose, he took a whiff of the mix of blood and grit and made a disgusted face, then wiped his hand on his pants, leaving streaks of red and black on the light fabric. He rubbed his hands together and held them over the worst of Tessa's wounds, emitting a pale, yellow light.

"They are. They're just taking longer than they should." He prodded at one of the deeper wounds, still seeping blood from her shoulder. "The venom wouldn't do this much damage to a Titaness, so I'm assuming using our father's lightning is what's causing her to remain unconscious. Idiot girl."

"She was trying to save her brother, Apollo. She did more than any of us could have."

"She did more than any sane person *should* have. Now let me work."

He continued to touch his hands and magic to her wounds, sealing off one, then another. After a few minutes, he stood and wiped his hands on his pants again. "The wounds are closed, but I'm not sure how long it will take the scars to fade completely."

Just then, the front door burst open, and Prometheus and Epimetheus came in, dragging Atlas between them, his head lolling to the side.

"Take him into the spare bedroom," I said, pointing down the hall. "Get him cleaned up. We'll figure out what to do with him once we've got them both settled."

Wordlessly, they dragged their unconscious brother down the hall toward the second bedroom.

"Right," Apollo said, wiping his brow as he looked down at his now-filthy clothing. "Have fun with that. I'll return shortly."

"I'm going to go clean this mess off of her and get her dressed." I met his eyes. "Thank you, Apollo."

Once he was gone, I soaked a washcloth with warm water and slowly began cleaning off the blood and venom that coated her skin. The wounds the empousa had inflicted were still red and puckered, taking far longer to heal that I would've liked.

Once she was clean, I dressed her in the softest clothes I could find—gray pajama pants and a tank top—and laid her down on my bed, pulling the covers up around her.

I'd just sat down in the armchair in the corner when a knock sounded at the door.

"Come in," I called quietly.

The door opened and the twins walked in, their faces drawn.

"How is she?" Epimetheus asked, staring down at her.

"Sleeping, for now. Apollo dealt with her wounds and I got her cleaned up." I propped my elbows on my knees and ran a hand over my face. "For now, we just wait. How's Atlas?"

"Asleep, as well," Prometheus said. "We cleaned him, dressed him, so now, I suppose we'll just have to wait."

"We could put them together," Epimetheus suggested. "They might heal better if they're near one another."

I considered his suggestion, then shook my head. "I don't think that's the best idea. We don't know what his state of mind will be once he wakes."

Prometheus exhaled and sat down at the foot of the bed. "Agreed."

Someone knocked, then Hermes voice came through the door. "You all need to come out to the living room."

I stood and looked down at the twins. "Come on. Let her get some rest."

"You go," Epimetheus said softly, not taking his eyes from his sister. "I'll stay with her."

Prometheus hesitated for a moment, then nodded. "Come get us if she wakes."

When we left the room, I looked at Hermes. "What's going on?"

"Persephone called Hades to the Underworld just after you got Tessa out of there," he said as we walked out to the living room. "They're back, and she's got news."

Hades and Persephone were waiting for us in the living room, and Dionysus stood over my liquor cabinet, pouring tumblers of wine for everyone.

"Wonderful, we're all here," Persephone said. "While you all were off on your rescue mission, I took another trip to Tartarus to follow up on Tessa's theory that river fire may have been tampered with. As it turns out, she was right."

Hades pulled a small jar from his pocket and held it up. Inside, a small, greenish flame danced slowly against the glass.

"River fire, straight from the Phlegethon. Someone or something has been draining its power."

"Hades, you idiot, I told you to leave that at home!" Persephone tried to snatch the jar from his hands, but he stepped just out of her reach.

"Goddamned lunatic, is more like it," Apollo muttered.

Dionysus paused, his wine glass halfway to his lips. "Why in the ever loving fuck would you bring that *here?*"

"As I said—" Hades tossed the jar toward me, and I caught it just before it hit the floor. "It's been weakened."

"Can we please not throw primordial fire around in my house?"

Ignoring me, he gestured toward the small, unimposing glass jar that I was holding by the lid. "Well?"

"It should be hotter," I said, turning it over in my hands, watching the flame flicker and beat against the glass. "This barely feels warm, at least to me."

"Hephaestus made the jar, so it can withstand a good deal of heat before melting," Persephone explained, folding her arms across her chest. "You're right, though. Even with his skill, if the river fire was at full strength, that jar, and this house, would be dust by now. It's nowhere near strong enough to maintain the magic needed to keep the wards in place much longer."

"Well, that is unfortunate, isn't it?" Apollo leaned back in his seat and ran a hand across his chin. "Are you able to stop it?"

"For now, we've got the guards doing additional patrols with added forces," Persephone replied. "Hecate is working on a spell that will strengthen the wards around the walls of Tartarus, but the magic in the river fire will need time to regenerate."

"That'll keep them in, then?" Prometheus asked. "Our father and Cronus?"

Hades nodded. "So long as Hecate gets those wards up before the river is weakened any further, those two won't be going anywhere."

"As much as she's loathe to admit it, due to the sheer size of the realm, she needs additional witches to help place them, and she's unsure who she can trust," Persephone added. "Scylla will be heading down to help, of course, but I'm going to pay a visit to the Pleiades who haven't been taken. They should be able to offer Hecate and Scylla enough backup."

I turned the small jar over in my hands, watching as the flame danced around. "Has anyone checked the wards that surround Olympus?"

"I was just about to suggest that," Apollo said, nodding. "Before the witches go down to the Underworld, I'd like them to confirm the strength of the wards here. We need to be sure those unwelcome on Olympus are kept out."

"Of course," Persephone said. "Anything else?"

I jerked my chin at Hades. "Have you fully questioned your guards? There's no way this could happen without inside assistance."

"I have, but I haven't had the chance to interrogate them properly." He eyed me speculatively. "You know, the assistance of a Coercer would come in quite handy. Probably speed the process up a notch or two. It takes so long for me to sort through all those memories."

"I'm sure Rudolfo would be more than willing. He hasn't had a good trial in ages."

He tsked and shook his head. "Your Coercion would be far more effective at drawing out the truth and you know it."

"I'm staying here," I said firmly. "You and Rudolfo are more than capable of interrogating a few giants. Unless you don't think your normal methods of interrogation are sufficient?" I barely held back a smirk when Hades bristled.

"They're more than sufficient. Coercion is just quicker."

"Nathaniel—"

I shot a finger at Apollo. "No. Drop it."

"There's nothing for you to do here right now, Nathaniel." Persephone gave me a sympathetic smile. "You're just going to drive yourself crazy sitting around and waiting."

"Is there any chance Atlas won't recover from this?" Dionysus asked.

"From Menoetius or the lightning?" I asked.

He blew out a breath. "Both, I guess."

"I don't have any doubts he'll recover from the first, especially now that he's got Tessa back. She'll strengthen him. As for the second..."

"Considering Father's lightning isn't meant to be fired off inside someone's *brain*," Apollo said, "and she's only just gotten her true powers back, it's very possible she could've melted her twin's mind into muck when she expelled that creature."

"Or she could've used it effectively and simply evicted the demon from his mind," I countered.

"Which is the more likely scenario," Hades added. "She has done this before, you know."

"Three thousand years ago, after a significant amount of training," Apollo replied, shaking his head. "So, she could've healed him or turned his brain to muck, like I said."

Dionysus pulled a throw pillow from behind his back and threw it at Apollo, narrowly missing his wine glass. "Pull the stick from your ass for five minutes and be positive for once, Apollo! Atlas is home! This is a good thing!"

"I'm being realistic, which is something you might benefit from now and then," Apollo snapped. "We've gotten our missing Titan back, but it's quite possible he's worse off now than he was an hour ago."

I closed my eyes and leaned my head against the back of the chair. Listening to the two of them argue was nearly as bad as hearing our parents.

Dionysus laughed. "You know what your problem is, Apollo?"

"You?"

"No. You need a good romp. You're too damn uptight. Someone needs to loosen your girth a bit."

I snorted, then lifted my head to see Apollo's reaction.

"I'm not a damned horse," Apollo gritted out, his face a surprising shade of pink.

"I'm sure even a horse would be a little more positive in our present situation." Dionysus smirked.

"Back to the matter at hand," Persephone said, raising her voice above my bickering siblings. "Nathaniel, I think you should consider coming with us. Your Coercion could help quicken the process with the guards."

'I'm awake...Can you come in here?'

"I'll be right back," I muttered, standing and leaving the room before anyone could question where I was going.

When I entered the bedroom, Tessa was still lying in bed. Her eyes were open, but she looked exhausted. Epimetheus stood just inside the door.

"I'll let you two talk," he said, patting me on the shoulder before leaving the room.

"Hey," she said, her voice rough. She cleared her throat and tried to sit up.

I sat down next to her, then helped ease her into a sitting position. "Atlas is in one of the guest rooms. He's asleep, but you should give yourself a few minutes to wake before going in to see him." I touched a finger to her shoulder. "Can I take a look at the wounds?"

She nodded absently, rubbing her fingers against her forehead.

I slid aside the strap to her tank top and examined the area where the creature had slashed at her skin. The vicious gashes had faded into thin, puckered lines.

Brushing a thumb across her collarbone, I smiled. "They're healing up well."

"That's good to hear." She sighed, then settled herself against me.

I kissed her forehead. "How are you feeling?"

"The wounds don't hurt much, but my head's all fuzzy," she murmured, wrapping her arms around my waist and resting her head against my chest.

"I would imagine," I said dryly. "Setting off lightning inside your twin's mind while doing a mind link and fighting off a demon will do that to you."

"Things must not be so bad if you're making jokes." She was quiet for a moment, then tapped her finger against my chest.

"What is it?" I asked.

"I panicked in there, Nate. That was my one chance to get that thing out, and I nearly failed."

"But you didn't fail. This wasn't exactly a well-planned mission, love. You had an hour's worth of practice before going in, if that. Considering that the last time you did any sort of combat was three millennia ago, I think you did splendidly."

"I guess."

I pulled myself away, then gently nudged her backward and tilted her chin toward my face. "Stop that. This is not the time to doubt yourself."

Her eyes ran over my face. "Did you see what happened?"

"I did. And I saw you fight back."

"With you and Hades yelling at me."

I shrugged. "It's what you needed."

"I know. Thank you." She chewed her lower lip for a moment before continuing. "I heard what you were all talking about just now."

"Tessa—"

She held up a hand. "No, just let me speak. Hades mentioned something in our dream walk about your responsibilities back when you were younger, outside of training Ischyra and acting as a liaison."

My heart gave an uncomfortable thud as I realized what she was about to ask. "What did he say?"

"That I needed to talk to you if I wanted to know what those responsibilities were."

I dragged a hand through my hair. "And you want to have this conversation now?"

"Yes." She pulled back and sat up so she could face me. "I'm honestly surprised at myself for not asking sooner, but I guess I never really thought about it. I just want you to be honest with me."

I cupped her face in my hands and looked in her eyes. "Always."

"Okay." She took a deep breath. "Rudolfo is the Coercer who handles inquisitions with Ischyra and demigods who are suspected of crimes against Olympus, right?"

"Yes, he is."

"And you trained him?"

I pulled back and ran a hand across my face. "Yes, I did."

"Meaning, before that was his job, it was yours?"

"It was."

"So, when Hades said you had other responsibilities…"

With a sigh, I rested my head against the headboard, unsure of the best way to explain what I used to do on this mountain.

"He was referring to my former duties as an interrogator for Olympus."

Silently, she waited for me to continue, giving me time to work out my explanation.

"He and Zeus—" I pinched the bridge of my nose and took a deep breath before continuing. "He and Zeus were very particular about the state they wanted a traitor's soul to be in once he or she reached the Underworld. It was my duty to adhere to their specifications, if you will. I forced the truth from them during an interrogation, ensuring their guilt, then the two of them took care of their punishment and death."

"Were the ones you questioned always guilty?"

"No, although most of the time, at least back then, Zeus didn't believe that."

She was quiet for several seconds, her eyes boring into mine. "How many?"

"How many what?"

"How many innocents did you torture trying to figure out if they were guilty?"

My eyes widened at her insinuation. "Gods, Tessa, it wasn't like that, I swear! Those who were innocent, well, their innocence was apparent almost immediately. I barely had to demand the truth before I could see it. There were times Zeus didn't believe me and took matters into his own hands, but there was nothing to be done for that. He was overly paranoid for well over a millennia after the war ended, so his interceding was a common occurrence."

"And the guilty ones?"

"The interrogation process for them was...more painful," I acknowledged. "They usually fought against me, even when they knew it made things harder. Then for the Ischyra, I would remove the powers of those who were outside the normal lifespan of a mortal, which would cause them to age and die within a few days. Those who weren't, along with deities and demigods, were executed by Zeus. Hades handled placement of the souls afterward."

"Why didn't Hades do it? Or you, even?"

"My father believes in carrying out sentences for traitors himself, not having someone else do his dirty work, so to speak."

She closed her eyes and exhaled slowly, and I reined in my instinct to read her mind and see where her thoughts were. "Alright. When were you finally able to stop?"

"The Ischyra were created about two centuries after I was born, and it was another six centuries or so before another Coercer came along that I felt could take on my prior responsibilities."

She was quiet for a moment, absently tapping her fingers on my chest before responding. "This is why Hades said you'd be good at training me for mental combat, isn't it?"

I nodded. "It is. I should've—"

"Don't." She took a deep breath and met my eyes. "I'm not going to judge you for doing your job, even if it did result in people dying. If they were traitors, then presumably they got what they deserved. I just wish you'd told me. When Hades insisted on mentoring me again, you should've told me. We agreed we were past this. No more holding things back because you're afraid of upsetting me." She rolled her eyes. "And yes, I realize that sounds a bit hypocritical right now."

"You not telling me about your mother is very different, Tessa. I don't begrudge you for keeping that to yourself." I took her hands in mine. "You've barely had time to deal with your own memories. Logically, I would not expect you to blurt out every bad thing that happened to you back then. As for my past...you're right. When you decided to let Hades resume training you, I should have told you. But to be quite honest, it's not something I particularly care to dwell on."

She placed her hand on my cheek. "You were doing your job back then, just like Rudolfo is doing his job now. I've known him most of my life as an Ischyra, and I've never once looked down on him for what he does. You made the choice to take control of your life and how you used your powers. It takes a lot of strength to turn your back on what you were raised to do."

I leaned forward and rested my forehead against hers. "Thank you," I whispered. "In my entire lifetime, you're the first one to see it that way."

"You just have to remember that these aren't the kinds of things that will scare me off. Maybe the Ischyra version of me, but not the Titaness. I have a different perspective on things now, and while I don't exactly like what you had to do, I also know what it's like to be young and fall in line. I let my parents control what I did for hundreds of years before finally breaking free of it, and that small period of time where I did what I wanted, did things for *me*, was amazing." She twined her fingers through mine and smiled up at me. "We both have pasts that consist of things that are less than rosy, to say the least. I'm willing to acknowledge that and move forward if you are."

"Tessa, you have to know that I would've had this conversation with you as soon as I could."

"I know. I also know I've never seen an ounce of cruelty in you, Nate."

"I'm not cruel. That's why I stopped."

"Then you may not like what I have to say next."

"What's that?"

Her gaze was steady on mine. "I think you should go with Hades and Persephone to question the guards."

"What? Why?"

Anger and annoyance flashed across her face. "Dammit, Nate, you know why! You're the best Coercer on this mountain and we need to know if there's a traitor helping someone weaken Tartarus. My father and Cronus *cannot* get free!"

I ran my eyes over her face, searching for any hint that she was uncomfortable asking me this, surprised when I found none. "It's very difficult for me to consider falling back into that role again."

"I'm pretty certain we're all going to take on roles we don't like before this is all over."

"Is this manner of thinking another one of Hades' lessons?"

"Some," she allowed, ignoring the bite to my words. "It's also logic."

A quiet knock sounded at the door, then Prometheus' voice filtered through. "Can I come in?"

"Yeah," Tessa called.

Relief flooded Prometheus' features when he saw her.

"Thank the gods." He crossed the room and pulled her to her feet, then wrapped her in a tight hug. She bit her lower lip, concealing a wince of discomfort when he pressed against her healing shoulders. "We were so worried."

When he set her down, Tessa loosed a heavy breath. "How is he?"

"I can't really say," Prometheus said, frowning. "He's still asleep."

Tessa gnawed on her bottom lip. "Gods, I'm such an idiot," she muttered, burying her face in her hands.

"Stop that, Tessa." I tugged at her wrists, gently pulling her hands away. "You did what you had to do, what had the best chance of success. It was risky, but it worked. That's all that matters."

"He's right," Prometheus said, coming to stand beside me. "Look at me."

Eyes watering, she did as he asked.

"Our brother is out of that hole, and as far as we can tell, that thing is gone from his head. He's unconscious, but he's here."

"Right." She took a deep breath and nodded. "Right. Okay. Take me to him."

"Of course," he replied.

She turned to me and took my hands. "We can talk more later if you want, but please consider what I said."

"I will." I brushed my thumb along her chin. "Try not to worry."

"Thank you." She gave me a shaky smile. "Can you send Hermes into the guest room? I want to try a dream walk. I think I can do it on my own, but I'm still feeling a little off."

"Consider it done." I gave her a quick kiss. "Good luck. Call if you need me."

20

TESSA

Despite the knocking in my brain that was left over from using Zeus' power, I rallied my strength and let Prometheus lead me to the guest room just down the hall. Everything hurt, but I needed to know Atlas was okay, that I hadn't done more harm than good.

Prometheus and Epimetheus had bathed Atlas and changed his clothes from the filthy rags he'd worn in the cave. Now he looked exactly as I remembered. His blond hair was soft, his golden skin unmarred, aside from the scar on his cheek given to him by Menoetius. A peaceful expression rested on his face.

I leaned down and pressed a kiss to his forehead, then sat down on the bed and took his hand, closing my eyes against the emotions that were flooding me.

After three thousand years, my family was slowly stitching itself back together. I'd missed out on so much when my soul had been shut away in Chaos, but right now, touching my twin's hand, seeing him in front of me, I had a sliver of hope that my brothers and I might be able to make up for some of our lost time.

"Are you sure about this?"

I glanced at Epimetheus. "Have either of you tried a dream walk with him yet?"

"I did," Prometheus replied. "I wasn't able to get through, though."

I nodded. "Then yes, I'm sure."

The door behind me opened and closed quietly, and I felt the bed dip. I looked up and saw Hermes sitting next to me, smiling.

"Nathaniel said you might need a hand?"

I smiled gratefully. "I'm exhausted and my brain hurts, but I need to get in there and make sure he's alright."

"I'm happy to help. Just tell me when."

"Thank you." I looked up at the twins. "Would you two mind giving me some privacy? I know you want to be here, but—"

"You'll work better without an audience." Epimetheus nodded. "We'll wait outside."

Prometheus looked like he wanted to protest, but Epimetheus pulled him through the door before he had the chance.

Once they were gone, I turned back to Hermes. "I really appreciate you coming in. I don't know what I'll do if I did more harm than good."

Taking my hand, he gave it a reassuring pat. "You're putting a lot of pressure on yourself right now, Tessa. If this doesn't work, we'll find another way to get him back to you." He touched a finger to my chin and smiled. "But that's not something we have to worry about, alright?"

Smiling, I nodded.

With a flick of his wrist, Hermes exposed the veil between the waking world and the dream realm. Without giving myself a chance to back down, I sent my consciousness toward the veil, setting my thoughts toward Atlas.

Moments later, I was in.

The first thing I noticed when I entered Atlas' dream was the clarity, which immediately gave me hope. I wasn't blasted by pain, anger, and grief like I had been just the day before. We were on the edge of the woods just outside our home, and unlike last time, the air was fresh, and a gentle breeze was blowing. A feeling of contentment flowed around me.

"Tessa?"

His rich voice was strained and full of disbelief.

Turning, I sucked in a breath when I saw my twin sitting on the ground, his arms resting on his bent knees.

I tried to say his name, but it barely came out as a whimper. Instead, I collapsed next to him and threw my arms around his neck. Tears dripped down my cheeks as I buried my face in his soft hair.

His body stiffened, then he placed both hands on my shoulders and gently pushed me back. His eyes—bright, beautiful green eyes—were wary as he took me in. "How is this possible? I watched you die."

"It's...gods, it's insane." I laughed as I wiped away my tears, letting my eyes run over his face once more. My twin was *here*, right in front of me. It was an effort to force a beaming smile from my face. "I'm still struggling to wrap my mind around it all."

"Start at the beginning, then."

I launched into the story of how our mother had gone to Hecate and begged her to send my soul to Chaos to keep me safe from Cronus. I explained how my powers as a Mimic had emerged not long after my transformation, then how Zeus' lightning had shattered the spell that had erased all memory of me from the world.

By the time I was done, his eyes were filled with tears. Slowly, he reached out a hand and cupped my cheek, his eyes running over my face, wide with disbelief. Tears began to roll down his cheeks as he pulled me against his broad chest and rested his chin on my head. I wrapped my arms around his waist, then sobbed myself into a hiccupping mess as I felt another missing piece of myself fall into place.

After a few minutes, he let go and looked into my eyes. "I thought —I blamed myself."

"I know, the twins told me." I shifted so I was facing him directly. "You know none of this was your fault, don't you? Even if I'd actually died that day, it would not have been your fault, Atlas."

He pressed his fingers to the corners of his eyes, staunching what remained of his tears, then nodded. "I know. I've known for some time, now."

"Then why didn't you leave that awful place? They said you imprisoned yourself."

"I put myself there, yes. I think about fifteen hundred years had passed before I decided to leave. That's when I realized I was unable to."

My eyes widened. "You couldn't—wait, Menoetius has had you prisoner this whole time?"

The thought of my brother fighting to get free, feeling himself go insane for so long nearly broke me in two. I refused to start crying again, so I let him twine his fingers through mine, needing to remind myself that he was right here in front of me now.

"Once Menoetius discovered where I was, well, mostly I was just held prisoner. There were times he enjoyed tormenting me with visions of your death, of my part in it. After Hecate cast her spell and all memory of you was erased, he became so angry. No matter how much he tried to convince me of your existence, I didn't believe it. I slowly felt myself begin to return to normal, for the most part, once he lost the ability to use your death against me. I don't know how long ago that was, though."

"Almost nineteen years ago," I whispered. "I was reborn almost nineteen years ago, and when I was, she erased everyone's memories of me."

I felt my lower lip begin to tremble as I stared at him, imagining all the horrible things our brother had done.

"Ah, no need for that," he said, pulling me into a hug.

"I can't help it."

"As I said, once my memory of you was erased, he couldn't use your death against me anymore. He tricked me in other ways, though," he said, his voice turning dark. "That was when he brought the empousa in."

"You thought I was a trick," I said with a nod. "When I came to you in that dream walk, you didn't believe it was me."

"I did. All my memories of you had just returned, and I thought he'd concocted some new method of torture. I'm sorry if I hurt you."

"It's alright. I think I probably would have done the same thing." I wiped my eyes again, unable to get the tears to stop. "Gods, he tortured you, Atlas."

"And then my sister came to rescue me. Using Zeus' lightning, of all things." He smiled, then tapped a finger to my nose. "I must say, I never would have expected that."

"Yes, apparently I'm full of surprises lately," I said dryly.

He loosened his hold on me, leaving one arm around my shoulders.

"Indeed. Now tell me, where are we, in the waking world?"

"Olympus. Once we're sure you're not under the influence of the empousa anymore, we're going to have to tell Zeus what's happened. Prometheus and Epimetheus are staying in the guest wing at his palace."

"Zeus' palace." He smiled softly. "I've never seen it, you know. I'm assuming Cronus' was destroyed?"

"Yes, not long after Zeus took over. They razed it and built the new one on the same site. It's beautiful. A little extravagant for my taste, but still beautiful."

He nodded, then started picking at a blade of grass near his feet. After a moment, he looked up at me.

"Has he been a good leader?"

"I think so," I said carefully, realizing Atlas hadn't even begun to have a chance to forgive Zeus for the things he'd done so long ago. "He seems to have mellowed out over the centuries."

"How so?"

"From what I know of our history, he was pretty awful back when the war ended. Seeing him now, I think those actions may have just been the after-effects of fighting his own father and winning such a huge victory, you know?"

"Yes, I could see some of that, toward the end. I was concerned his anger toward Cronus would become detrimental to himself. I was convinced that had happened when Menoetius showed me the ways

Zeus punished Prometheus and Epimetheus." He went quiet for a moment, lost in thought. "How have the twins been fairing?"

"It's hard to say. When I first came to Olympia, Epimetheus never spoke, at least not publicly. I didn't know him at the time, but it was clear he was broken. He's slowly getting back to his old self, though. Every so often I see a bit of his carefree nature. Prometheus is just... Prometheus, I suppose. Always worrying, protector of us all."

"I suppose they've had sufficient time to work past Zeus' cruelty," he muttered.

"Maybe. Although, I think Prometheus acknowledges that holding that grudge will do nothing to help us going forward."

"Yet Zeus could not undo what he'd done to Epimetheus and the humans."

"No, but I think the aftereffects of Pandora may have shown him how far he'd fallen. He and the other Elders created the Ischyra not long after and have been working with the humans ever since. Zeus has been trying to free you for some time now, though."

"Because there's another war coming," he stated flatly.

"Yes, and it's being led by our brother and father. There aren't many Titans left, but it would be nice to have those who are still around on our side."

He sat quietly for a moment, flicking absently at a tiny, yellow flower near his feet.

"Who's left?" he asked quietly.

"Honestly, I'm not sure. I died before the war ended and have only just started finding out more about what's going on with the rebels. I know Hyperion and Theia tend the agricultural operations with Demeter, and Crius helps command the giants who guard Tartarus. There are others, I just don't know where. Nate mentioned a while back that they're scattered around, though. I don't how many are dead or just in hiding."

"This Nate. Is he your lover?"

I smiled and felt my face flush. "Yes, he's Zeus' youngest son." I frowned. "That we know of."

He smiled at that. "Is he good to you?"

"The best, and the twins like him, so he's already passed that test."

He put his arm around my shoulder and rested his cheek against my hair. "Well that is certainly good to hear."

I laced my fingers through his and grinned up at him. "Are you ready to wake up?"

"No, not yet. I just need a bit more rest, if that's alright. It's been a long time since it was quiet up here," he said, tapping his temple. "I think I'd like to enjoy a bit longer."

I smiled. "Of course. I slept for two days after I broke Hecate's spell, so I understand."

"I'll be alright, Tessa. I want you to know that. I already feel lighter than I have in a long time."

I gave him a shaky smile. "You don't know how happy I am to hear that. Wake when you're ready, we're not going anywhere."

He leaned forward and pressed his forehead to my shoulder.

"Thank the gods for that."

When I left Atlas' mind, I called the twins back in.

"How is he?" Prometheus asked.

"He's good," I replied, standing up. "Worn out, but good. He asked for a bit more time to rest."

"What did he say?"

"He tried to leave, but he's been held prisoner by Menoetius for about fifteen hundred years," I replied. "It seems Menoetius spent this whole time using my death to torture him, and once everyone's memories of me were erased, he switched to possession."

Epimetheus stepped around me and stared down at our brother.

"How did we not know?" He looked back at Prometheus. "How could we have gone to that cave and believed our brother had gone so mad?"

"I don't know." Prometheus dropped down on the bed near Atlas' feet, frowning as he watched Atlas sleep. "You think he'll be alright?"

"Yes. He said he hasn't felt this clear in a long time. It seems like he's just tired, is all." I patted Prometheus' shoulder and smiled. "Which I am, as well, so, let's go update the others. There's nothing we can do here right now, and I'd like to get a bit more rest before we do whatever we're doing next."

The four of us turned and left the room. Once we were out in the hall, I told the twins we'd catch up, then turned to Hermes. "Is Nate going to the Underworld?"

"He is," he replied. "He wanted to wait for you, though."

"Why?"

"I don't think he quite believes you're alright with him going."

I sighed and rubbed at my brow. "I may not be happy about it, but I also acknowledge there's a war brewing and we need to keep my father and Cronus inside the walls of Tartarus. If he's up for it, then he should go."

He gave me a questioning look. "Would you go, if Hades had asked?"

"If I thought I could do anything close to what Nate can do, then yes. Without question."

He put his hands on his hips and stared toward the living room. After a few seconds, he exhaled slowly. "I'm happy to hear that, Tessa. There are times when I worry that Nathaniel has drifted too far from his roots. I've said as much to him on more than one occasion, but it helps to know where your mind is."

"My mind is on whatever will keep those bastards locked away. If that means I have to go down there and Coerce those guards into talking myself, I will. Nate's skills are far stronger than mine, though, and we all know it."

"Indeed. He knows what needs to be done, but he hasn't had to perform an inquisition since Rufolfo came along."

"So why not get him to do it?"

"While he may not show it, Hades has a great deal of respect for Nathaniel and his abilities. He'd never trust an Ischyra with a task like this."

"I guess that's not surprising. Hades probably wouldn't trust an Ischyra to do his laundry. He's an elitist snob."

Hermes barked out a laugh. “Too true, Tessa, too true.” He slung an arm around my shoulder and started walking us down the hall. “Come, see them off. Unless you’d like to go with them?”

“Definitely not.” I grinned up at him. “I feel like I haven’t slept in days.”

We’d almost reached the living room when Nate stepped into view. He gave a slight head jerk to Hermes, who quickly made himself scarce. When he was gone, Nate turned to me.

“Are you sure you’re alright with me leaving?”

“Yes!” I gave him a reassuring smile and forced back a yawn. “We need to find out if those guards know anything. My brothers are here, and I’m just going back to sleep, anyway.”

He stepped closer, then put a finger on my chin, tilting my face toward his. He kissed me softly, with just a hint of heat. “Stay here,” he whispered. He brushed his lips against mine again. “Be careful. If anything happens—”

“I’ll send up the bat signal.”

He closed his eyes, then gripped my face in his hands and touched his forehead to mine. “I love you,” he murmured.

And despite everything, despite who I was or where we were or what had just gone down, those three words melted everything inside of me. Biting my lip, I tapped his temple. When he opened his eyes, I smiled up at him. “I love you, too. Be safe.”

With one last quick brush of his lips across my forehead, he turned and left, leaving behind the quiet murmurs of Dionysus, Hermes, and Apollo in the living room.

I contemplated joining them, but instead, I returned to the bedroom and collapsed on the bed, exhausted.

The moment the dream walk began, I knew Hecate’s spell had failed.

21

TESSA

Menoetius brought me to a rocky cliff side that stood a hundred feet above a blue-green sea, his face serene as he stared out over the water.

If I didn't know him, didn't know who he was or anything about him, it would've been easy to say he had a pleasant face—when it wasn't twisted with malice. He looked a bit like the twins, just with darker features, and with his hands resting on his hips, he even seemed to mimic Epimetheus' relaxed nature.

"It's about time," he drawled, not bothering to look at me, his tone shattering any misconceptions one might have based on his appearance. "That witch's spell was nearly as tiresome as her last one."

Reminding myself that I'd just blasted an empousa from Atlas' mind, I squashed down my panic and straightened my shoulders.

"What do you want, Menoetius?"

He turned toward me, his expression eerily calm. "Do you know what this place is, baby sister?"

I folded my arms across my chest and arched a brow. "A cliff?"

He chuckled and took a step forward. As he moved, the dagger in his hand caught my eye, sending chills through me.

"Yes, but do you know the significance of this spot?" He pointed downward with the knife.

"I don't. Care to enlighten me?"

"This is the spot where I captured an empousa, just before sending its spirit to live inside our mother." The corner of his mouth curved up in a leer. "You remember that, don't you?"

I swallowed hard, then nodded. "I do."

"I must say, you surprised me when you defeated her," he said. "Hades trained you well."

"And if you were anyone else, I might take that as a compliment. Why am I here?"

"You killed my demon and took my prisoner."

"You can get another demon, and I rescued my twin. Our brother, who you've been torturing for more than a thousand years. Did you really think I wouldn't go to him?"

"Once I knew you'd been to visit him on the astral plane, I actually hoped for it." He gestured in my direction with the knife. "You see, your strength is your weakness, Tessa. You've got the ability to use an element as powerful as Zeus' lightning to exorcise a demon from a Titan's mind, yet that same power also caused the pathetic spell you had blocking me out to fail, leaving that frail little mind of yours unprotected."

My heart sank as I realized what he was saying. I hadn't even considered what that lightning would do to Hecate's spell, even though it had very clearly obliterated her last one.

"I'm stronger than you think." I tried to force conviction into my words.

"Do you truly believe that?"

"Of course I believe it."

"Come, Tessa, you know you can't lie to me."

He took a few more steps toward me, and I scrambled backward in an attempt to get away. My foot caught on a rock, and I nearly tumbled over the edge of the cliff, when Menoetius grabbed me by the neck and pulled me back up. He held me off my feet, bringing his face just inches from mine.

"My sister, the all-powerful, can't even keep herself from tripping over her own feet." He clicked his tongue and shook his head, then tossed me to the ground.

Ignoring my stinging palms, I tried to latch onto my power. I felt it there, hovering in the back of my mind, trapped. Each time I poked at the cage that surrounded it, I felt a hard force shove back.

"Oh, go on! Let's see you try to access that power of yours." Menoetius crouched down so we were eye-level. "What will you use on me? Coercion? A mind link? Maybe just brute force, like last time?" Sneering, he smacked the side of my head. "Come on, let's see!"

Fight him, you idiot. Do something.

But I couldn't. I was weak here. Useless.

The thoughts had tears springing to my eyes.

"Fuck you," I spat, scrambling backward.

His eyes turned to narrow slits of fury. With a quick snap of his fingers, the scenery changed, and we stood in front of the stone house we'd lived in so long ago. Before I could even flinch, he gripped the back of my neck, and I felt his hot breath on my ear.

"I have a surprise for you," he whispered in a sing-song voice. With a hard shove, he sent me stumbling toward the front door.

Desperately, I beat at the barrier surrounding my magic, but every effort was wasted. Anger at my inadequacies crept into my thoughts as I imagined all the ways I wished I could kill my brother.

I cried out as he lifted me by my hair, twisting the strands around his fist as he dragged me into the house. I scratched desperately at his hands, dragging my nails across his skin in an attempt to break his grip.

He just laughed and tugged harder, drawing a pained whimper from my throat.

Once we were inside, he tossed me onto the floor, then waited until I'd righted myself before speaking.

"Tell me, Tessa. Aside from our brothers and that lover of yours, whose mind is quite the vault, I must say, who do you love most?"

"Something tells me you know all about who I care for," I

snapped, trying not to let it show how much it scared me that he'd tried to get into Nate's mind. "So get on with whatever it is you're going to do."

He smirked. "You've gotten smarter over the years, haven't you?"

I forced myself to meet his dark, furious eyes. "I'd like to think so."

"Alright, then. Let's see how useful that newfound intelligence is. Out of curiosity, have you ever done a shared dream walk?" He sneered when I didn't respond. "They're quite useful, really, especially if you want to maintain privacy."

"Great. What does that have to do with me?"

With another snap of his fingers, the bodies of Eric and Mary appeared on the floor beside him, bound and gagged.

"No!" I jumped to run to them but received a swift kick to the chest by Menoetius' booted foot, sending me sliding back several feet.

"Ah, ah, ah." He lifted Eric to his feet and pressed the dagger to his throat. "No heroics this time. I caught these two napping, you see. Gave them a hefty dose of nightshade to keep them asleep until I could bring them to you."

I lunged forward again but hit an invisible wall that sent me sprawling back to the floor. Like I'd done with my power, I tried to beat against the wind barrier he was using to hold me back, but it was useless. I slumped, unable to hold back a cry when Mary's wide, hazel eyes met mine. She gave a small desperate cry, sending an ache shooting straight through my heart.

"Do you remember our first dreamwalk, Tessa? What I told you?"

Clenching my teeth, I scowled up at him. "Why don't you refresh my memory?"

"I told you I was curious what would happen if someone died during a dream walk." His lips curved into an excited smirk.

When I realized what he was planning, I had to swallow back bile.

"These two creatures must be pretty high on the list of those you love, correct?" When I didn't answer, he grinned, then kicked Mary in the back, causing her to scream out against her gag. "Pick one."

"You're insane," I whispered, unable to pull my gaze from my friends.

"Pick one, or they both die."

Eric began to struggle against Menoetius' grip, mumbling something against his gag.

Ignoring his struggles, Menoetius pressed the knife to Eric's back, causing my friend to wince. "Come on. Time to choose."

"Please don't do this," I begged. "Please."

"You took from me, Tessa. It's time to repay the favor."

"I saved my brother!" I cried, my voice thick with tears, trying again to beat against the wall he had constructed in front of me. "He was never yours to take! *Please*, Menoetius, don't do this!"

He tilted his head to the side and gave me a curious look. "I find it funny that you think begging will help them. If anything, it's making this much more fun."

I gritted my teeth, trying to keep the emotion from coming through in my voice. "Let them go. Do what you want to me, just let them go."

He waved the hand holding the knife dismissively. "Tying you up and torturing you doesn't hold the same appeal it once did. You'll get your time, though, don't worry. Now." He brought the knife up to Eric's throat and gave me a level look. "Choose."

I looked at Eric, then down at Mary as hate toward my brother began to consume me.

Think, Tessa.

"The clock is ticking, Tessa. A few more seconds and I'll make the choice for you."

Tears streamed down my face as I tried desperately to figure out what to do. I was asleep, alone, with no one beside me to help wake me so I could send for help. My stupid, weak mind was making it impossible to do anything but sit here as the people I loved were used as pawns to torment me.

But deep down, logic told me that something wasn't right. It was the middle of the day; all of the recruits would be down at the arena.

Opening my eyes, I looked back to my friends, focusing on their appearance. Something was...off. I couldn't put my finger on it, but something deep in the back of my mind told me to question what was in front of me.

They'd be at training right now, and Olympus has wards to keep him out.

Tilting my chin defiantly, I prayed to any god who would listen that I was right, then hit my brother with a level glare. "You're a sick bastard, and I won't give you the satisfaction of forcing me to choose. Either let me wake up and leave them be, or get on with it."

He inclined his head to the side, brushing the blade of his knife against Eric's skin. I tried not to watch as Eric struggled against Menoetius' hold on him, unable to avoid the pain the poison-coated blade was causing.

"I see the hesitance in your eyes, baby sister. You speak as though you're heartless, but I know it's breaking you, not knowing whether I'm lying or telling the truth." He tightened his grip on Eric, pressing the blade of the knife harder against the thin flesh of his throat. "Not knowing whether this is truly your friend or if it's just me, doing what I do best."

Panic overtook Eric's features when I didn't move forward, did nothing to help him. Again, I forced myself to look at him more closely, examine his features. There was something about the color of his eyes...

Training. They're at training.

"Nothing you do to me or the people I love will scare me away from destroying you, if that's what you're after."

"Are you sure about that?" The corner of his mouth curled up in a cruel smile. "There are so many things I could do to you...to them. You really shouldn't test me."

"I'm not going to repeat myself."

He made a small sound that was a mix of amusement and surprise, then nodded. "Alright, then. As you wish."

I barely held back my scream as he drew the dagger across Eric's throat, spraying blood across the floor in front of me. Mary's anguished cry reverberated throughout the house as she watched Eric's blue eyes go blank, but I bit down hard on the inside of my cheek to hold in my reaction.

Don't back down don't back down don't back down.

Dropping Eric's limp body to the ground and kicking him to the side, Menoetius grinned at me, his eyes flashing with malice.

He gave me an appraising look, and I prayed he couldn't sense the bile that was roiling in my stomach. Whether it was truly Eric on the ground or not, seeing him there nearly made me vomit.

"Impressive, truly. You barely flinched, little sister. I would imagine this newfound backbone has to do with the return of your memories." He grabbed Mary by the hair next, drawing a pained hiss from her lips as he dragged her to her feet. She glared at me, her eyes full of fury, and her face streaked with tears.

Don't back down. It's not real.

He jerked Mary's thrashing body against his, then pressed his cheek to hers, his knife poised above her belly. "Can you feel the fury coming off this one, Tessa?" He ran his nose along her jaw, gripping her chin when she bucked against him. "She'll never say it, but she hates you, you know. Your new life, your new friends. She hates everything about you. I should probably just put her out of *your* misery, don't you think? Give you one last thing to fret about."

My jaw was set so tightly it felt as though it might snap. Even if that wasn't really Mary in front of me, I still wouldn't let him see that his words were striking a chord, fueling fears that had been stewing in my mind for days.

"I know it was Hades who gave your memories back to you." Menoetius' hand slid from Mary's chin into her hair. He jerked her head back, then drew the knife slowly up her torso until it hovered just over her heart. "Was he fucking you when he forced them from your mind, or was it just his version of foreplay?" He chuckled, a low, dark sound, then pulled Mary tighter against his body, dragging the blade along the collar of her shirt, perilously close to her skin. "I should've known you'd whore yourself out to him the moment you returned."

Looking down at Mary, he gently caressed her cheek with the back of his hand, the tip of his blade barely an inch from her eye. Revulsion filled her features as he slowly kissed the spot he'd just touched. His eyes flicked up to mine. "I could have a lot of fun with this one, you know."

He's distracting you. Focus on her.

Refusing to look at him, I painted a devastated look on my face as I stared at Mary, examining her features, the way the edges of her body seemed to fade into the air around her.

An illusion. It had to be.

Forcing my fear as far into the recesses of my mind as I could, I clung to my fury, at the anger that sparked within me as I realized how easily I'd let him trick me.

Mary began to struggle and scream against him as the point of his knife pricked at her collar. Her eyes were wide with fear, and her mouth worked furiously against the gag as she tried to force it away from her face.

Don't back down. Don't falter.

"This is getting tiresome," I said through clenched teeth.

Menoetius' eyes ran up and down my body, his mouth twisted with disgust. "Your pain must be like a drug to him. It's no wonder he keeps you around."

Ignoring the small hurt that accompanied the idea of Hades using me just to feed off my emotions, I shook my head. "Not everyone is a sadistic opportunist like you."

He let out a laugh, and for a heartbeat, I thought he might drop Mary. "You think Hades *isn't* a sadistic opportunist?" He shook his head, then pointed the knife in my direction. "You're fortunate he's got a fondness for you, Tessa."

I kept my feet rooted to the floor, refusing to give him the joy of watching me beat against his invisible barrier again. "Oh? And why is that?"

"Deep down, he's even more of a monster than I am." He frowned, examining me with what looked to be genuine curiosity. "You know that, though. And yet here you are, consorting with him once again. It makes me wonder if my own fondness for inflicting pain runs in your veins, as well."

Without warning, he pressed the broad side of his blade to Mary's cheek, and her movements slowed, her eyes rolling back in her head as the godsbane seared her skin.

"Let's test that theory, shall we?"

22

NATHANIEL

The entrance to the Underworld was a cold, stone antechamber that could only be reached by teleportation. Torches lit the wall on either side of the archway that led to the bank of the swirling Acheron, the river that surrounded the entire realm. The air was thick and cloying, making it nearly impossible for those of us used to the air topside to breathe comfortably.

I looked over the steep, rocky riverbank, taking in the turbulent waters in front of me. The Acheron was deep, the current was strong, and it was entirely impossible for anyone to navigate, aside from the ferryman who transported the dead to their final resting place. As if sensing my presence, a smooth, black tentacle belonging to one of the hydra broke the surface and moved languidly toward where I stood, sending a clear reminder that I didn't belong here.

"Where's Charon?" I asked, taking a step back and watching as the tentacle slowly slipped back beneath the roiling water.

"He'll be along shortly," Persephone said, adjusting the leather sheath attached to the waist of her dark pants. "He'll take us down to where the Acheron meets the Phlegethon, and we'll travel to the gates on foot from there."

I dragged a hand through my hair, annoyed that I'd agreed to come. This was the last place I wanted to be. Plus, I kept having a nagging feeling that I should return home, that I was forgetting something.

"Oh, come now, Nathaniel." Hades clapped me on the back. "I know it's been a while, but there's no need to be nervous."

I shook off his arm. "It's not that. Something doesn't feel right."

The darkness upriver shifted, and a moment later, Charon appeared at the dock, clad in a dark robe, holding a dual-ended oar in his hand. He stood silent at the prow of the small boat, awaiting orders from his rulers.

"You haven't been here in centuries," Persephone said, gesturing toward the boat. "The air isn't terribly kind to newcomers, but you'll get used to it."

Hades hopped into the boat, then held out a hand for his wife. After he'd helped her in, I jumped down and sat on the bench that ran along the rail.

"No, I don't think that's it." I frowned. "My head feels clear."

"Figure it out later," Hades said with a wave of his hand. "Onward, Charon."

With a silent nod, the ferryman began to take us downriver, moving smoothly along the swiftly flowing current.

"Really, though, Nathaniel, try not to get so worked up over this," Hades said, resting his foot on his knee. "From what I understand, you're planning to scan the minds of the recruits and mentors. This is no different."

"It's completely different," I replied. "It takes hardly any effort to read the minds of Ischyra. Your giants are the children of our creators. Picking through the minds of Gaia and Ouranos' offspring requires more force, which means more pain."

"Yes, yes, and you don't like to inflict pain on the innocent." He leaned forward and rested his arms on his thighs. "I understand your hesitance. I even respect it. But you weren't alive for the last war. You don't know what it's like to be in the midst of a rebellion. Innocents will be hurt, some at our hands, some at the hands of our enemies."

"I know—"

"Nathaniel." Persephone cut me off and took my hand, giving me a gentle smile. "Don't you think by now, you're able to perform an inquisition painlessly?"

"Of course, so long as they're cooperative," I replied, annoyed that I had to spell it out. "When someone is actually guilty of something, they tend not to be, which makes pain during an inquisition much more difficult to avoid."

Hades narrowed his eyes as we turned a bend and the blue-green flames of the Phlegethon came into view. "Self-doubt is your lover's wheelhouse," he murmured. "Don't fall prey to the same monster."

"Ignore him," Persephone said, rolling her eyes.

I leaned back in my seat and stared at the rock wall that was rapidly flying past.

As much as I hated to admit it, he wasn't wrong.

Hades stood as the boat slowed, and Charon rowed us to the ancient-looking dock that sat about twenty feet back from the head of the fiery river. "We'll return shortly, Charon. Wait here for us."

The ferryman nodded, then took a seat on the prow as the three of us climbed out of the boat onto the charred, rocky bank of the Phlegethon. Keeping well outside the scorch line, we made our way upriver to where the entrance to Tartarus loomed before us. Flames from the river quietly licked at the shores, but despite the abundance of fire, there was a noticeable absence of heat.

I cast a questioning look at Hades. "Has it gotten weaker since you first met with your guards?"

"A bit," Hades replied. "We're just now noticing the decrease in temperature, although the wards remain intact, for the time being."

When we arrived at the dark wood and iron gates, Cottus, the leader of the giants who guarded Tartarus, lumbered forward to meet us. Crius, a dark-haired, burly Titan who'd been charged with the security of the realm, stood beside him.

Ignoring me, Crius addressed his rulers. "Hades, Persephone. I did not expect you back so soon. Has there been news from Olympus?"

"Nothing of note. We just had a few questions for Cottus' men, and I thought Nathaniel here might be able to give me a bit of assistance." Hades' eyes drifted toward the giant. "Speed things along a bit, you know."

Cottus stared down at me from a height of nearly ten feet, his thick lips spreading into an angry line, then he turned his glare on Hades. "You already questioned my men," he growled. "Now you bring this Coercer here to torment them further?"

Persephone smiled sweetly. "Now, Cottus. If your men are innocent, they'll barely notice Nathaniel's intrusion at all. No one will be tormented unless they're deserving."

"Which means there's nothing to worry about," I said, sliding my hands in my pockets. "I can't imagine you'd be content not knowing whether there was a traitor in your midst."

He spit on the ground, then put his sword to my chin. "Do not come down here and act as though you know us, Olympian."

I arched a brow, trying to ignore the painful prick of his godsbane-infused blade. "If one of your soldiers is intentionally weakening the walls around the realm you're supposed to be protecting, that's a problem that needs to be resolved sooner rather than later." I slowly pushed his massive sword aside, then inclined my head toward Persephone. "As your queen said, if they're innocent, there shouldn't be an issue."

"If someone has betrayed me, I will find him and put him down myself. No need for your mind games."

"If someone has betrayed you, then they have betrayed me," Hades said coldly. "A swift beheading at your hand will be the least of his worries."

"Now, gentlemen, let's all take a step back," Crius said, stepping between us. He peered up at Cottus. "Your ruler has given you a command. If you choose to disrespect him and those who enter our realm as guests, I'll have you flogged as I would any disobedient soldier."

The giant's lip curled in disgust, but he sheathed his sword. "Do what you want. And I won't be calling them forward, if that's what you're after." He leered down at me, his wide, sunken eyes boring into mine. "As you said, the walls are weak. We cannot go unmanning them for you to go fishing in their heads."

"We'll call them forward in groups. None of us has time to trek around the whole damned realm," Hades snapped. He waved a hand, dismissing Cottus. Crius watched as he stormed off, then, shaking his head, turned back to us.

"I have to apologize for his behavior. Cottus is quite protective of his men and has taken personal offense at the accusation that any could have knowledge about how our wards are failing."

"He should learn to watch his tongue," Persephone mused as she began cleaning her fingernails with one of her bronze daggers. "Unless he'd like it to become forked."

Crius gave her a hesitant smile. "Yes, of course. I'll speak with him. Would you like me to summon the first round?"

"Please do," Hades said. "And Crius?"

"Yes?"

"Make sure to remind them who their true leader is before you send them forward."

Crius' eyes darted between the three of us, then he nodded. "Of course."

"You know, others hating me on sight because of what I am is one of the main reasons I left this job," I muttered once Crius had left.

Hades chuckled. "You act as though I don't know how that feels. The only reason anyone topside puts up with me is because of Persephone."

"Of course it is. She's the only thing that keeps you in line."

"She's quite vicious when she wants to be." He smiled down at her. "Isn't that right, my love?"

She preened up at him and tapped her blade against his chest. "Only when you deserve it, dear."

Despite my current circumstances, I couldn't help but feel a sense of relief as I was reminded just how deeply they cared for one another. It helped to ease some of the jealousy that kept rearing its head whenever I thought of him and Tessa together.

The first set of guards arrived, each wearing matching scowls as they assessed me.

"This won't take long," I told them. "If you have mental walls up, it will be easiest if you can take them down now."

"Is that not your duty?" the taller of the two sneered.

"Alright, then." I ignored his satisfied smirk. "It's your choice."

I reached out toward his mind, gingerly examining the walls he'd constructed to block out intruders. As expected, they were nearly impenetrable.

"You're not making this very easy on yourself," I commented as he winced in response to my attempts to break in.

He scowled at me, then dropped his walls, allowing me through.

'Tell me about the witch,' I demanded.

Gritting his teeth, he continued to glower at me as he fought to resist me.

"I haven't met with any witch," he spat. "Now let me go."

Quickly, I examined the memories attached to his denial, then, finding nothing of interest, moved on to the next round.

With Crius teleporting the guards forward, it took an hour to get through all one hundred and fifty of them. We were on the last round before any gave us trouble.

"You've already interrogated us!" one of the last guards yelled. "Just let us get back to work."

Hades clicked his tongue. "You're sounding awfully guilty, Jura. I'm just doing a follow up, being thorough, you understand. Not that I need your understanding, of course."

The burly giant bristled at his words. "I am not guilty of anything."

I poked at his mental walls, earning myself a vicious glare. "You're blocking me awfully forcefully for someone who has nothing to hide."

He stared down his nose at me. "Maybe you aren't as strong as you think, Coercer."

I bit back the instinct to plow my way through his walls, a skill that was just as painful as it was effective. "It'll be far less painful than what Hades will do to you if he assumes your reluctance equates to guilt," I replied.

"I am not guilty of anything," he repeated.

"Open him up, Nathaniel," Hades ordered impatiently.

A flicker of fear flashed across Jura's face as he looked between me and Hades.

"Is that what you'd like me to do, Jura?" I kept my voice calm, despite my irritation. "I can tear through those walls of yours if you'd like, shred them like paper, but the outcome will be the same. I'll still know what you're hiding, but you'll be in a lot more pain."

"Then do it," he sneered. "I can tell you don't want to. Your discomfort in exchange for mine will make it worth it."

Irritation finally won out. I hit him with my strongest blast of power, disintegrating his mental walls within seconds. Ignoring his cries of pain, I forced my command on him.

'Tell me what you know about magic weakening the river fire.'

With a snarl, he fought against me, but eventually gave the answer I was searching for.

"He met with a witch," I said, maintaining my hold on him as I dragged forward the memories attached to his response. His chest heaved as the ropes of Coercion kept him from running, kept his mind from closing. "Two weeks back. Short, male, dark hair. Ring a bell?"

"Let me see," Hades snapped.

I dropped my own walls, allowing him to see the thoughts coming from Jura.

"No, that's not possible." Shoving me aside, he kicked a heavy, booted foot into Jura's groin, causing the giant to fall to his knees, groaning. Hades grabbed him by the hair, twisting his head as far as it could go. "Who is he?" he roared.

"I don't know!" Jura cried. "He only came down the one time!"

"Who is it?" I asked. Persephone stood beside me, a perplexed expression on her face as she watched her husband read the thoughts I was pulling from Jura's memory.

"Xander," Hades bit out after a moment.

"The witch that helped Menoetius?" I asked. "How is that possible?"

"It's not, so I can only assume they're using a glamour." Tightening his grip on Jura's hair, Hades glared in my direction, his eyes black as pitch. "Thank you for your assistance, Nathaniel. This went much more quickly with you here. Now, go home to Tessa while I finish up with this one."

A small amount of pity washed through me as I thought about what was about to happen to Jura.

Persephone patted my shoulder. "Come on, I'll take you back to the dock. We don't need to be here for this. Hades will let us know when he finds something useful."

I nodded, then with one last glance at Jura, I turned and began walking back up the blackened shores of the river.

Halfway there, I stopped in my tracks as my earlier feelings of unease hit me again.

Persephone touched my arm and looked up at me with a frown. "What is it?"

"I'm not sure." Frowning, I went over everything that had happened today, not quite sure what was gnawing at me. "Something still doesn't feel—shit!"

I broke into a run, mentally kicking myself for not considering it sooner. When I reached the dock, I leapt over the edge into the boat, setting the whole thing rocking and startling Charon.

"Take me back to the docks!"

Persephone scrambled onto the dock after me, stopping just short of jumping in the boat. "Nathaniel, what's going on?"

"Hecate's spell...the one blocking Tessa's mind." I shoved my thoughts at Persephone, and she gasped in understanding.

Her face full of fear, she turned toward Charon. "Take him back to the entrance, now!"

Without hesitating, he pushed us away from the dock and stuck his oar in the water. I drummed my fingers impatiently on my thigh, urging the boat faster.

We reached the dock, and the boat had barely stopped before I scrambled out and teleported back to my house.

Prometheus, Epimetheus, and my brothers all leapt to their feet when I burst through the front door. Ignoring their shocked expressions, I tore through the living room and into my bedroom, where I found Tessa thrashing in bed.

Without hesitating, I dropped down next to her and broke into her mind, forcing her awake with as much power as I could without hurting her.

Her eyes flew open and she sucked in a lungful of air, then immediately started to fight against me.

"Tessa! Snap out of it!" I put my hands on her arms, holding her down as she tried to slap and kick me, her eyes wild with fear.

Footsteps sounded behind me, and then I heard Prometheus' angry voice, demanding to know what I was doing.

Ignoring him, I gave Tessa's struggling body a small shake. "Apollo!"

My brother was beside me in an instant, pressing his hands to Tessa's arms and forcing his power into her. Almost immediately, her panic began to ebb, and she was left lying on the bed, chest heaving. Epimetheus pushed Apollo and me out of the way, then dropped to his knees on the floor beside his sister and brushed a hand across her forehead.

"Tessa, look at me," he whispered.

She blinked a few times, then I saw her grip tighten in his as she turned her head toward him.

Smiling down at her, he cupped her cheek in his hand. "There you are, little sister. Come on back."

Confused, she took in her surroundings. "What—what happened?"

"You were dreaming," I told her.

Suddenly, she sat bolt upright, then threw off the covers and shoved her brother out of the way.

"Whoa, hold on." I held her by her arms and met her eyes. "What happened?"

"We need to get down to the arena," she said as her eyes filled with tears. "Menoetius—he had Mary and Eric. I need to see—I need to know if he—"

She let her walls slip, allowing me a brief glimpse of the dream walk.

"Shit." I jerked my head toward Hermes. "Go down to the arena, check on things."

"I want to go," Tessa argued as he disappeared.

"No."

"Nate—"

"Hermes will be able check on things discreetly," I explained. "If you go down there and there is someone feeding Menoetius information, he'll know immediately that he succeeded, that he got to you."

Her eyes searched mine, and a number of arguments flashed across her face. Finally, she slumped.

"Fine," she whispered.

I kissed the top of her head, then Apollo crouched down in front of her.

"Now tell us what happened."

23

TESSA

I'd just finished sharing the memory of Menoetius' dream walk with everyone when Hermes returned.

"They're fine," he announced. "Eric was setting things on fire with an Earth user, and Mary was doing archery with the centaurs."

"You actually talked to them?" I asked, refusing to just accept his words.

"Talked to them, touched them." He grinned, then rubbed at his bicep. "Mary's ice arrows are impressive. I had her shoot me to demonstrate how they worked. She's got quite the aim."

Letting out a shaky breath, I slumped back against the pillows and covered my face with my hands. I took a few seconds to collect myself, not yet trusting myself to speak. I knew Menoetius had been fooling me in that dream walk, and I'd stupidly let him in, let him taunt me into a panic. I'd just needed to know for myself; I'd needed proof that Eric and Mary, my two oldest friends, were alive and whole and hadn't been butchered by a monster.

Running a hand down my hair, Nate put his arm around me and pulled me close, then touched his lips to my hair.

I leaned against him, closing my eyes as I let relief finally wash through me. I hated—*hated*—that I'd believed Menoetius just enough to make me seek confirmation that they were safe. I'd let him in that far, and if I hadn't been able to latch onto that small fraction of logic that nagged at my mind when I saw him, it's quite possible that one dream—that one feigned act—would've broken me.

I considered kicking everyone out so I could close my eyes and attempt to sleep again. Now that Menoetius knew I was with someone who could wake me, it was unlikely he'd try another dream walk.

Yet, when I considered how monstrous my own dreams—nightmares, really—had been recently, sleep immediately became something I wanted to avoid, at least for the time being.

"I need something to drink," I announced. I dragged myself out of bed, waving off the hands that reached out to help, refusing to let them see how shaky I still felt. "I'm fine, really."

When we got out to the living room, I headed straight for Nate's liquor cabinet, needing something stronger than wine or water to settle my nerves. Before I could lay a finger on the handle, Dionysus shooed me off.

"I'll make you something. Go sit down."

Narrowing my eyes, I pointed a finger at him. "I'm only letting you help because I acknowledge your superiority when it comes to making drinks."

He inclined his head toward me. "Many thanks, my dear."

I joined the others on the sofa and snuggled up to Nate, as Dionysus clinked and banged around in the cabinet. No one spoke, each of us temporarily lost in our own thoughts as the events of the last couple of hours weighed down on us.

We'd gotten Atlas back. Even if he wasn't awake, he was home. Menoetius may have ruined a good part of the happiness I felt at having my twin home, but I refused to let it drag me down. Nothing he said, no illusion or bit of magic he threw at me, would take away from the sheer joy of having my family back.

Dionysus came over and set several tumblers of amber drinks down on the coffee table, then handed one to me.

"Here you go. That should help take the edge off."

I held up the glass, inspecting the contents warily. "Do I even want to know what's in this?"

"Ambrosia...wormwood. Some other things." He shrugged, then sat and took a sip from his own glass. "Just drink it."

Hesitantly, I took a sip. The pale green liquid burned, then immediately warmed me, the flavors changing smoothly from floral, to anise, to earthy.

Dionysus sat down on the sofa across from me, propping his legs on the glass table and crossing them at the ankle. "Well...despite the more, shall we say, difficult events of today, we've been pretty damn successful, wouldn't you say?"

Apollo let out a quiet snort.

My eyes widened "I'm sorry, but what?"

Dionysus waved off my angry protest. "Atlas is home, your friends are fine, and if you set aside your upset for a moment, then you might be able to glean something useful from that ordeal Menoetius just put you through."

"Useful?" I shook my head. "Do you have any idea what it was like for me in there?"

"Not a lick, but what I will point out are two very important details." He held up his thumb. "First, Menoetius knows who your friends are, which, to me, is simply further proof that he's got someone on this mountain feeding him information about you, most likely someone well-connected to the Ischyra recruits, if not one of them specifically."

"We already knew he has someone up here—"

"*Second.*" He stuck up his index finger. "And most important. Menoetius can't cast illusions, nor can he use wind to create a barrier. Which means..."

"Shit," Nate said. He ran a hand over his face and huffed out a breath. "Shit."

A heavy silence fell over the room as we all absorbed the meaning behind his words. There was only one way Menoetius would be able to cast his own illusion, and the thought of what he'd likely done to gain that ability sent chills through me.

"Is it possible he's just got a wind user and an Illusionist working with him?" Prometheus asked carefully.

"Possible, but unlikely," Apollo said.

"No, he's using the power himself," I said, shaking my head. "He was so damn smug...he wanted me to see what he could do."

Apollo stood and straightened his jacket, his expression grim. "I'll reach out to Ares and find out if any Mentalists or wind users have gone missing. I'll check back in later."

"You think he's finally managed the spell to steal someone's power, then?" Prometheus asked as Apollo vanished.

"It's the only thing that makes sense," I said. "We're assuming he's got the missing witches. If he's managed to take their ability to cast, all he needed once he got them was to find someone to steal power from to perform the spell on."

"Which is more information than we had yesterday," Dionysus said. "It's not necessarily good news, but..."

"We're better equipped to deal with him if we know what he's got at his disposal," Epimetheus finished.

There was a quiet knock at the door. Nate called for whoever it was to come in while I took another hesitant sip of whatever Dionysus had just given me. It wasn't bad, necessarily, but not exactly good, either. It sent warm tingles through me, though, which seemed to help settle my frayed nerves.

"Tessa."

I stiffened as Hecate stepped into the living room, then gave her a curious look as I took in her appearance. She wore tight black pants and a long white sweater, with tall leather boots, all of which looked to be smudged with dust, soot, and mud.

"Hecate," Dionysus said, smiling. "You look quite...dirty."

I pasted a smile on my face and set my glass down. "Ignore him. How are you?"

"I'm well," she replied. "I was working on the wards for Tartarus, and Persephone told me Nathaniel's concern that the cloaking spell I placed on your mind may have failed." She looked around the room, taking in everyone's somber faces. "Should I assume from your expressions that it did?"

A sense of dread washed through me when I realized she probably knew exactly why the spell failed. We hadn't told anyone of our trip to get Atlas, and the last thing we—or he—needed was for Zeus to come banging down the door, demanding explanations. The tense silence around me told me the others were likely sharing my concerns.

Forcing the worry from my face, I nodded. "It did. I'm guessing Persephone sent you to replace the spell?"

"She did, but only if you'd like me to."

I scratched my head, then nodded. "Yeah, I guess. I haven't had a chance to practice my shielding while I sleep yet."

"Of course." She gestured toward the sofa. "May I sit?"

I nodded, then she sat down next to me and took my hands in hers.

She gave me a questioning look. "Are you sure you're alright?"

I forced another smile, then nodded. "I am, thank you."

"Alright, well, this will just take a second, then you can get back to what you were doing." She raised her hand, pausing a few centimeters from my face. "Are you ready?"

"I am."

She placed her hand on my cheek, murmured a few unintelligible words, and a few seconds later, I felt that same *prick* as before.

"There you go." She smiled. "All set. I think you should practice working on those walls tonight, though. I'd like to remove it sooner rather than later."

I dragged a hand through my hair and nodded. "So would I."

Standing, she gave me one last smile. "Let me know if you need me again."

"I will. Thank you, Hecate."

She looked around the room and pursed her lips, pausing for a moment before speaking. "Persephone didn't tell me exactly why my spell failed, and I'm going to choose not to ask questions just yet. The only thing I ask, is that you proceed carefully with...whatever you're doing."

Prometheus gave her a tense nod. "We will. Thank you."

With one last glance in my direction, she disappeared.

"Well, that's done," I muttered. Standing, I stretched my arms over my head, then let them drop to my sides. "I want to go check on Atlas again...maybe try to get some more sleep."

The twins looked like they wanted to argue, but I didn't have it in me just then to explain the extent of my exhaustion.

"I'm fine," I told them, forcing reassurance into my words. Glancing down at Nate, I asked, "We're still planning on going to Athens to check on the Siren reports, right?"

"We are," he nodded. "Once you're up for it."

"I'm up for it. Just figure out when." I leaned down and kissed his forehead. "I'm going to go pass out. Feel free to wake me with coffee later," I added teasingly.

Giving a brief wave to the others, I made my way back toward the bedroom, then paused as I passed the door to the spare room where Atlas slept.

I glanced toward Nate's—our—bedroom, picturing the giant bed with its down comforter and overstuffed pillows, then looked back to Atlas' door.

With a sigh, I pushed it open, shutting it quietly behind me. I needed to be close to my twin, to feel his presence, know that he was truly here with me, with our brothers.

So, I sat down on the wide armchair in the corner and propped my feet up on the matching ottoman. Crossing my fingers Hecate's spell worked, I closed my eyes and drifted off.

24

NATHANIEL

The mood in my living room was somber as we watched Tessa leave. She'd seemed so fierce that morning, determined to rescue her twin, no matter what it took. Now she was emotionally beaten down. Menoetius had gotten into her head, hit her exactly where he knew he needed to, and I fucking hated him for it.

When I said as much to Prometheus, he let out a slow breath. "Yes, if Hades insists on resuming training with her, then shoring up her mental walls needs to be his first priority." He lifted his eyes to mine. "Yours, as well. You're likely to have a softer touch, which I think she'll need."

"Hades should probably stick to mental combat," Epimetheus said. "He was damn effective when it came to that in her earlier life."

Prometheus' only response was a noncommittal huff.

A part of me wanted to back Epimetheus up, point out to Prometheus what he knew but didn't want to admit, that Hades was an effective teacher and Tessa had learned more from him than from her brothers. As much as I loathed the idea of Hades being around her regularly, I agreed that she needed teachers she could trust to push her to and past her limits, something she was desperately going to need after this most recent encounter with Menoetius.

The other, more logical part of me knew it just wasn't worth the potential argument that would ensue.

Before I could say anything, though, I heard Apollo's voice in my head, summoning me to his home.

Letting out an annoyed sigh, I set down the glass I'd been holding and stood to leave. "If you'll all excuse me, I'm being summoned elsewhere."

"Apollo?" Hermes smirked. "God forbid he just teleport back here."

"You're not wrong," I muttered.

I arrived on Apollo's manicured front lawn seconds later, face stinging from the brisk wind that cut across the mountain at the higher elevations. The air was clear up here, with hardly a cloud in sight, but much colder. The view over the valley made up for the temperature change somewhat, but not enough to make me ever reconsider moving further up the mountain.

Shoving my hands in my pockets, I made my way up the shining marble steps and let myself inside.

"You could knock, you know." My oldest brother's deadpan voice came from the door to his study, which was just off the main hall.

"You knew I was coming. Why did you need to see me?"

He slid his hands in his pockets and inclined his head toward the study. "We need to discuss a few things."

I followed him into the study, taking in the scene around me that wildly contradicted the rest of the house. Books lined the shelves on either side of the fireplace, some shoved haphazardly on their sides, while others were lined up neatly. A dozen different globes were scattered on a long table to the right, and a large cabinet full of old documents and records, with its doors flung open, stood on the left. Scrolls were piled unceremoniously on top of a wood filing cabinet inside. Two of the drawers sat half open, with papers poking out of the top.

Dragging my eyes from the disarray, I looked expectantly at my brother, who'd taken a seat in one of the armchairs that flanked the fireplace. He gestured with his hand toward the chair across from him.

"What's so important that we couldn't discuss it in front of the others?" I asked once I sat.

"Not everything needs to be a group discussion," he said, picking up a glass of wine and taking a small sip. "We need to decide when to tell Zeus that we've retrieved Atlas, and I don't think that's a decision his three siblings need to be involved in."

"You think he doesn't already know?"

"Father sees only what's right in front of him, and he wouldn't expect us, or me, at the very least, to go so blatantly against his wishes."

"And yet you did." I gave him an inquisitive look. "Why?"

He shifted in his seat, then stared into his wine glass for a moment before responding. "I felt as though I owed that much to Tessa, considering the hand I had in her current circumstances."

I tried to hide my surprise at his admission. "It's unlike you to seek atonement. What happened?"

"Hades is a sadistic prick who likely enjoyed Tessa's trip down memory lane far more than any sane deity should." His jaw tightened in annoyance. "I should have known what he would do when he saw her, when he realized she hadn't gotten her memories back. Had I considered the repercussions of Hecate's spell a bit more, I could have better prepared her for what kind of memories would be returning to her."

"Agreed on all counts. Shouldn't you be telling her this?" I arched a brow, and he rolled his eyes in response.

"You asked a question, it's been answered," he said tiredly.

I closed my eyes and shook my head, not caring to get further into that discussion. "I'd just assumed we'd speak with Father tomorrow before we leave for Athens. Did you have something else in mind?"

He pursed his lips, then drummed his fingers on his glass. "We should wait until after Atlas wakes, then tell him. We need to make sure Atlas has his wits about him before exposing them to one another. Prometheus and Epimetheus may have mended fences with Zeus, but Atlas has yet to have the opportunity."

"We can't exactly wait until he's fully acclimated to life outside that cave," I pointed out. "That could take years."

He waved off my concern. "No, of course not. Waking up to the man who imprisoned him isn't the best course of action, either."

"Obviously." Staring into the fire, I sighed. "Tessa should speak with him again, try to get him to reconsider coming out of the dream realm."

Apollo cocked a brow. "I believe he was quite explicit, when Tessa spoke to him, that he wanted more time to rest."

"It can't hurt to ask, and we can't wait around for him to decide to wake up any more than we can wait for him to forgive our father."

His face turned speculative. "You don't think she's given him a full picture of what's going on?"

"I think she's trying to shield him from it, at least for now."

"Can you blame her?"

"Not at all. I'd want to do the same." Having a strong desire to change the subject, I asked, "Has there been any news from Ares?"

"That was actually the other reason I wanted to speak with you." He took another sip of his wine. "It turns out a few Ischyra have, in fact, gone missing."

My eyebrows shot up. "From where? And why didn't we hear about this sooner?"

"Two from South Africa and two from the US, just reported this morning. Ares has sent out requests for all lead Ischyra to contact their soldiers and report any who fail to respond. We should know within a day or so if there are any more unaccounted for."

I rubbed my hands over my face and leaned back in my chair. "Is it safe to assume an Illusionist and a wind user are in that bunch?"

He nodded. "Two of each, actually."

I exhaled a sharp breath. "So, he's got the power of witches to cast his spell and immortals to steal power from. If he's taken two of each, I'm guessing that means the power of one Ischyra isn't enough for him to wield efficiently."

"More than likely. They hold a paltry amount of power compared to a god or Titan, so he'd likely have to drain several to get the level of power he's after. Even then, that's likely only enough for temporary use."

I didn't even want to consider the ramifications if that were true. "Have we got any clue where he's holed up? He's got to be keeping them somewhere."

"None, so when we go to Athens, we should have Tessa try to get a read specifically on him. We need to get an idea of his whereabouts."

"We?"

A look of mild surprise crossed his face. "You think I'd stay behind for Tessa's first assignment?"

"Actually, yes."

"Considering how her last excursion went, don't you think it would be wise to have a healer on hand?"

"We can call for help if we need it."

He let out a frustrated groan. "You're being stubborn."

When I didn't respond, he leaned forward and rested his arms on his knees, then looked down at the floor. After a few seconds, he took a deep breath.

"Tell me what to do, Nathaniel."

I looked back at him, then waited for him to lift his head and look at me. "About what?"

"This." Finally lifting his gaze to mine, he waved a hand between us, and I saw annoyance flash across his face. "Your incessant dislike for me."

"There's nothing *to* do, Apollo." I gritted my teeth, hating the turn our conversation had taken.

A muscle in his jaw twitched as he took in my expression. "You know I've only ever wanted what was best for you. As your brother—"

"When have you ever acted like a brother to me?" Frowning, I eyed him curiously. "No, really, when in my entire life have you acted like a brother to me? Was it all those centuries you spent demeaning me when I was younger? Or was it that time you sent my lover off to fight a battle she had no chance of winning?"

He laughed incredulously. "Is that what this is about? I didn't play big brother well enough?"

I pointed a finger at him. "No. *That* is what this is about."

"What is 'that,' exactly?"

"You being an insufferable prick. You're condescending, sanctimonious, and arrogant. That's what's kept me away."

Irritation sparked in his eyes. "All of which could be said for any number of our relatives. What else?"

Jaw tense, I tapped my fingers on the arm of my chair, trying to decide if this was really a conversation I wanted to have. We'd managed to go years—centuries, even—barely speaking, the space between the duties we performed giving us ample ability to remain separate. Discussing this now, dragging my issues with him out in the open like this, was causing irritation that I didn't care to waste time on just now.

He lifted his brow in a sardonic expression. "Well?"

"Alright. You regularly make choices for others without consulting them first, treating anyone who disagrees with you like a child. You insert yourself in my business when you've got no place doing so, and you take every opportunity you can to try and make me feel like garbage about the choices I've made about my own life."

He slammed his hand down on the arm of the chair. "Because you turned your back on your family!"

I jabbed a finger at him. "That's exactly the problem! I didn't turn my back on my family. I turned my back on the rotten things Father and all the rest of you expected me to do! Did you ever stop for *one second* and think about what those expectations—those *duties*—did to me? Do you think I enjoyed picking apart minds, setting them up to be tortured? I don't care if I was born for it, Apollo. I *hated* it. Every damn second of it." I shook my head in disgust and slumped back in my chair. "You're a healer, Apollo. You've got no idea what it's like."

"You don't like the power you were given? Fine. Tell me, what kind of god is it you want to be then?" He folded his arms across his chest. “Do you want to be the kind of god who spends his days with Ischyra and humans, ignoring your heritage? Because that’s all I’ve seen of you for more than two thousand years. You were dealt a shitty hand, then something bad happened to you, and you took the easy way out of dealing with it.”

“The easy—what’s that supposed to mean?”

“You blame me for Karis’ death, yet you take none of the blame yourself. You didn’t like your power, so you dampened it, ignored it, instead of finding something worthwhile to do with it. Instead of dealing with the things in your life that you didn’t like, you hid from them, ignored them, as if doing so would make them go away!”

“You know, for someone who wants to mend fences, you’re making it very difficult.”

“I’m just being honest.”

“You can stop at any time,” I bit out.

I could feel his glare on me as I stared at the wall behind him, and it was a struggle not to meet it with one of my own. Finally, I stood.

“I’m going back to check on things at the house.” I pinched the bridge of my nose and sighed, then dropped my hand to my side. I recalled my discussion with Athena, the sadness and frustration in her eyes when she asked me to work things out with our brother. Forcing as much hardness from my tone as I could, I said, “I’ll see you in the morning.”

Before he could respond, I left.

25

NATHANIEL

By the time I returned home, Dionysus and Hermes had gone to deal with their own business, and Persephone and Athena had arrived, Athena having just returned from a meeting with Zeus.

She smiled at me when I walked in. "Ah, Nathaniel! I was just telling everyone—I think we may have found a lead on where Menoetius has been gathering forces."

"Well, that's good news," I said as I sat down next to her. "Did you send for Apollo?"

"No, because it's a loose lead, at best,' Athena replied. "I've got Ischyra stationed in Florida and Panama looking into it now, but it will likely be a few days before they have anything concrete. Hopefully, once we get back from Athens, they'll have gathered more intel."

"Speaking of Athens...I'm still not certain Tessa is up for heading out into the field," Prometheus said. "After today, it seems like it would be too much to ask of her just yet."

"Tessa is perfectly willing and able to head into the field," Athena countered. "She'll be fine. I'm certain of it."

"You were also certain dragging two recruits to Scylla's cave was fine," he replied dryly.

"While that may not have been the best idea, it gave her friends a dose of what they're in for, should they choose to remain in her life. They need to know who Tessa is now so they can make that choice." Athena turned a smile on me. "Now, how was your visit with our loving brother?"

"Wonderful as usual." I dropped down on the sofa beside her, then relayed the news of missing Ischyra and Apollo's concerns for what that meant regarding Menoetius' power.

"Well, that's just dandy," she said with a huff. "So now we've got that to deal with along with the matter of how Menoetius discovered a Mimic had been awakened."

"Zeus is quite certain there's a traitor floating around up here," Prometheus said.

"Zeus is also notoriously paranoid and distrustful," Persephone pointed out.

"No, it's a valid concern," I said. "One thing at a time, though. Let's focus on the next trip to Earth, first."

"Which will be when, exactly?"

We all jumped when we heard Tessa's voice from the doorway. Her face was drawn, making it clear she hadn't even begun to get the rest she needed. When she saw my look of concern, she smiled sheepishly. "I couldn't sleep, and you guys sound a lot more interesting than rest right now, anyway." She took a seat on the couch next to me, so I lifted my arm to let her snuggle into me.

"It's fine," I said. "Just make sure you get some sleep tonight."

"I will." She looked around the room. "So, what's the plan for going to Earth?"

Athena opened her mouth, her eyes darting to the twins, then back to Tessa. "I'm hoping to send teams out tomorrow to investigate a few other areas, but I'd like to get to Athens in the morning. Do you still want to join us?"

"I do." Tessa's eyes drifted to the twins. "I'm sure one of my brothers can stay here with Atlas. I don't want to leave him, but I need to get out and do something productive."

Prometheus looked as though he wanted to argue, then arched a brow when Tessa shot him a look. "Alright," he said reluctantly after a few moments. "I can stay."

"Where are you planning to go?" Persephone asked Athena. "After Athens, I mean?"

"I'll be off to deal with a few empousa nests." Athena rubbed a hand across her forehead in a rare show of exhaustion. "Want to come?"

"To fight empousa?" Persephone laughed. "Hades and I will be reaching out to the other Underworld deities over the next few days, otherwise I'd say yes."

Athena frowned, then looked at Persephone. "Here's a thought. Do you think Hades can handle speaking with the Underworld deities himself, at least tomorrow?"

Persephone shrugged. "He can, it's just a matter of whether he wants to. Why?"

"Well, we still need to deal with these crop failures. Father tends to brush them off as less important, but I think we can agree that's not the case."

"True. What are you thinking?"

"If you and Demeter can go deal with those, or at least some of them, perhaps you can do something to heal the land, avoid Ischyra having to get too involved. Do you think your mother will be up for it?"

Persephone shrugged. "I don't see why not. I'll have Hades manage on his own for a few hours so she and I can get those dealt with."

Tessa gave Persephone a curious look. "You can do that?"

"Of course we can." Persephone smirked, challenge sparking in her eyes. "You should come with us. If you think you can manage to work some Earth magic, that is."

Tessa's grimaced. "I don't know. My elemental work isn't all that great."

'Your elemental work is fine,' I told her. *'This will be good for you.'*

She chewed on her lip for a moment, her brow furrowed in thought, then nodded. "Alright. I can try. I can't promise anything, though."

"Sounds great," Persephone said with a grin as she stood. "Mother and I will come by tomorrow afternoon. I'm going to head back and make sure Hades hasn't decapitated anyone before getting any useful information."

Tessa's eyes widened as she looked up at me. "Did you find something?"

Persephone looked at me, surprised, then sat back down. "You didn't tell her?"

I shot her a silencing look, and I immediately felt Tessa's curiosity shift to annoyance.

"No." She pointed a finger at me, and I nearly flinched under her glare. "Don't even think about it. What happened?"

I took a sip of my drink, avoiding her eyes. "I scanned the minds of all the guards and found one who was consorting with a witch."

She arched a brow, waiting for me to continue.

I sighed, then set my drink down. "A witch who, according to Hades, bears a striking resemblance to the one who assisted Menoetius in your past life."

"But that's not possible." She sent a panicked look to her brothers.

I held out my hand into hers, hoping she'd accept the minor offer of comfort, and she wrapped her fingers through mine.

Her eyes were wide. "Scylla killed Xander, didn't she?"

"She did," Prometheus said, frowning at me. "When you say he bears a striking resemblance, what do you mean?"

I rubbed my free hand over my eyes, then rested my elbow on the arm of the sofa. "I've never seen Xander in the flesh, of course, but if Scylla was truly successful in destroying him, then it's either a descendant or a glamour."

"Hades is still dealing with the guard, Jura, so we should know more soon," Persephone added. "Don't worry, Tessa. We'll find out who it is."

I felt Tessa tremble slightly, and her refusal to believe this was happening flowed right into me. It stoked my own fear and anger, and not for the first time, I was struck with an urgent need to take her away, hide ourselves somewhere until this war was over and no one was after her. Until everyone who wanted to either use her or kill her was destroyed.

Dionysus propped his feet up on the coffee table and leaned back. "The Telchines have made their reappearance. My money is on one of them."

Pursing her lips, Persephone shook her head. "No, they can shape shift, but they can't cast."

"A descendant of Xander's would be more likely, right?" Tessa asked. "Someone who looks like him?"

"That would be my guess. Hecate said she never heard of Xander having children, but with the way deities were procreating back then, it would've been easy to miss one or two." She rolled her eyes.

Dionysus snorted. "They were a bunch of horny bastards, weren't they?"

"Still are," Hermes muttered.

"So, for now, we wait," Persephone said with a shrug. "Hades will get what information he can from Jura, speak with the other guards if necessary, and share the memory of Jura's meeting with the witch with Hecate and Scylla."

"And then what?" Epimetheus asked.

"Then, it'll be time to hunt a witch." She looked around at the rest of us expectantly.

Tessa huffed out a nervous laugh. "Oh, is that all?"

Persephone straightened her jacket. "As I said, we'll find him. This isn't something you need to worry about, at least not just yet." She gave Tessa a sympathetic smile. "This is what I do, Tessa. I find the bad guys. I've got some of the strongest trackers, both deity and Ischyra, working for me. We *will* find whoever this is and take them down. Do you hear me?"

Tessa took in Persephone's confident expression, then held her gaze for a few seconds before nodding. "Okay. If you say so."

"I do. Now, get some sleep. I want you bright-eyed tomorrow."

With a wink, Persephone vanished.

Sighing, Tessa looked at her brothers. "Do you two want to stay down here with us? There's plenty of space."

"I'll stay," Epimetheus said. "I can keep watch over Atlas while you sleep."

"Are you sure?"

He flashed her a quick smile. "You did the legwork, so I can manage this."

"And I'll come back in the morning to relieve you," Prometheus added. He tilted his head toward Tessa and me. "You can go to Athens with them."

Tessa glanced over at Athena, frowning. "How many are going on this field trip?"

Avoiding my eyes and those of the twins, Athena grinned at Tessa.

"Well, about that. This should be a fairly mundane mission. I was going to see if you wanted to give your friends another go at joining us."

Prometheus crossed his arms. "Athena—"

She shot him a glare. "Shush. This wouldn't be the first time we've brought recruits out into the field for a taste of what their duties will be."

"Nate and I actually already talked about that," Tessa told them. "We haven't gotten a chance to run it by any of them yet, though."

"I'll go check in with them," Athena offered. "Epimetheus can come, too, soften them up a bit."

Epimetheus' eyebrows rose. "Why in all the realms would you think I'd be able to soften them up?"

She gave him a sweet smile. "Just a hunch."

'What are you up to?' I asked her, immediately suspicious.

'Not a thing.'

"There's one last thing we need to discuss," Tessa said, looking at her brothers. "We need to decide when to tell Atlas about the missing witches. Three of his daughters are missing, and he deserves to know as soon as possible."

"Not to sound callous, Tessa," Athena began, "but considering his relationship—or lack thereof—with the Pleiades, do you think it's something that will matter all that much to him?" Athena looked to the twins, then back at Tessa. "I realize how that might sound, but—"

"You're not wrong," Epimetheus said reluctantly. "At least not about his relationship with them. He was an absent father at best, but he still deserves to know."

Prometheus nodded his agreement. "The sooner the better, although I think it might be best to determine that once he's woken up and we can better assess his frame of mind."

We talked for a while longer, making plans for the next day before everyone said their goodnights. Epimetheus retired to the spare room, intending to spend the night on the armchair, while Prometheus returned to the palace, and Athena went home.

Once they were gone, Tessa turned to me. I could feel her accusing stare even before I shifted my gaze to hers.

Grimacing, I shifted so I could take both her hands. "I know what you're going to say."

"Oh?" She pulled her hands back and folded her arms across her chest. "And what's that?"

"You're angry I tried to keep Persephone from telling you what I found out in the Underworld."

"Annoyed is more accurate." She let her hands fall to her lap and gave me a pleading look. "Nate, please stop trying to protect whatever delicate sensibilities you seem to think I have." Holding up a finger, she leaned back when I made to take her hands again. "And don't start thinking you can just give me those bedroom eyes and make me forget why I'm irritated. I'm still angry about Menoetius' dream walk, so this isn't helping."

I waited a few seconds, assessing her expression. When it appeared she had settled a bit, I held out my hands, palms up. With a huff, she let me lace my fingers through hers. I drew one hand to my mouth and kissed her knuckles. "Anger is better than fear, Tessa."

"It is," she acknowledged, covering my hand with hers and closing her eyes. Her face retreated into the drawn, tired look she'd had before, so I pulled her into my lap and wrapped both arms around her.

"He's such a fucking bastard," she whispered. "I let him get to me, Nate."

Shifting her back a few inches, I tilted her chin toward me, hating that he was continuing to beat at her, long after the dream walk had ended.

"Show me," I whispered when she looked at me. "Let me see the whole thing one more time."

"What?" She frowned. "Why?"

"I just need to see something, that's all."

She sent me the memory of the dream walk, and as I watched the events, I focused on her thoughts, her reactions.

Her eyes turned wary when she saw me smile. "Why are you smiling?"

"Because," I said, tapping her knee. "You didn't back down."

"But—"

"No buts. Caught off guard, that ruse would've taken in anyone. He baited you, and you called his bluff. Yes, he probably knows he hit you where it hurts, but you also didn't give him the satisfaction of seeing you break." I brushed my thumb across her jaw, waiting for the tension to ease from her brow before continuing. "Just do me a favor? Hold onto that. Every time you doubt yourself, hold onto that."

Swallowing hard, she nodded. "I can do that, I think."

"Thank you." I stood, then set her on her feet and cupped her face in my hands. "Tomorrow, after we're done on Earth, I think we should invite your friends up. You should spend some time with them, especially after today."

"I guess." She leaned forward and rested her forehead on my shoulder. "Gods, Nate. Even though I knew deep down they weren't real, it made me so sick. I think the worst part was feeling so trapped when I couldn't get to them, you know?"

"I know, love." The pain in her voice was like a punch to the gut. Everything in me screamed to fix it, to make it better, but nothing I said or did would make things right. The frustration that accompanied that fact hurt nearly as bad.

She pulled back and looked up at me, then smiled. It was shaky, but it was a smile, nonetheless. "I think you're right. Every time I close my eyes, I see what he did to them. Having them here in front of me...I think that will help."

"I'm happy to hear we're in agreement," I teased. "Am I allowed to kiss you now? Or are you still angry?"

Finally, a full smile bloomed on her lips. "I suppose," she said with an exaggerated sigh as she twined her arms around my neck.

Drawing her mouth to mine, I infused the kiss with everything I felt for her, my need to make her happy, content. Her body relaxed as the tension she'd been holding on to faded.

When she pulled back, she was breathless. "Has anyone ever told you you're a really good kisser?"

Smiling, I laid one last kiss to her forehead. "It may have been mentioned."

26

TESSA

Hades visited me in my dreams that night. I expected to be annoyed, to want to eject him with as much force as I could muster, yet after today, after the dream walk with Menoetius, I simply didn't have it in me to fight him.

"You need to fight me, though," he said when I told him as much.

We were sitting in those same high-backed chairs as the last time, only tonight, we were in what appeared to be his living room. A large, dark red and brown carpet dominated the floor, which was made of narrow, dark boards. Intricately carved wood furniture, upholstered in deep reds and browns, matched the wood molding around the doors, windows, and fireplace. It had his decorative touch all over it.

"That's the whole point of this arrangement, Tessa. I anger you, you kick me out of your head, then we repeat until you're not quite so dreadful at it."

Closing my eyes, I rested my head against the chair and sighed. Exhaustion was taking me, even in sleep. All I wanted was to be back in bed, burrowed under the heavy down comforter with Nate's arm around me.

"Open your eyes," Hades ordered.

I opened one. "Tell me what to do."

"Your brain is a muscle. Figure it out."

Dragging myself out of a slouching position, I rubbed my hands over my face, attempting to wipe away the sleepiness. "Can I use my power?"

"On the first try, but only because in doing so, you'll be better able to examine the mechanism that allows your mind to operate as it does. After that, you'll need to *will* me away."

"And once I'm able to remove you?"

"I'll keep coming back until I'm no longer able to get in. Once you've mastered locking up your walls in your sleep, to the point where I'm unable to chip away at them in the slightest, then we'll be done, at least with this portion of your education."

I cocked a brow. "This portion?"

"All of your abilities need to be tested and improved if you're to be the kind of warrior you're capable of being."

A warrior. The thought of that word being applied to me was thrilling, terrifying, and amazing, all at once. My brothers were warriors, and all my life, I'd wanted them to include me, teach me what they knew, help me be as strong as they were. But all they'd given me was basic training in physical combat. It seemed that might change now, but I knew for a fact Hades wouldn't let me down when it came to this. He was as pragmatic as he was loyal, so if he still thought I had a chance at becoming a true fighter, I trusted him to help me get there, even if my brothers hated it—and him.

"Is there a specific skill you feel I should start with, once we're done here?" I asked.

Tapping his fingers to his chin, he eyed me shrewdly for a moment before responding. "Coercion, certainly. You've already got a leg up on that, and Nathaniel has a great deal to offer you in that area." A slightly unsettling smirk twisted his lips. "You know, together, the two of you could be quite formidable, once you've gotten yourself handled."

I rolled my eyes, refusing to acknowledge how much I actually wanted that. "Okay. Anything else?"

"You could work on tracking with Persephone, if you'd like. She's quite skilled."

"Would she be okay with that?"

He angled his head to the side in a curious gesture. "Why wouldn't she be? She sees the benefit in a Titaness who knows her full strength, just as I do, and she's got a very specific skill set that you'd likely excel at."

I chewed on my lip as I thought about all the people who were getting involved with my training. It was wonderful, knowing so many wanted to help, but at the same time, I had a hard time not feeling like a burden. Taking a deep breath and forcing the thought from my head, I nodded. "Okay, ask her. If she's willing to work with me, I'd be honored."

"Consider it done. Now, let's begin."

"Hang on. I have a question before we start."

His eyebrows raised. "Oh? What might that be?"

"Did you find out any more about that witch your guard met with?"

He made an annoyed grimace. "Unfortunately, no. It appears he or she placed an interdiction on Jura, so we're working to reverse it now. If you know anything about interdictions, you know they're nearly impossible to reverse until their terms have been met."

"And what do you think the terms of his were?"

"Most likely to keep quiet until he either died or Cronus gained control of the mountain. So, our choices are to wait for one of those things to happen or reverse it ourselves."

"Will you let me know once you find something?"

"Of course." He gave me an expectant look. "Any more questions, or can we begin?"

I waved a hand for him to continue. "My mind is yours."

We practiced for hours. Half the time was spent trying to remove him from my mind. After a few verbal assaults, a lot of sweat, and maybe a few tears, I finally managed to kick him out. No matter how hard I tried, though, I'd been unable to keep him from reentering my mind, which was, to me, the most important.

When I opened my eyes the next morning, the sky was just beginning to shift from periwinkle to pink, visible through the skylight and giant picture windows beside the bed. Despite feeling mentally drained from my practice session with Hades, physically, I was surprisingly refreshed.

I smiled when I felt Nate's lips brush against my ear. He slid his hand across my stomach, pulling my body against his. "I had a dream about you," he whispered.

I giggled as he rolled on top of me and started kissing his way down my neck. "What, exactly, was this dream about?"

"You." He pushed the strap of my tank top out of the way and dragged his lips across my shoulder. "And me."

"That sounds interesting." I bit my lip as his hand slid up my thigh and pulled my leg around his waist. More than happy to start my day this way, I hooked my arms around his neck and tightened my legs around him. "What were we doing?"

He let out a quiet laugh, then slowly dragged his teeth along the sensitive skin of my neck, nipping my ear and sending tingles through my body. "Things that would keep us right here for the better part of the day."

"It's early. We've probably got at least an hour before one of your siblings comes barging in."

I knew he would say no, but I wanted—so badly—to shut the rest of the world out, forget the pain of the last few days, and spend the day in bed with him. The roller coaster of emotions that had encompassed every day since I'd awoken had been exhausting; all I wanted to do was ignore it all, just for a little while, in this big, comfortable bed in Nate's nice, quiet house.

Gripping my hips, he shifted me so I was straddling him, then he sat up and pulled my lips to his. He let out a ragged breath as I wrapped my legs around him, pulling him flush against me. Dragging his mouth from mine, he drew his hands up my sides, his thumbs brushing lightly along my skin. "When we're done saving the world, I'm taking you away," he whispered. "I want more than an hour with you."

"That sounds like a fantastic plan. Where are we going?"

His midnight eyes looked up at me, full of emotion, as he ran his fingers through my hair. "Somewhere that isn't here."

I struggled to keep my voice from shaking as he tangled his fingers in my hair, then gently pulled my head back so he could feather kisses along my collarbone. "What if I want to go to Antarctica?"

He pulled back, and a lazy smile tugged at the corners of his mouth, his eyes sparkling. "Then we'll go to Antarctica."

Just as he leaned in to kiss me again, his entire body stilled, then he dropped his head to my shoulder and made an annoyed sound.

"What's wrong?" I asked, frowning.

"It's my—"

The door opened and Apollo strode in.

"—brother," Nate finished, falling back onto his pillow and pinching the bridge of his nose.

I glared at Apollo. "Knock much?"

He waved a hand dismissively as I adjusted the strap of my tank top, which was still hanging over my shoulder. "He never does, why should I? Get up. We're leaving for Athens in an hour."

"And they sent you to wake us up?" Nate rolled his eyes. "I'm guessing that was—"

"Athena's idea, yes. Apparently, she's too busy to play alarm clock, but she seems to think I've got all the time in the world."

"You're second in command of the whole damn mountain," Nate grumbled. "Since when do you take orders from her?"

"I didn't feel like arguing."

"She knows Nate has an alarm clock," I said, pointing at the clock on his nightstand as though it wasn't sitting in plain view. "And you could've called telepathically."

"Do you know how annoying it is, trying to wake someone that way? We're meeting at my house in an hour. Be there or we're going without you."

When he was gone, I turned to Nate. I'd barely opened my mouth when he stopped me.

"Don't. Please."

"You don't even know what I was going to say," I grumbled.

He stared up at the ceiling, not meeting my eyes. "You think I should work on my relationship with my brother."

"Okay, yes, but—"

"I am." He turned his face toward me. "I'm trying to, anyway."

I hesitated a moment, gnawing at my lip. "You said you forgave him for Karis."

"I know. It's not about that."

"Then what is it?"

He held up his hands, then let them drop. "It's just...him. Even before I met her, he and I were constantly at odds. Our relationship was better before she was killed, but we were never close. Not like I am with the others."

"He wants a relationship with you."

He clenched his jaw but didn't respond. The unspoken words were written on his face, clear as day.

I know.

I sat up and looked down at him. "I may have missed out on a few thousand years of getting to know him, but the Apollo I knew back then—and, it would seem, the god he is now—isn't a bad guy. Kind of an arrogant prick at times, sure, but only on the surface. Look what he did for me, Nate. We were acquaintances, at best, in my past life, yet he agreed to have an interdiction placed on himself to keep me safe. He went behind Zeus' back and kept a massive secret from him, the ruler of goddamn Olympus, to keep me safe."

"And while he was keeping said secret, he was an excessive dick to *me* while trying to warn me away from you." He rubbed his hands over his face, then gave me an irritated look. "It just...brought back memories, that's all, especially since I'm here more permanently now."

"Okay. It's none of my business how you decide to handle things with him. He's your brother, it's your family." I started to climb over him and off the bed. "It's not—"

"Don't say it's not your place," he said softly, gripping my hips to keep me from leaving. "You should never feel as though you can't share your thoughts with me."

I forced a smile and traced my finger over his lips. "Okay."

He pressed my hand to his mouth and kissed it. "We should get moving. Athena and Epimetheus are going to get your friends around seven."

I hesitated, then exhaled a long breath. "Hades came into my dream last night. We practiced my shielding."

His eyebrows lifted slightly, and his eyes became cautious. "And how did that go?"

I gave him a quick run-down of our training session, leaving out the part about Nate training me to use Coercion. I knew he'd be wonderful at it and would have plenty to teach me, but I was struggling with the idea of asking him to teach me to do things he very likely didn't want to do.

"At least you made progress." His eyes ran over my face, turning slightly wary. "Are you sure you want him training you again? It seems like it doesn't take much to set you two into an argument."

Narrowing my eyes, I gave him a playful smile. "Nathaniel, are you jealous?"

His cheeks reddened, then he rolled his eyes. "I'm trying incredibly hard not to be, but I won't lie and say it's easy watching you pick back up with him."

"Understandable." Considering something, I frowned. "You do trust me, though?"

He brushed his thumb across my cheek. "Of course. It's him I'm wary of."

"Well, if it makes you feel any better, Persephone is going to help teach me how to use Earth magic to track. So, now I get to get beaten down by not one, but *two* Underworld rulers."

"She's an incredibly skilled tracker," he acknowledged, barely concealing his relief that Hades wanted his wife training me as well. "You'll be able to learn a great deal from her."

"I certainly hope so." I slid off his lap and stood up, then leaned back down and kissed him. "Thank you. For the concern and the wake up."

The corner of his mouth pulled up in a half smile. "Happy to oblige." He stood, snagging a shirt and jeans from his side of the dresser before heading into the bathroom.

I changed, then followed him in, hip bumping him away from the sink so I could get at my toothbrush.

"That's not very nice," he mumbled around a mouthful of toothpaste.

"Hogging the sink isn't very nice, either," I said, hopping up to sit on the counter while I brushed.

"Uh huh." He wiped his face with a towel, then turned and leaned against the counter, waiting for me to finish my morning routine. When I finished brushing my hair, I bit my lip as I took in my reflection. Grabbing a hair tie, I hastily twisted it up into as decent a braid as I could manage. It was loose, a little wispy, and kind of pretty, if I was being honest.

Nate must've noticed my perplexed expression, because he came over and turned me to face him. Wordlessly, he took my face in his hands and gave me a deep, plundering kiss that shot heat straight through me.

I pulled back, breathless. "What was that for?"

He smirked. "Your hair looks kind of cute when it's intentionally messy."

"Jerk." I leaned up and gave him a quick peck on the lips. "But thank you. I'm going to go check on Atlas before we go."

I made my way down the hall to the guest room and quietly opened the door. The morning sun hit this side of the house indirectly, so the light filtering through the curtains was still fairly dim. Epimetheus had already left with Athena, and Prometheus had arrived a little while earlier and was in the living room reading, so I was happy to take a few quiet moments alone with my twin.

Sitting down gingerly on the edge of the bed, I stared down at him. Atlas had rolled onto his side, his shoulder-length hair spilling across his forehead and onto the pillow, concealing the top part of his face. Gently, I brushed the tangled strands away and tucked them behind his ears, taking in the hard angle of his jaw and high cheekbones. I ran a finger lightly over the scar on his cheek, and anger flashed through me as I recalled how Menoetius had given it to him.

I hadn't witnessed the fight between my two brothers; I'd only been given vague details of the confrontation by Epimetheus. The most he would tell me was that Atlas had disarmed and stabbed Menoetius through the heart with his own blade, but not after taking a slice to his own face, the spelled knife leaving a thin, pink scar running from chin to cheekbone. Atlas had said it was a small price to pay for vengeance, but I always thought he regretted not just killing Menoetius outright.

"We're going to destroy him," I whispered.

I sat there for a few more minutes, lost in thought, when there was a quiet knock.

Nate came in, shutting the door quietly behind him. He sat down on the ottoman beside the bed and leaned forward, holding his hands out to take mine. When I slid mine into his, he smiled as he took in my expression.

"Are you alright?"

I nodded. "I am." I brought my eyes back to Atlas' sleeping face and sighed before turning back to Nate. "Can you do me a favor?"

"Of course."

A small smile formed on my lips. "That's it? No questions asked?"

"Are you going to ask me to do something you know I won't be comfortable with?"

"No, it's just—never mind. Can you help me with my mental walls tonight? Hades was really helpful last night, but I don't know that I'll be able to deal with his tough-love teaching every night, and I obviously can't wait for Atlas." Drawing my hands from Nate's, I brushed a hand over my brother's brow. "It's worse than I thought it would be," I murmured.

Nate sighed, then tapped my knee. "Look at me."

Reluctantly, I dragged my eyes away from Atlas and met Nate's.

"You saved your brother. Right now, his mind is recovering, just like yours had to. He's been through an ordeal, but he *will* come back to you." His eyes matched the fervent tone of his voice, making it hard not to believe every word he was saying.

I gave him a rueful smile. "Promise?"

"If I could, I would. What I *can* say is that you woke up. You shattered your own mind and managed to come back from it." He inclined his head toward Atlas. "As will he."

Frowning, I let my eyes run over his face, seeing the emotion that was written there as he brought back the memories of my own ordeal. "Is this how it felt when it happened to me? When I was still asleep?"

Staring down at the floor, he nodded, then took a few seconds before speaking. "It was incredibly difficult seeing you that way. I would imagine it was infinitely harder for your brothers." He cleared his throat, then rested his arms on his knees and looked at me. "Epimetheus refused to let you out of his sight. Prometheus just... paced. All through the halls of the palace."

"And you?"

He held out his hand, and I let him twine his fingers through mine. "The moment Hestia told me I still held a place with you, that you still...wanted me, I was there in that room with you."

"And here I am getting ready to go off with my friends," I murmured as guilt washed through me.

He must've felt it, because he took my other hand and pulled me into his lap, letting me snuggle against him. "This is much different. An aspect of their lives had just returned after being missing for a very long time, Tessa. They thought they hadn't protected you enough in the past and were afraid of forgetting you again. You're leaving to help Ischyra—to help protect people—and I think that's something your twin would admire in you."

Desperately, I hoped he was right. I couldn't just sit here and wait for Atlas to wake up, any more than he would if he were in my shoes.

As time went on, I was beginning to see similarities in our personalities that, until now, I would've denied the existence of. My twin was a fighter, not one to sit idly by, and more and more, I saw that in myself. There was an unrelenting need to contribute, to be useful, strong, and someone the others would want around when it came down to a fight that I couldn't seem to quiet.

I stared down at my hands, absently picking at a fuzz on Nate's shirt as darker thoughts toyed with my mind. Finally, I spoke the words I'd been holding in, refusing to speak even to myself. "Nate... what if it happens again?"

"What do you mean?"

I raised my eyes to his and met his puzzled stare. "What if it gets so bad that someone decides to make the choice to send me away again?"

Fury sparked in his eyes as tears filled mine. "That won't happen."

His words left no room for argument, but I asked anyway. "How do you know? Even Hecate said she did it to protect the mountain, not just me. What if it comes to that again? What if—"

His lips were on mine in a hard, forceful kiss meant only to silence me and nothing more. He pulled back, and his eyes bore into mine.

"That won't happen," he repeated. "You're stronger now. You won't allow anyone to force you to stay behind. Anyone who continues to question your abilities is simply denying what's in front of them." He brushed his thumb over the back of my hand. "And I won't let it happen."

Relief flooded me but was clashed with annoyance that, once again, I felt as though I was relying on someone else to tell me I was strong, that I could be something and someone worth having. Quickly, I averted my eyes, not wanting him to see that my fear had so quickly transformed to anger.

"Stop that," he whispered. He put a finger on my chin and gently turned my face back toward his. "You don't need reassurance from me or anyone else. You know what you can do, you know your own strength. Stop looking to everyone else to validate what you already know."

I clenched my jaw, annoyed at his bluntness, but more irritated that he was right.

"It's very difficult," I said carefully. "I spent so much time being told I couldn't do these things, and by the time someone came along who convinced me I could, I died. That last century of my life, the last nineteen years as an Ischyra, it's just a blip, you know? How can that short amount of time make up for so many centuries of being told no?"

"I understand. Tell me this, though." He smiled up at me. "What's so different now compared to when you were an Ischyra? You questioned yourself then, but not nearly to this extent, so what's changed?"

I smiled ruefully. "My entire life as an Ischyra, I was supported. Now, I've got centuries of memories of people I loved telling me I couldn't do it. It kind of puts things at an imbalance."

He cupped my face in his hand, and I leaned into the comfort he offered. "No one is telling you that now. Focus on that."

"It's easier said than done, Nate."

"Which is why I'm not telling you to 'get over it' like some gods would."

I smirked. "Like a certain ruler of the Underworld we know?"

"Among others." He gave my thigh a light pat. "Come on. Sitting here dwelling on what-ifs isn't going to make you feel any better, nor will it wake your twin any sooner."

Looking back down at Atlas, I thought about trying another dream walk, but knew if I were in his place, I'd want as much rest as I could get. Instead, I kissed his forehead, then followed Nate out to the living room.

"Are you sure you're alright to sit with him?" I asked Prometheus. "We can try to find another Psychometric and send them in my place. Getting a read for Siren activity really isn't all that complex."

"No, that'll just waste time. You should go." He rested his hands on my shoulders. "You need to get out there and work on rebuilding the skills you acquired in the past."

I gave him a surprised look. "Why the sudden change of heart?"

He closed his eyes and let his hands fall, and when he opened them, he smiled. "Logic, in the form of an angry goddess of wisdom and a twin brother, may have had something to do with it."

I smirked. "See? Athena's not a bad influence."

He pulled me in for a hug, then patted my back. "Not that bad, anyway. Now, go. I know how much you want to help. I'll hold things down here and call if he wakes."

Standing on my tip toes, I pressed a loud kiss to his cheek. "Thank you, Prometheus. Really."

With one last smile, Nate and I teleported up to Apollo's to wait for the others.

27

TESSA

When we arrived at Apollo's, Nate went inside to let him know we were there, so I sat down on the lawn and leaned back on my hands, spreading my fingers in the soft grass and tilting my face up to the morning sun. Apollo's mansion towered behind me, a quiet, yet commanding monstrosity of gleaming marble and white stucco. It was chilly up here on the mountain, the wind cutting right through the thin black sweater I wore, but there was something so peaceful about just enjoying the earliest rays of the day as they slid silently over the range. Under different circumstances, I could sit out here all day.

I felt the air shift beside me, and when I opened my eyes, Epimetheus, Eric, Mary, and Yana all stood above me, all in their regular black training uniforms.

"Morning," I said, grinning up at them. Frowning, I looked at Epimetheus. "Where's Athena?"

He kissed my cheek, then sat down next to me. "She had to run back to the palace, but she'll be along any time now."

Yana arched a brow in my direction as the others joined us on the grass. "Your hair is a mess," she observed. "You still have not learned to braid it?"

Epimetheus snorted as he leaned back on his hands, copying my position. "Of course not. She knows I'll do it."

"Hey, at least I tried!" I exclaimed.

Giving me a chastising look, she scooted closer, then gestured for me to turn around. "I find it quite silly that you lived nearly one thousand years in your previous life, yet you never took the time to learn to do your own hair." She tsked as she pulled apart my messy attempt at a braid and twisted the strands around in her fingers. "You can shatter spells with the power of Zeus, yet a simple hairdo flummoxes you."

When I tried to turn to the side to argue, she gave a hard yank on my hair to keep my head in place. "Stay still."

"Yes, ma'am," I grumbled.

A few moments later, Yana snapped a hair tie in place and smoothed back any flyaways. "There, it is done."

Reaching back, I patted the tight braid she'd woven and smiled. "Thanks."

Mary nudged Epimetheus with her elbow. "Better watch out. I think someone's gonna take your job."

He cast her an amused, sidelong look and shook his head.

Eric started fidgeting with his fire, igniting and extinguishing a tiny flame in his palm. "So...How are you doing? After that dream walk yesterday?"

"Better, I guess." I studied his expression, trying to see where his thoughts were without actually reading them, knowing I would be more than a little freaked out if I'd been in his place. Forcing a smile, I looked between him and Mary. "I'm just glad you guys are safe."

"Who's safe?"

Athena had just appeared behind Mary, clad in a dark gray, fitted tunic and black pants with boots that laced up to her knees. She'd left her bow and quiver of silver arrows behind, and instead carried her preferred weapon—a spear made of yew with a razor-sharp bronze head.

As she settled down on the lawn next to us, I inclined my head toward my friends. "We were just talking about the dream walk Menoetius did yesterday."

"Ah." She nodded and a tightness set over her mouth. "Yes, Apollo filled me in. Good on you for standing your ground, though."

I flashed her a brief smile, forcing myself to accept—and actually believe—her words.

"Tess, I gotta ask...should we be worried?" Mary bit her lip and gave me a reluctant look. "I mean, now that we know he knows who we are."

"Honestly? I don't know. After we get back today, it might not be a bad idea to talk about what to do going forward. The wards around Olympus are strong enough to keep him out, but if he somehow manages to get into your heads for a dream walk—"

Eric frowned, tilting his head to the side in curiosity. "Wouldn't he have done that already?"

"No, not necessarily," Athena replied. "He'd have to be able to track your minds, which he can only do if he's been in contact with you before. He knew enough about you to fool Tessa with an illusion, but that's the extent of what he knows of you."

"But he said he tried to get into Nate's head," I said, shaking my head. "He's never met him."

"Nathaniel stopped the second dream walk Menoetius did, when the twins infiltrated it to help her," she explained. "Menoetius would've gotten a whiff of his essence then. Fortunately, my brother's mental walls are rock solid."

"Do you know how he is getting information about Tessa?" Yana asked.

Athena gave her a careful look. "What do you mean?"

I refrained from shooting her a frown. It was obvious to anyone with a brain that someone was giving Menoetius information; I didn't see any sense in playing coy with my friends.

Sensing as much, Yana looked back and forth between Athena and me before responding, her eyes turning uncertain. "I was only curious...since he did that first dream walk back before she regained her memories, it seemed as though he knows a good bit about what's going on up here."

"We're looking into it," I said before Athena could give her any more non-answers. "No one knows anything for certain just yet."

'What are you doing?' I asked Athena. *'She just asked a question.'*

'Yes, and we still don't know who has been giving Menoetius information about you.' Avoiding my gaze, she added, *'You've only just met her, Tessa. I'm not saying she's the one who's been blabbing, but until we know for sure who is, this isn't something we need to be discussing in mixed company.'*

"So how's Atlas, anyway?" Mary asked, dragging my attention from Athena's mental chastising.

"Still sleeping." I plucked a blade of grass and started twirling it between my thumb and forefinger. "Prometheus is going to stay with him while we're gone, but I really want this to be a quick trip."

Mary patted my knee. "Try not to worry. He'll wake up soon."

I smiled my thanks, but I could tell it didn't reach my eyes. Looking for a change in topic, I pointed toward where Athena had laid her spear on the ground. "Why'd you bring the spear this time?"

She shrugged, smirking when she saw Mary eyeing it with interest. "It's simpler to carry than a bow and arrow, plus it's my Old Faithful. Would you like to see it?" She lifted it and handed it to Mary, who looked down at the weapon, wide-eyed. Athena's brow lifted. "I'm assuming you'd like to model one of yours after it?"

Mary turned the spear over in her hands, examining every facet of its craftsmanship. "Yes—how did you know?"

"Chiron has told me how skilled you've become at creating weapons from ice. I'd be curious to see how you manage a spear. Hephaestus designed this one, so I'm the only one who can use it, otherwise I'd let you give it a go. I'm sure you could model something after it, though."

"Her ice arrows are particularly impressive," I said, shooting Mary a glare. She stuck her tongue out in response, then went back to examining the spear, focusing on the way the bronze tip gleamed in the morning sun.

"Yes, he mentioned those," Athena said with a nod. "Chiron said the shaft breaks off and the head actually splinters once it's inside?"

"It does," Mary said, blushing a bit as she set Athena's weapon down. "It took me a few days to figure out the splintering part because I had to make sure it was strong enough to actually get lodged into a body before shattering. Just having the shaft break wasn't going to do much in terms of damage, so I wanted it to actually mess things up inside, too."

"And how did you finally figure it out?" Epimetheus asked.

Mary grinned, and self-satisfaction glinted in her eyes and in the slight curve of her mouth. "Speed, science, and accuracy. I know how to fire fast, and I'm an excellent shot, so as long as I've got my aim right and have the ice at just the right freezing level, they'll go where they need to go and do what I need them to do."

"Show off," Eric muttered, sounding annoyed.

"And so modest," I teased.

Smiling, Athena turned toward Eric and Yana. "So, are you kids ready for your first field trip?"

"What exactly will we be doing?" Eric asked, still looking a bit perturbed.

She wrinkled her nose. "Not a whole lot, honestly. Tessa will be reading the area to see if we can substantiate the claims of Sirens coming onto the mainland. You'll get to meet Cornelius, though. He's our lead Ischyra in the Athenian region. He's been around for quite some time now, so feel free to pick his brain a bit, if you'd like."

Eric's eyes brightened at that. "Really? He won't mind?"

"It's the job of the older generations to teach the younger. He may not be your mentor, but it's still his duty to ensure the continued success of the Ischyra. So long as you don't become bothersome, ask away." Athena shifted her stare to the girls. "You two, as well. I can feel your hesitancy whenever you're around us. While I know some of us are less hospitable than others—" she shot a look at Apollo, who was coming down the stairs with Nate "—many of us are quite nice and more than willing to help you learn."

"Time to go," Apollo said when they reached us, not bothering with any sort of greeting.

"Good morning to you, too," I mumbled. Ignoring me, he clamped his hand on Eric's shoulder and disappeared. Athena and Epimetheus quickly followed suit with Yana and Mary. Alone on Apollo's front lawn, Nate laced his fingers through mine and kissed me.

"Are you ready?"

Taking a deep breath, I nodded. "Let's do this."

Seconds later, we arrived in Athens, just beside the Parthenon that overlooked the city from the ancient Acropolis.

Hot summer air blew around us, and the smell of the ocean several miles off, imperceptible by human senses, just barely brushed my nose. Dropping Nate's hand, I walked toward the short wall that ran along the edge of the hillside and took in the view. Crumbling ruins and evergreens dotted the steep hillside beneath me, leading to the cramped and crowded city streets below. Red-roofed houses and apartments stretched all the way to the coast, where the mist covering the water was slowly beginning to give way to the morning sun.

In just a couple of hours, the hill we stood on would be teeming with visitors eager to explore the ancient ruins. For now, though, it was quiet.

Since the return of my memories, I hadn't thought much about what the outside world would look like, now that I had two viewpoints of it. Yet here, standing in the shadow of the Parthenon, just above the entrance to the underground Ischyra headquarters, I struggled to reconcile my old memories of the area—long before cars, hotels, and even the ancient citadel on which we stood were even imagined—with my more recent trip, one when I was twelve, with John and Analise, that involved tour busses, selfies, and sandwiches from carts on the side of the road.

The world was a different place when I was a young Titaness. Very little of what existed then still stood today. Giant marble monuments, statues, and cities that once seemed able to stand the test of time had since been reduced to rubble, torn apart by one natural or manmade disaster or another. Most of what humans looked to today as signs of our antiquity—Pompeii, the Roman Colosseum, Delphi, and the very place I now stood—had come and gone hundreds of years after my death, while my soul had whiled away the years trapped in Chaos.

I was older than this place, but in so many ways, I felt much, much younger.

"Are you alright?"

I started when Yana spoke beside me, then smiled at her. "I am. It's just weird. I remember it from just a few years ago, but also from how it was...before."

Her voice was quiet, hesitant when she spoke. "What was it like?"

I stared out over the city and felt a faint smile form on my lips. "Everything was changing back then, and the humans lived so much differently than us. Athens was barely half of what it is now. I only came a few times because my brothers...they didn't think it was safe." Slowly, I drew in a breath through my nose, then slowly exhaled. "But I remember it being amazing."

She inclined her head toward the massive Parthenon, a near mirror image of the ancient Agora on Olympus, and raised her eyebrows a fraction. "And this?"

I slid my hands into my back pockets, then bit my lip as Mary and Eric came to stand on my other side. "They hadn't even begun to build it yet. This was just a rock." Looking down at the ground, I kicked the dirt with my sneaker. "A big, empty rock."

Avoiding their eyes, I looked again at the city that appeared both familiar and foreign. I didn't want to see their reactions to the reminder of just how much had changed in just a few days, to how much *I* had changed.

I also didn't want to acknowledge just how painful a reminder this place was of what I'd missed out on.

"It must've been wonderful," Mary commented, slipping her hand into mine.

"Yeah." Eric chimed in. "No car horns, no annoying tourists."

"No underground sewage or air conditioning," Yana added dryly. "No showers."

I let out a quiet, relieved laugh, then nodded. "Exactly."

A throat cleared behind us. "If you four are done?"

"Way to ruin a moment, Apollo," I called back, rolling my eyes. Linking my arm through Mary's, I smiled down at her. "Come on, let's go before Apollo gets grumpy...er."

"Is that possible?" she whispered.

We made our way over to where everyone else stood, waiting at the bottom of the ruined steps of the temple. I shot a thankful look toward Nate. I knew without asking that he'd been the one to give me those few moments with my friends.

"It's beautiful here," Mary commented, taking in our surroundings.

Athena wrinkled her nose and looked up at the crumbling structure in a haughty expression. "As far as temples dedicated to me go, I suppose it's alright."

Eric's mouth popped open, as though just realizing he was walking around with the very goddess not only for whom this temple had been built, but also for whom this entire city had been named.

"You gave them an olive tree," Apollo muttered, his tone tinged with bitterness. "They gave you a temple and patronage of an entire city. You should be thankful."

"Don't be jealous," Athena added with a smirk, jabbing him with her elbow. "It's unbecoming."

Biting back a smile, I turned to Nate. "Where are we going, anyway?"

He gestured toward a long, narrow building that sat behind several large signs that offered information about the structures. "The entrance to the Athenian headquarters is just over here."

Athena and Apollo led us forward, and when we reached the structure, Athena opened an unassuming gray door, then gestured for us to move forward. Exchanging a glance with Mary, I shrugged, then stepped through, finding myself on a landing at the top of a metal spiral staircase.

"What keeps humans from wandering in here looking for a bathroom?" Eric asked as we started to descend.

"It's spelled to repel curious eyes," Epimetheus explained.

The stone stairwell that descended into the rocky hill and the thick, steel door with only a single window were reminiscent of a dungeon, but when Athena pressed a code into the keypad attached to the frame and pushed open the door into the Athenian headquarters, the interior looked anything but.

Smooth concrete made up the walls, floors, and ceiling of the hallways inside. The entrance hall was fairly short, continuing only fifteen feet or so before bisecting into two separate halls.

A stocky man with dark blond hair came through a doorway about halfway to the intersection, followed by a handful of other Ischyra, all dressed in the standard gray field uniform. He then strode forward to meet us as we walked toward him, while the others made their way in the opposite direction.

"Athena," he greeted her when he came to a stop in front of her. "Thank you for coming."

"Cornelius." She gave him a brief nod. "I hope you don't mind, we brought a few recruits along." She inclined her head toward Mary, Eric, and Yana before shifting her attention to me. "This is Tessa. She'll be your Psychometric for the day."

Smiling, I held out a hand to Cornelius'. "It's nice to meet you."

He gave my hand a firm shake and flashed a quick smile of welcome to the recruits. "Good to meet you, as well." He gestured down the hall. "Come, I can give you the latest on this Siren nonsense before we head out."

We veered left at the end of the hall, entering another hall that looked nearly identical to the first, only this one was nearly triple the length and had heavy, steel doors dotting the walls. The quiet murmur of voices spilled out through an open doorway about halfway down, which was where Cornelius led us.

The room we entered was a meeting room, of sorts. A large,

square table, capable of fitting at least thirty people, took up the bulk of the space. Cork and white boards dotted with papers, maps, and photos ran the length of three of the walls, while the fourth was dominated by a large map of the Athenian region. About a dozen Ischyra milled about, some leaning over papers on the table, others examining the things that were hung on the walls.

"Just this way," Cornelius said, gesturing toward the map. We followed him over, stopping several feet from the wall.

"Tell us what you know," Apollo said, frowning as he looked at several black Xs that dotted the map, all of which were several miles away from the coast and far beyond the boundaries of where the Sirens' curse allowed them to travel.

"Each marker represents a Siren sighting," he explained, tracing a circle in front of the map where the sightings had been recorded. "I've not been able to substantiate any myself, but the reports have come from trusted soldiers."

"Which is why we've brought Tessa," Athena said. "She'll be able to substantiate quite quickly, so once that's done, we can go from there."

Sliding his hands in his pockets, Nate stepped forward and examined the map. The Athenian region consisted of central Greece, from the southern tip of Athens up to the southern border of Thessaly. "Which sites do you think will yield the most information?"

Stepping beside him, Cornelius pointed to two spots about two feet apart. "A security guard at the archaeology museum in Lamia reported seeing a 'green-skinned woman with long, dark hair and wings' on the grounds just after sunset to the local police department who contacted us. One of our own soldiers had a similar sighting in a park in Maroussi."

"It would be easier to get a read on a location that doesn't otherwise have a lot of traffic," I said. "Are any of the other locations more secluded?"

"The park is small and overgrown, not one that gets a terrible number of visitors," Cornelius replied. "The museum has been closed for the last month for roof repairs, so providing you can stick to just recent events when you do your reading, you shouldn't have too much to sift through."

I gave him a tight smile, then pretended to refocus my attention on the map. I'd used psychometry as an Ischyra and managed it well enough, so there was no logical reason to doubt my abilities in this case.

"Well, get started, then." Athena sent a look toward the recruits. "I've got some things I need to take care of here before we head back. How would you three like a tour while Tessa takes care of business?"

She gestured toward Epimetheus, and the two of them led Eric, Mary, and Yana out of the room. My friends hardly spared me a glance as they left, the barely concealed look of excitement on Eric's face telling me they were likely going to have a lot more fun than I was.

When they were gone, Cornelius turned to me. "This shouldn't take long. I trust the sources but having confirmation from a deity can't hurt."

"I'm happy to help," I told him.

Cornelius, Apollo, Nate, and I teleported to Lamia, nestled in the foothills of the Óthrys Mountains. We arrived on a sloping hillside that overlooked the small city, just outside the stone wall that surrounded the museum. Seconds later, a tall, dark-haired female Ischyra appeared.

"This is Clarisa," Cornelius said, introducing us. "She's head of the local liaisons' office and reported the sighting to us."

"Thank you for coming," she began, her voice laced with a heavy Greek accent. "If you will follow me, the guard claimed he saw the creature just this way." She turned and led us toward a copse of trees that sat about a hundred yards down the hill, stopping about fifty feet away. "He said she stood just here, between those two large trees."

"Did she see him?" Apollo asked.

"Not that he believes," Clarisa responded. "I assume she would have taken or injured him if she had."

"Maybe," I murmured, eyeing the area she'd indicated where the Siren had been seen. "Okay, let me see what I can find."

I waved Nate and Apollo off when they moved to follow me toward the trees, needing the space to feel out the area on my own. I'd gotten maybe ten feet away when I heard Nate strike up conversation with the others, effectively occupying them and giving me the space to work without anyone hovering over my shoulder.

Being able to touch an object and learn all about it had become one of my favorite Mentalist abilities as an Ischyra, but I only ever used my Psychometry for weapons training. This type of situation was new to me. My eyes scanned the area as I approached the trees, looking for any signs of disturbance in the grass or lower branches. Seeing none, I stepped between the two trees Clarisa had indicated and crouched down. Running my hands over the soft blades of grass, I closed my eyes and focused on all activity from the last few days. Cornelius had been right; foot traffic had been light. Only a few security guards had been through on their normal path as they kept watch on the grounds.

Then I saw her. The Siren had pale green skin, large, feathered wings, and long dark hair. Where normally there would have been a scaly, green tail, there were two thin, twig-like legs. I focused on her thoughts and intentions, surprised when I found her mind hesitant, not full of malice. It seemed as though she were waiting, watching, hoping for someone to come near and see her.

"Huh. That's odd." I slowly shook my head as I tried to reason out her actions.

"What did you see?"

Standing, I turned and faced Apollo, who was frowning at me curiously. The others had just come up behind him.

Brushing off my hands, I loosed a breath. "There was definitely a Siren here, and she was *definitely* standing on two legs."

"Anything on Menoetius?"

Shaking my head, I looked back to where the Siren had been standing. "No, nothing. I'm sorry."

Apollo sighed and his face fell. "Well, I guess that's that, then."

"Thank you," Clarisa said. "I trusted the guard's story, but I thought it best to get confirmation."

Frowning back at the spot where the Siren stood, I nodded. "Of course."

"Alright, let's head to—"

Apollo hadn't finished his sentence when Prometheus' voice sounded in my head.

'Atlas is awake.'

28

TESSA

Seconds later, I was sprinting up the steps to Nate's door. When I burst inside, I skidded to a stop.

My twin stood in the living room with Prometheus, looking perfect and healthy and *alive*. He was taller than I remembered, more broad, terrifying to look at to anyone who didn't know him the way I did, the way our brothers did.

Shock coated his features when he saw me. He stood, frozen in place as we took each other in. A moment later, a huge smile bloomed across his face, softening the lines of his angular jaw and causing his sharp eyes to sparkle. He crossed the room in three strides, swooping me into his arms and spinning me around as he buried his face in my hair. Tears streaming down my cheeks, I wrapped my arms around his neck and pressed my face to his shoulder.

"Gods, it's really you." His deep voice was thick with a mix of exhaustion and emotion. He wasn't crying, but the cracked edge to his voice, the tightness of his embrace, said more than enough about his emotional state.

All I could do was nod, unable to form the words that wanted to tumble from my mouth.

"I never thought I'd be the one thanking you for saving me." Leaning back, he tapped me on the nose. "I'm supposed to protect you, remember?"

I let out a watery laugh as he set me back on my feet. Clutching his arms, I beamed up at him. "I didn't think I could do it, Atlas," I whispered. "I thought—"

He cupped my chin with a massive hand and smiled softly as his green eyes—identical to my own—stared into mine.

"It doesn't matter. Anything you did would've been better than being there."

I grinned, then tugged at his hands and pulled him over to the sofa. The others all took seats, and Nate sat directly across from me, a soft smile on his face. Even Apollo looked slightly less rigid than normal. Prometheus sat on my other side, while Epimetheus took a seat on the floor, just beside the fireplace.

"Where's Athena?" I asked.

"Debriefing the recruits, then she's checking in with Zeus," Epimetheus explained.

Atlas put his arm around my shoulder and pulled me into his side, then rested one foot on his knee. "Now, tell me what else is happening. What has Menoetius been brewing?"

Quickly, I brought him up to speed on everything we'd found in the last few days, including the weakening river fire and the witch who had met with one of Hades' giants.

"You've already seen Hades?" Atlas shot me a disapproving look.

"He's the reason she was able to save you," Epimetheus said quietly. "So I wouldn't press that issue."

'Thank you,' I said. He responded with a quick wink but nothing more.

Atlas gave our brother a long look, and I could only guess at what he was thinking when he heard the approval in Epimetheus' words, reluctant as it was. "Have you spoken with the other witches about who could be weakening the Phlegethon's fire?"

"Tessa has spoken to Scylla—"

"Scylla?" Atlas held up a hand and cut Prometheus off, then gave me another chastising look. "*Really*, Tessa."

"She's my friend, Atlas." I threw up my hands in frustration. "Why do I keep having to explain this to people?"

"If we could not do this right now, that would be lovely," Apollo said. "Prometheus? You were saying?"

Atlas sat back in his seat, his brow drawn down, but he didn't question me any further.

Prometheus cleared his throat. "Scylla is putting out some feelers to see who might be playing both sides, and Hades is investigating things in the Underworld," Prometheus replied.

Atlas exhaled, then rubbed a hand across his face in a tired gesture. "Alright, then. What are our next steps?"

"Your next step is to rest," I said firmly. "You just woke up."

"I feel as though I just slept for a year," he said with a sigh. "Tell me what plans you've made."

Nate and Epimetheus exchanged a look before Nate spoke.

"Tessa's mental barriers should probably be the first thing we address," he said, flicking a glance at me. "Hecate has put a shielding spell on her mind for the time being, but it would be best if Tessa could do it on her own."

My twin looked at me in alarm. "A shielding spell? Why?"

"Menoetius has done three dream walks," I explained, not wanting to get into too many details. "My walls are weak when I'm asleep—"

"Yes, I remember. Of course, we'll resume your lessons immediately."

"No, it's fine, Atlas. I've got plenty of people to help me with that. You need to focus on getting yourself reacclimated."

He clenched his jaw, then looked around the room.

"She's right, brother," Prometheus said gently.

"You want me to rest, yet you've allowed Tessa out to face *Sirens*—"

"No one has allowed me to do anything," I said carefully. "But I took nearly two days to rest once I awakened and got my memories back. You should do the same."

"Does Zeus know I've returned?"

"Not yet," Apollo answered. "We needed to be sure Tessa hadn't turned your mind to sludge before informing him."

"Real nice," Nate muttered, shaking his head. Apollo shrugged but didn't look the least bit apologetic.

"I can assure you, she hasn't," Atlas said firmly.

"Then we'll inform him tomorrow, once you've had another night to recuperate," Apollo said. "Tessa is planning to help with a few minor issues on Earth in the meantime."

"I'm sure Persephone will understand if Tessa would rather stay here," Prometheus said, frowning.

Atlas turned to me. "Persephone?"

"Hades' wife," I explained. "Demeter's daughter. She's a harvest goddess, as well, and there have been some crop failures on Earth recently. They've asked me to help them replenish the land, if possible."

His eyes widened. "You can—you can do that?"

I shrugged. "I don't know. I'm going to try, though." For some reason, his shock made me even more confident I would be able to help.

Something in his eyes shifted, and my twin stared at me as though seeing me for the first time. "What other abilities have you acquired?"

I gave him a rueful smile. "None that I wasn't born with."

His gaze turned accusing as it shifted to the twins. "And you two have allowed her to do these things? With Menoetius still after her?"

"As she said, no one has allowed her to do anything," Epimetheus said.

Shifting so I could face my twin, I took his hand in mine. "I'm strong, Atlas. You need to know—understand—that I'm not going to sit idle anymore."

He held my gaze for a moment, his expression unreadable. Withdrawing his hand from mine, he looked around the room, taking in the faces of people who'd all changed over the centuries.

Crestfallen, I realized I'd spent so much time fussing over my own troubles, my own problems with meshing two lives together, that I hadn't thought for a second that he might have to do the same.

After a few moments, he looked back to me, his eyes full of confusion.

"I think I need to rest some more, after all." He patted my hand, then stood. "We'll speak again later."

"Of course," I said quietly, trying to ignore the sinking feeling in my stomach.

My eyes brimmed with tears as he left the room without so much as a backward glance.

I BRACED my hands against the kitchen counter and stared through the window over the sink, trying hard not to let Atlas' behavior upset me.

I should've known, should've considered how he would feel about my change in circumstances. The sister he knew was a completely different person now.

"Are you alright?"

Hastily wiping my eyes, I forced a smile at Epimetheus as he leaned against the counter beside me.

"Yeah. He just—I know he just needs more time."

"You'll always be the sister he feels he needs to protect, Tessa. It's hard enough for Prometheus and me to accept that. Atlas is..."

"Atlas." I smiled ruefully as I turned and mirrored his position. "I know."

"Just try to remember that he hasn't lived in this world. He doesn't know what it means to have been raised as an Ischyra and likely doesn't trust the training you received from your guardians or mentors."

"I just wish he would trust *me*." I tucked a piece of hair behind my ear that had escaped my braid. "The way he looked at me...he still sees me as naive. Unable to make choices for myself."

Epimetheus draped an arm around my shoulder and grinned down at me. "Then we'll have to prove that's not who you are, then, won't we? Show him how you can crack open the ground beneath you, beat Hades to a bloody pulp—"

I smiled wryly. "Would that be more for your benefit or his?"

He chuckled. "He'll come around, don't worry."

There was a knock at the door, and Nate appeared wearing black combat pants, a fitted black shirt, with a long trench knife dangling at each hip. He opened the door, and Persephone walked in, followed by a tall, golden-haired goddess.

I hadn't seen Demeter since my transition ceremony, and I'd only seen her in passing in my previous life. Her gold tresses were styled in a high bun that highlighted her sharp facial features, drawing focus to her light eyes. The dark blue leggings and gray sweater she wore would've reassured me that our mission to heal failing crops was a simple one, had her daughter not been standing right next to her.

Persephone wore dark leather pants, a fitted white shirt under a leather vest, and a matching belt that held no fewer than five knives of varying sizes attached. She grinned when she noticed me examining her weapons, then pulled open her vest to reveal half a dozen throwing stars, all razor sharp.

I raised a brow as I took in her and Nate's attire. "Are we expecting an ambush?"

"Apollo and I are heading to Polynesia to give Ares a hand with cleaning up the empousa nest down there," Nate said. He jerked his chin toward Persephone. "I'm not sure I want to know what her plans are."

She shrugged innocently. "You can never be too prepared." Unclipping a sheath from the back of her pants, she handed it to me. "And you shouldn't go in unarmed, regardless of what your powers are."

Wrapping my hand around the crude wooden hilt of the dagger, I smiled in thanks.

"Over preparation is one of Persephone's more irritating qualities," Demeter remarked, casting a sidelong glance at her daughter. Her voice was rich, carrying subtle hints of power. She inclined her head in my direction, the motion seeming forced. "Tessa. How are you?"

"I'm good, Demeter." I paused, unsure what her tense expression was about. "You?"

She gave me a tight smile. "Well, thank you."

Not having the patience or inclination to decipher the meaning behind her tense expression or our awkward exchange, I focused on attaching the dagger Persephone had given me to my waist. Frowning, I struggled to connect it to my jeans, not wanting to admit that knife work had never been one of my greatest skills. Passable, but nothing compared to how I could wield a staff.

"Let me," Nate murmured, turning me to the side. *'We can practice when you get home, if you want.'*

I gave him a grateful smile, then looked back to Persephone and Demeter. "Where are we going, anyway?"

"There are a number of corn fields that have died off in New Jersey and two of the largest vineyards in Argentina's Mendoza province have dried up," Demeter explained. "Those are two of the biggest crops in those regions, so the loss will affect their economies a good deal if they aren't replenished."

Nate gave the sheath a tug, then brushed a hand across my lower back and a kiss across my temple. "All set."

I glanced down at the dagger, the weight of it on my waist a foreign but not entirely unwelcome feeling.

'It looks good on you,' Nate murmured.

Smirking, I nudged him with my elbow. *'How good?'*

'Very good.'

I tried to ignore the tendrils of lust his tone sent snaking through my mind. *'I'll hurry back, then.'*

He tucked a strand of hair behind my ear and smiled. "As soon as you get there, use your Earth magic to summon up another weapon. A vine, a staff, something simple that doesn't require your magic to exist. If Menoetius shows up and somehow manages to disable your power, you don't want to be left with just one dagger."

"Will do."

'Are you sure you're alright to go without me?'

I wanted to say no, that I wanted him to come with us, but I bit that back. I needed to be able to go out and do these things on my own, explore my powers without him or my brothers or Hades barking at me. So, I patted his cheek and smiled up at him.

'I'm good to go.'

"Where is Athena?" Persephone asked. "I expected her to be here."

"She was checking in with Zeus, then she has some business in the US," Epimetheus said. "Prometheus and I will stay here with Atlas."

My heart clutched at the mention of my twin's name, and I reined in the desire to speak with him again before we left.

He needed space. I needed to give him that, regardless of how badly it hurt.

Demeter held out a hand for each of us. "Let's get to it, then."

I gave Nate one last quick kiss, then took one of Demeter's hands, while Persephone took the other.

Moments later, we stood on the edge of a barren wasteland.

Dried up grape vines woven through trellises stretched as far as the eye could see, curving along gently-rolling hills. Brown, rotting fruit hung from dead branches and littered the ground beneath, which was nothing more than yellow grass spotted with patches of dirt.

I dragged my eyes away from the fields in front of me to look at Demeter. "What could've done this?"

"That's what we're here to find out." She took a few steps forward and plucked a leaf from the nearest vine. It disintegrated at her touch, sending brown dust to the ground. She glanced back at Persephone. "Get a sample of the soil. I want it tested for poison. If that's what's causing the failure, we may be able to come up with an antidote to distribute to the Liaisons to give to other farmers. It will be far less time consuming then trying to heal them all ourselves."

Wordlessly, Persephone pulled several vials from a pouch on her belt and began filling them with soil.

I looked around the quiet field. "Where are the farmers?"

"They don't know we're here," Demeter replied absently.

"Why not tell them?"

Persephone wrapped the vials in cloth to keep them from breaking and stowed them back into her pouch. "They don't need to know just how directly we affect their lives, Tessa. If they did, they'd begin to rely on us too much."

"I see." It seemed wrong, not telling them that we were here to fix the blight on their land, but it wasn't my place to argue. "So, how do we do this?"

Persephone and her mother exchanged a glance.

"The same way you'd use any of your other abilities," Persephone explained. "You just...tell your power what you want it to do."

"Will it into being," Demeter added.

I stared out over the desolate field again, the sheer size of it sowing seeds of doubt in my stomach. There was just so...much.

Persephone nudged me with her elbow. "Now do you see why we asked you to come?"

"This should be second-nature to you, Tessa," Demeter said, her voice slightly less rigid than before. "You just have to let your power do what it was created for."

The smile I gave her wavered, but I nodded. "You're right."

"Alright, then." Demeter sat down on the ground, then held out her hands for us to sit with her. "Sit down and let's get to this."

Persephone and I mimicked her position, and I watched as they closed their eyes and gently prodded the earth with their hands. Following their lead, I let the soil cover my hands, then tapped into my Earth magic, not quite sure what to expect.

There was a faint prickling sensation along my arms that seemed to originate both inside me and from the Earth. The feeling intensified, and a few seconds later, I sucked in a breath and opened my eyes. Green, earthy magic spread out around me, my own mixing with Persephone and Demeter's as it wove through the dirt. The further out it went, the more I could *feel.* Trees growing, plants dying, animals burrowing—I could feel it all. Everything my power touched spoke to me and I knew, without question, what I needed to do.

I let my power dance along the vineyard's paths, caressing the deadened fruit and dried ground. I felt it in every fiber of my being, as the three of us cast our power over the field, inspecting everything that was supposed to be alive, blooming, producing, questioning why it wasn't. Then, gently, it sank into the ground, digging deep into the soil, swirling around the roots and infusing everything it touched with life and rightness.

The only other time I'd experienced something that beautiful was when my own power was awakened as an Ischyra. The feel of magic as it sought out each cell, making everything function the way it was meant to, was amazing.

The fact that *I* was the one helping to infuse that magic into the earth had a stupid, dopey grin forming on my lips. I wasn't breaking things or fighting anyone; I was helping to restore life in something that had fallen victim to a war it had nothing to do with.

When my eyes refocused on the goddesses in front of me, Demeter was eyeing me speculatively, but Persephone's dark eyes were twinkling.

"It's something, isn't it?" she whispered.

"It's..." I let out a shuddering breath as tears sprang to my eyes. "Gods, I can feel...everything."

With a nod, Demeter stood up and dusted off her hands. "Alright, then. I think we've done all we can here. Let's go take care of that corn field then head back. I'd like to get that soil tested as soon as possible. We'll check back here in a few days to make sure things are turning about."

I wanted to stay, watch the magic do its work, but they assured me it would take time for things to turn back around. So, wordlessly, we joined hands, then teleported to our next stop.

The scene that met us in New Jersey looked far worse than the vineyards of Argentina. Twelve-foot corn stalks, yellowed with disease, spread out in every direction. It was hard not to feel suffocated, dwarfed under their height.

"This will take a bit more effort than the vineyard, due to its size," Demeter warned.

"How far out does it go?" I asked, looking around.

She gave me a grim look. "In total, it's about fifteen hundred acres, non-continuous."

I choked back a laugh. "Gods, I think I was better off not knowing." I took a deep breath. "Okay. Same process?"

"Same process," Demeter confirmed.

The three of us sat down and, once again, dug our hands into the dry dirt. It was easier to tap into my Earth magic this time. Immediately, I felt the Earth's response when our combined magic reached out.

As Demeter had warned, the corn fields were more taxing than the vineyard. By the time we'd gone through the process of infusing our shared magic into the earth, pulsing life into the crops, I felt tapped out.

Wiping a hand across my brow, I leaned back on my hands and let out an exhausted sigh. "I think I need a nap."

A small smile ghosted across Demeter's lips. "It can be tiring, but you'll learn to get used to it. We don't do things like this often."

"It's nice that you do, though." Despite how tired I felt, I truly believed this was the kind of thing I could do every day.

The three of us sat there quietly for a few more moments, listening to the sounds of summer around us. Blue jays squawked somewhere nearby while the *tap tap tap* of a woodpecker sounded relentlessly in the distance. Farther out, on a road that was blocked from view, a tractor rumbled past.

"We should head back," I said. "Otherwise I could sit here all day."

"It *is* peaceful, isn't it?" Persephone mused.

We were about to leave when I heard Athena's voice.

'Where are you three?"

'We just finished up in New Jersey. Why?'

'Head down to Saboga, Panama. This empousa nest is a bit larger than we anticipated. I'll meet you on the beach on the southeastern side of the island.'

"Athena—"

"We heard," Persephone replied. "She needs us in Panama."

The two of them exchanged a quick glance before looking back to me.

"Are you sure you're ready for that, Tessa?" Persephone asked, her expression dubious as she took in my jeans, sweater, and Converse. "You did wonderfully here, but—"

I exhaled a short breath through my nose.

"Yes. I'll—I'll do what I can. If I end up just being a hindrance, I'll leave."

Demeter eyed me shrewdly. "Alright then. Let's go."

ATHENA MET US ON A SMALL, boulder-dotted beach that ran along a dense forest on the tiny island of Saboga. Her fist was clenched around her spear, the bronze tip coated in black empousa blood.

Persephone put her hands on her hips when she saw her. "What have you got?"

Athena gestured with her weapon down a tree-lined dirt road that disappeared into the forest. "Empousa nest about two hundred yards that way. We've evacuated the locals to the other side of the island, and there are eight Ischyra working on it now, but I'd like to avoid calling in more. I need you two—" she looked at Persephone and Demeter "—to head in and lend a hand to the Ischyra for now. We'll meet up with you shortly."

Persephone drew two of her longest knives from her belt and twirled one in her hand. "Consider it done."

When they were gone, Athena took my hand and teleported us to the edge of a large lake that ended in a bulkhead about twenty feet off to our right.

Confused, I looked around. "What are we doing here? Where's the nest?"

"I need you to do something else first. An empousa tried running this way. I want you to see what she was heading for."

Forcing down the nervous trembling that was threatening to come to the surface, I swallowed. "Shouldn't we help the others?"

"With Persephone and Demeter here, they've got it handled." She rolled her eyes and sighed when she saw my dubious expression. "They're *fine,* but trust me, if anything goes wrong, they'll call us in. This will only take a minute, then we'll join them."

I rubbed the bridge of my nose and grimaced. "Okay. Tell me what you need."

Athena narrowed her eyes at me. "Are you sure you're up for this?"

"Yeah." I cleared my throat. "Yeah, I'm up for it."

She pointed toward a spot on the ground coated in black blood. "We caught one right here sneaking through the trees. Considering the empousa's aversion to water, I'm assuming there was a boat waiting, or one they expected to be waiting. I was hoping you might be able to use your psychometry on the creature's blood to determine her intentions." She shrugged. "It might be a long shot, but..."

"It's worth checking out. Yeah." Crouching down, I examined the spots and splatters of blood in the broken grass. Hesitantly, I touched a finger to the blood.

Curling my fingers in the grass, I focused on the intent of the creature who'd bled here, her emotions, plans, the last things she did.

"She was scared, that's for sure." I frowned, trying to push past the emotions that were obvious on the surface, toward the more complex factors that floated just beneath. "But also confident. She was very certain whoever was back here would take her to safety."

"Focus on her thoughts, her memories," Athena said, sounding a bit impatient.

Ignoring her tone, I tried to drown everything around me out, aiming for specifics—who she was looking for, where she was planning to go, why she was here to begin with. After a few moments, I exhaled a heavy breath.

"She was thinking about Menoetius. I can't tell you if he was actually here or not, though." Looking around the quiet space, I shrugged. "I don't know why he would've been, honestly."

Her eyes narrowed in a pensive expression. "Well, it's a lead, possibly, so we'll mark it when we get back to the palace."

Shouts rang out from the direction we'd just come from.

'We need all hands on deck,' Persephone told us.

I sent Athena a panicked look. "I thought you said they had it handled?"

Athena grinned at me. "Come on. Let's go take out some of those bloodsucking bitches." Seeing my hesitation, she rolled her eyes. "Even if we pretend for a moment that you're nothing but an Ischyra, you've been trained in nearly every form of fighting there is since you were ten. Now, let's go put that to the test."

When I hesitated again, she smacked the side of my head. "Enough, Tessa! We're going and that's the end of it."

Without giving me a chance to protest, she grabbed my arm and teleported us...into the middle of mayhem.

A small shack surrounded by palm trees was overflowing with screeching empousa, fangs dripping with blood and venom. The bodies of two Ischyra lay prone on the ground near the door, while Persephone and Demeter took on five apiece, each moving so quickly, they were little more than violent blurs.

With a shove, Athena sent me into the melee. "Pick a weapon, Tessa, but do it quick!"

I had no time to respond before an empousa launched herself at me, fangs bared and dripping blue.

Godsbane.

I called on Earth and made a sharpened staff, shoving it into her torso when she was only inches away. Snarling, she thrashed against it, her body sliding further down the staff as blood poured from the gaping hole in her chest, coating my hands and causing them to slip. I flipped her onto her back, driving the staff further into her stomach and into the ground below.

Hissing, she struggled against my weight, trying to sit up.

Shit shit shit.

"Knife, Tessa!"

Putting my full weight on my staff, I snagged Persephone's knife from my waist and dragged it across her throat in one smooth motion, spraying blood across my front. With a final gurgling hiss, she went limp.

I barely had time to look up before another empousa hurled herself at me. Reflexively, I grabbed her by the neck and pinned her to the ground, then slammed my knife into her neck, hilt-deep. Her long, jagged nails dug into my neck and arms, and I received a mouth and face-full of black, oily blood as I pulled out the bronze blade and sliced her neck open. Gagging, I jumped back, turning just in time to see a third coming at me. My blade went through her torso like butter, her collar bone making a disgusting crunch as the knife shattered it in two. More blood sprayed as she fell, hissing.

There was a small sound behind me, and I spun, bringing my knife up and tearing through the sternum of a fourth female when her fangs, dripping with blue godsbane, were mere centimeters from my neck. Her eyes, full of fury, bore into mine. Something inside me snapped as I stared into the pure malice reflected in her expression as the light faded from her eyes.

All my training with John and Analise, all of my training with my brothers and Hades, fell into place. I knew what I was doing and that I could absolutely hold my own here. I knew, without a doubt, that I didn't need to question myself or my skills any longer. They were part of my being, part of *me.* A few thousand years in Chaos couldn't take that away.

I shoved the dead empousa to the ground, then adjusted my grip on the handle of my knife and pulled the staff from the body of the first one I'd killed.

"I can do this," I murmured, bracing myself as a fifth came at me. When a sixth joined her, I dropped my staff and formed a vine, using it as a whip to catch one around the neck while I dispatched the other. I let my training take hold, slicing through muscle and sinew. With each kill, something buried deep inside that had been dormant for too long awoke in me, fueling the knowledge that, no matter what anyone said, I could *absolutely* do this.

Finally, the area surrounding the shack was quiet. The ground was littered with dead empousa, and the two injured Ischyra were sitting up, drinking the antidote to the venom Athena had given them.

Chest heaving, I let the vine fall to the ground and sheathed the knife, then made my way over to the others.

I watched as the Ischyra rested against the wall of the shack, breathing deeply as the godsbane was eradicated from their system. Looking at Athena, I questioned why the godsbane didn't affect them.

Athena stood and dusted off her hands. "Anka, here, is an Original Ischyra, so she's able to withstand higher doses of godsbane than others," she said, indicating the tiny brunette who looked to be nearly a foot shorter than her male companion. "And it looks like not every empousa had their fangs coated, which is what saved David. He just got a heavy dose of venom, but the antivenin will fix that." She tilted her chin in the direction of the shack. "We lost three inside, though. The rest are gathering up the ones who tried to get away around back."

She offered a hand to Anka and David, helping them both to their feet.

"Thank you," Anka said, dusting herself off.

Athena nodded absently as she wiped a smudge of blood from her cheek with the back of her hand. Aside from a few smears here and there, she barely had a drop of blood on her. Looking down at my body, I saw that my arms were coated in black, nearly to the elbows. My shoes, Converse that had once been gray, were black with dirt and more blood. Splatters of shiny black slashed across my shirt, soaking through and sticking to my skin.

Wiping Persephone's dagger on the back of my jeans, I held it up to my face and took in my blurry reflection. The same gory spray that coated my shirt was streaked across my face.

"We need to get you some proper fighting clothes," Persephone remarked, tucking a throwing star—tipped in bronze, the only metal the empousa were vulnerable to—back into her vest as she eyed my jeans and long-sleeved shirt. "Those flimsy things won't do."

Athena picked up her spear from where it had been leaning against the wall of the shack and slid it into its sheath, then turned to me, tightening the strap across her chest. "Well, how'd it feel?"

Slowly, I turned around, taking in the scene around me.

Bodies of dead empousa, looking no different than regular human women, save for their fangs and black blood, were scattered about, torn and slashed to bits. Swallowing hard, I looked back to the others. Athena was biting her lip and wincing, while Demeter and Persephone stood behind her, waiting for...something.

"I...I think I'm going to be sick."

Athena darted forward and caught me under the arms just as my wobbly legs gave out.

"Oh, dear. Alright. Are you two good to clear this out? I'm going to run her home."

"Yes, we'll be fine," Demeter muttered. "Go on and take her."

"Home." I tried to suck in a breath, but it lodged in my throat. "Yes. Home would be good."

29

NATHANIEL

The beach on the southern shore of the atoll in Polynesia we landed on was overrun with screeching empousa by the time Apollo and I arrived.

"I thought Ares said it was just one nest!" I shouted over the din.

'It was,' Ares replied mentally, sounding strained. *'Just handle it.'*

"Great." Apollo groaned as half a dozen empousa suddenly noticed our presence. He slid a glance at me, then formed a small ball of blinding white light in his hand, far brighter than what he'd normally use to heal. "Stun and burn?"

"Stun and burn," I agreed grimly, watching as the females dropped their current prey—three Ischyra and one human—and took off running toward us. I waited until they were about ten feet away, then stunned them with a blast of Coercion, freezing them in place while Apollo hit them with a blinding burst of light, turning them immediately to ash.

Footsteps sounded behind us.

"On your six!"

Apollo and I spun at the shouted warning, repeating our process with three more empousa as they bore down on us.

'Where else do you need us?' I froze three more creatures in place, allowing Apollo to take them out as I awaited direction from Ares.

'Deal with them hand-to-hand on your own; Apollo needs to get over to the less-populated islands and wipe out the smaller nests.'

"I'll be quick," Apollo said before teleporting off, leaving me to fend off the rest myself.

Unsheathing the bronze daggers at my waist, I did a quick scan of the minds around me. The three Ischyra on the ground were alive, but unconscious, the human, very near death. A few more Ischyra were on the other side of the building, fighting off a slew of their own.

Another female came at my side, barely giving me time to grab her by the hair and drive a blade through her heart. Shoving her off, I stunned two more behind me, turning and slicing their throats in one quick motion before moving on to the rest.

I'd dispatched another ten before Apollo returned, accompanied by Poseidon.

"Nathaniel." Smirking, he held up his gold trident and blasted through five females who had just emerged from behind the main building. "Are you in need of assistance?"

"A bit." I parried a blow by another female, slicing through her chest and kicking her off in a single motion. "Are the other nests dealt with?"

"Done," Apollo replied.

Without a word, my brother and I got back to work while Poseidon began mowing them down with his trident. The three of us combined our powers smoothly, taking out the remaining empousa quickly.

When we were done, we were surrounded by several dozen small piles of ash and dead bodies.

Poseidon gestured around with his trident. "Someone care to tell me how a single empousa nest turned into half a dozen islands overrun?"

"Excellent question." Apollo flicked a bit of dried blood off his otherwise clean sleeve. "Where's Ares?"

'Southern tip of New Zealand,' Ares said. *'Get over here, now.'*

The three of us teleported to a small auxiliary building that acted as an offshoot of our South Pacific headquarters. Ares and a small group of Ischyra stood out front, faces grim.

"How did this happen?" Poseidon demanded. "You said one nest, Ares."

Ares gave our uncle a weary look as he secured his shield on his back. "Our lead Ischyra reported a single large nest in Tahiti. When I arrived, Tahiti and six other smaller islands were overrun. It appears he was mistaken."

"Where is he?" Apollo demanded.

"Niko?" Ares shrugged. "Gone by the time we arrived."

"Have you sent for a psychometric?" Poseidon asked, sheathing his trident on his back. "See if you can determine his intent?"

"There's one stationed in Japan on her way here now. She's a few hours from the nearest portal field."

Poseidon jerked his chin toward me. "Why not call for Tessa?"

"She's off with Persephone and Demeter dealing with some other things," I told him. "Crop failures in the US and Argentina."

Ares cocked his head to the side, confused. "Last I spoke to her, Athena had called the three of them down to Panama to help handle a nest there."

"They're doing *what?*" Recalling the dagger Persephone had equipped Tessa with, I rounded on Apollo. "Did you know about this?"

"I knew Athena was working on a nest, yes."

"Apollo..."

"I also knew there was a *chance* she would call those three for backup if necessary." He shrugged. "Persephone made sure Tessa was armed with a bronze dagger before going in."

I closed my eyes and counted to three before looking at him again. "And you didn't think that was worth mentioning to anyone else?"

"That three very powerful goddesses might be called to help

another very powerful goddess?" With a small smile, he shook his head. "No, I did not think that was 'worth mentioning.' We had enough to deal with here. Tessa can handle herself, and you didn't need to be distracted."

"Which you would have been," Poseidon said, clapping a hand on my back. "Now we have killed two birds with one stone. The nests have been handled, and Tessa has finally gotten a small taste of physical combat."

Ignoring him, I sent my thoughts toward Athena, but hit nothing but a brick wall.

"She's fine," Ares told me. "They're doing clean up as we speak."

"Then why is she blocking me?"

Apollo quirked a brow. "Do you blame her?"

"Fuck off."

Poseidon chuckled, then tightened the baldric that held his trident, securing it against his chest. "On that note, I have potential allies to court. We'll be meeting at the palace tomorrow to discuss the outcome of today's events." He flicked a glance between me and Apollo. "And I have a feeling there will be other matters to discuss, as well."

Before anyone could ask what he meant, he was gone.

Ares stared at the spot where Poseidon had just stood, then faced us. "What did you two do?"

Apollo held his hands up and shrugged. "I truly don't know what you're talking about."

Ares brow lifted. "Nathaniel?"

"We'll discuss everything tomorrow," was the only answer I gave.

He eyed the two of us shrewdly for another moment before shaking his head. "I'm not sure what's worse; you two bickering, or you two scheming."

"No one's scheming," I muttered.

He made a sound that told me he was unconvinced, then turned to scan the area around us. Several Ischyra were dragging off the bodies of dead empousa to be burned, while a few humans that had been unlucky enough to be in the area were having injuries tended to by healers.

"You should get back to the mountain," Ares said, turning to face us. "They've got it well handled here, and I think you may need to be present when Tessa arrives to ward off the twins." He shook his head. "They're not going to be happy about Athena throwing her to the wolves like that."

"It needed to be done," Apollo said, ignoring my derisive snort.

"Yes, but it doesn't mean they're going to be any less angry, and that type of reaction from them needs to be dealt with and squashed sooner rather than later." Ares lifted a brow in my direction. "She's in this, Nathaniel. Like it or not."

I felt Apollo's eyes on me, awaiting my reaction.

I stared past Ares, where a male Ischyra was getting a broken leg reset by a fellow soldier. "Let's head back."

Ares gave a short nod. "Good. We'll discuss matters further tomorrow morning. Be at the palace at nine."

As I watched my brother walk off, his bloodied shield slung over his shoulder, I tried to temper my emotions as I thought about the danger Athena had put Tessa in. The twins were going to be furious; there was no doubt about that, and I couldn't particularly blame them. Athena had made a call that many would consider foolish or ill-timed.

"Before you turn that angry look into words or actions," Apollo said, "let's see what the outcome of Athena's little experiment was first."

"She could've gotten her killed."

"She's a Ti—"

"Do *not* tell me she's a Titaness, Apollo. If Menoetius had shown up and gotten his hands on her, she'd be as good as dead."

"And if he had, we would have heard about it by now." He waved a hand in frustration. "This is your problem, Nathaniel. You assume the worst when you have no proof of it even coming to pass. Athena is a war goddess; she wouldn't throw someone into a situation unless she knew they could handle it."

"Oh, I'm sorry, have you forgotten the field trip to Scylla's cave?" Sarcasm dripped from my words.

"A teachable moment. Those recruits needed to know what kind of life their friend would be living, and Tessa needed to find a use for herself."

"A teachable—are you kidding me?" I shook my head and laughed. "You know, I don't know why I'm surprised you'd think that."

"It wasn't the wisest of Athena's decisions, I'll grant you, but when it comes to tactical matters, Athena is unmatched. She would not have called Tessa in for assistance if she didn't believe Tessa could provide it."

I gritted my teeth, forcing myself to rein in my concern. Despite Tessa's self-doubt since recalling her old life, she'd been a phenomenal fighter as an Ischyra. I needed to set aside my own fear for her safety and try to accept that she was more than capable of defending herself.

ARRIVING ON MY LAWN, I heard the raised voices of Athena, Tessa, and Prometheus filtering through my front door. I immediately contemplated returning to Polynesia to help the clean-up crew. Based on the grim look on Apollo's face, he likely felt the same.

"...take her into a situation like that without even consulting us!"

"That's enough, Prometheus!" Tessa snapped.

Athena's derisive laugh filled down the steps. "Why on Earth would I consult you? You're not her keeper."

Slowly, Apollo and I trudged up the steps. A pair of gray Converse coated in black sat forlorn outside the front door.

"We could go back," Apollo muttered when he saw Tessa's dirty shoes. "Dealing with dead bodies will likely be more productive than yet another argument about who's in charge of that damn girl."

When we reached the open door, I leaned against the jamb, crossing one ankle over the other and folding my arms, taking in the scene in front of me. Prometheus and Epimetheus stood facing Tessa and Athena, who had their backs to the door. Tessa was barefoot, arms folded across her chest, as Athena stood with her hands on her hips in challenge to Prometheus.

"Prometheus, give her a chance to explain," Epimetheus said quietly. I thought I saw a hint of mirth in his eyes as he looked at his sister.

Tessa threw her hands up and groaned. "*She* doesn't have to explain anything!"

"You could barely walk when she dragged you in here!"

"It was my first battle, Prometheus! I'm more than capable of stabbing a few empousa, in case you haven't figured it out. It just...startled me."

Prometheus glared down at her. "Yes, it's quite obvious just how *capable* you are."

"Oh, like you never got a little messy in battle," she shot back.

Athena patted her back and gave her a tight smile. "It's alright, dear. We'll work on your reaction time. It'll just take some practice, that's all."

"Just look at her, Prometheus," Epimetheus said, his eyes now clearly full of laughter. "Clearly she can handle herself."

Jaw clenching, Prometheus closed his eyes, opening them after a few seconds with a slightly calmer expression. He stared down at Tessa, and one corner of his mouth quirked up.

"See?" She held her hands out, palms up. "Still in one piece."

Prometheus' eyes drifted over Tessa's shoulder to where we stood, and I thought I saw relief flash across his face. "Thank the gods. Maybe *you* can talk some sense into her."

Before I could respond, Tessa turned to face us, and I heard Apollo choke back a laugh. I bit the inside of my cheek to keep from letting out one of my own.

She was covered from head to foot with black, oily blood. It was streaked through her hair, splattered across her legs, torso, and face, and coated her arms nearly to her elbows. Smears of what looked like her own blood were on her forehead and the back of her left hand,

and there were a few cuts on her neck that looked suspiciously like attempted bites. Persephone's bronze dagger still dangled at her hip, the sheath smudged with a single, black handprint.

Narrowing her eyes, she shot a finger at me.

"If you even think about laughing, I will punch you in the face."

30

TESSA

"Did you even *try* to avoid arterial spray? At all?" Apollo wrinkled his nose as he stood in the doorway, looking me up and down. "And why do you look like you've been rolling in the dirt?" He turned to Nate with a look of disgust. "Nathaniel, why are you even allowing her in your home?"

Nate's lips quirked, but he didn't respond.

"Be nice, Apollo," Athena chastised. "She did wonderfully."

I was pretty sure she meant to be comforting, but the way her lips were trembling as she took in my appearance kind of made me want to hit her.

Looking over at the twins, I scowled when I saw Epimetheus trying—and failing—to cover his laughter. Prometheus' furious expression from moments before was slowly sliding into amusement.

"What the—can you please not make fun of me? This isn't exactly old-hat, you know. No one ever taught me how to 'avoid arterial spray' before. *Or* take on a bunch of empousa on my own, but you know, whatever."

Apollo gave me a disbelieving look. "You're a Titaness, Tessa. Your speed is all you need to get out of the way. Of anything."

"You're right," Nate said, forcing back a grin. "We shouldn't laugh. It's just—"

"Just *what*, Nathaniel?" I put my hands on my hips and gave him a challenging look, knowing my appearance likely made it fall flat.

"You look like something Charybdis regurgitated," Apollo said with a grimace.

Nate snorted, then clapped a hand over his mouth when I glared at him.

I shifted pleading eyes at my brothers, but they weren't even trying to contain their amusement anymore.

"You all suck," I snapped before storming off toward the bedroom to shower.

As I passed the spare room, the door opened and Atlas stepped out.

"Atlas!" I stepped toward him, then stopped, remembering my current state of grossness.

"Tessa, I thought I heard—" He blinked down at me, then his eyes widened. "Is that blood?"

I cringed, realizing how bad I must look. After our conversation earlier, this was probably the last thing he needed to see. "Um...yes."

His face flushed, then he stared at a spot over my shoulder. When he spoke, I could tell he was struggling to keep his tone measured.

"Why are you covered in blood, Tessa?"

"Um...Because killing empousa is a dirty job?"

His nostrils flared. "Emp—Prometheus!"

Wincing at his bellow, I held up a hand. "It's really not—"

"What's wrong?" Prometheus came to a halt beside us, followed by the others.

Atlas pointed a finger at me and spoke through gritted teeth. "Why was she fighting empousa?"

"Uh oh," Athena muttered. Grabbing Apollo and Nate's arms, she dragged them both back out to the living room, muttering something about family business and leaving me to deal with my brothers alone.

Prometheus raked a hand through his hair. "Try not to overreact, Atlas. She went with Persephone and Demeter—"

"I went with Persephone and Demeter to heal some farmland," I interrupted, needing to speak for myself. "When we were done, Athena called us for backup on an empousa nest and because she got a potential lead on Menoetius down in Panama."

"You went after him *alone.*" Atlas turned his glare on the twins. "You *let* her go after him alone?"

"I didn't go after him alone," I said before either of the twins could respond. "I went to get a read on an area where he *may* have been with three other very powerful goddesses."

"And a nest of empousa, apparently."

"Which we dealt with."

A muscle in his jaw twitched as a number of emotions flickered across his face. I bit back a smile when interest won out.

"How many did you kill?"

"Six. I think."

"By yourself?"

"By myself."

Shaking his head, he shifted his gaze to the twins.

"I don't care for it any more than you, brother," Epimetheus said, arms folded across his chest.

Biting my lip, I looked to Prometheus. His eyes flicked down to me, then to my twin.

"Athena showed me the memory." He gave me a disapproving look. "And although I wish she hadn't done it without at least checking in with us first..." He trailed off, then sighed before finishing. "You would have been proud."

Jaw tight, Atlas appraised my current state, taking in the blood spattered across me from head to toe.

"Alright, then. Let me see the memory."

"Let Prometheus show you. I need to get all this goo off of me before I start to stink, and I'm sure Athena's viewpoint is more entertaining than mine," I added, rolling my eyes.

He raised one brow, then the other. "Goo?"

Epimetheus clapped a hand to his shoulder. "She spent eighteen years as a twenty-first century human, Atlas. Get used to it," he said, then turned and walked back out to the living room.

I stood on my toes and kissed Atlas' cheek, trying to avoid getting blood on him. "I know it's hard, coming back and finding out so much has changed. I get it. I just need you—" I looked to Prometheus, then back at my twin "—*all* of you, to trust me."

Atlas' mouth curved into a sad smile, then he pulled me into a hug.

"I love you, Tessa," he murmured. "And I will do my best. Just give me a bit of time, alright?"

"That's—sure, but, um...I'm getting empousa blood all over your shirt," I mumbled into his chest.

He stiffened, then placed his hands on my shoulders and nudged me back, wincing as he looked down as his now-filthy shirt.

Smirking, I patted his cheek. "And I love you, too. Now, go change. I'll be out in a bit."

He gave me a tight smile, then turned and walked back into the guest room.

"I think he handled that well," Prometheus commented once Atlas had shut the door.

"I suppose." I pulled the tie out of my hair and started undoing my braid. "I guess we'll see how things go from here."

He reached up to ruffle my hair, then thought better of it and patted a mostly blood-free spot on my shoulder, instead.

"Go get washed. If you want, we can work on your speed at some point so you can learn how to avoid getting quite so messy next time."

"Really?" I bounced a little on my toes, excited at the thought of training with the one brother who'd refused to join Atlas and Epimetheus in training me when I was younger. "You'd help me?"

"Yes, I'll help you." He held up a finger before I could thank him. "On one condition."

"What's that?"

"Just...tell us if you're planning on diving into a situation like that again."

I held my hands up and started backing down the hall. "Hey, I just thought I was going out to fix some corn."

He snorted. "Alright. Go get cleaned up."

When I got into the bathroom, I stripped out of my clothes and shoved them all in the trash can under the sink, fully intending to burn them as soon as possible. I turned the water on as hot as I could stand and stepped under the spray. After scrubbing the crusted blood from my skin and hair, using almost half the bottle of shampoo, I finally felt as though all traces of grime had been removed.

I'd just finished wrapping a towel around myself when there was a knock at the door.

"Who is it?"

"It's me," Nate said. "Can I come in?"

"Yep." I secured the towel around my chest, then grabbed a brush and started dragging it through my hair.

He shut the door behind him, and I smirked when his eyes roved up and down my towel-clad body before he came up behind me and wrapped his arms around my waist.

I narrowed my eyes at his puppy-dog expression. "Can I help you?"

"I'm sorry I laughed at you."

"Uh huh." I continued wrestling with the tangles in my hair, refusing to look at him. "I'll remember that next time you're the one covered in demon blood."

"I'm sure you will." He kissed my bare shoulder, dragging his lips along the skin toward my neck. "I really am sorry I laughed. You just looked so...disheveled. It was unexpected."

Closing my eyes, I tilted my head to the side as his mouth traveled up toward my ear. "And here I thought you'd be mad at me for going down there to help."

Tightening his arms around my waist, he met my gaze in the mirror. "I was, at first, but more with Athena, to be honest, even though I know that's not fair. But...I told you I would stick by you when it comes to things like this. I might not like the thought of you fighting those things, and that's not likely to change, but I promise to have your back when I can."

Turning to face him, I smiled as I adjusted my towel. "And I appreciate that more than you know. Now, kiss me and go, because I need to get dressed."

His lips slowly curved upward as heat filled his eyes. Trailing his fingers down my arms, he brought my hands up to link behind his neck and brushed his lips against mine. Pressing a hand to my waist, he pulled me closer, eliminating the space between us.

Sliding my fingers through his hair, I deepened the kiss.

In one smooth motion, he'd lifted me up and set me on the counter, then caught me in a deep, searing kiss, silencing the surprised yelp that had bubbled out of me.

Heat shot through me, mixing with the remaining adrenaline of my fight with the empousa, so I wrapped my legs around his waist and pulled him against me. With a quiet groan, he braced a hand on the wall behind me, running the other up my leg, his strong fingers digging into my hip as I tightened my hold on him.

I'd just gotten to the button on his jeans when his entire body stilled.

"Tessa, wait," he whispered, his breathing ragged.

Frowning, I leaned back and looked into his eyes, still raw with lust. "What's wrong?"

He closed his eyes and rested his forehead against mine. "Your brothers...are barely twenty feet away."

I let out a shaky breath. "Oh."

I put my hands on his chest as he slowly eased himself back, and I readjusted my towel. "I'd definitely say it's time to go, then."

The corner of his mouth tugged up in a smile as he buckled his belt. "I think you're right." Caging my body between his arms, he brushed a chaste kiss across my cheek and another on the tip of my nose, belying his assertiveness from just a few moments before. "Besides, Epimetheus went down to get your friends. Considering the day we've had, I have a feeling things are going to be crazy from here on out, so we thought you might like a night to spend with them."

"That sounds amazing, thank you."

Once he'd gone, I put the lid to the toilet down and I sat, letting my shaking legs finally give out.

"There are bigger things than sex to worry about, Tessa," I muttered, then snorted as Mary's words from the other day came back to me.

"You could be dead tomorrow. Do you really want to die not knowing what it's like to have sex with him?"

Bigger things to worry about or not, the answer was a resounding *no.*

31

TESSA

Wrinkling my nose, I stared into the dresser drawers Nate had designated for me. Now that I was no longer required to wear the Ischyra training uniform six days a week, I was going to need more regular clothes. I considered grabbing Mary and Yana to hit the shops in Olympia soon, but the thought of shopping didn't excite me nearly as much as it would have a few months ago.

I finally settled on black leggings and a thigh-length navy sweater, and I'd just finished twisting my hair into a high bun when I heard Eric's voice through the door.

"You decent, Tess?"

"Yeah, come in!"

He came in, followed by Mary and Yana, then grinned as they sat down on the bed. "So...I hear you killed some monsters," he said.

My eyes darted back and forth between them, then I groaned when I saw Yana smirk and Mary arch a brow.

"Go on, get it over with," I said, gesturing with my hands for them to continue.

"Did you know that gods can share memories with each other?" Yana's wide blue eyes twinkled. "And with Ischyra."

"Epimetheus showed us what you looked like when you got home," Mary told me with a self-satisfied look. "Eric and I agreed that you've now officially been paid back for taking us to Scylla's."

"My soon-to-be-least-favorite brother will be getting an earful from me shortly, don't you worry."

"Oh, don't be mad," Mary said, smiling. "It's all in good fun."

"At my expense," I muttered.

"Do not worry," Yana said, stretching out on the bed and shrugging a shoulder. "I am sure it could happen to any of us."

"Doubtful," Mary said. "We've been working on our speed since day one, remember?"

Eric shot her a silencing look that made me smile.

"Don't be mad at him, Tess," Mary said. "He was so miserable before; now he actually seems...well, not miserable, I guess. If that's at your expense, well, then, whatever. You killed the bad guys. If laughing at what you looked like afterward keeps him from getting angry about what you did, so be it."

"I guess." I smiled as I recalled what it had been like growing up with a Trickster god for a brother. "It shouldn't really be that surprising. He thinks it's funny when I get embarrassed about things like this."

"Really?" Yana wrinkled her nose. "I cannot see that in him."

"He tempers it with his sensitivity." I smiled wryly. "Prometheus used to get so angry when we were younger. Epimetheus was always playing tricks on him."

Yana gave me a curious look. "But not on you?"

"I was usually helping him."

"Totally not surprising," Eric muttered.

"Yeah. Prometheus and Atlas were always wound so tight. Epimetheus took it upon himself to provide a little levity, and I just liked needling them from time to time." A smile flickered across my lips at the memories. "It's nice, seeing him smile more."

"It seems like you guys are doing well," Eric said, his voice cautious. "Are you okay...since getting your memories back?"

I climbed on the bed next to them and sat with my legs folded under me. "I am. I was angry when I first remembered everything, especially with Hades for forcing my memories on me, but once I calmed down, I could acknowledge that he was right, at least in that I needed to just get it over with. I still want to maim him for how he handled it, but that's par for the course with him."

Eric shook his head. "I still can't believe you and he..."

I stared down at my hands and picked at my fingernail. "It was a different time back then. We were all different. Now, it's just a matter of adapting, I guess."

"And how are you adapting?" Yana asked carefully.

I shrugged. "Today helped. Going to Athens, healing those crops with Persephone and Demeter...doing something that didn't involve fighting and destroying things—that helped. I've gotten so used to others looking at my powers as a weapon over the years that I kind of forgot what else I can do."

Eric's face twisted into a perplexed expression. "Um...am I the only one who finds it ironic that the queen of the dead was the one to show you that?"

Mary snorted, then hit his chest with the back of her hand. "Idiot."

Yana gave me a sympathetic smile. "Well, it is good that you were able to do that, even if your day still ended with killing things."

"Yeah." I forced my hands to stop their idle movements. "I think I needed that, too. Not the killing, necessarily, but the knowledge that I can actually do the things I was trained for. Not just as a goddess, but as an Ischyra, too."

"Well, good," Mary said, patting my knee. "I'm happy to hear things are looking up. Now, come on. I think I heard Dionysus say something about wine."

"Of course he did," I said with a laugh. I slid my feet into a pair of sandals, then we made our way out to the living room, where I found Atlas and Prometheus seated on the sofa, talking quietly.

Mary, Yana, and Eric stopped in their tracks, uncertainty painting their features, and I looked at my twin, trying to see what they saw.

Despite how much he and I looked alike, he wasn't like me, or even like the twins. My friends had known me as an Ischyra, and while Prometheus and Epimetheus were new to them, they were, if nothing else, personable—at least to some extent. They had the validation of Nate, Apollo, Athena, and the rest of the Elders as deities who were our allies, skilled warriors who could help train our soldiers.

Atlas was a Titan who'd once fought for the wrong side. A deity who'd been imprisoned, freed, then locked himself away for centuries, only to become a prisoner once again when he tried to leave. He was a god who'd lived in solitude for millennia, had been recently possessed by a demon, and was suddenly thrust into a world full of sounds, color, and life.

He didn't have Prometheus' desire to protect or Epimetheus' need for love or my need to just...*be*. He was the personification of strength, both in body and presence. Nothing about him was soft, and one look at his hard, set jaw and furrowed brow made that abundantly clear.

To me, he was my other half. To my friends, I would imagine just the thought of sharing a room with him would be terrifying.

"I'll meet you outside, okay?" I gave my friends a quick smile. "I just need a few minutes."

"Of course." Yana gave my hand a quick squeeze, then the three of them filed through the front door.

I watched Atlas track them to the door with his eyes, continuing to stare after it closed. Prometheus sat quietly, assessing our brother to see how he would react to this other change in circumstances.

His eyes drifted to me. "You said they're called Ischyra?"

Gently, I sat down next to him on the sofa. "Yes. The Elders' response to tricking Epimetheus into taking Pandora."

"Human children gifted with power so they can remedy the mistakes the gods made?"

I exchanged a look with Prometheus before responding. "Essentially...yes."

Atlas tapped a finger on the arm of the sofa, and a small muscle in his jaw ticked as he stared into the fire someone had lit in the hearth. "And you're friends with them?"

"I *was* them." I slid closer and touched his hand. "I was reborn as a human, so I was raised with them, I came to Olympus with them, trained with them."

He nodded his head slowly, his eyes darting to the window when I heard Mary let out a bawdy laugh.

"They're comfortable in such close proximity with the gods," he observed. "Why?"

I smiled wryly. "Not all of the gods. Dionysus probably just said something stupid."

"There are four Titans and five gods here, three of whom are Elders. They're lesser beings yet behave as though they're equal."

"Atlas..." Prometheus warned.

My twin's gaze shot to his. "Am I wrong?

"Yes, you are," I said quietly. Annoyance flicked across his face, so I pushed forward. "A lot has changed, Atlas, for both of us."

His eyes, full of questions, searched my face. After a moment, his body relaxed, but a look of melancholy took hold. "I don't know what I see when I look at you, Tessa."

"What do you mean?"

"You're not...the sister I had."

I forced back the lump that formed in my throat, the sadness that acknowledged the truth in his words, then slid my hand into his. When he brought his eyes to mine, I smiled. "No, I'm not. That girl died in a clearing in the woods three thousand years ago. And you need to learn to live with that."

The corner of his mouth lifted in a slight smile, and he brushed his thumb against my knuckles. "I will. Now, go spend some time with your...friends." I nearly laughed at the perplexed expression as he said it. "I hear tomorrow is going to be a big day."

Frowning, I looked to Prometheus. "It is?"

"It is." He gave me a stiff smile. "We're meeting with Zeus and the others in the morning to discuss how we're going to move forward. We'll also be informing him of Atlas' return."

"So soon?"

"We can't wait around forever," Atlas said. "This war seems to be starting, whether we're ready or not." He clenched his jaw before continuing. "Zeus deserves to know who is living on his mountain."

"Uh huh." I gave him a dubious look. "And are you alright with seeing him...seeing Zeus?"

"I'll have to be, won't I?" He jerked his chin toward the door. "Go on."

"Are you sure? It's not too noisy?"

He smiled softly. "I've been in silence for eons. I thought the noise would bother me, but instead, I feel as though I'm truly back among the living. So, enjoy your friends. It pleases me to see you happy."

"You could come out there with us, you know." I gave him a hopeful smile. "You might like my friends, you never know."

"One step at a time, dear sister. One step at a time."

After about an hour and at my friends' insistence, I found myself on the lawn with Eric, Yana, and Mary, practicing my elemental work. Nate and Mary had both been right; taking some time to train with them was doing me a world of good.

"Okay, Tess, again," Eric instructed as he ignited the tips of his fingers. "And try not to splash me this time."

Narrowing my eyes on the tiny flames, I proceeded to snuff each one out, alternating between tiny bursts of wind and small streams of water.

Eric wiped his face with the back of his hand, removing the spray from the water I'd tried to aim directly at his hands. "That was... better."

"It's just like what Charlise told you," Mary explained. "It's just another sense."

"A wobbly, unwieldy sense," I grumbled, taking a sip of my wine and setting it back on the grass. "Mentalist stuff is much easier."

"Remember your emotions, Tessa!" Chiron called down. He was sitting on the porch with Nate, Athena, Hermes, the twins, and

Apollo, catching up for the first time in nearly two weeks. Every so often, he'd shout down some bit of encouragement or advice.

"Yeah, yeah," I muttered.

"It's not unwieldy, Tessa," Mary said impatiently. "You just need to —god *damn* it!" Mary jumped as Dionysus appeared on the lawn beside her.

"Hey there, water girl."

Shaking off her shock, Mary ignored him and continued to focus on me. "Pretend the water is another tool. It's no different than fire in that sense."

Dionysus nudged her leg with his foot.

I pursed my lips as Mary continued to avoid looking at him, the annoyed expression on his face comical.

"For example." She held out her hand and gestured for me to do the same. "Form a ball of water. Just a plain old ball, nothing fancy."

When I'd complied, she nodded. "Now, picture it rearranging itself, just like you did when you made ice. Make it form a line instead of a circle. You have to hold it together while also breaking it apart, if that makes sense."

The ball of water that undulated in her palm slowly began to unravel until it was a long, thin rope.

I did the same, taking a few seconds longer than she did to get the right shape. "Now what?"

Her eyes slid to the side, where Dionysus was poking her arm, then she took a deep breath. "Now, you send it where you want it to go." With a flick of her wrist, the water rope turned into a whip, and with a *snick*, one end had bound Dionysus' wrists together, while the other end was poised next to his cheek.

His mouth popped open in shock.

Tilting her head to the side, she smiled sweetly. "Was there something you needed?"

I clapped my hands over my mouth, barely holding back my laughter at his stunned expression.

Narrowing his eyes, he broke through the water in a smooth

motion, then pointed a finger at her. "I think you just declared war, water girl."

"I think I'll put my money on the recruit." Epimetheus dropped down on the ground beside me, resting his elbows on his knees, then grinned at Dionysus. "She's clever. You didn't even see that coming."

"*I'm* clever," Dionysus argued. "And I absolutely saw it coming."

I lifted a brow. "Would you like me to show you the look of shock on your face that speaks to the contrary?"

Mary held up her hands in an apologetic gesture. "I'm sorry, Dionysus. It will never happen again, I promise."

"Damn right it won't," he said. "Because I'll—"

Biting my lip, I formed a basketball-sized ball of water and dropped it on his head.

Someone barked out a laugh on the porch.

"You asked for that, Dionysus!" Athena called down.

Apollo muttered something about idiotic children, so I sent a gust of wind his way, ruffling his perfect white-blond hair. He shot me a glare, which I returned with a sunny smile.

"Tessa, you've officially become my least favorite of Nathaniel's girlfriends," Dionysus said, wiping water from his eyes and flicking it in my direction.

'He's never liked my girlfriends, so don't take offense.'

'And why is that?'

'According to him, they're never fun enough.'

I smirked, somehow not surprised by that. *'Come sit with us.'*

A second later, I felt Nate sit down behind me, so I leaned back until his arms were around my waist.

"Nathaniel, can you please tell *Tessa*—" Dionysus shot me a playful glare "—to control herself? And her *friends?*"

"Tessa, love?" Nate murmured as he rested his chin on my shoulder.

"Hmm?"

"Go for wind next time. He hates having his hair messed up."

Dionysus narrowed his eyes at me. "Don't you dare."

I help up my hands and smiled. "Wouldn't dream of it."

Letting my hands fall back to Nate's, I looked at Yana. "Electricity?"

"Of course." She pulled herself into a sitting position from where she'd been laying on the grass. "What would you like to learn?"

I shrugged. "No clue. I know how to zap things, and when I used Zeus' lightning, I just kind of...threw it out. I was able to aim yours pretty well, though."

"How well are you able to control it?" she asked.

Pursing my lips, I held out my hands and let my electrokinesis flow, letting green sparks coat my hands like crackling gloves, then I shot a few sparks at the ground.

Nodding, she smiled. "That is good!" She opened her hands and did the same, her electricity slightly quieter than mine.

"How do you make it so quiet?"

She shrugged. "Practice. It is good, though, because it allows you to sneak up on someone and—" Without warning, she clamped a hand on Eric's shoulder, causing him to jump to his feet. "—Zap them."

"What the fuck, Yana!" Eric swatted at his shoulder, where the fabric of his shirt still smoked. "I like this shirt!"

I snickered, earning myself a look from Eric as he rotated his shoulder to ease out the sting of Yana's power.

"I don't think I like your friends anymore," Dionysus commented, looking between Yana and Mary. "They're far more evil than I expected."

Epimetheus raised his eyebrows in question. "As an Elder, shouldn't you be the one instilling fear?"

Nate's forehead came to rest on the back of my head, and I felt his shoulders shake with laughter.

"He's right!" Hermes yelled from the porch. "You're a disgrace to your position!"

"Nobody asked you, you dick!" Dionysus shot back. He turned his eyes to Nathaniel. "You're more than welcome to take over, you know. I'll gladly step aside. I'm sure Apollo would *love* that."

Nate barked out a laugh. "Not a chance. Politics and bureaucracy are for my older siblings."

Leaning back against his chest, I patted his cheek. "And you're just content to be the baby, aren't you?" I crooned.

"Watch it," he murmured, nipping my ear. "I know where you sleep."

I smiled in contentment as my friends continued to banter, setting aside all desire to train any further. Instead, I rested against Nate's chest and watched as the sky continued to darken, as the lights of the upper half of the mountain—the gods' homes—began to wink on and stars began to dot the sky.

It felt like it had been ages since I'd looked at the night sky, truly taken it in. I'd gone stargazing with John and Analise so frequently growing up that I'd begun to take it for granted, assumed it would always be a part of my life. The last time I really got to see it was when Nate brought me to the summit of Olympus, back when we'd only just started to get to know each other. Something had shifted that night, as we laid together in the wooden shelter, buried beneath heavy, wool blankets to block out the blustery wind. We'd stayed there and talked for hours as I snuggled against his chest while he stroked his fingers through my hair, enjoying what seemed like the most peaceful spot in all the realms.

Letting my eyes scan what parts of the horizon I could see, they landed on the giant, K-shaped constellation that my guardians and I had made our common point. Taurus.

My eyes drifted toward the lower right end of the constellation, where they always went when I sought it out. The small blur of stars was barely visible to the naked human eye, but to my Titaness eyes, the seven Pleiades were crystal clear.

I blinked as a memory popped into my head, one from my childhood as an Ischyra, that had gotten buried under the years of more significant memories since.

. . .

I BOUNCED *on my toes as John fiddled with the controls on his telescope, a giant green device that stood nearly four feet tall, a good six inches above my head. My fingers were growing cold, so I curled my small hands around the cup of hot chocolate Analise had just poured.*

"What are the coordinates, again?" John asked.

Analise rattled off some numbers that I didn't understand, and John punched a few buttons.

"There." He put his hands on his hips and looked down at me. "You ready, kiddo?"

I nodded eagerly, shoving my cup into Analise's outstretched hand. John hooked his hands under my arms and lifted me onto the bumper of his Jeep.

"Look right through there." He pointed at a black eyepiece that stuck out of the side. "Tell me what you see."

I did as he instructed, standing on the bumper and squinting as I tried to see what he was showing me. Pulling back, I frowned at him. "Some white spots. And a blob."

He chuckled, then pulled out his beat up copy of Petersen's Field Guide to Astronomy. *Flipping toward the dark blue pages that showed the different constellations, he pointed to a spot on one of them.*

"The Pleiades," he said. "Also called The Seven Sisters." He pointed up at the sky, his index finger outlining a giant group of stars. "They're a tiny part of that bigger constellation up there. It's called Taurus. The Bull."

"It doesn't look like a bull," I observed. I looked back into the telescope, then back down at the page. "Are there horns?"

Gesturing to two spots in the sky, he nodded. "Just there. Elnath and Zeta Tauri."

"Huh." I looked back though the eyepiece, trying to get a better glimpse of the Pleiades. "How do you know there are seven sisters?"

He smiled and ruffled my hair. "Because astronomers with far better telescopes than ours have seen them."

Squinting, I looked again. "Do they have names?"

"They do. Would you like to hear them?" When I nodded, he sat down next to me and pointed each one out in the book. "Sterope, Merope, Electra, Maia, Taygete, Alcyone, and Celaeno."

"Those are weird names," I commented, wrinkling my nose. "I'm glad you didn't give me one like that."

He chuckled, and Analise ran a hand across my hair.

"They're very old names, sweetheart," she explained. "Weird to you, but everyone's name has a meaning to the people who named them."

"Who gave them their names?"

"A goddess named Pleione was their mother. She watched over the seas, and it was her job to protect sailors." John tapped a spot on the page. "She's right there, beside them. A binary star."

"What's that?"

"It means she was so special she got two stars."

I was quiet for a moment as I stared up at the sky again, tilting and turning my head this way and that so I could see the sisters without the telescope. I took the book from John's hands and examined the picture again.

"There are lots of little stars there, too. Do they all have names?"

"No," he said, smiling. "Most just have numbers."

"That's not very fun," I said, frowning. Biting my lip, I traced my finger over the page. "Can I name one Tessa? I want one of my own."

There was a beat of silence before Analise responded. "Of course, sweetheart. You can have as many as you'd like."

After some deliberation, I pointed to one that sat on the outer edge of the constellation. "There. I want that one."

"That one looks perfect." Analise pulled a permanent marker from her bag and wrote my name in tiny, perfect letters right next to the little star I'd chosen for myself. I tried not to be shocked that she'd just written in a book. With marker.

Instead, I smiled and rested my head on her shoulder. Deep down, I knew naming a star for myself didn't mean anything; no one would recognize it aside from us three. Still, though, it felt special, almost like a secret.

"So...who was their dad? The Sisters?"

There was another second of silence before John spoke.

"Their father was one of the strongest Titans who ever lived," he whispered. "His name was Atlas."

"Does he have a star, too?"

John smiled and kissed the side of my head. "He's got three, actually, just there beside his daughters. Would you like me to show you?"

"Yes, please."

JOHN AND ANALISE had always directed me to that one spot in the sky —that one group of stars that promised to offer comfort when I was separated from my guardians. Our common point—the promise of home, of unconditional love, and of people who would always be there, looking out for me, no matter what or who I was.

Because they'd known. They'd known exactly what it would mean to me, placing myself in the stars beside my twin. Before I'd even made it to second grade, they'd made sure my twin and I were always by each other's sides.

I don't know how long I'd been crying when I felt thick, strong arms lift me up, and I was pulled into someone's lap. Another hand, more gentle, pressed against my back.

"It's alright, Tessa. I'm here."

Burying my face in my twin's chest, I let out a keening sob that shook through my entire body as tears ran down my face in torrents. Letting me cry into his shirt, he whispered comforting words as he rocked me back and forth.

I cried for him, for the life he'd lost, for the grief and guilt he'd endured alone while our brother tormented him. I cried for our brothers who'd lived an eternity trying to right the wrongs of others. For Epimetheus, who'd spent three thousand years buried under a mountain of regret and guilt after losing the first woman to offer him love, and for Prometheus, the god who'd done all he could to protect his family, only to feel as though he failed in the end.

I cried for myself, mourning the life I'd missed out on—the three thousand years that had been taken from me in the blink of an eye. Years with my family, with myself, and with the world, that I would never get back.

And I cried for Clymene, the mother I'd never had a chance to properly grieve. Her death, her *sacrifice*, hit me with the force of a freight train, the realization that I hadn't yet cried for her, bearing painfully down on me. Another choking sob tore from my chest.

I hadn't been able to watch her body burn on a pyre, holding the comforting hands of my brothers because I had been right there, burning with her.

Atlas' arms tightened around me, and I clung to him as his own shoulders shook with tears. I felt Prometheus rest his head on my shoulder as Epimetheus squeezed my hand.

And in that moment, for the first time since I'd gotten my memories back, as the four of us cried on Nate's lawn together, I allowed myself a small sliver of hope that my brothers and I might be able to be a family again.

32

NATHANIEL

I'd seen Tessa upset before. I'd watched her buckle in pain, watched her cry tears of anger and fear.

The grief—the devastation—that tore through her as she slowly broke down into inconsolable agony had a lump forming in my throat, anger building inside of me for everything that had been taken from her, everything she was now struggling to get back, and everything she never would. Watching as her twin rocked her like a child, seeing his own grief clear in his expression, further sparked the fury I felt.

I grunted a goodbye to the recruits before Dionysus took them home, then stormed into the house, slamming the door so hard the windows rattled. Ignoring whoever had been stupid enough to follow me in, I pulled a bottle of brandy from the liquor cabinet and poured myself two fingers' worth.

"Nathaniel."

I gritted my teeth when I heard Apollo's voice behind me, then tossed back the contents of my glass in one swallow and poured another.

"Get out."

"Slamming doors isn't going to help anyone."

I slammed the glass down then rounded on him, furious. "Do you know what would've helped?" I pointed toward the front lawn where Tessa and her brothers still sat. "Preventing that! There should not be three fucking Titans sitting on my front lawn consoling their sister because her soul was ripped from her body and shoved in the fucking Void for three thousand years!"

"What exactly is it you think I should've done?" He cocked his head to the side in question, his pale eyes curious, his tone infuriatingly even. "I wasn't there when Hecate cast her spell. So what would you have had me do?"

When I didn't answer immediately, he shook his head, then jerked the bottle from my hand and poured himself a glass. "This was not my doing, Nathaniel. Hestia and I helped keep Tessa protected once she was reborn, ensured things were on track to return her memories once she reached Olympia, but that's it. It's unfair of you to hold this whole ordeal over my head."

"Then send Hecate down, because I've got plenty of blame to toss at her," I snapped.

"Can you put aside your irritation for one damn minute and consider *why* Hecate did this?"

"She did it to protect the realms. And do *not* try to spin me any bullshit about doing it to protect Tessa," I added when he opened his mouth to speak. "We both know damn well that wasn't the case, regardless of what Clymene wanted."

His jaw snapped shut, then he exhaled a slow breath before speaking.

"Fine," he said quietly. "I suppose it's also worthless to try to convince you to view things objectively, because I know exactly how far I'll get with that request."

"Look out there, Apollo! She's fucking breaking!" *I* was breaking. "How in all the realms do you expect me to look at this objectively?"

"By acting like a god for one damn minute! It is possible to be angry for Tessa and her brothers while acknowledging the logic behind Hecate's actions!"

"The logic? That day in the clearing, instead of *killing her*, did

Hecate even consider just fighting for her? Helping her and Atlas take on Cronus and Iapetus?"

"The Tessa of the past was half the fighter she is now," he hissed. "Weak in almost every sense of the word. She very likely would have been a hindrance."

"So now you're insulting her? Is it ever possible for you to *not* be a dick?"

"Spew whatever insults you want, but it's the truth. If you think she's got issues with self-doubt today, how do you think it was back then, when she was told daily that she couldn't do the things she can do now? When the best teacher she could find spent most days emotionally abusing her in order to make her stronger? Do you think that made her someone who could or would kill her own father? Her ruler?" He tossed back his brandy, then set the glass down on the cabinet with a thud. "The years she spent as a human were a small point in time for an immortal, but during that time, she was surrounded by people who pushed her, taught her to believe in herself, her abilities. A true support system. The only reason she questions herself as much as she does today is because she was denied the chance to be a true goddess in the past."

"Did Hecate consider the emotional damage her stunt would do to Tessa? Even once?"

"Her 'stunt' likely saved a lot of lives, Nathaniel."

Raising my eyebrows, I inclined my head toward the door. "Do you want to go tell Tessa that? Tell her she shouldn't be upset because her death saved lives?" I picked up my glass and leaned against the cabinet. "You don't understand what's killing her right now, do you?"

He clenched his jaw but didn't answer.

"She never got to mourn her mother, Apollo. Clymene died right in front of her, and she never got to mourn her until now." Shaking my head, I took down the rest of my drink and set the glass down. "On top of everything else, she's faced with that."

"She seems to be doing just fine making a life for herself here," he said quietly, folding his arms across his chest. "You've seen to that."

"But not without you trying to warn me away first."

He let out an annoyed huff. "I will admit that I might have been wrong in that approach. I thought you would be a distraction, but it appears you've been much the opposite."

The way his face took on a pinched expression at his admission nearly had me laughing. "Did you just admit you were wrong about something, Apollo?"

His lips twitched, but he pushed back whatever emotion he almost let through and sighed. "Don't get used to it. It happens quite rarely."

"What, you admitting you're wrong?"

"No. Me actually *being* wrong." He glanced toward the window beside the front door, his jaw set in a hard line. "I'm going home for the night. I'll be back in the morning and we can discuss the best course of action regarding Father. I don't see any point in trying to hash that out tonight."

Following his gaze, I nodded.

Without bothering with any farewell, he vanished.

Sitting down on the sofa, I settled in to wait.

TESSA HAD BEEN on the lawn with her brothers for over an hour, and by the time Atlas handed her off to me before bed, she'd fallen asleep, her tear-streaked face finally peaceful. Her brothers had looked defeated as they said their goodnights, the twins back to the palace, Atlas to the spare room. I lay awake for what felt like hours, trying to figure out something, anything, I could do for her, for them.

By the time she woke, she'd looked herself again, with the exception of the sadness that still seemed to linger in her eyes. She was quiet as she brushed her teeth, a pensive look on her face that I wasn't quite sure what to make of.

"I think we should get the news of Atlas out of the way first," Apollo said now as we waited in the living room for Tessa to finish getting dressed.

"You don't think that might derail the more important discussions we need to have today?"

He waved off my concern. "I'm his second, he trusts me to make decisions in his stead. He may not like that we brought Atlas back without consulting him first, but he's been trying to get him back for some time. Just because we didn't follow his lead doesn't mean the outcome isn't the same."

"Are you discussing me?"

Apollo and I both jerked our heads toward where Atlas had appeared. He dropped down on the sofa across from me and raised his brows.

"We are," Apollo replied. "We're just trying to figure out the best way to inform Zeus of your return."

"Why not just bring me with you when you go?"

"We think it might be best if Apollo heads up first so he and the twins can speak with our father first," I explained. "Tessa and I will bring you up once they're done."

He nodded slowly, his expression thoughtful for a moment before he looked back at me. "Who else will be at this meeting?"

"Hades and Poseidon, along with a few others," I replied.

"Likely the rest of the Elders," Apollo added.

Atlas leaned forward and rested his forearms on his thighs, then tapped his thumbs together. "I'm going to be very clear with you both. This is not likely to be a terribly civil reunion."

Apollo got to his feet. "Which is why I'll be going first, to help soften the blow."

"We're hoping the need to discuss other aspects of the coming war will be his main priority," I added.

"Alright." Atlas nodded at Apollo. "We'll await your word, then."

Once Apollo had left, Atlas eyed me, and I realized this was the first time he and I had been alone together. An irrational, or perhaps, rational, considering the circumstances, unease came over me at his appraisal.

"You're Zeus' son."

"I am."

"And your mother?"

"Hera."

He gave me a curious look. "You're a child of the Olympic rulers, yet you aren't on the Elders Council."

I smiled tightly. "That wasn't ever something I wanted."

"I see." He narrowed his eyes and assessed me again. "Are you good to my sister?"

"I'd like to think so."

"He's wonderful to your sister," Tessa said, coming in and kissing his head before sitting down next to me. "And I already told you, Prometheus and Epimetheus have approved." She cast a glance between us. "Did Apollo already head up?"

"He did," I replied. "So, now we wait."

Not five minutes later, we were outside the palace doors.

Tessa took Atlas' hand and smiled at him. "Are you ready for this?"

He gave a noncommittal grunt.

"Atlas..."

"Let's get this done," he muttered.

I pushed open the heavy doors, leading the way into the entrance hall. About halfway down, two servants came around a corner, both skidding to a stop when they took in the massive Titan behind me.

With a brief nod in greeting, I continued past them, silently hoping we didn't come across any more.

Zeus and Apollo's raised voices carried down the hall from the war room, and when we entered, they stood face to face, arguing in a way I hadn't seen for some time. Prometheus and Epimetheus stood off to the side, seemingly avoiding any interaction, while Poseidon stood slightly behind Apollo. We hovered just inside the door, waiting.

"I should demote you for all of your deception!" Zeus bellowed.

"Go right ahead!" Apollo shouted back. "I'm certain you'll have great luck finding someone else to take my place!"

"If I didn't know better, I'd think all of you were attempting to shut me out of my own damn mountain!"

Poseidon laughed and shook his head. "Listen to yourself, brother. You sound just like our father, paranoid to the bone."

"How dare you—" Zeus lunged toward him, then stopped when he hit an invisible barrier. His head whipped toward the door, eyes narrowing when they fell on Tessa.

Frowning, I looked down at her and saw she was staring at him impassively.

"We're not going to fight today," she said, her voice calm, taking my hand as it slid into hers. "Let's get this over with and move forward."

The tension in the room increased several degrees at her blatant use of power on our ruler. After a moment, she released the barrier of air she'd put up between Zeus and Poseidon. I expected him to lash out, rebuke her, at the very least. Instead, he held Tessa' glare before shifting his to the Titan at her side.

There was a moment of silence as Zeus and Atlas assessed each other.

Adjusting his jacket, Zeus gave Atlas a curt nod, then seamlessly shifted his demeanor. "Atlas. It's good to see you out of that hole. How are you feeling?"

"A bit like I've been trapped in a cave for three thousand years," Atlas replied dryly.

His eyes moved past Zeus and over to Poseidon. "Poseidon."

"Atlas. I'm happy to see you well again," Poseidon replied, inclining his head in greeting. "Your brothers said you were in quite the state, last they saw."

"Indeed." Atlas put a hand on Tessa's shoulder and squeezed. "Fortunately, Tessa managed to bring me back."

"Yes, Apollo just filled us in on just how well Tessa has been acclimating," Zeus said, arching a brow in her direction.

"Getting my memories back helped," she said, putting a smile on that was anything but genuine. "I'd still like to throttle Hades, but what's done is done."

"Well, it's good to see you've found a silver lining in an otherwise unfortunate situation, right?" Zeus clapped his hands in a false show of ease. "Now, let's get caught up. Have you all filled Atlas in on the current state of affairs?"

There was a tightness in his voice that I could tell he was trying to conceal.

'He's furious at us all,' Apollo said. *'Be prepared for a reaming later. And you may want to tell Tessa to restrain herself.'* His face remained blank, but trepidation rang in his tone.

"They have," Atlas responded, walking toward the table Zeus stood beside that held a map of Earth. "What more can you tell me?"

"I'd expect more, after today. We've been out courting allies for the past two weeks. There are still several we need to lean on a bit more, but thus far, it appears we're in good company."

The tension in the room seemed to lift as conversation switched to the topic of war, a common language for my father and Atlas.

"And the problems you've been encountering on Earth? Crop failures, empousa attacks? What of those?" Atlas asked.

Zeus raked a hand through his hair and huffed out a breath. "Those are clear attempts to occupy our forces on Earth, keep them busy running errands when they should be planning for battle."

Atlas frowned down at the map of Earth, then examined the matching one of Olympus on the other side. "Where have the attacks occurred?"

Stepping forward, Zeus pointed toward a number of wooden markers that were scattered across the map of Earth. "Each marker is a demon attack. The red ones are empousa, which have been the most widespread."

A curious look came across Atlas' face. "Yes, I've been wondering about the empousa ever since Tessa returned home covered in blood. How exactly *did* Hecate lose control of her minions?"

"They proliferated," Epimetheus said blandly. "In great numbers and eventually shunned her as their leader."

Atlas' lips twitched, and I watched as my father's face turned a strange shade of red. "I'll assume their...proliferation...was due to the release of Pandora's magic?"

A pained look came over Epimetheus' face, and I saw Atlas' gaze shift to his brother's for the briefest of moments.

"It was, and it's long over," Zeus replied. "The lamia have since taken their place and will be joining us when called upon."

"I suppose second class vampires are better than none at all."

"Atlas, that's enough," Tessa murmured.

His brow lifted, and they exchanged a look, then he shook his head and turned back to the map. "The blue markers? What are they?"

"Crocotta," Zeus said grimly. "They've been terrorizing the more remote areas. Mountain villages and indigenous groups, mainly, murdering or taking the men, the strong, and the skilled villagers, leaving behind the women and children."

"So their methods haven't changed then," Atlas murmured. "Take the strong, leave the weaker of the species to die."

"What are the Ischyra doing to combat those attacks?" Tessa asked, folding her arms across her chest as she frowned at the large number of blue markers scattered about.

"Providing provisions when they can," Poseidon said. "Although those can only take a village so far when nearly all of its working population has been taken. The crocotta in their animal forms are quite stealthy, one of the more difficult creatures to catch or hunt."

"Trackers?" I asked. "Have you deployed any to hunt them down?"

"Persephone will be taking a small team to the villages who have been most severely affected," Zeus said. "I won't spare them all, though."

I nodded. "What form have they been taking?"

"Deer, although some have reported goat, as well," Apollo replied. "These attacks have only just started, though. We can have Artemis send some of her archers out. They'll be able to see through the crocotta's shifted form easily enough to know which creatures to take out."

Zeus pursed his lips, then nodded. "Only a few, though. They can take some of the villages the Ischyra can't. We can't afford to spread either of those assets thin just now."

The sound of murmured voices filtered down the hall, through the closed door.

"It sounds as though the others have arrived," Zeus said. "I suppose that means it's time to get started."

ALTOGETHER, nearly thirty deities had crowded into the war room. In addition to the thirteen Elders, the Titans, and myself, Hecate, Scylla, Chiron, Hades, and Persephone joined us.

"Our main concern at this point is staunching whatever flow of power Cronus is amassing on Earth," Ares said. He gestured toward a region that surrounded southern Europe. "With the exception of the Siren sightings in Athens, this area has been relatively free from activity, so our assumption is that his forces are trying to keep us occupied elsewhere, turn our eyes away from where the true problem lies."

Atlas folded his arms across his chest and looked at the area where Ares was pointing. "So what do you suggest?"

"We can't leave the other areas of the world without protection, but we need more forces in the vicinity of southeastern Europe."

"I'll go down and meet with Cornelius," I said. "He's got sway with the other Original Ischyra; he may be able to bring them back on board."

"I'll join you," Apollo said, frowning as he looked at the size of the region. "I've managed to maintain good relations with most of them."

Zeus tapped his index finger on his lips, then lifted his eyes to Tessa. "Tessa, I want you to go meet with Oceanus down in Volos. He's being stubborn. You're Clymene's daughter and more personable than your brothers. You may be able to sway him better than I could, considering Cronus is the reason his daughter is dead. Athena will go with you, as she's got some experience with them."

Hera huffed beside him at the reference to one of my father's many former lovers, Metis; an Oceanid and Athena's mother.

"How many does he have?" Tessa asked.

"The Oceanids number at around three thousand," I told her. "Not including their offspring."

She inhaled a breath through her nose, then let it out slowly. "Okay, I'll see what I can do."

"We've confirmed that the bulk of the Underworld deities will be working with us," Hades said. "With the exception of the death spirits. The Keres are, unsurprisingly, remaining neutral."

"Shocker," Dionysus muttered.

"We'll be heading out to meet with the centaurs and the satyrs tomorrow," Chiron said, gesturing toward Dionysus and Hermes.

"Try not to get them too drunk before requesting their allegiance, please," Apollo said dryly. "Last time you visited them, you came back reeking of Centaur piss and had nothing even remotely productive to report."

Dionysus pressed a hand to his chest. "Your lack of faith wounds me, brother."

Hecate stepped forward. "I've managed to speak with all of the primordials, as well as the necromancers. All say they'll commit to our cause, but I've had no luck figuring out who has been helping Menoetius."

Zeus grunted. "Keep on that one," he ordered. "We need the allegiance of your witches, but not at the risk of bringing on a traitor."

Hades looked to Hecate and folded his arms. "What of your parents? Will Perses and Asteria be joining us?"

"My mother will likely remain on Earth, although that remains to be seen. Father has already confirmed he's for our cause." She cast a quick glance at Tessa before continuing. "Also, Scylla was able to find out a bit more about our mystery witch."

"What did you find?" Zeus asked, turning toward the sea witch who stood beside Hecate.

"Not a terrible amount, unfortunately. He's been living on Earth for quite some time now, non-practicing, which was how he slipped under our radar."

"How long has he gone unnoticed?" Zeus asked Scylla.

"We can't say," she replied. "My source was another witch who'd only heard whisperings of him. Now that he's been practicing his magic, I'm going to attempt to track it."

"You can do that?" Tessa looked surprised at the notion of tracking an individual's magic.

"It's not so different than what a regular tracker does," Scylla explained. "I'll be speaking with Jura, the guard Hades has been questioning, shortly so I can attempt to get a read on the witch's essence."

"And based on that, you can track him down?"

Scylla nodded. "It shouldn't be too difficult."

"Who else has Menoetius acquired?" Artemis asked, arms folded across her chest.

"Currently, the empousa, the crocotta, the Telchines, and a number of water deities—the Naiads, along with the Potamoi," Athena replied. "We're not sure who of his former brethren he's approached."

"Considering the Sirens are the children of a Potamoi, I think it's safe to assume they're on his side, as well, then?"

"More than likely," Athena confirmed. "Cronus is using the removal of their curse as a carrot on a stick." She cast a glance at Demeter. "It would certainly help if we had a similar offer," she said pointedly.

Demeter arched a brow, but didn't respond.

Artemis tapped her fingers on her bicep, her eyes darting across the map of Earth. "Alright. I'm going to take twenty of my archers to deal with the crocotta. Contact me when you need me elsewhere."

"Take thirty," Apollo said, not looking at her.

Annoyed, Artemis faced her twin. "Twenty will be more than sufficient."

"The number of villages affected will likely increase over the next few days. Thirty will ensure you've got the numbers you need."

"*Twenty* is the number I need."

"Enough." Zeus jerked his chin toward Artemis. "Take twenty-five. Apollo's got a point."

Scowling at our father, she turned and left, not bothering with goodbyes.

'Do they not like each other?' Tessa asked.

'Not particularly.'

Amusement laced her tone when she responded. *'Ah. That seems to be a theme for him.'*

'What's that supposed to mean?'

'The siblings he has the most in common with are the ones he spends the least amount of time with.'

'Funny,' I remarked, then brought my focus back to the conversation.

"I've spoken to Thetis," Poseidon said. "She and the other Nereids are with us, so combined with the Oceanids, the water gods should give us another five thousand fighters."

"Air support?" Atlas asked, frowning.

Chiron held up a hand. "We'll check in with the Harpies and griffins. They'd be good to have on hand."

"And Aphrodite, Hera, and I will seek out the rest of the Titans," Hestia said, sighing as she stared out the window. "Although I'm not sure how successful we'll be."

"The old fools have gotten lazy, if you ask me," Aphrodite said, her dark eyes flicking back and forth between Tessa's brothers, who looked noticeably uncomfortable under her perusal. "Some, anyway."

"Rein it in, Aphrodite," I muttered.

Pouting, she hopped up on the table behind her and crossed one leg over the other. "I'm just being honest."

"Well, stop," Zeus snapped. "We need their allegiance, so keep your opinions to yourself or I'll send someone else." Stroking his beard for a few seconds, he nodded. "Alright. We'll adjourn for now. Everyone, check in once you have news."

As everyone began to file out, Zeus walked toward where Tessa, her brothers, Apollo, and I stood.

Patting me on the shoulder, he inclined his head toward the door.

"Come, we've got plenty more to discuss."

33

TESSA

By the time Zeus had dismissed everyone, only Nate, his parents, my brothers, Apollo, Athena, Hecate, Demeter, and I remained. Once the room cleared out, we moved to the sitting room, where Athena poured wine for everyone before dropping down on the sofa with a huff.

"Well, that was exhausting," she said. "Thank the gods it's over."

Hera sat down beside her, adjusting her skirts as she looked back and forth between me and my twin. Smiling, she took a sip of her wine. "Atlas, despite my husband's less than hospitable welcome, I'd like to offer a place in the guest wing for you while you're on Olympus. It's the least we can do."

"That won't be necessary, Mother," Nate said, sounding annoyed. "I have the space for him."

"And we have more," she countered, ignoring Zeus' sharp look.

"Thank you, Hera," Atlas said with a nod. "That's...much appreciated."

"You can stay with us," I whispered, surprised and a little hurt that he was so quick to accept her invitation. "Really."

He ran a hand over my hair and smiled. "No need. I'll be content up here with our brothers."

'And I'd prefer to be closer to Zeus than halfway down the mountain.'

I bit back my retort, acknowledging the logic behind remaining with our brothers in the palace. He'd been betrayed by Zeus once; it would be far easier to keep an eye on him in his own home than Nate's.

"Right, then." Hecate pulled a small jar out of the pouch at her waist and set it on the coffee table, then inclined her head toward Demeter. "Demeter and I have finished extracting the poison from the dirt at the farms you all healed. It's definitely the work of the Telchines. One of their earlier formulas, but it's theirs, alright."

Nate picked up the vial and examined the green liquid inside. "What is it?"

Hecate leaned back in her chair and propped an elbow on the arm. "The main ingredient is black walnut root, which can be found all over the world. It's highly toxic to other plants, so in large quantities, like what was found in this soil, it could easily wipe out a thousand acres of crops in a matter of days."

"It's not harmful to humans, though," Demeter continued. "The castor seed and hemlock that make up the bulk of the remaining ingredients, on the other hand, are, meaning, any crops that aren't susceptible to black walnut toxins could still transfer the poison to human populations."

"Have you developed an antidote?" Zeus asked, frowning down at the bottle.

"Persephone is working with Maia, Sterope, and Electra to develop something to distribute as quickly as possible."

"Maia—" Atlas sat up in his seat. "The Pleiades? What do they have to do with this?"

Zeus shot a confused look toward Apollo, then me. "You haven't told him?"

Atlas turned to me, and I thought I saw my two other brothers shift slightly from where they stood beside the fireplace. "Told me what?"

Wide-eyed, my eyes darted between the twins and Hecate. "Gods, Atlas..." I closed my eyes and took a deep breath. "With everything that's been going on, we wanted to wait to tell you. Taygete, Celaeno, and Alcyone have gone missing."

Atlas stared at me, wide-eyed, then leaned forward and rested his elbows on his knees and pressed the heels of his hands to his forehead. When he spoke, his voice was a deadly calm. "Three of my daughters have gone *missing*, and you didn't think to tell me the moment I woke up?"

"We're the ones who suggested waiting, Atlas, so don't take it out on Tessa," Epimetheus said.

Atlas' head shot up, and his harsh gaze went straight toward Prometheus. "I suppose this was your idea?"

Prometheus folded his arms across his chest and nodded. "It was."

A muscle in Atlas' jaw twitched as he and Prometheus stared each other down. Without shifting position, he looked at Zeus. "What's being done to find them?"

"It seems as though Menoetius has taken them as a power source to be able to cast," Zeus replied. "Once we find him, we assume we'll find them."

"You assume." Atlas shook his head and let out a quiet laugh. "Just like you assumed I was guilty?"

"You *were* guilty," Hera said, any prior niceties gone. "In case you've forgotten."

Sitting forward, I placed a hand on Atlas' arm in an attempt to calm him, but he just shook it off.

"I had washed my hands of Cronus and his cause years before the war ended." His brow lifted. "Had you listened to reason, you would've known that."

"That has little to do with the situation we're in now," Zeus replied. "We all played our parts in the war and how it ended—"

"Yes, and if you hadn't imprisoned me in that damn mountain, we might not be in this mess!" Atlas shook his head and made a sound of disgust. "You took away any chance I had of killing that bastard."

"Cronus has been locked away for thousands of years—"

"As if that would do anything to staunch his need for power!"

Atlas rose to his feet, drawing himself to his full height, which was a good six inches over Zeus. "He should be dead!"

"I did what was best for this mountain," Zeus hissed. "For the gods and deities of this mountain and all the other realms—"

"Yes, please play the part of the pious ruler." Atlas' voice dripped with disdain. "We all know the only reason you imprisoned him was so you could draw out his torture for your own enjoyment."

"I did nothing of the sort!"

"So you showed him mercy, instead?" Atlas jabbed a finger into Zeus' chest. None of our siblings made a move to calm him. "You're nothing but a foolish child."

"Don't you touch me," Zeus warned, smacking Atlas' hand away and taking a step closer, putting them mere centimeters apart. "If you hadn't sided with him in the first place, I never would've locked you away!"

"If you gentlemen are going to fight, do you mind if we start taking wagers on who the victor will be?"

Hades appeared in the doorway and was eyeing Zeus and Atlas with a curious expression. Smirking, he walked toward the arguing gods.

"I mean, this is a confrontation we've been waiting on for centuries, right?" He held out his hands and glanced around the room. "Personally, my money is on the lunatic who's recently been exorcised, but what do I know?"

'You couldn't have just walked in and said hi?'

Hades shot me a wink, and I could've sworn I heard my twin growl in response to the obvious attempt to bait him.

"What are you doing here, Hades?" Zeus snapped.

Hades shrugged, coming to a stop behind the sofa across from us, then gave his brother a sardonic smile. "I just figured I'd come witness the fireworks, that's all."

I pasted a smile on my face. "You're certainly getting your share of misery topside these days, aren't you?"

"Indeed," Hades murmured. He waved toward Zeus and Atlas. "You both might as well sit down. I've got news."

Atlas' jaw clenched as he glared down at Hades. Ignoring his request to sit, he moved to the fireplace, bracing his hands against the mantle and staring into the flames.

Zeus sat down with a huff. "What now? You've only just left."

"Yes, well, funny how these things have a way of not waiting until a convenient time to happen."

"What is it, Hades?" Hera asked wearily.

"Crius has gone missing. According to Cottus, Crius was none too pleased when I had Nathaniel interrogate my giants."

"Considering all the grievous things you've done in the last few thousand years, that hardly sounds like a valid reason," Nate commented.

"Agreed," Hades offered. "Which is why I'm assuming it's bullshit."

"You think he's turned, then?" Zeus asked.

"I'd say it's more than likely."

Prometheus snorted. "And this surprised you?"

"Considering we didn't force him to live out eternity in Tartarus, it's somewhat upsetting, yes," Hades replied.

"Exactly how does a Titan escape from the Underworld?" Hera asked.

"He wasn't imprisoned, and I didn't place sanctions on him to remain there, although he never struck me as the type to want to do anything other than ensure the torment of prisoners for all time."

"What does your ferryman have to say?" Demeter asked.

"I've spoken with Charon," Hades said. "He confirmed he didn't ferry him or anyone else across the Acheron."

"Have you confirmed this?" Prometheus asked.

"I just said—"

"You said Charon confirmed it. That's not what I asked."

Hades paused, then folded his arms across his chest and gave my brother a level stare. "Please don't insinuate my ferryman is not to be trusted, Prometheus."

"I'd be remiss if I didn't ask the question."

"He's got a point, Hades..." I said reluctantly.

He shot me a warning glare. "Don't start. You know better."

My brows shot up, and I held up a hand when Atlas turned and faced us. "Don't take that tone with me. Charon is the son of two primordial deities and has access to all five rivers. If it were anyone else, you'd be just as quick to question."

"You're back barely a week, and already you're placing blame on someone you used to call a friend?"

"It's been over three thousand years, and you expect me to take it on faith that everyone I knew back then is the same person today?"

"My ability to judge others is just as sound as it was then," he snapped. "Do not mistake me for someone so easily manipulated—"

"As who? Me?" I shook my head. "Don't even go there."

"You've spent nearly two decades with humans. Are we to believe none of their weaknesses rubbed off on you?"

"Oh, go fuck yourself."

Hera let out an amused snort.

"I'll take that as proof of my point," Hades said cooly.

"Okay!" Athena said. "As entertaining as all of this bickering is, can we get back to the matter at hand? What, exactly, are you doing to locate Crius?"

Hades shrugged. "At this point, what would you have me do? I'm not going to hunt down one Titan who has no special powers to speak of when we've got plenty of other issues to contend with. Our success in this war isn't contingent on his allegiance, so I don't particularly care to waste any more time on him."

Nate nudged me with his elbow. *'Are you alright?"*

I scowled at him but nodded. *'Yeah. Irritated, but yeah, I'm fine.'*

'Let me know if you need to leave.'

"Speaking of other concerns," Hades said, turning toward Demeter and Hecate. "Persephone said the antidote for the poison is just about ready."

"How quickly will they be able to make enough to distribute globally?" Hecate asked.

"A few days, at most," Hades replied.

"Wonderful," Athena said. "That's quite a relief."

"There's one more thing we needed to discuss," Hera said, a smile curving her lips as she sat forward in her seat. Instantly, I became uneasy. "Nathaniel, Athena, Apollo—you should know that I've asked Eris and Enyo to return to Olympus to assist us in the coming war."

Athena rolled her eyes at the mention of their two sisters and glared up at Zeus, ignoring Hera. "Are Ares and I not war gods enough for you? You have to bring those two in to pick up the slack?"

Zeus clenched his jaw but forced his voice to stay even. "Their methods are different than yours, effective in other ways. Hera suggested bringing them in, and I agree. We'd be fools not to call all hands on deck, and you and Ares have other responsibilities."

"*Hera* suggested," Demeter scoffed. "We'll be lucky if they don't bring down this damn mountain themselves."

Hera narrowed her eyes at Demeter. "I don't appreciate you speaking so ill of my own children," she snapped. "Considering your daughter's line of work, I'd think you'd be a bit more understanding of the good they can do."

"Enyo is a war crime in the making," Hades pointed out. "Violent and unstable. Coming from me, that's saying something. Comparing her to Persephone's ability to help me carve up some monster's soul is like comparing apples to oranges."

Hera huffed. "She's a hunter and assassin, Hades. Don't bother sugarcoating it."

'She is?' I asked Nate. *'I thought she was just a big-time tracker.'*

'That's exactly what she is,' he replied. *'She tracks criminals, though, so they generally end up dead.'*

"Well, you're certainly making it clear, once *again*, just where Eris and Enyo get their incessant need to piss people off," Demeter shot back.

Hecate threw her hands up and stood. "I don't have time for this nonsense. Athena, I'll be in touch."

Without another word, she vanished, allowing us to deal with their family discord without her.

With a sigh, Nate pinched the bridge of his nose, then let his hand fall. "And Eris? How do you plan on controlling her? All she does is cause problems. She'll be more trouble than she's worth."

"Isn't she the one you said was like Mary?" I asked quietly.

"That mousy little recruit from a few days ago?" Hades chuckled. "Oh, yes, please. Let's put the two of them in a room together."

"Mary's not mousy, you jackass," I snapped.

"Alright, enough!" Zeus turned toward Athena. "They'll be arriving in two days. As Ares is choosing to remain in the field, you, Apollo, and I will fully debrief them when they get here. Until then, you'll deal with the recruits, figure out who might be sharing information, and go with Tessa to Volos to speak with Oceanus. Is that clear?"

Athena folded her arms stubbornly across her chest. "Fine. But so help me, Father, if either of them attempt to cross me, they'll get a spear straight through the eye."

"Now, Athena—" Hera began.

Athena sent her a level glare. "And an arrow for good measure."

As the five of them continued to argue about the stability of Enyo and Eris, I looked at Atlas and tilted my head toward the door.

'Come out in the hall for a minute?'

Wordlessly, he turned and strode from the room. Following him, I closed the door quietly behind me.

"I'm sorry we didn't tell you about the sisters sooner," I said, turning to face him.

He waved a hand dismissively. "I wasn't exactly a father to them before I went into that mountain. What right do I have to be concerned for their well-being when I hardly gave a damn before?"

"Don't say that." I smiled sympathetically. "Things were...different back then."

He sat down in a carved wooden armchair and stroked his chin as he stared absently down the hall. "That's no excuse."

I bit my lip, then leaned against the wall across from him. "Can I ask you something?"

"Of course."

I cocked a brow. "Without you getting angry?"

He gave me a crooked smile. "I suppose that depends on what you're asking."

"Back then—before the war. Your relationship with Pleione was so...fleeting. It never seemed as though you cared to have a relationship with her or the Pleiades. Why the sudden change?"

He leaned back in the chair and stretched his long legs out in front of him, then stared down at the floor for a moment before speaking. "I suppose I didn't see the benefit of being a father. I think I took after our own, in that respect."

"That couldn't be further from the truth, and you know it."

He lifted his eyes to mine. "Is it? I sired seven daughters for Pleione, yet all I truly know of them are their names."

I shrugged. "So, get to know them. We can go down and visit with the three who are staying with Demeter and the Titans down in the valley, if you want. Once the others return, you can get to know them, too."

He huffed out a breath. "You truly think it will be that simple?"

"Not simple, but certainly possible." I slid down to a sitting position, stretching my legs out and crossing them at the ankles. "You know, when I was younger, my guardians used to take me stargazing. Guess what the first constellation they showed me was?"

"Which one?"

"Yours." His brow furrowed in curiosity, so I continued. "On our very first camping trip, John and Analise took me to Utah to watch the Taurids meteor shower, and John explained all of the stars in Taurus. When he pointed out your star, he told me you were 'the strongest Titan to ever live.'" I smiled fondly at the memory, a happier one, now that I'd gotten my emotions out the night before. "I even named a star for myself, right next to yours. After that, Taurus became our common point, the place we would look when we were apart and know that we'd always be connected by that one spot in the sky."

"Your guardians—they knew of your past, then?"

I nodded. "Hecate placed interdictions on them just like she did for Apollo and Hestia. They weren't able to tell me who or what I was, but from the time I was a little girl, they made sure I knew that you were special to me, that you had a place in my heart."

A smile flickered across his face. "They sound like good people."

"They are. They treated me like their own, even though I wasn't."

He let out a long sigh. "I'm assuming there's a point you're leading up to?"

"My point is that you've got good people who love you and want to support you. You've been given—our *family's* been given—a second chance, Atlas. Don't waste it on grudges and fighting and regret. If you want to get to know your daughters, then get to know them."

He gave me an amused smile. "Are your guardians the source of your newfound wisdom, as well?"

"You wouldn't believe the number of one-liners John had when it came to advice," I said, grinning. "Analise was a total mom, but John was like a real, live Yoda."

He frowned. "I don't know what that is."

"Oh. Right. Never mind." I made a mental note to introduce my twin to pop culture as soon as I had the chance.

"I appreciate the talk, Tessa. Really." He stood and helped me to my feet. "You've given me a lot to think about."

"Are you sure you won't come stay back at Nate's?" I hated the idea of him being up at the palace and not right next door, but I was also somewhat looking forward to Nate and me having the house to ourselves again.

As though sensing my thoughts, he smirked. "I think I'd prefer the company of our brothers than that of two deities in a new relationship. It's a wonder you haven't wrecked his home yet."

My mouth popped open and my cheeks flamed, but I didn't bother arguing. Hades and I had certainly wrecked plenty of things in our time together.

He laughed, the genuine smile brightening his entire face, then draped an arm around my shoulder. "Not to worry. He can't be any worse than Hades. Or any of those other ruffians you consorted with when you thought we weren't paying attention."

I dropped my face to my hands and shook my head. Apparently,

I'd been worse at keeping my love life a secret than I'd thought back then.

He ruffled my hair, then kissed the top of my head. "Go home. I'll be fine. Tomorrow we'll talk about where we go from here."

"Thanks, Atlas." I leaned into him, letting him give me a tight, one-armed hug. I wrapped my arms around his waist and smiled. "It's so good to have you back."

He put his other arm around me and rested his chin on my head. "Thank you for bringing me back."

OUR TRIP to the palace had taken hours longer than I'd expected, and by the time Nate and I got home, I was exhausted from the amount of thinking and talking and planning we'd done. The silence when we entered the house, the emptiness of it, was utterly glorious.

As I changed into my pajamas, I thought about what the next few days would bring. Soon, Athena and I would be visiting Oceanus, the father of both her mother and mine. It would be my first time attempting to court an ally, and the concern that I was out of my depth kept gnawing at me.

Fighting, I could do. I liked to think I'd proven that to myself quite sufficiently in recent weeks, as hard as it might have been. Politics were a whole new ballgame for me, which made me thankful I wasn't going to be visiting him alone.

I met Nate's eyes in the mirror. "So, how many more of these meetings are we going to have?"

He walked over to me, then took the brush from my hand and set it back on the dresser, turning me to face him. With his finger on my chin, he tilted my face toward his. "I don't want to talk about that anymore. We've been doing that all day."

"Oh?" My hands fell to rest on his hips. "What *do* you want to talk about?"

He took a step closer, his lips a hair's breadth from mine. "I'd like to talk about how you're wearing one of my shirts again, even though I specifically told you not to."

My lips curved into a smile as I ran my hands up his arms. "Technically, I never agreed to that."

"They're my shirts, though."

"At least I have pants on this time."

He tilted his head down and flicked up the hem of the shirt to eye my shorts and smirked in amusement.

"Barely." He let the hem drop back down but kept his hand on the bare skin underneath.

"I mean…if it's bothering you that much, I could just take it off," I suggested, leaning up and kissing his neck.

One side of his mouth pulled up in a smile, then he pressed his lips to my ear.

"You're infuriating, you know that?"

I smirked. "Yet you still love me."

"Even more after these last few days, if that's possible," he murmured. "I knew you were amazing, but watching you fight, watching you save your brother…I've been wanting to do this ever since you came home yesterday."

Slowly, he laid a soft kiss to the underside of my jaw, then moved slowly to the sensitive spot beneath my ear. One hand slid under my shirt and splayed against my back, pulling me into him.

He brought his lips to mine in a kiss so deep and full of emotion, it set my whole body tingling. When he pulled back, I sighed in contentment and gave him a slow smile.

"I should go on rescue missions and kill monsters more often."

He let out a quiet laugh. "No, you definitely shouldn't."

"You know, I think we should celebrate," I said playfully. "Take a page from Dionysus' book."

"Is that so?" He arched a brow and began to trace slow circles along my back with his thumb, drifting slowly toward my waist. Hooking his thumbs in my waistband, he began backing me toward the bed.

I sucked in a breath and struggled to keep my voice from

wobbling as his hands ran slowly down my spine. "I mean...considering no one died this past week, I'd definitely say that's cause for celebration."

He let out a quiet laugh. "Tessa, are you trying to entice me?"

"Is it working?" I bit my lip and grinned.

"Definitely working," he murmured as he pulled his shirt off and tossed it aside, trapping my lips in another long, lingering kiss. He laid me down on the bed, caging me between his arms and legs as he slowly began to undress me.

I don't know what I'd expected our first time to be like. The times I thought it might happen—on the summit, in the bathroom, even at the springs when I was still just an Ischyra—had a certain...frenzied feeling attached to them. I'd wanted him, every inch of him, then and there. Now, as he took his time with me, touching me and kissing me in ways I'd never been touched or kissed before, the last thing I wanted was to rush.

Other lovers in my past had been good to me, but nothing compared to the emotion I felt pouring from his body as we made love for the first time. I opened my mind to his, letting him feel what I felt, letting him know what he was doing to me, what his touch, his words did to me.

When I was seconds from tumbling over the edge, he put his lips to my ear.

"I love you, Tessa."

34

TESSA

Any residual glow that might've been left over from my night with Nate—one that hadn't ended until the early hours of the morning—was demolished when I woke up to a strange woman in bed next to me.

She grinned when I opened my eyes, her head propped on her fist. "Hi, there."

Turning my face to the pillow, I kicked Nate. "I think I found another one of your siblings. Make her go away."

"I'd like to see him try," she said snarkily, then poked my arm. "You must be the new Titan in town."

"Go away, Eris," Nate muttered into his pillow. "And please don't tell me you brought Enyo with you."

So, this was Eris; Nate's goddess of discord sister who apparently reminded him of Mary. Based on the snark alone, I could kind of see it.

She was pretty, in a non-traditional way. Dark brown hair streaked with vibrant red, crystal blue eyes, a pert nose, and a sharp jaw made for an incredibly striking appearance. There was something in her expression, though, an unsettling gleam, that told me to keep a close watch on her.

"Enyo stayed down in...somewhere." Frowning, she thought for a moment, then shrugged. "I don't know where. She said someone's getting tortured or something. You know how she is." With a wink, she sat up, then reached across me to pull the pillow from under Nate's head and smacked him with it. "Now, get up! I missed you!"

Grabbing the pillow, he threw it back at her with so much force, it knocked her off the bed.

"Prick!" she exclaimed, laughing.

With a huff, I wrapped the blanket around myself and stood. "You two can continue your reunion without me." Plastering on a smile for Eris, I said, "It was lovely to meet you. I'm going to get dressed now."

Irritated, I grabbed the first clothes I found and stormed into the bathroom, slamming the door behind me.

Arguing ensued as soon as the door was shut, but I was too aggravated to bother eavesdropping. Once again, one of Nate's siblings had decided to stroll into his room, invading *our* privacy, interrupting *our—*

I paused in the middle of brushing my teeth. With a growl, I rinsed, spit, then slammed the faucet off.

"Sower of fucking discord," I muttered as I opened the door and glared at Eris, not caring a lick about propriety. "Can you turn your... whatever it is that's making me pissed off, down a notch?"

Nate groaned, and Eris snorted, then clapped a hand over her mouth.

"Wow, that Mimic shit is powerful, isn't it?" With a flourish of her hand, she bowed. "Ask and you shall receive, ma'am."

Almost instantly, my body relaxed and the aggravation of just a few seconds earlier receded. Letting out a relieved breath, I smiled at her. "Thank you. I appreciate it."

"Now go away so we can get dressed," Nate ordered her. I bit my lip, amused at the uncharacteristic annoyance in his tone.

When it came to making people want to fight, Eris seemed pretty damn gifted.

With another wink, she vanished, and I turned pleading eyes on Nate.

"For the love of us all, Nate, can you *please* talk to your family about boundaries?"

"Eris has no goddamn boundaries," he muttered as he got up and started pulling on a pair of jeans.

Softening, I walked over to him and covered his hands with mine, stilling them as they picked up a shirt, then turned his face toward me and looked into his eyes. "She's gone. Take a deep breath and stop letting her piss you off."

Closing his eyes, he rested his forehead against mine, his fingers clenching and unclenching on my hips.

"You're right. I'm sorry. She just—"

"Takes her job very seriously?" I stood on my toes and brushed my lips against his, annoyed when I barely got a response due to the tension in his jaw. "Stop that," I whispered as I ran my fingers down his bare chest. Gripping his chin, I drew his mouth to mine, kissing him until I felt him relax and the tension began to fade away.

Slowly, he pulled back, then touched his thumb to my lower lip and gave me a soft smile. "Were you using Dionysus' magic to calm me down?" he asked quietly.

"Nope. Just me."

'Why is there a psychopath on your front porch? Get out here; you need to train.'

I snorted when I heard Hades' angry voice in my head. "Hades is here. I think he found Eris. Are they safe to be alone together for a few minutes?"

Nate grimaced. "Uh...probably not." His eyes went distant for a moment. "Ah...Apollo just called, and he needs my help with something. So I'm going to have to leave for a bit."

Eyes widening, I smacked his chest. "Don't you dare leave me alone with those two! We'll be lucky if we last an hour!"

"Just don't get mad." He smiled playfully. "Or let Hades get mad. Maybe don't let him and Eris interact with each other at all."

"Oh, is that all?" I put my hands on my hips. "You know, I vaguely recall you telling me you thought I'd like her."

He winced. "Yes, well, I may have been mistaken, although she's not always as...Eris...as she was just now."

"I might kill you by the time this day is over."

A devious smile curved his lips as he slid his hands over my hips, still sheathed in the blanket I'd pulled from his bed. "You know...I could use a shower before I leave. What about you?"

I gave him a speculative look, refusing to give an inch. "Didn't you just tell me not to make Hades mad or allow the two of them to interact? Wouldn't forcing him to wait out there with Eris be doing exactly that?"

"No one is forcing him to do anything," he murmured, leaning down to run his lips over mine. "And this way, you'd be starting whatever it is he's got planned for you in a good mood."

I narrowed my eyes. "This spiteful little rebellion you've got going on...is that you, or is it Eris, trying to instigate a fight between us and Hades?"

He shrugged. "Probably both. I don't really care."

Seconds later, he'd backed me against the bathroom door, the blanket I'd had wrapped around me falling to the floor. I made quick work of his jeans, then he carried me to the shower and turned the water on, not bothering to wait for it to warm up before stepping inside. The cold water bit at my skin, so I sent a little of my fire magic through the pipes, turning the water hot within seconds.

"They're going to be waiting a while, aren't they?" I murmured against his lips.

"A very long while," he agreed.

Hades glared daggers at me when Nate and I made our way onto the front porch.

"It's incredibly rude to leave the person who wants to help you waiting on the porch for nearly an *hour* just so you can roll in bed with your lover."

"Technically they were in the shower," Eris stage-whispered. Her power rolled off her, an overall feeling of irrational anger and irritation. Combined with Hades' typical orneriness, I was suddenly in the mood to punch things. Hard.

"It was twenty minutes," I muttered. "Don't you have an Underworld to rule? And I thought I was supposed to be going to meet with Oceanus?"

"Anyone with any sense knows he'll stand with us, so it can be put off for a day or two. And, unlike a certain brother of mine, I have a queen who is perfectly capable of ruling in my stead."

Rolling my eyes, I sat down on one of the porch chairs. "Whatever. You could've come back later."

"Enough with the petulance, Tessa. You've done all of five minutes of training since you returned. If you're going to be at all useful, you need to regain any skills you might've lost." He inclined his head toward Eris. "You should be blocking her out with hardly any effort, yet here you are, not doing it."

"She got to Nate, too!" I exclaimed. "Don't act like I'm the only one."

"Do you see Nathaniel acting like a child right now?" He folded his arms across his chest and arched a brow. "No, you don't, because unlike you, he's got a modicum of self-control."

"Damn, who pissed in your Cheerios?" Eris laughed. "I bet you two are fun at parties."

"My what?" Hades stared at her, flummoxed. "What did you just say?"

"Excuse me," I said, getting his attention once more, "but I vividly recall kicking some ass at that empousa nest right *after* healing a ton of crops the Tels poisoned." I waved a finger in his direction. "While you were off *not* getting anything useful from your guard-turned-traitor."

"Eris," Nate warned. "Tone it down."

"Seriously, you should stop whatever it is you're doing." I jerked my chin at Hades. "His pissiness is bad enough. Do you really think we need your help instigating arguments?"

She laughed, then leaned forward and ruffled Nate's hair. "Oh, Nathaniel, I like her."

Smacking her hand away, Nate scowled at her. "Do you have any idea how Mimicry works when it comes to empaths, Eris, or do you just not give a shit?"

Shrugging, she hopped up on the porch railing, nudging Hades out of the way. "Educate me."

"Now she asks," I mumbled.

"Don't make me dose you harder, little girl," she said, narrowing her eyes.

"'Little girl,'" I scoffed. "I've got five hundred years on you, easy."

Hades choked back a laugh. "Oh good gods, this is wonderful." Pausing, he tapped his chin and took on a thoughtful expression. "You know, come to think of it...sending the two of them into enemy camps together could win this war before it's even begun."

Eris held up her hands and grinned. "Sounds like a plan. Let's do it."

Frowning at her, I nodded. "That actually...isn't the worst idea."

"Okay, that's enough." Nate held up a hand and faced his sister. "You're oozing discord constantly, Eris, and when you're around a Mimic—"

"As in, someone who isn't normally a perpetual bitch," I added with a smile.

Nate shot me a warning look before continuing. "Someone who isn't accustomed to carrying that type of power around regularly, it affects them differently than it does you." He tilted his head toward Hades. "We have a hard enough time keeping the two of them from beating on each other when he gets angry. It doesn't help when you piss him off on top of it. Just...keep that in mind when you start trying to cause trouble."

"Fine," she groaned. "I'll use my words from now on, I promise."

Slowly, whatever her power had been doing to me eased up, and my body started to relax. Almost immediately, mortification at the way I'd spoken to her—Nate's *sister*—hit hard. "Gods, I'm—"

"Do *not* apologize to her," Hades said, shaking his head. "She enjoys your embarrassment almost as much as angering you."

Eris wrinkled her nose and smiled apologetically. "He's right."

Hades pushed off the railing and arched a brow. "Speaking of which, we should start training."

"I thought you said Apollo was coming over?" I asked Nate.

Eris snorted. "Apollo won't come within a hundred yards of me unless Daddy tells him to."

"You could surprise him," I suggested. "Apollo loves surprises, right?"

"I'm not bringing her with me," Nate said. "I wanted to wait to make sure you three weren't going to kill each other before I left." He gave us each a pained look. "Although, I'm still not certain."

"We'll be fine," Hades said, waving him off. "Eris will likely get bored before long, anyway."

"Is that supposed to be an insult?" I eyed him warily. "I can't really tell."

"Right." Nate stood, then looked between the three of us and nodded. "Have fun." He pointed at Eris. "Stay here."

Leaning down for a kiss, he added, *'Call me if you need me.'*

I turned to Hades once Nate had vanished and raised my brows expectantly. "So, what are we working on today?"

"Your speed. According to Athena, you did well enough fighting the empousa, but Persephone showed me what you looked like once you were done. It was horrific."

"Ooo can I see?" Eris asked.

Gritting my teeth, I watched as Hades sent her the memory. The urge to hit something returned when Eris let out a bawdy laugh at the sight of me covered in empousa blood.

With a huff, I looked at Hades. "So, are you going to have me run laps around the mountain?"

"No, and let's move this to the lawn. Quarters are too close up here."

I followed him down the steps to the center of the yard as Eris dropped down on the bottom step to observe. I'd just opened my mouth to ask what he wanted me to do, when he spun and swung his fist toward my face. I'd barely ducked before he kicked his leg out and knocked both of mine out from under me.

"What the fuck, Hades!" Pushing off my shoulders, I leapt to my feet, ignoring Eris' snickering.

Hands on his hips, Hades stared at me with a perplexed expression.

I cocked a brow and waited for him to continue.

"From what I understand, you fought well against your brothers prior to your reawakening, but Athena and Ares often beat you bloody," he began.

"And?"

"I'm quite certain that's because your body and mind have been trained to fight your brothers, and in some deep part of your brothers' subconscious, it was ingrained in them not to harm you. You knew their moves, their styles, even before you knew who they truly were. Ares and Athena's styles were wholly unfamiliar to you. Also, you were learning to fight as an Ischyra, not as a deity. You've got a whole new set of skills that need to be incorporated into your fighting. You're faster now, for one, but you're also able to mind-read and communicate telepathically. Your gifts are an asset that need to be wielded."

Logical. "So then, how are you going to be able to help? I've fought you plenty of times."

"As I've said, I'm not concerned with hurting you. The same can't be said of your brothers."

"And I'm not concerned with hurting you, so I suppose this will work out well." I smiled sweetly.

"Indeed." He glanced up toward the top of the mountain, where the golden roof of Zeus' palace was just barely visible. "Will you resume weapons training with Atlas?"

I sighed as I followed his gaze. "I don't know. Maybe?"

"It might help."

"Help who?"

"You. Him." He shrugged. "Or not."

"Hades... are you being *nice?*" I teased. "For no reason at all?"

He gave me a withering look. "I'm simply acknowledging the disadvantage to having two broken Titans on this mountain."

"I'm not broken!"

"You're repairing yourself, slowly." His brow lifted in an expression of superiority. "It's why I gave you back your memories. Do you see, now, why I was right to do so?"

"It wasn't right for you to force them on me, and you won't get me to say otherwise." I ran a hand through my hair, avoiding his gaze as my eyes drifted back toward the palace. "But I will acknowledge that having them back has been...advantageous." I pointed at him. "And *no*, that is not me saying you were right and I was wrong, so don't let it go to your head."

His lips twitched, but he just nodded. "Alright, then. Show me the memory of your fight with the empousa. I want to see it from your perspective. We'll start there."

So, I did. After that, he walked me through each step, everything I'd done wrong and everything I'd done right, frequently bringing Eris over to stand in as an empousa while he called out moves.

Once we were done going over—and over—my ability to kill and move on, Hades informed me he'd be visiting in a dream walk each night to practice my shielding.

"I'll be asking Nathaniel to join us, if that's alright."

"How come?"

"Your main focus should be on accessing your powers when they've been disabled; countering Menoetius' ability," he explained. "Nathaniel will be able to help by coercing you into suppressing your power. Once he does that, you'll need to work on removing him."

"How will that work, though? I've resisted his Coercion from day one."

"Menoetius doesn't actually remove your powers, only subdues them. They're still there, they just need to be accessed."

"And Nathaniel will be able to trick that little mind of yours into thinking he's done the same thing." Eris nodded approvingly. "A real mind-fuck. Good to know the kid's finally stepping up."

Hades leaned back on his hands. "It's not quite the same, but it will have to suffice."

I picked at a blade of grass, recalling how I'd felt when Menoetius had disabled my power. I'd been mentally and emotionally stripped bare, my weaknesses fully exposed. I didn't mind Hades seeing me that way, because he'd already seen me at my absolute worst—he'd seen the aftermath of Menoetius' attacks, what they'd done to me, my brothers. He'd been one of the ones to help me move past them.

But I also didn't love Hades. I never had, and that made being exposed...easier. In contrast, with each day that passed, my feelings for Nate grew more and more intense, more real, and the thought of him chaining my power, making me feel the way Menoetius had done so many times, seeing me broken and weak...it was gut-wrenching.

"Tessa."

I lifted my eyes to Hades, surprised to find a softness in his expression. Eris, thankfully, was silent as she watched us.

"You've got misery pouring off of you. Whatever it is that's causing you to feel this way, shut it down."

My eyes filled with tears, threatening to overflow, but I took a deep breath and forced them back, then tried to smile.

"I'm okay," I told him. "I'll be okay."

He nodded slowly. "I know you will."

35

NATHANIEL

I felt bad leaving Tessa to fend for herself with Hades and Eris, but Apollo's insistence that I meet him at his house left me little choice. She'd manage, of that I was certain, but that didn't mean I was happy about it.

"Father is insisting we visit with the recruits today," Apollo said when I arrived. "He's gotten more irritable the last few days, so I'd like to get this part out of the way quickly, if we can."

Rubbing the back of my neck, I grimaced. "Well, we've got to make it quick. Eris is back."

His eyes widened in shock. "At your home? And you left Tessa alone with her?"

"And Hades, so you'll understand why I'd rather not be gone long."

For once, my brother was speechless.

"Don't look so surprised," I muttered. "Tessa can hold her own."

He cleared his throat, then nodded. "Alright, well, we'll be quick, then. Hopefully they'll all be in one piece when we return." Pausing, he gave me an assessing look. "Are you sure you're alright with this, Nathaniel? It's quite possible one of the recruits or mentors could be guilty of something."

I gave him a dry look. "If I tell you I'm not alright with it, will you get Rudolfo to do it, instead?"

"You know father won't allow—"

Jaw clenched, I took a deep breath. "Then that's it, isn't it? If he doesn't want one of the other Coercers to do this, then there's nothing to be done for it."

We teleported to the arena and were met by Chiron at the front entrance. The sounds of recruits chattering and laughing filtered through the archway, following him onto the lawn. Glancing over his shoulder, Chiron came toward us.

"Good morning, gentlemen. I wish I could say it was good to see you."

"Don't we all," I said, glancing over his shoulder toward the arena. "I'm sorry about this."

He waved off my apology. "No need, Nathaniel, truly."

Chiron began to lead us toward the entrance of the arena. *'Do you truly believe one of the recruits could somehow be feeding information to someone on the outside?'* he asked.

'We have to cover our bases,' I replied. *'A recruit or a mentor is the most likely culprit, considering they're who Tessa was closest to. Several knew about her relationship with me, despite how early on it was.'*

'As unfortunate as it is, we can't put our full trust in anyone just now,' Apollo added.

Chiron folded thick arms against his chest and his dark tail twitched irritably as he looked around at the recruits milling about.

'Well, I certainly hope you're wrong. I'd hate to think I've had a traitor under my nose this whole time.'

'You can't be expected to know everything, Chiron.'

Shrugging, he pulled out his bugle and let out a short blast. "Line it up, everyone!"

The recruits began falling into their lines, grouped by affinity. I ignored the curious looks we received as I halted a few yards from where the recruits stood, Apollo moving to stand beside Chiron. The mentors had ceased all discussion and stood silently just behind him, wearing expressions of wariness as they took in Apollo's presence.

Once the recruits had settled, Chiron put his hands on his hips and faced them. He stared at the ground for a few seconds before addressing them, seeming to wrestle with his conflicting emotions.

Taking a deep breath, he lifted his head and looked out at the recruits. "As you all know, one of your fellow recruits has gone through quite an ordeal. While I understand many of you may have questions, you should know that the Elders and all interested parties feel it is best that information pertaining to this ordeal remain confidential."

'You're on,' Apollo told me.

As Chiron continued to speak about teamwork and the importance of focusing on a recruit's duty to the realms, I ran my eyes over the recruits and, pushing aside my reluctance, let out my Coercion. Slowly, it trickled through the rows, sniffing at the minds of each one, prying them open as discreetly as possible. I pushed more of my power toward the mentors, gingerly prodding at their minds until they were open.

I noticed a few of the Mentalists flinching, so I reeled it in slightly. Charlise's eyes darted toward me, questioning the intrusion, as Rudolfo gave me a curious look of his own.

Ignoring them, I sent out the command for information, allowing my power to prick at the minds of each Ischyra until what I wanted to know sat at the forefront of their minds.

'What is that?' a panicked voice asked.

Something black flashed through their mind, too quickly for me to see.

'Shut your mind down!' another recruit sent out.

'I can't!' the first voice cried.

Tilting my head to the side, I eyed the two recruits who were having a desperate internal exchange in the back row, earmarking their places before I continued to examine the minds of the rest. None of the others seemed to notice my presence, and with the exception of the two whispered voices, none possessed any modicum of guilt. Once I'd finished scanning them all, I reeled the Coercion back in.

'There,' I told Apollo. *'Back row, far right.'*

"Chiron!" Apollo called, sauntering to stand beside the centaur, interrupting whatever he'd been saying. "It appears you've got a couple of recruits who'd wish to speak."

Chiron's eyes shot to me, his expression pained, then nodded as Apollo began calling out the names of the two recruits. Sliding my hands in my pockets, I moved to stand beside them.

"Anette! Andrei! Please, come forward."

My expression turned grim as I recognized Mary's former roommate and Eric's current one. Neither recruit made a move to come forward, so I sent out another command, forcing them to walk toward Apollo and Chiron.

'What are you doing?'

I gave a quick shake of my head when Mary questioned me, then purposely avoided making eye contact with Yana and Eric.

When they reached the front of the crowd, I released my mental hold, and Apollo gave them a tight smile, one he only reserved for situations in which he was attempting to hide how furious he was. He approached Andrei, then touched a finger to the recruit's chin, tilting it upward, forcing him to look into his eyes.

"Andrei, is there a reason you didn't respond when one of your leaders called you?"

Furiously, he shook his head. "I—I'm sorry, sir, I—"

"Apollo is just fine." He let his finger drop. "Now, tell me. What is so important that you're advising your friend here to shut her mind down?"

"Please—" Anette stepped forward. "Leave him be."

Surprised at her show of concern, I examined her mind further. There, toward the back, were the tell-tale claw marks of a mind who'd been subjected to a long-term mind-link. Whoever had been connected to her mind had been there for quite some time, lingering discreetly in the background, most likely unnoticed.

'Someone has linked into her mind,' I told Apollo. *'We'll have to examine it more later but watch what you say.'*

Apollo's eyes flicked up and down Anette's body, his eyes bored yet curious, before he turned back to Andrei.

"Tell me, or I will send my brother into your mind to find out for me. I don't give a damn if he has to shred those mental walls you've built to bits to do it."

Andrei's eyes widened as they darted toward me. Gently, I pushed past his walls, searching.

"I am sorry, it is just—Tessa has not been to training in weeks, and we have been worried—"

"Worried?" Apollo's eyes widened in disbelief, then he waved a hand in annoyance. "Alright, Nathaniel. Find out what he's hiding."

Someone in the crowd sucked in a breath, but the rest remained stock still, quiet as death.

I raised my eyebrows at Andrei, giving him one last chance to cooperate.

A pleading expression took over his face, although insincerity was clear in his eyes. Seeing that, I pushed through his walls with enough force to hurt, but not do damage.

'What are you hiding?' The command echoed through his mind, calling his response forward. He resisted the pull of my power with more strength than I expected, causing me to double what I hit him with, prying open the deepest parts of his mind until I pulled out his secrets.

When I had what I needed, I nodded at Apollo. *'Take them both. She's compromised, but I don't think she knows it. He's been in contact with someone on the outside, only, whoever they are is blocking their essence. A more thorough inquisition is needed, so you may want to grab Rudolfo.'*

'We are not bringing any more outsiders into this. Rudolfo stays here. You'll do the inquisition.' His tone left no room for discussion, which left me gritting my teeth.

With a quick snap of his fingers, both recruits' wrists were bound in heavy metal cuffs. Andrei let out a hiss, and for the first time, anger flashed in his eyes.

"They're laced with godsbane," Apollo whispered with a smirk. "Just enough to keep you from fighting."

I looked out at the other recruits and mentors, trying to avoid the looks of shock on their faces as they looked at me. Not two weeks ago, they'd seen me as a mentor, one of them. Now, not only did they know I was Apollo's brother, I was taking away two of their fellow Ischyra to be interrogated.

Resigned, I placed a hand on Andrei's shoulder, causing him to recoil.

'To the palace?' I asked my brother.

Apollo shook his head. *'My home.'*

I exchanged a grim look with Chiron who looked as though he was holding back a devastated expression.

'Good luck,' I murmured, then teleported away.

When we arrived at Apollo's, we cuffed the two recruits to straight-backed chairs in the middle of his living room. Andrei had given up any pretense of fear, showing nothing but anger as he glowered at me while Apollo secured him to the seat.

Desperately, I hoped Anette and Andrei would make this easy on themselves—and me. I hoped they had some inkling as to the price this would cost them if I had to force myself in and pick apart every layer of mental protection they'd built up since arriving on the mountain.

'You don't want to get Zeus?' I asked.

'Not until we've got something definitive to tell him. If we go to him before then, he's likely to do something rash. We'll go to him when we're done.'

Staring down at the recruits, I contemplated how to go about getting information. Discovering who'd linked into Anette's mind might take a different type of power than I had access to—someone who could track a being mentally, not just dissect someone's mind.

I crouched down in front of them, examining their expressions. Anette showed nothing but fear, her wide blue eyes full of it. Andrei, on the other hand, was full of contempt, an air of superiority flowing from his mind.

Ignoring his condescending look, I sighed. "You both need to listen to me very carefully. You can either tell me the truth, which I can easily confirm with a quick look into your mind, or you can keep quiet, and I will force myself to dig around until I find what I need. Which would you prefer?"

Anette began to tremble, her pale blond hair falling out of its braid and sticking to her sweat and tear-stained face. Her entire body shook as I watched her recall everything she'd learned about Coercers in her lessons growing up. Stories flashed through her mind of mental torture, scalpels of magic tearing through minds. All things I'd done before, things she now realized I could do to her.

"I'll tell you whatever you want," she said, her words tumbling out. "Please."

Pursing my lips, I nodded. "We'll get to that." I shifted my focus to Andrei. "For now, I'd like to know what Andrei has been up to."

"Then you will have to get it yourself," he spat.

I eyed him curiously. "And why is that? Why wouldn't you just spare yourself the pain and discomfort and tell us what we want to know?"

A smirk twisted his lips as he sneered at me, straining forward against his restraints. "Because I know you do not want to."

My brow lifted as I shared a look with Apollo.

"Interesting reasoning," he commented.

"Very." I gave Andrei an expectant look. "This used to be my job, one of my sole duties to Olympus. Why would you think I don't want to do it now?"

A brief look of panic flashed through his eyes, vanishing almost as quickly as it appeared, replaced by a smugness. "It is no matter. You will find what you are looking for, one way or another."

"Can't you just read his mind?" Anette's tone was pleading.

"Of course, but tearing down mental walls is painful business, no matter how weak they may be."

"And you choose pain?" Apollo arched a brow at Andrei. "Whoever your master is must be quite proud." Considering Andrei for another moment, he added, "Or disappointed in your stupidity. I suppose it could go either way."

"Andrei, just tell him what he wants to know!" Anette hissed.

"It's good advice," I told him. Silently, selfishly, I begged him to cooperate, to do this the easy way. Despite his guilt, the thought of what this could do to his mind—strong, but not half as strong as those of the giants I'd questioned just two days earlier—caused me far more discomfort than I cared for.

"I see that you're conflicted," he whispered, the corner of his mouth pulling up in a sick smile. "So, go ahead, Coercer. Do your worst."

Closing my eyes, I took a deep breath, bracing myself for what I was about to do. If he was truly guilty of high treason, he would be content to see me and all my brethren, every being on Olympus, dead. If he was against Olympus, that meant he believed a world led by the vilest of all the Titans would be better than the one we lived in now.

"Alright, then. Let's begin."

ANDREI'S SCREAMS of pain were still echoing in my mind when we left him and Anette in the palace dungeon. Shredding his mental walls, digging into the deepest parts of his mind, forcing his power to retreat into a dark corner so I could find every last bit of information he knew, was torturous, for both him and me. And yet, once I'd seen what he'd done, what he'd allowed to happen, I knew what I'd done was necessary.

After dropping them with the jailers, Apollo and I met with Zeus in the war room. Our father was pacing back and forth between the maps of Earth and the Underworld, stroking his beard thoughtfully. I sat down in a chair beside the fireplace, content to let Apollo handle the report of what Andrei had given us.

Zeus looked at Apollo. "Tell me again exactly what you saw."

"Andrei has been sending information to the empousa in exchange for safety once the war is done," Apollo explained. "Information regarding Tessa's progress, some details of her time here, and so forth. It seems that began not long after we discovered her powers as an Ischyra."

"And how has he gotten this information? I was under the impression her progress had been kept under wraps."

"Andrei is the roommate of one of her close friends," Apollo explained. He sent a glance in my direction before continuing. "It would appear the friend disclosed some of the information to Andrei, and the rest, Andrei gleaned via eavesdropping."

"You know this roommate?" Zeus asked me.

"I know him," I replied, not looking up from the floor. "He's harmless. Anything he told Andrei was fed by stupidity and perhaps jealousy, but not treason."

"You'll check his mind, regardless, along with those other friends of hers," Zeus said before turning back to Apollo.

I looked up to argue, but Apollo shot me a silencing look.

"What of the rebellion itself?" Zeus continued. "What does he know of that?"

"He knows that there are efforts at work to free Cronus and Iapetus from Tartarus, although he's unaware of any specific plans," Apollo said.

Zeus stopped his pacing, his blue eyes furious as they met mine. "You're certain of this?"

"Yes," I said tiredly. "He met with Kira, the leader of one of the empousa nests we took out in Polynesia. I don't know who she was reporting to, though."

"And she's dead?"

"She is."

He was quiet for several moments as he processed the news. When he spoke, his voice was tight. "And the girl?"

"Anette has been victim to a mind-link," I told him. "That's all I've been able to ascertain."

"We'll need someone especially skilled at mental tracking to determine who or what had hold of her," Apollo said. "I've sent out a call to Ares to track a trusted Ischyra down, and Hecate will be here shortly to place a block on their minds."

Zeus shook his head. "No, we keep this to our own. Get Scylla up here, not an Ischyra." Tapping his chin, he continued to pace. "Who else knows about this?"

"About the specifics?" Apollo shook his head. "No one. The recruits, mentors, and Chiron all watched us take them away, though."

"Put the recruits on lockdown for now," Zeus ordered. "No one in or out of the dorms, except for training." He flicked a glance at me. "I'm going to have Hades have another go at this Andrei. He may be able to get more from him."

"He doesn't *know* anything else," I snapped. "Hades won't do anything but hurt him further."

Arching a brow, Zeus paused his pacing and folded his arms across his chest. "And that's a problem? This recruit has been consorting with the enemy, Nathaniel!"

"There's no more information to get. As ruler of the Underworld, don't you think Hades has more important things to do that run your fool's errands?" I lifted my brow expectantly. "We know Andrei is guilty. Hades should be focusing on—"

"Don't you tell me what he should be focusing on," Zeus snapped.

"I did what you wanted." I rested my elbow on the arm of the chair, then propped my head in my fist, not caring how petulant I might look. "Can I go now?"

A heavy silence hung between us as we stared each other down. There was a satisfied gleam in his eye that I met with a cold look of my own. Somehow, he'd succeeded, at least temporarily, in forcing me back into the mold he'd built for me thousands of years ago. He'd done what he'd set out to do, more quickly than either of us expected, and the animosity I'd had for him that had slowly faded over the years was beginning to creep back in.

Apollo cleared his throat. "I think we're done here. We'll reassess the situation once Hecate and Scylla have given us more to go on."

Not sparing my father a parting glance, I gave Apollo a nod and teleported home.

36

TESSA

A short while later, Hades left after receiving a call from Zeus. He reminded me that he'd be back later to do a dream walk, then vanished.

"So." Eris sat down on a porch chair once he was gone and propped her feet up on the rail. "You and my baby brother, huh?"

I took the seat next to her and nodded. "Yep. Me and your baby brother."

She eyed me shrewdly, and I got the strange sensation she was trying to figure out what made me tick.

Rolling my eyes, I shook my head. "Just ask what you want to ask, Eris. It'll be a lot easier."

Narrowing her eyes, she tapped her fingers on the arm of the chair. "You used to have a thing with Hades. That's pretty obvious."

"Yes, I did, and it began and ended long before Nate was even born. Your point?"

She arched a brow and took a sip from the bottle of wine she'd filched from Nate's liquor cabinet. "Did it? End?"

"Yes, it did. Doesn't his marriage to Persephone and my relationship with Nate say that?"

She shrugged. "He thought you were dead. Now you're not, and here he is, back in your life again. I just want to know you're not going to screw over my brother, that's all."

"I love Nate, Eris," I said, suddenly feeling very exhausted. "What more do you need to know?"

"Why does Hades insist on helping you?"

Irritation pricked at me, and I struggled not to let it show, knowing it was likely what she was going for. "That's complicated."

"Then un-complicate it." Her voice held a challenge that I saw reflected in her blue eyes. She wanted me to slip up, wanted to find something that contradicted my insistence that Hades had no romantic place in my life anymore.

I met her gaze, unflinching. "In my past life, my family kept me under lock and key. They didn't want anyone to know how powerful I was or what I could do, so they prevented me from learning how to wield my power. Eventually, Cronus got word of it, but instead of teaching me to defend myself, my brothers protected me." Taking the bottle from her hand, I took a long swallow before continuing. "Hades did the opposite."

Eris scowled when I set the bottle on the arm of my chair furthest from her. "And how did your family take that?"

"My father called me a traitor, Prometheus and Atlas called me naive and locked me in my room to keep me from him." Snorting, I took another sip of wine. "They actually thought locking me away would stop me."

She jerked the bottle from my hand and set it on the opposite arm of her chair, earning a smirk from me. "So you snuck behind their backs to see your lover? That's a dangerous thing to do when a world is at war."

"I needed to learn. Eventually, Atlas gave in and started training me in physical combat, but he couldn't do much in terms of my other powers. Or maybe he wouldn't...I don't really know."

"Do you blame your brothers, then? For your death and your mother's?"

I looked at her, shocked. "Of course not!"

"Hades does," she countered. "It seems logical. If they hadn't shut you away, you probably would've been fighting right there beside them, instead of cowering behind them." She cocked her head to the side and gave me a curious look. "Do you ever wonder how it would be now, if you hadn't died? Whether you'd be his queen instead of Persephone?"

A dozen curses threatened to spill through my lips. Grimacing, I clenched my fists and reined myself in. "Stop trying to cause problems, Eris, please."

"Sorry." She twirled her finger around the neck of the bottle, then scrunched her nose and looked up at me. "You know how it is, right? With Hades? When you get upset, he feeds off of it? It's the same for me. Even if you don't actually blame them, I can still feel your resentment. It's hard not to—Hey, baby brother!" A smile lit up her face when she saw Nate appear on the lawn, quickly fading when she saw the look on his face.

"What's wrong?" I stood and jogged down the steps to meet him. His jaw was tense, eyes tight, and something—some emotion I couldn't quite name—was pulsing off of him. "Nate, what happened?"

Wordlessly, he shot a look to Eris. Frowning as I watched the silent exchange, I tugged on his sleeve. "What's going on?"

Eris' eyes darted toward me, then she smiled. "It was good to meet you, Tessa. I'll see you guys tomorrow, 'kay?"

Before I got a chance to say goodbye, she was gone.

Confused, I looked back up at Nate. His hands gripped my hips and his eyes were closed.

Brushing my thumbs across his cheek bones, I whispered, "Look at me."

When he did, his eyes were full of so much hurt I nearly buckled. Taking a deep breath, I twined my fingers through his. "Come on, let's go inside."

He let me lead him into the house, trudging slowly up the steps behind me. When we got inside, I sat him down on the couch, then dug through his liquor cabinet until I found something that wasn't wine. I poured, then sat down on the table in front of him and put the glass in his hands. "Drink."

The corner of his mouth twitched as he met my eyes, then he downed it in one gulp. Immediately, he winced, then looked at the glass in disgust. "Who put cheap vodka in my liquor cabinet?"

Smiling, I took the glass from him and set it on the table next to me. "My guess would be Dionysus, so we'll have to talk to him about his idea of a joke. Now tell me what happened."

Leaning forward, he rested his forehead against mine, running his hands up my thighs until they came to rest on my hips. He sat like that for a few moments, so I waited for him to gather his thoughts.

"I went with Apollo to scan the recruits' minds, see if we could find out who was getting information to Menoetius."

My lips moved to form questions, but I bit them back and waited for him to continue.

"Eric's roommate has been feeding information to the empousa." He dragged his eyes to mine. "Information about you."

I jerked back. "Andrei? But I barely know him! What could he possibly have to tell anyone?"

Nate's eyes searched mine, and there was a reluctance there that had my heart pounding. "It seems Eric has disclosed quite a bit about your situation. Prior to your demonstration for Zeus, he told Andrei about your powers, your training...me."

I was shaking my head before he'd even finished speaking. "No, Eric wouldn't have said anything. He promised to keep quiet."

"Well, he did." His voice rang with tired annoyance, which I tried to ignore. He let his head fall to my shoulder, and the extent of what he must've had to do to get information from Andrei was like a lead weight bearing down on us.

I ran my hands up his arms, letting my fingers tangle in his hair before kissing his temple, needing to give him the contact as much as I needed it for myself.

I couldn't believe Eric would've done something like this. Everyone had known I'd been pulled from regular training to work with Ares and Athena, but no one outside of my trainers, Mary,

Eric, and Yana had known exactly what I was or what I could do. Even now, everything was just speculation. When I'd let Mary tell Eric what was going on with me, she'd made him promise ten times over that he wouldn't tell a soul. We all knew my power wasn't something that would be kept a secret forever, but when we were first learning about it, well, there were reasons—this being case in point—that we didn't tell the whole world a Mimic had been awoken.

"Zeus is insisting that I question Eric and your friends," he said quietly.

I stiffened. "Why? Didn't you already get what you needed from Andrei?"

"Probably," he whispered. "That doesn't matter to him, though. He's already got Hades working him over a second time."

I realized now that the indescribable feeling I felt coming off of Nate when he arrived was a mixture of disgust and anger, at both himself and his father, and that only fueled my own fury. The version of Nate who'd been with me that morning—the one who'd told me he'd loved me as he took me against the shower wall, the one who left with a smile on his face—was gone. Whatever he'd done to get his information from Andrei had taken that person and replaced him with someone I barely recognized.

Gently, I pulled Nate's head back so I could look at him. "What will you have to do?"

"I'm not going to do it, Tessa." Brow furrowed, he shook his head. "The bastard can find someone else to do his inquisitions. Hades can do it."

"Hades won't be able to rein in his need to feed on their pain. They won't fight you, so it would just be simple Coercion, right? You ask a question, they answer it? As long as they don't try to hide anything—"

"It's hardly simple, Tessa." His eyes became pained. "What happens afterward, once I've treated them like criminals, when I'm still your lover and they're still your best friends?"

I considered his question for a moment, turning it over in my mind as I thought about the best answer. Taking a deep breath, I straightened my back. "Then I'll do it."

He jerked his face from my hands. "You most certainly will not!"

"Why not? You don't think I'm able to?"

"You know that's not true."

"Then what is it?"

Pain-filled eyes ran over my face. "You don't need them looking at you the way others have looked at me. You don't need to shatter the image of their friend that they're still holding on to."

"I think that ship has sailed, Nate," I said, taking his hands. "Let me help."

"We'll see," he said quietly. He brushed his thumbs across my knuckles, then kissed the back of my hand. "There's something else you need to know. It's about Anette."

I listened, stunned, as he explained how he'd seen evidence that Anette had been unknowingly mind-linked. Everything she'd seen, everything she'd done, would've been seen through the eyes of someone else, completely unnoticed to her and everyone around her. The realization that I may never have actually met the real Anette hit me like a cement truck.

"How long?" I asked, my voice raspy. "How long was someone linked to her?" *How long was someone watching us?*

"We don't know. Weeks, most likely. Scylla is going to come up and try to find out. She's good with tracking someone's power, so we should know more soon. For now, the recruits are on lockdown, only allowed out of the dorms for training."

The question of whether anyone else could've been mind-linked, watching me or my friends without our knowledge, bubbled to the surface.

"No one else was compromised," Nate assured me.

I let out a relieved breath. "Where are they?"

"The palace dungeon. Andrei, for his crimes, Anette, for her safety. Once Hecate and Scylla have examined them, we'll know better what to do with her."

"And him?" I raised a brow. "What will they do with him?"

His eyes held mine for a moment before speaking. "He'll be executed for treason."

Nausea rolled in my stomach at the thought of what that would entail.

"Who will do it?" I whispered.

"My father performs all executions," he replied. As if anticipating my next question, he tightened his hands on my waist. "You won't have to be there."

Tears filled my eyes. Whether they were from fear, sadness, or relief, I wasn't sure. I didn't know how I felt right then, knowing one of the recruits I'd come to Olympia with—a recruit I'd once shared a dinner table with—was likely going to be executed in the near future.

I remembered wondering at the transition ceremony just how many executions Zeus had doled out over the years, thinking his warning was just that, because no one would be stupid enough to go against him. The naivety of that sentiment was nearly comical.

Taking Nate's face in my hands, I kissed him, sending as much love and strength as I could in the small gesture.

Standing, I held out my hand. "Come on. Let's go to bed."

Fractured dreams woke me several hours later. Moonlight was spilling in through the windows, bathing the bed in pale, blue light, disorienting me at first. Nate was asleep on his stomach beside me, one arm thrown across my waist, the other shoved under his pillow. Any remnants of his feelings from hours earlier were gone, the expression on his face peaceful as he slept. Smiling, I traced a finger across his jaw, then his lips, before brushing his hair from his forehead.

His eyes opened for a brief moment, then he tightened his arm around my waist and pulled me closer, nuzzling my neck. Almost immediately, his breathing became even, his breath warm against my skin.

Gently, I pushed him off me, rolling him onto his back and straddling his hips. He opened his eyes again, more alert this time, and I leaned down and laid a soft kiss to his lips. I slipped my shirt off, then slid my hands up the smooth planes of his chest

His sleep-clouded gaze stayed locked on mine as his hands grazed up my thighs and he shifted under me. Sitting up, he pulled my legs tight around his waist, then ran his hands up my back, tangling in my hair as he drew my mouth to his in a deep, bruising kiss.

Our love-making that night wasn't rushed. Once again, Nate took his time, and I was content to let him, knowing how badly he needed to be surrounded by something that didn't involve pain, fear, or distress.

If I was being honest with myself, I needed it, too.

37

NATHANIEL

Hours had passed since Tessa had woken me up, dragging my mind from the darker places it had been retreating to. She hadn't erased the feelings I'd had when I came home from the palace, but the emotion that had poured from her as we moved together in bed had helped extinguish some of them, just a little.

Any remaining peace I'd gotten from her vanished the moment Apollo's voice snapped me from sleep.

'Get to the palace, now. Something's wrong in Athens.'

Ten minutes later, Tessa and I were in the war room with Zeus, Apollo, Eris, and Athena.

"Ares hasn't been able to reach Cornelius since yesterday," Zeus explained. "It's unlike him to ignore a call from his leader, so I need you all to get down there and find out what's going on. He's still tied up down in Polynesia, otherwise he'd go himself. My gut tells me something isn't right, though."

Athena and I exchanged a glance. "Any thoughts on what could've happened?" she asked.

"No. I'd say it could be nothing, but he's been trying to reach out to other soldiers in the area for the last hour with no response."

Athena tightened the strap on her baldric and nodded. "Alright. Let's go, then. Tessa, weapon up before we go."

Wordlessly, Tessa formed a whip from a vine, then looped it over her shoulder. I unclipped a knife from my belt and attached it to hers, then made a mental note to get her something of her own as soon as we returned.

Moments later, we stood just beside the Parthenon, in front of the entrance to Ischyra headquarters. I opened the door and led the way inside.

Our steps echoed off the cool stone walls as we made our descent into the dark stairwell until we reached the steel door at the bottom. Apollo pressed a few keys on the keypad by the frame, then turned the thick handle and shoved it open. I expected the bustling sound of a fully manned headquarters. Instead, eerie silence greeted us, followed by a quiet scraping sound.

Apollo hesitated a moment, then stepped inside, his face grim as he took a few steps into the hall.

'That's not at all unsettling,' Eris said, unsheathing a long trench knife.

Athena pushed past her, silently drawing her spear from the sheath on her back and gripping it tightly in her hand.

We made our way down the hall in silence, our footsteps barely making a sound on the concrete floor. When we reached the intersection at the end, we stopped.

'What's going on?' Tessa asked.

'Something isn't right,' I told her. *'No headquarters is this quiet.'*

She jumped as a thud echoed from the left, the sound of something heavy and blunt hitting metal.

Athena jutted her chin in the direction of the sound, indicating we should follow, then led us toward the muffled thumping sound. From where I stood, it seemed to be coming from the meeting room we'd been in just a few days before.

As we approached, the stillness of the building seemed to intensify. Apollo formed two small balls of light, one in each hand. Athena positioned herself with her back to the wall next to the door, then inclined her head toward me. I took up position opposite her and turned the knob, finding it locked. Putting my full weight behind it, I tried again, this time snapping the locking mechanism apart so Athena could nudge it open with her spear.

Almost immediately, I felt the sting of godsbane in the air and a burning in my lungs, just as a male voice rasped for help from inside. The door opened a few more inches, revealing a pair of black-booted legs clothed in the thick gray of an Ischyra uniform. The air coming from the room reeked of godsbane.

Athena shoved the door open the rest of the way and we rushed in. I heard Tessa suck in a gasp when she entered the room behind me. What I saw had nausea rolling in my stomach and fury boiling my blood.

Bodies of dead Ischyra were strewn around the room. Some were slumped over tables, others looked like they'd been trying to reach the door when they fell. Eyes, wide and lifeless, stared outward from faces that were frozen in pain and panic. Whatever had happened here had happened quickly, and they'd been trapped like animals.

"What the fuck happened here?" Eris whispered, her voice stunned. "Who—"

A rattling breath sounded from the floor, and I tore my eyes from the bodies around me. Turning, I found Cornelius slumped against the wall beside the door, his eyes glassy, breaths coming in ragged gasps. Without waiting for any orders, I slung his limp body over my shoulder and teleported outside, then set him on the ground against the wall. I'd just opened my mouth to ask what happened when the others appeared beside me.

Gritting my teeth, I watched as Apollo knelt to assess Cornelius' condition.

Tessa looked back and forth between Athena and me. "What happened back there?"

Athena stood beside me, hands on her hips as she stared at the entrance to headquarters. "The room was full of poison. It must've been released into the air once they were all enclosed in there."

I closed my eyes against the image of Ischyra trying to drag their dying bodies toward the door, desperate to get out.

There was a loud retching sound as Cornelius sucked in a deep breath, then hard coughing as he allowed Apollo to help him sit up.

Without giving him time to fully come to, Eris crouched down in front of him and smacked his cheek with the back of her hand. "What happened?"

Cornelius squeezed his eyes shut, then shook his head, causing his dark blond hair to spill across his forehead.

"I don't know," he rasped as he sat up and rubbed his forehead. "We were in a meeting last night, then they just started dropping." He looked around at all of us. "Were there any survivors?"

"Not that I could see," I said quietly, trying to force back the fury that wanted to unleash. "I'm sorry."

"No one was alive in that room," Apollo confirmed, shaking his head.

Tessa frowned at Cornelius curiously. "How come you survived?"

"I'm an Original Ischyra," he said, waving off Apollo's offer of assistance as he struggled to his feet. "I'll be fine in a few hours."

Suddenly, the stench of seawater hit me, then Eris gave a shout. I spun to see two hissing Sirens rise up in the air on the other side of the wall. Their large, green wings beat lazily as they hovered just above us, their thick tails swaying back and forth.

The leader of the two glared down at us. "Well, well. I was wondering when we might finally get some gods down here. Your Ischyra have been quite busy, you know."

"Saia, Mila," Apollo said dryly. "Have you come to see the result of your stunt?"

Arching a dark brow, Saia shook her head. "I don't know what you're talking about." Her gaze shifted, then narrowed when she saw Tessa. Slowly, her tail began to transform as she lowered herself to the wall, forming two thin, emaciated legs. "Mimic." She folded her arms when her feet touched the stone, ignoring the blood that still seeped over her skin. "I thought that was you."

"Oh?" Tilting her chin in a defiant gesture, Tessa let the vine she'd looped around her shoulder slip to her wrist. "I wasn't aware we'd met."

"We haven't," Mila hissed. "You killed our mother."

Apollo and I exchanged a glance.

'Take her and get out of here,' he ordered.

'Don't you dare,' Tessa snapped before refocusing on Saia. "Is she the one who tried to kidnap me and drag me back to Cronus? That was my twin, actually, but I certainly enjoyed beating her bloody before he hacked off her head."

Mila let out a low snarl, shifting to hover just behind her.

"You should have heard the sounds her wings made when we snapped them." Tessa inclined her head toward Saia's legs, gesturing with her whip. "It was almost as satisfying as hearing Atlas shatter the bones in her legs. You'd think by now you would've tried to find a better way to get your feet back than trusting some power-hungry psycho."

I tried to rein in my surprise at the malice in her tone.

'Eris,' I warned. *'Ease off.'*

'Not me this time,' she said, sending me a wide-eyed shrug.

'Leave her be,' Athena said. *'Let her handle this part.'*

Clenching my teeth, I gave her a quick nod.

"Menoetius is going to eat you alive," Mila snapped, lunging forward. "You defiled the body of our mother—"

"I defended myself against a pathetic sycophant who tried to kill me!" Tessa stepped forward, unfurling the whip. "So you can fuck off with your accusations."

"She only wanted her freedom!" Mila hissed. Pain, fleeting, but genuine, flashed in her eyes as she lunged toward Tessa. I hit her with a blast of Coercion, forcing her to stop mid-air. Hate-filled eyes met mine, but she stopped struggling.

"Menoetius was very unhappy to hear you took his prisoner." Saia jumped down from the wall. Her thin legs looked as though they might break on impact, but they held steady. "Or, so I've been told."

"Why don't you tell him to come tell me himself," Tessa shot back, taking another step toward the Sirens. "In person, not in a dream walk like some coward."

'Are we taking them in?' I asked Apollo, rallying my Coercion.

He watched the Sirens for a moment, brow furrowed, then shook his head.

'No. Not this time.'

Saia's brow raised as she put her hands on her hips. "You'd call Menoetius a coward? The Titan who plans to help overthrow Olympus? Brave words coming from a deity who's spent such a long time away from this world." Her eyes slid up and down Tessa's body, appraising. "As though you could defend yourself against the likes of him. He'd snap you in two before you could even take a breath."

"He's no conqueror," Apollo said tiredly. "Menoetius just does what he's told, nothing more. When will you puppets learn?"

Her eyes darted toward Apollo, then she shrugged. "His master doesn't, though. He does what he *wants*. And don't you ever call me a puppet again, Olympian."

Tessa laughed. "Cronus and my father are still locked up in Tartarus. They can't do a damn thing."

Mila raised a single, delicate brow at Tessa. "Not for much longer, from what I hear." She flapped her wings, lowering herself so she was eye level. "You might want to watch the things you say, Mimic."

Anger flashed through me at the cruel smirk that twisted her lips. I lashed out with my Coercion, using my mind to hold her in place as she continued to push against my power. "That's far enough," I growled. "Take your filth and spew it somewhere else."

I let her struggle for a few more seconds, then let the Coercion drop, causing her to freefall for a few seconds before she got her wings flapping again.

She glared at me as Saia looked back and forth between us, a curious expression on her face.

"That's enough, Mila. I'm sure you've made...whatever point it was you were trying to make." Her eyes traveled to each of us in turn.

"Enjoy your time on Earth, Olympians. I'm sure we'll meet again soon."

She snapped her fingers, jerking Mila's glare from me, and flew off, her legs reforming into a tail as she ascended. A moment later, Mila followed.

Tessa exhaled a heavy breath once they were out of sight, then turned toward Athena. "What was the point of that?"

"The point," Athena replied, sheathing her spear, "was to confirm what we already knew—that the rumors of their curse being lifted are true. They also probably wanted to ensure we saw their handiwork inside."

"I'd hardly call that lifted," Eris said. "Her legs were nothing but twigs."

"Then I don't know."

Wordlessly, Tessa turned and began walking back down the stairs.

I hurried to catch up with her. "Where are you going?"

"I'm going to get a read on that room and figure out what happened here," she said, her voice tense.

"I'll go in with her," Athena said from behind. Before I could argue, she added, "I want you to send out a blast of Coercion throughout the rest of the building, ferret out anyone who might be hiding. Apollo is going to get Cornelius back to Olympus for a full report."

We reached the bottom of the stairs, and I looked down at Tessa. *'Is that alright?'*

'Yes. I'll let you know what we find.'

I brushed a hand down her back and nodded. "Be safe."

"You, too."

Athena put in the code, then pushed open the door. Now that the door to the meeting room had been opened, the fading sting of godsbane in the air immediately assaulted my nostrils. I waited until they'd turned in the direction of the meeting room before leaning against the wall, then shoved my hand through my hair, trying to staunch the sickening hate that felt like it was taking over. We were on the verge of war. People were going to die, but this...This had been something else.

Unfurling my Coercion, I let it drift through the building. After a few minutes, I pulled it back in. Whoever had released the poison into that meeting room was gone.

Everyone else was dead.

38

TESSA

As we began to make our way down the hall, Athena pulled a piece of cloth out of her back pocket. "Here. Cover your nose and mouth. Breathing that stuff in will make you lightheaded and foggy pretty quick."

You don't have to tell me.

Keeping that thought to myself, I took the cloth and tied it around my head, covering the lower half of my face, then continued on to the meeting room.

Acid roiled in my stomach when I stepped inside. At least twenty dead bodies littered the floor around the door, as though the slaughtered Ischyra had been trying to escape, even as the godsbane had burned them from the inside out. Flashbacks of my own torture-by-godsbane pushed to the surface of my mind, but I quickly shut them down.

Stopping a few feet inside, I put my hands on my hips and turned in a slow circle, taking in the room and trying to avoid looking too closely at the bodies around me. I would mourn for them later, after I knew who or what had killed them.

"If Cornelius couldn't get out, that means someone or something must've locked them in," Athena remarked.

My eyes landed on the entrance. "I'm going to see if I can get a read on the door. Try to figure out how the poison got in."

Frowning, she looked around the room. "Do you think it was the Sirens?"

I shrugged. "Maybe. Poison isn't really their thing though, is it? I'd expect ears oozing with blood, not death-by-poison."

"No, I suppose you're right." With a heavy sigh, she started examining the room, stepping gingerly over the fallen Ischyra.

Placing my hand on the heavy steel door, I closed my eyes and dragged up my psychometry.

"Nothing," I said, dropping my hands after a few moments. "Just a bunch of Ischyra coming in and out."

"Were there any who left and didn't return?"

Gritting my teeth, I put my hand back on the door knob, this time watching the faces of the Ischyra who'd come and gone. "Nope, none."

"I may have found something." Athena crouched down in a corner and touched the wall, then motioned me over.

Kneeling beside her, I looked to where she was pointing and saw a small hole, about the diameter of a drinking straw, had been drilled just above the dark gray carpet.

"See what you can find," she said, standing as I leaned down for a better look. "It's not much, but it looks to be how the poison was released into the room."

I nodded and waved her off, then put my hand over the hole and closed my eyes.

After a few moments of sifting through information about the construction of the room, the vision of a male, small and pale, drilling a hole through the back of the wall appeared. Slender hands inserted a tube, then taped it securely to the drywall. Seconds later, the tube filled with gas.

"Dammit," I muttered.

"What did you see?"

"There was a tube on the other side, so I'm guessing that's how the poison was let in. Unless it's still in there, though, that's all I'll be able to see."

"Who put it there?"

"A male. Small, dark hair, really pale. Almost bluish. The color is off, but it almost felt like—"

Her mouth twisted into a disgusted sneer. "A Telchine."

"That's what I thought." I exhaled an annoyed breath. "Did you find anything else?"

"Nothing useful." Slowly, she looked around the room, her eyes tightening as she took in the fallen Ischyra once again. I began to feel crowded, cramped into this place that had gone from meeting room to tomb in what had likely been a matter of minutes.

Athena touched my elbow, then gestured toward the door. "Let's go fill in the others."

Carefully, we left the room, closing the door shut behind us.

"Who will come to take care of the bodies?" I asked, tugging the cloth from my face. The air still stung a bit, but it was better than the suffocating feeling of something covering my nose and mouth.

"I've already let Zeus know what happened. A team will be here shortly to remove the bodies and collect anything they think might be of use in catching whoever did this."

It felt strange to leave the bodies closed up in that room without waiting until the removal team arrived. I reminded myself that Athena likely had experience with these things, so I followed her back toward the outside door.

We'd almost reached the door when a frantic call from Chiron echoed through everyone's minds.

'Arena...attack.'

39

TESSA

If I hadn't trusted Chiron wholeheartedly, I would've thought he'd been playing a trick.

The lawn of the arena was deadly quiet, the normal sounds of recruits training, absent. There were no sounds indicating any type of disturbance, either.

'Do you feel that?' Nate asked.

'Feel what?'

'The wards are down.' Eris said.

My eyes shot to Athena, and my heart sank when I saw the expression matched the grim tone to her sister's voice. Her eyes went vacant, most likely calling in whoever needed to be called for something like this.

There was a quiet scraping from around the side of the arena. Cautiously, we approached and found Chiron leaning against the wall, a hand pressed to his side where blood flowed down his leg, his eyes barely open.

"What happened?" Nate demanded. He lifted Chiron's hand out of the way and prodded at the wound. "Why isn't this healing?"

Chiron slumped against the wall and winced. "Godsbane...healing...slowly."

His eyes flicked to me, but before he could speak, I heard a gurgling sound from inside the arena. Quiet, hardly noticeable, but it was enough to set me running.

'Tessa, wait!'

Ignoring Nate's call, I tore through the entrance, then skidded to a stop. I heard footsteps behind me, but I didn't bother to check who'd followed me in. I couldn't tear my gaze from what lay before me.

Like the meeting room, the arena had been turned to a slaughterhouse.

Most of the Ischyra scattered across the arena floor looked like they were sleeping, maybe just knocked unconscious in the midst of a training exercise. Logic, mixed with the harsh tinge of godsbane and the stench of death in the air, told me that wasn't the case. Bile rose in my throat as I forced myself not to look at their faces, not to look for Mary, Eric, or Yana.

They were all dead. My mentors, the other recruits. All slaughtered like beasts for sport.

A quiet chuckle drew my attention to the middle of the arena. Menoetius stood there, smirking, but he was easy to ignore.

Instead, my eyes drifted past him to the slender, unassuming blond Titan at his side. Setting my jaw and begging my heart to stop pounding so loudly, I released the vine that still hung at my wrist. Silently, I begged for whatever was in front of me to fade away, to be an illusion, another cruel trick on my brother's part.

Pale green eyes slid from the whip at my hand to my eyes, and a small smile graced my father's lips.

"Daughter," he said, the quiet familiarity of his voice like a knife through my heart. "It's good to see you. Alive."

Hatred, hot and consuming, burned in me as my body and mind urged me forward to fight him, but I felt frozen in place.

My father's lips twitched as he watched me, knowing how conflicted I must be feeling. Here was the man who'd raised me, who I thought loved me the way a father should love his daughter, only to prove completely the opposite once a need for power took hold of him.

'If you get a clear shot, take it,' Athena said. *'They've just put a protection spell around the whole damn arena, so no one else can get in. Hecate is trying to unwind the spell, and Zeus is trying to use his lightning to shatter it, but it's not working.'*

I shot out twin bolts of Coercion, one for each of them, only to have my power slam into brick walls surrounding their minds.

Ignoring my attempted attack, Iapetus turned his head a fraction of an inch toward Menoetius and gave a small nod.

Déjà vu hit me like a truck as Menoetius snapped his fingers, and the air in front of him shimmered. My heart sank as Mary, Yana, and Eric appeared, bound and gagged.

Nate's hand at my elbow was the only thing that stopped me from running toward them.

My lips began to shake as I took closer stock of my friends. Desperately, I searched their forms, praying I would find that telltale, subtle sign of an illusion. Blurred edges, eyes that were just a bit off...anything that would tell me this wasn't real, that it was just another one of Menoetius' cruel tricks.

It wasn't.

Swallowing back a sob, I took a step forward, stopping abruptly when Menoetius jerked Yana to her feet. Her hair was a knotted mess, and her blue eyes were wide with fear as he dragged her upright, wrapping his giant hand around the back of her neck. "It's killing you, isn't it, Tessa? Not knowing if this is real or another illusion?"

"I already know it's real," I snapped. I let out a quiet breath, then tentatively touched my power. Menoetius hadn't gotten it, so it was there and fully responsive. Zeus' lightning flickered at my fingertips, but I held it steady. I had no idea how much force would be behind it now that I had my Titaness strength back. If I let it out, I risked hurting or even killing my friends.

Yana struggled against Menoetius' grip, straining against her bonds as tears streamed down her cheeks. She screamed against the gag in her mouth, her terror nearly palpable.

"Daughter."

The sound of my father's voice had my fear for my friends temporarily turning to disgust.

"I have a name. You gave it to me, remember?"

A patronizing smile flickered across his lips as he interlaced his fingers behind his back. "Yes, of course. And when your mother and I chose to combine our energy, I gave you life as well."

"And when you killed my mother, you gave me death. What's your point?"

'Try not to antagonize them, but stall as long as you can. We'll be through soon.'

I nearly sighed with relief when I heard Epimetheus' voice.

"You were lucky back then, Tessa." He looked toward Mary, Eric, and Yana, then back at me. "If I had come up with the idea of a spell to steal a deity's power when you were a child, you wouldn't have made it far in the world. The small kernel of power you were born with would have been simple to take, simple to wield. It was pure chance the idea didn't come about until long after you were grown. It was perfected not two years after you died, did you know that?"

"Lucky me," I snapped through gritted teeth. "Why would you do this?"

His eyes searched mine, narrowed. "I would like you to come with us, Tessa. It will be better for everyone if you do not fight us."

I spared a glance toward Mary and Eric, both looking woozy but unhurt, then met my father's eyes. "I find that very hard to believe."

He held my gaze for several seconds, impassive, before nodding toward Menoetius.

Yana continued to struggle against Menoetius' grip. Before I could form words or summon my power, his wrist twitched, and the sound of her neck snapping echoed through the arena.

Mary and Eric screamed against their gags as utter devastation filled their faces. Acid churned in my stomach at the sickening sound, at the sight of her eyes rolling back in her head as the injury took her.

Struggling to contain my revulsion, I shifted a curious look to Menoetius.

Even for him, this was weak, as far as cruelty went. It wasn't a fatal injury for an Ischyra, nor did he draw out her torment. Or mine, for that matter. It would take her a few days to recover, but she would heal.

"Maybe," he said, picking up on my thoughts. He nudged her still form with his boot, and it took all I had not to launch myself at him. "Or maybe I drained all of her power first." A slow smile twisted his lips as he held up his hands. His palms danced with green electricity. "Do you know what a snapped neck does to a body when you've taken all of its immortal power?"

Realization slammed into me as I watched Yana's electricity writhe across his skin. Screaming, I threw myself forward, Apollo's light flickering to life in my hands, blindingly hot, incinerating the vine I'd been holding. Viciously, I wanted to shove it down my brother's throat, watch him burn from the inside out, just like *he'd* done to all the Ischyra that lay dead around us.

I barely made it two steps before Nate had me by the arms. Electricity sparked across me as my body tried to shake him off. I felt him flinch before his arms tightened around me.

'Get off me!'

'Get ahold of yourself,' Nate snapped. I felt the unmistakable twinge of Coercion in his words, forcing me to settle my thoughts, to be reasonable, not lash out. My chest heaved as I fought him, staring down at Yana, crumpled on the arena floor, surrounded by the dead bodies of her friends. A desperate need to rip my father and brother to bloody shreds began to consume everything inside of me.

'Stop it!' Nate hit me with another, slightly stronger blast of Coercion, and my body finally stopped fighting him. I took a few steadying breaths, even as irritation that he used his power on me rose.

He was right. I couldn't go after them now. We were nearly outnumbered; plus, we had two hostages to save.

"As I was saying," Iapetus continued. "You can either come with us willingly, or we will continue to kill your friends, then force you to come with us. As you can see, we've got the ability to take power, so either way, we'll get what we want. It will be far less painful for you, though, if you come of your own free will."

Straining against Nate, I glared at my father, hatred boiling out of me at the impossible choice before me.

Martyring myself wouldn't help anyone; if anything, it would only make things worse.

I couldn't martyr my friends, either, though. Not in that way.

I looked at Eric and Mary, each now gripped in one of Menoetius' meaty hands and closed my eyes. Any major power use against my father and brother was a risk but doing nothing was a greater risk. If it got them out of Menoetius' hands, we'd deal with the aftereffects later.

I knew my logic was shaky at best, but I couldn't dwell on that.

Making my choice, I lashed out with every ounce of power I had, funneling it all behind Zeus' lightning. Once again, I prayed I wasn't going to do more harm than good.

The *BOOM* echoed through the arena, the lightning throwing everything it touched back against the arena wall. I staggered on my feet behind the force of it, barely managing to stay upright as Nate's arms were ripped from around me. Menoetius' grip on Mary and Eric released as they were all thrown backward, my father right beside them. I didn't see what happened to the others, but a commotion at the entrance told me the lightning had done what I'd wanted it to do.

I glanced back, waiting long enough to see the twins and Atlas run in, followed by Zeus, Hecate, and at least a dozen others before making my move. I leapt to my feet and ran toward my friends. I needed to teleport them away, get them out of here.

Halfway there, Menoetius appeared in front of me, blocking my path. His entire body vibrated with violent fury, and for the first time since arriving, true fear for myself trickled through my veins.

Before I could summon any kind of weapon, my brothers were in front of me.

"Get out of here," Epimetheus snapped.

Menoetius' glare faltered briefly before transforming into a grin. Wordlessly, he held up his hands, curling his fingers in challenge.

"Go!" Atlas ordered as he moved toward Menoetius.

I tore past them to where Mary and Eric had fallen, just as the sound of fists on flesh met my ears. Mary looked like she was still unconscious, and Eric...

I froze.

Iapetus stood before me, hatred and malice twisting his features as he gripped Eric by the hair. A silver dagger, identical to the one he'd given Menoetius, was clutched in the long fingers of his other hand, gleaming and dripping blue with godsbane. Eric's eyes were barely open, still groggy from the impact of the lightning I'd used, mixed with whatever had already been done to him. As the cold blade of the knife touched his throat, searing his skin with godsbane, his eyes snapped open. Realizing what was happening, he started to struggle against Iapetus' grip.

I'd just unfurled a long, thin whip of fire, and had pulled back my arm to flick it, when my father sliced the blade across Eric's throat.

The world slowed and my vision clouded as I watched Eric's body fall, slumping to the ground with a quiet thud. I blinked furiously, trying to clear the shock from my vision. The quiet slide of my father's dagger followed by the jerk of Eric's body replayed itself in my mind over and over as the thin slice on Eric's neck began to gush with blood. His eyes widened in shock as he tried to form words, but all that came out was a wheezing gasp.

Screaming, I ran forward, the whip disintegrating. My father moved to grab me, but the moment his hands touched me, he was driven backward under another blast of lightning. I would kill him later, after I saved Eric.

My breath came in short, painful gasps as I slid on the sand beside Eric, hands scrabbling at his neck. Blood poured through my fingers, the poison that pulsed through it pricking my skin as I tried to staunch the flow. I pushed Apollo's light into his body, trying to heal the wound, but it was useless. Nothing could combat the amount of godsbane that had coated the knife.

Eric's bright blue eyes started to go vacant, and his hand drifted up to touch my arm.

"No. No, no, no," I whimpered, pressing my face to his chest. My fingers curled into his shirt as I rocked back and forth, wracking my brain for something else that could heal him, anything that could stop the inevitable.

Everything around me began to fade as his heartbeat began to slow, the rhythmic *thump thump* against my ear becoming a whisper as his lungs began to rattle. Blood gurgled from his lips and nose as the godsbane did its violent, quiet work, burning through his blood and organs, ensuring they could never be repaired.

Moments later, the light left his eyes and his hand slid from my arm, limp in the bloodied sand beside him. Then his body went still.

40

NATHANIEL

There was a momentary lull in the arena, only a few seconds or so after Tessa let out my father's lightning. The time we arrived at the arena until now had been only two or three minutes, at most, but watching Yana fall, hearing Tessa's screams, the blast of lightning that threw us all to the ground, had made those minutes feel like hours.

I watched as the twins latched onto Menoetius' arms, and Atlas knocked him out with a single blow to the head, preventing him from teleporting away.

Iapetus was moaning on the ground, thanks to Tessa's lightning blast directly to the chest.

And Tessa...

I took off running, jumping over the dead bodies of Ischyra as I tore across the arena to where she was hunched over Eric's body. Sliding to a halt by her side, I dropped to my knees and pried her hands from Eric's bloodied shirt. Pale hands replaced them as Apollo joined us, attempting to push his magic into Eric's body.

"I already tried," Tessa whispered hoarsely, leaning against me. "The knife was soaked with godsbane. There was too much..."

Apollo leaned back on his heels and gave her a grim look.

"I'm sorry, Tessa." His eyes shifted to me. *'I'm going to check on Yana, see if Menoetius was telling the truth about draining her power.'*

He vanished, and I turned back to Tessa. Her eyes shot up at a movement behind me, and I'd barely had time to follow her gaze when Iapetus was on his feet.

Tessa shoved me out of the way, ignoring my shouted warnings as she threw herself toward her father, screaming wordlessly.

Atlas reached her at the same time I did, and together we tackled her to the ground. She kicked and thrashed against us as Iapetus stood on wobbly legs. His pale eyes darted between us, then to Mary, unconscious on the ground not five feet away.

Zeus appeared beside him, lightning flying from his hands. Iapetus dove to the side, the concentrated bolt missing him by inches, tearing a giant hole in the arena wall behind him, instead.

Rolling, Iapetus clamped his hand on Mary's still shoulder and disappeared.

Tessa struggled even harder, lashing out with more Coercion than I thought she could manage. Electricity sparked across her body, sending shocks through both of us that were nearly impossible to fight through. My own Coercion fought against hers as I struggled to get her to stop fighting.

"Get off of me!" she screamed. "I have to go after them!"

A hand, long-fingered and pale, reached between Atlas and me and pushed down on Tessa's chest, just below her neck, helping to subdue her.

Fury sparked in her eyes as she took in Hades' added presence. A stream of curses poured from her lips as she renewed her struggles.

Seconds later, she was unconscious.

"Get her out of here," Hades snapped as he pulled his hand back. "Before she wakes and tries to track them. Throw her in the dungeon if you have to." He shot me a glare. *'Knock her out again if she tries anything stupid.'*

Atlas and I exchanged a glance, then I teleported all three of us to the palace lawn.

We lay there on the grass for a few seconds, catching our breath. I replayed the events of the last few minutes in my head, trying to wrap my head around what had happened, and how.

Atlas got to his feet, then held out a hand to help pull me up.

"Let's get her inside," he said quietly. "She needs to be cleaned up, and one of us should do a dream walk."

I nodded numbly, then lifted her into my arms and carried her through the palace doors.

My mother was there, eyes wide and full of shock as she took us in.

"Nathaniel—"

"I'm fine," I told her, not slowing as I walked past. "Get down to the arena, see if they need any help with the dead."

Atlas followed behind me as I carried Tessa into the same room she'd been in when she'd destroyed Hecate's spell at her demonstration for my father. Gods, it seemed like that had been months ago.

I laid her down on the bed and slipped off her shoes, then sent out a mental call to Athena to bring clothes.

I wasn't leaving her, and I didn't see Atlas going anywhere, either.

Jaw tense, I crouched down beside her, sliding my hand into hers as I rested my forehead on the edge of the mattress. Her screams as Yana fell, and the keening cry that poured from her throat as she clutched Eric's shirt were on a loop in my mind. A painful, stabbing loop that I didn't think would ever stop.

"I had no idea how strong she'd become," Atlas whispered, sitting down on the foot of the bed. "Has she been that way since you've known her?"

Lifting my head, I looked up at him and nodded. "She has."

He stared down at his sleeping twin, his eyes pained. "She's going to be furious with us for taking her."

"I know." I waited a few moments before speaking again. "Would you like to do the dream walk?"

He shook his head. "No, you know her better than I. Go in, do what you can to help her. I'll try to clean the blood off her."

I didn't miss the way his voice cracked over his words. The realization that his sister was truly no longer the goddess he'd known seemed to finally be cementing itself in his mind.

Closing my eyes, I pushed myself into Tessa's mind. The spell Hecate had placed was gone, once again destroyed by Zeus' lightning.

I mentally took her to a plain, white room, not wanting to draw on any additional emotions that might be tied to other places just now.

Words died on my lips as she turned to face me. Green eyes that had looked at me full of love and passion as she'd eased my pain the night before were now full of undeniable hurt and fury.

"You used your power on me," she said, her tone accusing, deadly even. "You used your power to stop me from going after my father. Why?"

"If you'd gotten your hands on him, he would've teleported you away. I had no way of knowing whether or not you'd be able to fight his attempt to take you, so I acted. I'm sorry."

"You're sorry?" She let out a disgusted laugh. "For making that choice for me or for letting him take Mary, instead?"

"That's not what happened, Tessa."

"It sure looked like it to me!"

Biting back my irritation, I took a deep breath. "I told you I would stop you if I thought you were in over your head. You were in over your fucking head back there, Tessa! That has nothing to do with faith and everything to do with logic. I wasn't going to let you try to martyr yourself in a fit of rage, after you'd *just* made the very rational decision not to do exactly that!"

"It was my choice to make!"

"And if you took two seconds to look at this situation reasonably, you would see that it would've been the wrong one. Gods, Tessa! If he'd taken you, he and Cronus would have your power by now. You would've bought Mary maybe a day and gotten yourself tortured and killed in the process! You want me to apologize for using my power on you to prevent that from happening? That's not going to happen!"

Her lip curled in aggravation as a dozen responses flashed through her eyes. "You had no right—"

"We stopped you from making a stupid mistake," I interrupted.

"He *killed* Eric, Nate!" Her voice broke on a helpless sob as she collapsed to the floor. "And Yana..."

"And going after Iapetus would not have brought either of them back," I said quietly. Slowly, I sat down next to her, tentatively placing a hand on her back. She flinched, and for a second I thought she would pull away. Then her eyes closed, and she accepted the arm I slid around her shoulders.

I expected her to cry again, to sob and scream.

Instead, she just sat quietly for several moments.

"Was it true?" she whispered. "About Yana?"

"I don't know," I replied, touching my lips to her hair. "Apollo was checking when we left."

Her lips began to tremble as tears started to streak down her cheeks. Turning her face to my chest, I wrapped both arms around her and held her. The anger that had weighed her body down moments before, eased, replaced by the tremors of sadness and grief.

I'm not sure how long we'd been sitting there when Hecate materialized in front of us. Her face was drawn, her eyes tight as she took in Tessa's demeanor.

Wiping her face with the back of her hand, Tessa sat up and looked at her morosely.

"Just say it."

Hecate opened her mouth, then shifted her eyes to me. Taking a breath, she looked back at Tessa.

"Menoetius stripped your friend of her affinity for electrokinesis," she began.

Tessa's body stiffened against mine, and I laced my fingers through hers as we waited for her to continue.

"It—well, it appears he took her power, but not her life."

"Yana's alive?" Tessa leapt to her feet, and I stood beside her, eyeing Hecate cautiously. "How is that possible?"

"She is, and we're not entirely sure," Hecate told her.

"And Mary? Do you have any idea where Iapetus might have taken her?"

"No, unfortunately. I'm sorry." Her eyes flicked to me again before speaking. "I think it's time you two return to the waking world. We've got quite a bit to discuss."

THE WAR ROOM was buzzing with conversation when we arrived. Every Elder was present, in addition to Tessa's brothers, Persephone, Hecate, Scylla, Eris, and Chiron, who still hadn't finished healing from the wound Iapetus had dealt him. Hades had taken Menoetius to a cell.

The room quieted when Tessa, Atlas, and I walked in.

Zeus stared at us for a moment, his face somber and still slightly shocked, then nodded. "Good, we're all here. Let's get on with it. Hecate, Scylla?"

"The wards around Olympus have been replaced and strengthened," Hecate began. "We've got Ischyra scouring the mountain, but it doesn't appear any of our enemies, aside from Iapetus and Menoetius, came through."

"How did this happen?" Tessa asked. "How did they take them down in the first place?"

Hecate and Scylla exchanged a look, then Scylla responded. "The best we can assume is that the witch who weakened the river fire in Tartarus somehow damaged the wards around the mountain as well."

"And those around Tartarus? Does anyone know how Iapetus got out in the first place?" Hera asked.

Persephone stepped forward, looking a bit shaken. "The wards around Tartarus are intact, and the river fire is slowly replenishing," she began. "However, it appears Iapetus and Cronus were able to slip through before the wards were back up to strength."

Murmurs erupted around the room. Zeus banged on the map of Earth to call order.

"Do we have any knowledge of where Cronus is?" Zeus asked, looking around the room.

"None, unfortunately," Persephone said. "Hades is currently

dealing with his guards, trying to figure out how this could have happened."

"When was the last time you confirmed they were inside?" Zeus asked her, teeth clenched.

"Two days ago."

"When Crius went missing," Atlas said flatly. "The Titan neither you, nor your husband, thought needed to be hunted down."

"We would have known if he brought two prisoners with him!" Persephone snapped.

"You didn't even notice there were holes in your goddamn wards until it was nearly too late! Pardon me if I don't take your excuse of 'we would have known' too seriously!"

"Alright, that's enough!" Zeus banged on the table again. "We're not here to argue. Persephone, get back down to the Underworld. Rally your best trackers and *find them*."

With a quick nod, Persephone vanished.

"Athena, Ares, gather your best, as well." Arms folded, Zeus continued to issue orders throughout the room. "Hestia, Hera, Aphrodite, get the word out to any who don't already know about what's happened. Demeter, finish replicating that antidote and get it distributed to the Liaisons. Anyone else who has not already been in contact with the groups we discussed two days ago, leave now and get it done."

Tessa and I waited quietly until he was finished and the room began to clear, until we were left with only her brothers, Hecate, Scylla, and my father.

Hecate exchanged a glance with Scylla, then set her mouth in a tight line as she looked at Tessa. "Tessa...first, you should know that Yana should be alright."

Tessa arched a brow and looked between the witches, confused. "Should? What does that mean?"

"It means we aren't quite sure what Menoetius did to her. It appears he took the affinity that was given to her as an Ischyra, but for whatever reason, he didn't kill her. Whether it was intentional or not, we don't know. Apollo is with her now, examining her further."

Frowning, I replayed Hecate's words. "He didn't take her life...is she still an immortal? Or did he do as he said and returned her to her mortal state?"

"Again, we don't know. Our current assumption is that Yana retains her immortality. If she hadn't, breaking her neck would have killed her instantly. Apollo is trying to discern that as we speak."

Tessa looked visibly relieved beside me. Letting out a quiet breath, she nodded. "Okay. Can I see her?"

"Not yet," Zeus said. "There's...more. And it may have to do with your friends from Renville."

Frowning, Tessa looked up at me, then back to Zeus. "Renville? What do you mean?"

Scylla stepped forward, her face somber. "Tessa...maybe you should—"

"Just tell me," Tessa bit out, the meager thread of composure she'd managed to hold onto beginning to fray.

Scylla took a deep breath, then met Tessa's gaze. "When you lived in Renville...did your guardians tell you or know of any supernaturals living in the area? Witches in particular?"

"No...why?"

"You were friends with some humans, correct? Other than those whom you traveled here to Olympus with?"

"Gods, Scylla, just spit it out!" Tessa snapped, her voice wobbling.

"I'm going to share a memory with you, one that I managed to glean from your friend Anette's mind when I was tracking the witch who performed the mind link." Her eyes shifted to me, then back to Tessa. "It appears he was using a glamour when he visited the Underworld, but I was able to see his true face. I think you might know him."

'Get in my head, now,' Tessa ordered me.

Casting a confused look toward Scylla, I complied, settling myself into Tessa's consciousness and waiting for Scylla to share the memory.

The moment she did, Tessa's entire body gave a jerk as the shock of recognition flashed through her.

Zeus folded his arms and stared down at her. “You recognize him, then?”

Pulling myself from Tessa’s mind, I took her hand and pulled her against my chest as I met my father’s eyes. She’d gone pale at the sight of her old friend, her features slack as she stared vacantly at the floor.

“Yeah,” she replied, her voice numb and barely a whisper. “I know exactly who he is.”

41

MARY

When I opened my eyes, the first thing that registered was the ache that throbbed through my skull and the searing pain in my wrists. Second, my wrists were chained to the damp, stone floor in some kind of dungeon. The small room I was in was almost completely bathed in darkness, save for a bright square of sunlight that streamed in through the ceiling directly above me.

I jerked to a sitting position, tugging at the thick metal links that shackled my wrists, hissing in pain when the burning increased. I could already see harsh red lines forming on the skin underneath.

"I wouldn't tug on those too hard," a raspy voice said.

Squinting, I peered through the darkness until my eyes settled on three, human-shaped lumps in the corner.

"Yeah?" Stubbornly, I gave the chains another light tug, wincing when they bit into my skin. "Why's that?"

One of the lumps leaned forward, and just enough sunlight touched her face for me to make out pale blonde hair and watery blue eyes.

"Those chains are laced with godsbane," she whispered.

"The more you pull—" a second voice said.

"The more you'll burn," the third finished.

"And the weaker I'll be. Fuck." I slumped back against the wall, wincing when the metal shifted against my skin. "Now what?"

"Now, nothing," the second voice said. "Now, you just wait until he comes for you."

"What is your power?" Number Three spoke this time.

"Water. Who's going to come?"

"Menoetius has been stealing power. Didn't you know? He's going to want yours, I'm certain."

"Yeah...he might be held up for a while." I sent up prayers to any gods who were listening that Tessa, or anyone, had killed that bastard. They'd come into the arena—our arena—flinging tiny balls of godsbane powder that exploded the moment they made contact. Before I could try to run, they'd tackled me, Eric, and Yana, keeping us away from the poison, but not well enough that it didn't make us groggy and weak.

That feeling of total helplessness was something I never wanted to fucking feel again.

"Yes, that's what his witch said," replied Number One. "He's been captured."

I squinted again, trying to see their faces more clearly.

"There are three of you over there, right? I'm going to assume you're Atlas' missing daughters? The witches?"

Number One spoke. "Yes, I am Alcyone."

Numbers two and three introduced themselves as Celaeno and Taygete.

"Do you know how long we've been here?" Celaeno asked. She leaned forward a little, and I could just barely make out features that were identical to Alcyone's.

"I'm not sure. Maybe a week?" Frowning, I tried to do the telepathy thing and reach Tessa, but I either had no idea what I was doing, or something wasn't working. "Why can't I use my power? Is the godsbane different in this neck of the woods or something?"

"It is the room," Alcyone said.

"The witch replicated Menoetius' ability to disable powers, worked it into a spell that surrounds the room."

"Telepathy? Can't you all do that? Or is there a spell blocking that, too?"

When I got no answer, I groaned. Trying not to jostle my chains, I rested my head against the wall and closed my eyes, still woozy from Tessa's lightning blast back at the arena. I was going to give that girl a giant piece of my mind for nearly killing us when I got back.

"Who's his witch, anyway?" I asked. "They haven't been able to figure it out."

"We do not know him," Celaeno replied.

"He is not one of ours," Alcyone added. "Raised human, we think."

Taygete leaned forward, but before she could add her two cents, harsh voices sounded from outside and a key rattled in the lock. Familiarity hit me, but I couldn't quite place it.

As the door opened, the witches seemed to slide into darkness, no longer visible in the dim light.

When I saw Iapetus back at the arena, he'd been calm, collected. Every movement was measured and precise, and he had this general aloofness about him. Now he looked triumphant. Gleeful.

As he stepped out of the doorway to let someone else through, I saw why.

The Titan who followed him rivaled Atlas in size. He was a wall of solid muscle with dark hair and cruel, calm eyes. Slowly, he stalked forward, stopping when he was a few inches away from me.

I squeezed my eyes shut, for once not giving a shit that I might look weak.

"Look at me," he growled.

Lips trembling, I forced a look of defiance and opened my eyes, tilting my face toward his.

Cronus, the former ruler of Olympus, looked down at me with a calm smile. He stood there for a few seconds, not moving, holding my stupidly stubborn stare before crouching down in front of me. Leaning forward, he picked up a lock of my hair and twisted it gently around his finger, then pulled, yanking my entire head forward and causing me to cry out in pain. He took a long, disgusting sniff, then shoved me back against the wall. I bit back another cry when the chains pressed harder against my skin and my head smacked against stone.

"You have the power of a god in you."

"No shit," I spat.

He chuckled. "You have the power of a god, but you're not one. You're one of those filthy Ischyra I've heard about, aren't you?"

When I didn't answer right away, he gave a sharp pull on my chains. Tears leaked from my eyes as I screamed in pain.

"Yes! Yes, I'm an Ischyra." I took several deep breaths, trying to slow the tears that were streaming down my cheeks.

"You're a perversion," Cronus said, giving me a look of disgust. "I should exterminate you here and now."

"Go right the fuck ahead," I bit out. "I'm a nobody. Who gives a shit if I die?"

Iapetus let out a dark laugh, then crouched down beside Cronus.

"You're not a nobody, Mary." Iapetus sneered down at me. "I've already killed the boy. What do you think Tessa is doing right now, not knowing whether or not you've joined him? No, you're anything but a nobody."

"The...boy?" Frantically, I tried to stand, but the shock of pain as the chains bit into my wrists sent me sliding back to the stone floor. "What are you talking about?"

"Ah, yes, I forgot. Your friend—that vapid blond creature—he's dead."

"You—you killed Eric?" I shook my head violently as fresh tears started to gush down my face, and denial screamed in my mind. "You're lying."

"He's not." A third voice spoke from beside the door, where someone I hadn't seen at first had been standing in.

My heart started to pound, and shock slowed my thoughts as recognition hit. The figure stepped forward, and brown eyes, ones that had once belonged to a good friend, stared down at me, shining with malice.

A million scattered thoughts ran through my head as I took in the face of someone I'd once thought I'd known. Someone I'd had lunch with every day since ninth grade, shared a limo with to prom, done so many normal human things with. He and Leila had been two of our best friends for years…

Iapetus shifted to the side, and Josh took his place in front of me. I didn't even have it in me to flinch away when he ruffled my hair and grinned.

"Hey there, Mare Bear. Good to see you."

IF YOU ENJOYED *Paradox* and want to see a bit more into the world of Olympus, signup for my newsletter here to get some exciting bonus scenes!

Continue reading for a preview of Entropy, the thrilling conclusion to Tessa's story...

MARY

1

I had a dream once when I was young where I fell down a well. I'd been about twelve, and completely unbeknownst to our guardians, had just spent a large part of the day swimming in an old quarry with Tessa, Leila, and Eric. When we got home, the three of us had gotten the mother of all scoldings. "Underwater currents" and "freezing temperatures" and "the gods only know what else" were a few things listed as the hidden dangers we'd been lectured on, along with the typical, "you're not immortal yet!" that we'd all received a time or three growing up.

That night, I dreamt someone tossed me down a well. I remember waking up thinking it was weird because I'd never actually *seen* one of those old-school wells with the bucket and rope, but there I was dreaming about one, anyway. All I remembered was a heavy push followed by one hit after another against a wet stone wall as I bounced down to the freezing water below that was most *certainly* filled with "the gods know what".

Now, seven years later, I felt an odd sense of deja vu. The damp walls that surrounded me in my cell weren't as physically tight as that well had seemed, but they were just as confining and just as gloomy.

It had been six days since Iapetus had kidnapped me from the arena and dropped me in a dank cell with three missing witches. Six days of being unable to move more than a few feet from the very *real* stone wall, thanks to the godsbane-infused shackles on my wrists. Six days since I'd been ripped from the massacred arena not knowing which of my friends had lived or died. Not knowing whether my captors were lying when they told me one of my oldest friends, along with the rest of the recruits and mentors, were dead at the hands of Tessa's father.

The days that the Pleiades and I spent in our small, damp stone chamber were long and dull, with only a small square of sunlight above our heads to show any passage of time. The sisters had kept track of the passing time with small scratch marks on the stone floor —there had been twelve on the day I arrived.

Once in awhile, the monotony would be broken when Cronus or Iapetus would come in and take one of the witches or dole out some punishment to me.

BANG!

The door flew open, crashing against the stone wall behind it and knocking me from my thoughts. Cronus strode in, filling up the small space with his enormous, vicious presence, followed by three guards. I tried to get a good look at them to figure out what species they were, but they kept their faces averted, so all I saw was dark hair.

"You know where to go," Cronus snapped, jerking his chin toward the three witch-sisters who sat slumped on the floor across from me.

A moment later, Cronus and I were left alone, his dark, intimidating presence causing the size of the cell to shrink in size. Tendrils of fear twisted around me as he stood, unmoving, above me, muscles straining against his shirt.

My trademark sass had evaporated days ago, replaced by a moroseness that scared even me. As Cronus glared at me, I simply stared back, hoping this wouldn't be the day he decided he wanted to drain my powers but knowing I was too weak to try to defend myself if he did.

Everything about him screamed "apex predator." He was the wolf, and I was the goddamn sheep.

As though sensing my fear, a small, cruel smirk twisted his lips. He loomed over me, standing so close that the toes of his heavy black boots were nearly touching my bare feet. One step and he could shatter every bone in my foot.

Folding his arms across his chest, he arched a brow. "What, no snappy remarks today?"

When I didn't respond, he sighed, then crouched in front of me.

My lower lip begin to tremble, and my heart thundered in my chest as his face filled my vision. I focused on the collar of his shirt, refusing to look at the cold, cruel face just above.

"Look at me."

I felt frozen, my eyes refusing to answer my mind's command to obey him.

Look at him look at him look at him.

You know what'll happen if you don't.

My silence was received with a backhand to the face.

I cried out, the sheer force of his blow nearly knocking me to the floor. My chains stopped me from face-planting, digging into my wrists and yanking me to a stop right before I hit the damp stone. Cronus latched on to my hair and gave a vicious twist, causing my neck to strain and the godsbane-infused shackles to dig into my skin.

"Please!" I began to sob, my entire body shaking. Physical pain mingled with nausea that pummeled through my body. "Please, stop!"

His only response was to backhand me again. My vision blurred with tears, and I wondered if this was how it'd felt for Tessa when Menoetius had taken and tortured her. Tessa was strong, even if she didn't know it, but even the strongest person could become weak in the worst of circumstances.

Don't try to compare yourself to her, a voice whispered in my head. *She's a Titaness. A Mimic. She's got infinite strength. All you've got is just a little bit of water.*

I squeezed my eyes shut, shrinking back from Cronus' next blow as I tried to silence the voices in my mind.

Cronus dropped his hand and angled his head to the side. "I

struggle to understand why the Fates saw fit to bless you with the power of my children. The power *I* gave them." Cruel eyes dragged across my filthy training uniform, blood and grime-encrusted hair, and tear-streaked face. "There must've been thousands of other humans they could've instilled with the gods' magic, who would've begged for it, but instead, they gave it to *you.*" He gave a lock of my hair another yank, and I hissed at the quick pain. "It's disappointing to see someone with such power reduced to this."

"Did you chain me up just to pull my hair and insult me?" I rasped, struggling to find some sense of myself through the pain. I shot him a smirk. "I guess that's all bullies are good for, huh?"

His expression remained unchanged as he delivered another backhand to my face, this time to the other cheek.

"Your water abilities... they belonged to my son once, you know." He shook his head as the look of disgust he wore deepened. "I wonder what Poseidon would say if he knew the drop of power he'd handed over had been wasted on such a pathetic—"

The heavy iron door opened, ushering in a gust of cool air.

"Cronus, I think she's had enough."

The pain of Cronus' beating transformed into a leaden feeling in my gut at the sound of Josh's voice. I slumped against the wall, my head still ringing from that last hit, and refused to look at him.

At my *friend.*

Former friend. Don't you forget it.

Cronus' lip curled in annoyance as he stood to face Josh. A moment later, he strode through the door, leaving me alone with Josh, who closed the door, and slid down to sit beside me. His knees were bent, forearms propped casually on top as he rested his head against the wall.

Tears stung my eyes as the air shifted, and I was hit with his familiar scent—either his soap or aftershave, or maybe just him, I wasn't sure. All I knew was that it was the familiar smell of family, of someone I'd shared nearly every day with for the past four years. The fact that he still smelled like the guy I'd loved like a brother was a torture all its own.

In the week I'd been here, I'd seen him only twice—the day Iapetus and Cronus dragged me back here after slaughtering the other Ischyra recruits in the arena and again a few days later. I'd been out of it when I arrived here, groggy from both the godsbane that had poisoned me and from the blast of Tessa's power that had taken everyone in the arena down. The second time had been two days before when he'd strolled into the room, looked around, and left, as though he'd come in for something and forgotten what it was.

The pain from Cronus' hits was receding, but it was a struggle not to focus on the boy—or whatever he was—at my side.

"How ya doing, Mare?"

"Fuck off," I muttered, wincing when my jaw protested at the movement.

He nudged me with his elbow. "You know, you shouldn't antagonize him. It takes a lot longer to heal in here than it does out there."

I shifted baleful eyes toward him. "Fuck. Off."

He sniffed out a laugh. "Do you want to know a secret?"

"Probably not," I grumbled, although secretly I was morbidly curious.

"*I* think it was silly of Iapetus to take you," he whispered conspiratorially. "I plan to let you go eventually, don't worry, but I thought it might be fun to make Tessa stew a bit first, get her nice and riled. What do you think?"

Slowly, I slid him a disbelieving look.

"You know, this isn't the girl I remember," he said with a click of his tongue. "Where's your fight, Mare?"

"I must've left it back on Olympus when you freaks poisoned me, beat me, and dragged me away from the people I love."

"Technically it's 'person,' now, right?"

"What?"

"You said 'people I love.'" He shrugged. "Tessa's the only one left."

"Shockingly, I met new people while I was there," I snapped. "Believe it or not, I'm capable of making new friends."

"Mary Miller brought people into her inner circle?" He stuck out his lower lip and nodded. "I don't remember you being so *inclusive* in

Renville. But yes, I suppose we *could* classify Yana and Anette in the 'people you love' category."

I rolled my eyes but tried not to let on how upset I actually was. As each day passed, I was losing more and more hope that I'd ever see the people I cared for again. Tessa was the only person left from my old life now, but the new additions—Yana, Anette, Nate and his stupid brothers, and Tessa's brothers—had surprisingly found a place in my heart, and the thought of not seeing them again hurt like a bitch.

I turned my head to resume my staring contest with the wall across from me, but Josh gripped my jaw and forced me to look at him, eyes narrowed.

My fingers tugged feebly at his arm. "What the—"

"Quiet," he snapped, dropping his human act. His cold brown eyes searched mine, then a satisfied smile curved his lips. "Sorry, Tess. This conversation is for our ears, only. It's good to see you got that mind link down, though. Keep up the good work."

My eyes widened as I took in his meaning, but before I could rally my brain to reach out to her, I felt a hard *flick,* then his eyes shifted their focus back to me.

He smirked. "Sorry about that. Can't have prying eyes looking in all the time, can we?"

I opened my mouth to tell him we most certainly *could*, but my lips refused to form the words.

"Now, let's chat."

TESSA

2

With a frustrated growl, I released Hermes' hands and dropped down on Nate's bed, then braced my hands on my knees as I sucked in heavy mouthfuls of air. Slowly, the magic that I'd used to link my mind to Mary's began to fade, along with any lingering feelings of her presence.

Hermes sat down next to me and slid a comforting arm around my shoulders, pulling me against his chest and resting his chin on my head as the sound of Cronus' hits replayed over and over in my mind.

"It'll be alright, Tessa," he murmured.

"Didn't you see what he did to her?" I cried as I shoved him away.

They were *beating* her. Hurting her. Probably draining her power at this point, too.

"And we're going to get her back," Epimetheus said soothingly, moving to stand in front of me. He leaned down and placed his hands on my shoulders, meeting my gaze. "That's why we're doing this."

"I know it's hard, but we have to keep trying, alright?" Hermes said.

"Gods, I *know* that!" I shoved my brother away and began pacing Nate's bedroom. I ran a hand roughly through my hair as fury and frustration began to mingle with fear for my best friend.

Over the last several days, Hermes had been acting as an anchor for my body while I sent my consciousness to other places on the astral realm, in the dream realm, and along the mental connections on the physical plane that, according to him, connected us all. We'd hoped to home in on Mary and the Pleiades, but we'd quickly discovered that was nearly impossible. Whatever magic was being used to conceal her prison rarely faltered, and when it did, it wasn't for more than a few moments. We'd had brief success with astral projection, but I was only ever able to see the space immediately around Mary and nothing more. Any distinguishing features of her prison remained hidden.

"What did you see?" Epimetheus asked carefully. "How is she doing?"

I wiped at my eyes and tried to compose myself. "She's doing... alright, I think. Scared, pissed off that she's scared, and she misses us." I gave Hermes a watery smile. "Including Nate's stupid brothers."

His blond eyebrows shot up. "She called us stupid? Dionysus will be heartbroken."

Epimetheus snorted. "Her spirits must not be so bad, then."

"I guess." I rubbed my fingers over my eyes, my hands shaking as I tried to forget the sound of Cronus' huge hand against Mary's cheek, the looks of fear on the three Pleiades' faces as they were dragged from the room. It took all I had not to break down in a sobbing mess.

Focus, Tessa.

After a moment, I looked at Hermes. "I thought a mind link would be harder to detect than astral projection."

"It *is* harder to detect if you're not looking for it." Hermes shrugged. "I wouldn't be surprised if Josh had been waiting for you to drop in."

"Pretty convenient he happened to pay her a visit right when you showed up," Epimetheus muttered. "Do you think he can sense intrusions, like that empousa that was in Atlas' mind?"

"That could be it," Hermes said. "Or maybe he was just waiting. He's a witch, after all. My guess is he's got some kind of warning system that will sense any type of magical intrusion. The dungeons here at the palace are set up similarly."

"Yeah, maybe," I said quietly, hoping it was something that simple. Systems could be taken apart. Maybe not easily, but it could be done.

Hermes laid down on the bed and folded his arms under his head. "Alright, let's look at what we know, then. What did you just see?"

I lay down next to him, mimicking his pose. Epimetheus took a seat near the end of the bed and frowned, awaiting my response. "A stone room, the three Pleiades getting dragged off, and Cronus and Josh."

"And what else did you learn?"

I clasped my hands over my stomach, tapping my fingers against the waistband of my jeans as I thought. "Mindlinking works, but only briefly. We got through, so whatever magic is being used to block the room is fallible. And now Mary knows I can get into her head. If nothing else, maybe that'll improve her morale a little bit, hopefully." Which was a good thing, relatively speaking, unless Josh did something witchy and blocked me out permanently.

"Exactly." Hermes propped himself up on his arm and looked down at me with a grin. "Considering how miserable she seemed, I would imagine that knowledge might improve her spirits a good deal."

I chewed my lip uncertainly. I didn't need to bother mentioning how little fight Mary seemed to have in her. It didn't seem as though they'd been draining her powers, but the sheer hopelessness that was plaguing her was like a knife to the gut. The girl I'd just linked to... that wasn't my best friend. That was a mere shadow of the feisty, stubborn, no-nonsense person I'd grown up with. That her experience was so similar to my own had pity surging inside me, which I quickly tamped down. Pity wouldn't help her right now; it would only make things harder for those trying to find her.

Closing my eyes, I reached back, desperately searching for something in her mind that had told me she wasn't entirely lost. It had been there, a small spark, but it was quickly dwindling.

"Mary's no idiot," Epimetheus said softly. "If she knows you were there, she knows you're doing all you can to find them."

Sitting up, Hermes patted my leg, his golden fingers giving my calf a reassuring squeeze. "Try not to worry. You got into her head once. It won't be a problem for you to do it again."

"You've been running yourself ragged," Epimetheus added. "You need to try and save some of your energy if you're going to keep trying to find her."

I shot him a look that told him I'd be doing no such thing, and he just shrugged in response.

"Gods, I just wish we could do a dream walk!" I exclaimed, exasperated.

"That didn't work the first five times we tried, so shelve that one for now," Hermes said. "We need to figure out our next approach. Have you ever used Splitter powers?"

"You mean that hive mind power?" I shuddered. "No. Telepathy is as far as I like to go with mental conversing." I stared up at the skylight, watching as the clouds slowly drifted past the cabin while I ran through my other powers. There were a few I hadn't tried that I could still tap into, although most of those were ones I hadn't had much practice with. "But...now that we know Mary is with the missing Pleiades, it might be worth a shot, as long as I can limit it to their immediate space. If I can get through to even *one* of them..."

"You may want to touch base with the sisters who weren't taken, then," Epimetheus suggested. "They might be better suited to help guide you."

Hermes arched a brow. "You think they haven't already tried to locate them?"

"It's more than likely, but it could be worth trying," Epimetheus replied.

"If they'd had any kind of success, we would've heard about it," I said.

"It's still worth a shot," Hermes said patiently. I could tell he was getting annoyed with my negativity, but these constant failures were wearing on me more each day.

I took a deep breath and nodded. "Yeah," I said quietly. "You're right."

"Will you bring Atlas?" Epimetheus asked.

His question gave me pause. In the short time Atlas had been back on Olympus, he hadn't been down to Demeter's house in the valley, where three of his seven daughters were living temporarily. From conversations we'd had, I knew he wanted to build a relationship with them, something he hadn't been able to do in the past. He was scared, though, something he would never openly admit.

"I don't know," I finally said. I rubbed my fingers across my brow, suddenly feeling overcome with exhaustion. "Probably. My brain hurts."

Hermes put his sandaled feet to the floor and stood, then held out his hand. "Come on, then. Let's head outside."

I gave him a dubious look as I took his hand. "For what?"

"So you can practice your elemental powers."

Epimetheus stood beside him and smiled gently. "You've been so focused on Mentalist abilities the last few days; your head needs a break."

"That's for damn sure." I slipped the hair tie off my wrist and twisted my hair up into a bun. "But don't you guys have places to be?"

Hermes shrugged. "Eventually. Besides, I told Nathaniel I'd keep you company, though."

"It'd be nice if Zeus gave him a damn break for once," I muttered. "He's been dealing with Menoetius all week."

"We're heading into war," he said simply. "This is how it goes, at least from what I've been told, and digging into prisoners' minds... well, that's what Nathaniel is good at."

I swallowed hard, knowing just how much Nate hated that fact.

Epimetheus gave my shoulder a quick squeeze.

'We're all going to do things we might otherwise find unseemly by the time this is all over. Nathaniel isn't one to lose sight of himself, Tessa.'

I patted his hand in thanks. *'I know.'*

As soon as he pulled the door open, the sounds of bickering from the living room reached my ears, nearly causing me to retreat back into the bedroom that had become our near-permanent residence the last few days. Epimetheus caught me by the shoulders and nudged me forward, stopping my attempt to flee from what was becoming an increasingly common annoyance.

"Change of plans," Hermes muttered as we listened to yet another argument between Apollo and Yana.

"It has been three days! You cannot keep me locked up here—"

"You are not locked up, Yana." Apollo's voice rang with irritation. "It's safer for you to remain here."

I couldn't help but smirk at the patience Apollo was struggling to force into his voice. Dealing with Yana the last few days had been... trying. She'd slept for three days after Menoetius had drained her powers and snapped her neck. When she woke up, she was a spitting ball of fury and fought almost every attempt Apollo made to heal the broken connections to her magic. They'd been futile attempts, as we all knew they would be, and I think they upset her more than if he'd done nothing at all.

And while he hadn't said it outright, I was pretty sure it upset Apollo more than anyone that this had become a problem he was unable to fix.

"Up until a week ago, we thought this whole mountain was safe!" Yana shot back. "Now you are saying I cannot even return to my room to get my things—"

"I've already *told* you we are sending someone to retrieve your belongings."

Yana dragged her hands through her short, black hair and let out a string of rapid-fire Romanian.

"Bringing my mother into this is highly improper," Apollo snapped.

"Screw your propriety *and* your mother," Yana growled. "I am going to get my things!"

Apollo's face took on a look of outrage. "How *dare* you speak to me that way!"

"You want to give him a hand?" Epimetheus murmured to me. "Apollo looks a bit out of his depth."

Bracing myself for Yana's ire, I stepped into the living room. "I can take her down to the dorms to get her stuff, Apollo."

He shot me an icy glare, clearly irritated I'd just circumvented his order that she stay put.

I smiled sweetly. "Don't you think I can keep her safe?"

"I can keep myself safe," Yana spat, turning her stormy eyes on me.

"She needs to get out of the house, and you need to stop playing babysitter," I told him, ignoring her.

"As far as everyone in Olympia knows, all of the recruits, save Mary, Andrei, and Anette, were killed in the attack," Apollo said slowly. "Menoetius thinks draining Yana's powers also drained her immortality, meaning she should be dead right now. If he or anyone else finds out she's still alive—"

"Menoetius doesn't care whether or not Yana is alive," I told him. "And even if he did, he's locked in the palace dungeons. She could parade around Olympia naked, and they'd never find out." I walked toward them and linked my arm through hers, then gave him a bright smile. "And we don't need your permission."

His mouth barely had time to twist into a scowl before I'd teleported us away, coming to a stop just inside the dorms that, up until a week ago, had housed all fifty of this generation's Ischyra recruits.

For a few moments, Yana and I stood there, taking it in. Nothing about the stone courtyard—the granite slabs that made up the floor, the stone fountain or the surrounding benches—looked different, but I could feel it. It was just...empty. Even the quiet sound of the fountain's burbling water seemed morose, as though it were sad there was no one there to enjoy its calming presence.

"It is so quiet," Yana said. Her voice was hardly more than a whisper, but it seemed to echo through the empty space.

"Yeah." I angled my head toward the archway that led to the female recruits' hall. "Come on, let's go."

Wordlessly, we made our way through the covered walkway that encircled the courtyard toward the hall. It'd been a month since I'd slept in my old bed, and nearly as long since Mary had moved out of her room with Anette and in with Yana. It felt more like years, though. Eons.

Neither of us looked at the closed doors that used to belong to the other recruits as we passed.

Yana pushed open the dark door with the elegant gold script that still bore both of our names and stepped inside, holding the door long enough for me to follow. She didn't spare Mary's unmade bed a glance as she tugged her large duffel bag from under her bed and began systematically opening drawers and emptying them. As she picked up a book that she'd left on the foot of her bed, she looked at me with lifted brows. "Do you want to get any of Mary's things while we are here? For when we find her?"

I felt a lump form in my throat as I thought of my best friend trapped in whatever dark hole Cronus and Iapetus had shoved her in. The fact that Yana was so certain we'd find her alive and in one piece made me think she hadn't lost as much hope as it had initially seemed.

"Yeah." I cleared my throat and nodded, then turned toward her bed. "Yeah, I'll grab her things."

So, while Yana finished packing up her things, I began to pack up Mary's, all the while making her a silent promise that she'd be the one to unpack them.

When we were finished, I hoisted Mary's suitcase off the ground and turned toward the door, not wanting to take in the room now that it appeared so desolate. We stepped into the hall, and I eyed the closed doors that ran along either side.

"The funeral is in two days," I remarked.

Yana pressed her lips into a thin line. "Each recruit should take something with them. Not just coins. Maybe photos? I think all of us brought at least one or two."

"I think the guardians would appreciate that."

Quietly, Yana and I went room to room, and I used my telekinesis to unlock each door. We'd all brought very few personal objects with us from Earth—books, jewelry, or some other small thing, but Yana was right. The one thing we'd all brought were photos, so we took those.

Once we'd gotten a stack of pictures to take back with us, we packed up the rest of their belongings in their respective suitcases or duffel bags and set them on their beds, just in case their former guardians wanted to take their things back to Earth. I didn't know if they'd all appreciate it or not, but I know if I'd been in their shoes, packing up the belongings of the person I'd raised for eighteen years by myself would be the epitome of painful.

When we reached Anette's room, I hesitated. Since they discovered she'd been connected to Josh through a mind link, Anette hadn't been released from the palace dungeon. No matter how much Nate or I tried to convince Zeus she would be fine, he wouldn't relent.

"Where will she stay once she is let out?" Yana asked, picking up on my thoughts.

"No idea. She's welcome at Nate's, obviously. He's got the room. There are apartments in Olympia, though, so maybe she'd want one of those?" I shook my head as I gazed around the room. "I don't know. I can't imagine any of you will be forced to stay here."

"I will refuse." Her tone left no room for argument. "This place is a tomb. I cannot stay here." She gave a small frown. "If they even allow me to. If I have no powers, what good will I be?"

I gave her shoulder a squeeze. "I wouldn't worry about that just yet. You're still badass, even if you can't electrocute us anymore."

She gave a small huff, then moved to Anette's dresser and opened the top drawer. "I am going to pack up her things. We can bring them back to Nate's for now, but they should not stay here."

We spent the next few minutes scouring Anette's room, piling clothes, books, and other knick knacks into her bag. Once the bag was full, Yana scrunched her face in confusion as she stared at the pile of clothes that was still on her bed.

"How in all the realms did she fit all of this in her bag?"

"Ziploc bags." I smiled, remembering that I'd asked the same thing when I met Anette. "She packed all her clothes in Ziploc bags, sucked the air out so they were flat. Just leave the rest. I'll come back and get everything else later."

We left the girls' hall and went across the courtyard to where the guys' hall entrance was. We repeated the same process in their rooms until finally, only one room was left.

When we reached Eric and Andrei's door, Yana gave me a reassuring pat on the back. "I will wait for you out here."

I smiled gratefully. Hesitantly, I placed my hand on the knob, knowing I would be hit with a thousand memories once I entered his room. Memories that I knew I needed to face alone.

When I entered, I sat down on his unmade bed and closed my eyes, my fingers curling tightly around the rumpled sheets. As I did, the painful scent of citrus mixed with cedar hit my nose, immediately bringing tears to my eyes. I'd always hated the smell of his body wash, but it was so unmistakably *Eric* that the tears I'd been holding back finally began to flow. Drawing his pillow to my face, I inhaled, breathing in my old friend, the guy I'd spent day after day with and who I'd never see again.

Quiet sobs shook my shoulders as my grip on his pillow tightened. There was nothing left of Eric except *things*—sheets and clothes and pictures. All I wanted was my friend back.

No. All I wanted was my old life back.

It angered me to think that, because I knew it wasn't entirely true.

And yet, if I were still the same girl I'd been when I came to Olympus, Mary wouldn't be missing. Eric—and all the recruits—would still be alive. I wouldn't need to clutch his pillow to remind myself of what it was like to get one of his bone-crushing hugs, the kind that spoke volumes about the kind of person he was.

Loving. Carefree. Happy. Loyal.

And now, gone.

Lifting my tear-filled eyes, I stared at the bed across from Eric's, perfectly made, and waves of fury rolled inside me as I thought of who'd once slept there. Andrei had been Eric's roommate and first friend on Olympus, and now he was rotting away in the palace dungeons, awaiting execution.

How in all the realms had it come to this? How had we gone from group dinners, crushes, and training, to murder and betrayal?

I shook my head and wiped the tears from my cheeks. Taking a few deep breaths, I tried to steady myself. There would be a day for dwelling on the things we all could've done differently, but today wasn't it. Grief wasn't a luxury I could afford just yet. Maybe ever, considering how things were going these days.

Standing, I swiped a few photos out of Eric's top drawer—ones of me and him with Mary and another of him and his guardians—and slid them into my back pocket. I hesitated when I saw the photo of us from prom—Eric and I had gone together, along with Mary, our human friend, Kellan... and Josh and Leila.

It had been one of the best nights in high school, one I knew I'd never forget. We'd celebrated that night, one last hurrah before Mary, Eric, and I left for Olympus. We'd danced like fools with the rest of the senior class before taking the party back to Josh's house, set deep in the woods outside Renville. It had been a night that celebrated friendship, our love for each other... the kind of love that would transcend the separation of our mortal and immortal lives.

Until it didn't.

Now when I looked at that photo, all I felt was rage, sharp and hot, mixed with an unrelenting sadness.

I tossed the picture in the trash can by Eric's dresser, then bent down to pull his duffel bag out from under his bed. Quickly, I packed up all his things, then set the duffel on top of his bed for his guardians, Joanne and Evan, to decide what to do with when they arrived.

Wiping the remainder of the tears from my face, I left, not bothering with any of Andrei's things. Maybe it was unfair to his guardians, but I couldn't handle taking the time and care needed to pack up his belongings when he'd wronged us so badly. If anything, I wanted to take them to the Underworld and toss them in the Phlegethon, letting its fire wipe all reminders of him from existence.

Yana was leaning against the wall across from Eric's room when I emerged a few moments later.

"Ready?" she asked.

"As I'll ever be."

NATHANIEL

3

Spending my days picking apart the mental shield of a creature like Menoetius was akin to having needles shoved under my fingernails. With each few threads of his magic I ripped free, one would bite back, nipping at my powers like a stinging insect. His powers were as vile as he was, twisting into thorny ropes around my own tendrils of Coercion as I tried to find out whatever it was he was hiding.

"It might help if you got my baby sister in here, you know." Menoetius' chest heaved as he stared up at me and Hades from where he was slumped against the wall of his cell. "She's finally coming into those powers of hers, after all. Tell me, which one of you gave her that last push to embrace what the Fates gave her?"

I gritted my teeth at was probably his tenth attempt to lure me into an argument with Tessa's former lover. If I didn't know how important it was for us to get through his walls, I would've thought my father sending me down here to work with Hades was some sort of punishment. Both of them were as antagonistic as they were vicious, but I only had the luxury of leaving one behind.

"Do you ever get tired of hearing yourself speak?" Hades asked dryly, narrowing his eyes as I pulled apart a few more strands of

Menoetius' shield. We'd been trying—and failing, for the most part —to get information from Menoetius for the last week. As I attempted to disassemble his shields, Hades tried to pull information from his memory.

But everyone had their weaknesses, and we would find his.

"Your shields are impressive," I commented, slowly sliding free another dull, brown thread of magic from his shield. "It's been three days, and I've barely been able to get anything from you. How long did they take you to build?"

"Centuries," he said with a smirk. "I'm curious to see how long it takes you to unravel them, to be honest." He angled his head to the side. "I wonder if you'll be happy with what you see once you do."

"If you want that to happen, why fight me?" Four threads.

"Are you *that* eager to see all the glorious things I did to Tessa, Nathaniel?" He grinned wickedly. "And here I thought Hades was the resident sadist." He gave Hades a considering look. "Or is it masochist? You're spending a great deal of time with your lost lover's new mate. Are you hoping he might share, or do you just enjoy torturing yourself?"

I swallowed back the urge to reach through the bars and throttle him, and Hades let out a quiet growl.

Ignoring them both, I went back to work.

'Did you see that?' Hades asked as an image flashed in the space where I'd just created a small crevice in Menoetius' shield.

'Mountains?'

'We'll share it with Persephone later. She may know the place he's remembering.'

I gave him a quick nod. All we'd gotten the last few days were small flashes—mountains, the sea, and a couple brief glimpses of Tessa's hometown of Renville. So far, though, we'd had no luck figuring out what any of it meant.

"Really, though. How long do you plan to do this on your own before you put your stubbornness aside and bring Tessa in here to assist?" Menoetius asked.

The corner of my mouth curved up. "Why do you think I haven't brought her in?"

He let out a low chuckle. "Well, then, if you're going to insist on sheltering her like my moronic brothers, might I suggest we bring in a bottle of wine to share since we'll be spending so much time together?"

"You don't strike me as the wine and dine type, Menoetius." Two threads.

Snap.

I held back my hiss of pain as his power stabbed at mine, but the wobble of his lips told me he'd caught my reaction. The pain was brief but intense, a shock that traveled through the tendrils of power I'd sent out.

"These shields take on a mind of their own after awhile, don't they? You'd think the witches would've concocted a way to spell these rooms to disable involuntary magic." He looked around his cell and shook his head. "It'd make things much easier."

"They have," Hades told him. "Why do you think we find yours so fascinating?"

Gritting my teeth, I stood up from the stool I'd been sitting on and cracked my neck.

"Leaving so soon?" Menoetius gave me an amused look. "And here I thought you might want to hear about the dreams Tessa had after Hades returned her memories." His expression turned wicked. "They were quite...vivid."

"Sorry to disappoint," I muttered. "I'll be back soon, don't worry."

Not bothering to wait for Hades, I turned and strode down the hall, away from Menoetius' cell. As much as I hated to admit it, I needed a break from his constant attempts to pit me and Hades against one another. Regardless of my trust in Tessa, there was no denying the fact that feelings had awoken in Hades for her that had been dormant for millennia.

He wouldn't stray from Persephone. I knew that as well as anyone. It didn't change the fact that the thought of Tessa dreaming of their time together made me feel a bit ill, even if it was just the result of memories resettling themselves in her mind.

As I traveled down the long hall of stone cells that made up the underground dungeon, I ruminated on how to handle Menoetius' shields. They were the most complex I'd ever seen; far more than the Giants I'd questioned in the Underworld, and they were direct descendants of Gaia and Ouranos themselves. The Giants' shields had been made of brute strength: effective, but easy to break through with the right amount of power, if not a little painful for them.

I had no trouble believing Menoetius when he said his own had taken centuries to create, but I also didn't believe for a second that he'd been the one to create them. They seemed to be made up of sheer intelligence and cunning. The trip wires woven in blended into the rest of his magic seamlessly, making it nearly impossible, so far as I could tell, to differentiate between the two.

As I neared the door that would lead back up to the palace, I paused when I heard a prisoner's voice from the second to last cell.

Andrei had been mostly quiet the last few days, with the exception of a few occasional taunts as Hades or I walked past his cell. After spending the first few days banging on his bars and screaming obscenities, he'd resorted to the occasional snide comment, seemingly accepting his fate and the fact that his masters would not be coming for him.

"Coercer!" Andrei's voice was rough with disuse. "I know you are out there!"

"Ignore him," Hades said, coming to a stop behind me.

"That's the third time in as many days he's tried to get my attention," I muttered as I continued past his cell. Frowning, I ascended the stairs that led back up to the palace. "It's irritating."

"Does our infallible Coercer think he missed something?" Hades mused.

I cocked a brow. "Considering recent events, I really wouldn't throw barbs about missing key pieces of information, Hades. And no, I don't believe I missed anything."

His amused expression immediately slipped into a glower, and he remained silent as we made the trek through the gilded halls of the palace to my father's war room.

A heated argument could be heard through the door, the raised voices of Zeus, Atlas, Prometheus, and Poseidon carrying clearly through the heavy wood. It had been typical the last few days—one would suggest something, Zeus would shoot it down. Rinse, repeat.

"Ah, Nathaniel, Hades!" Zeus smiled when we walked in, ignoring the looks of annoyance on the other gods' faces. "How are things with Menoetius? Any luck?"

I nodded a greeting at the other three gods, then shook my head. "His walls are too complex to break with brute force, so it's taking longer than I'd hoped, but it'll get done."

"If I didn't know better, I might think he was enjoying this," Hades said, shaking his head. "Whoever helped build his shields—"

"Knew exactly what they were doing," I finished.

"Are you planning on asking Tessa for assistance?" Atlas asked.

I cast him a look. "I am. We need the help, and it will be good for her."

"Brother, you're admitting you need assistance?" Zeus appraised Hades, his tone taunting. "That's somewhat unlike you."

Hades gave Zeus a withering look. "Knowing when to put my pride down and accept help is *quite* like me, actually. You'd do well to take a page from my book now and again."

My father's lip curled in annoyance.

"When do you plan to bring Tessa in?" Poseidon asked me wearily, cutting off yet another spat between his brothers.

"Tomorrow after the briefing," I said.

"Is it really necessary to include her in this?" Atlas asked, his face stormy.

"She'll be fine," Prometheus said reassuringly. His expression was reluctant, but he'd come to acknowledge Tessa's abilities for what they were in the last two weeks. "You need to trust her."

"I do," Atlas snapped. "I just don't want her near him. He can smell her fear, feeds off it." He shook his head. "Her being there will be amusing to him."

"She won't be alone," I pointed out, my patience waning. "Hades and I will be with her."

"And fear isn't what's driving her now," Hades said. "Vengeance is. She's well-prepared."

"Is that any better?" Atlas murmured, more to himself. He ran a hand through his hair and sighed.

"The others will be here tomorrow morning for a full briefing, so I'm hoping you'll have more information when you go back in," Zeus said. "Dionysus and Chiron have brought back representatives from several groups, and the Titans who've agreed to help are all on their way. I need you all here first thing."

I braced my hands on the table and looked over the wooden markers that indicated sightings of Cronus' allies. Red circles dotted areas throughout Earth, marking attacks by empousa, which seemed to be the most widespread of Cronus' forces. Blue marked the shapeshifting crocotta, and marked in green were the crop failures and other incidences of poisoning that had been facilitated by the Telchines—including that of the attack on the Ischyra compound in Athens. Several red markers that hadn't been there the day before were scattered across northern Asia.

"Those are new." I pointed at the swath of circles in Siberia. "What's happened in Russia?"

"Empousa attacks," Poseidon said, his expression grim.

"I thought the lamia had them in hand?" I asked, confused.

"They do now." Poseidon shrugged. "There are far fewer lamia than there are empousa, though, and Hecate had sent the bulk of them to other regions where large numbers of empousa have been reported."

"There were only a handful in Siberia," Prometheus said. "They released poison into the water supply in a few small towns there." He took on a pained expression. "Everyone was killed, man, woman, and child."

"How many have they killed?" Hades asked, frowning down at the newest addition to the map.

"A few thousand humans," Prometheus replied, his face pained.

"There doesn't seem to be any rhyme or reason to where they've chosen to attack."

I rubbed the bridge of my nose, then dropped my hand to my side. "We need to take them out," I said flatly, looking at my father. "The Tels. They've got a hand in everything."

"Agreed," Atlas growled.

"Yes, I'd like to come up with a plan to deal with them fully as soon as possible," Poseidon replied.

"Do we have any idea where they're holed up?" I asked. "Where they're getting their supplies? Why they chose the area they did?"

"Eris is doing some reconnaissance tonight, so we should know more when she returns," Zeus replied. He tossed another green marker over Norway. "At last report, however, she thought they were in Scandinavia, possibly somewhere in Iceland. We're hoping she'll be able to pinpoint a location soon."

"That's their only location?" I asked dubiously. "That doesn't seem terribly prudent."

"They're cocky," Hades said. "That doesn't have a tendency to mix well with prudent."

"No, it does not," Zeus said. "Once she has a more precise location, I'll have Artemis send out teams to monitor their activity."

"If they're in one spot, we should just take them all at once," I said.

My father nodded. "That would be ideal. Although an attack like that requires careful planning, so we need to be smart about it."

"Send Tessa in with Eris," Poseidon suggested. "With Tessa absorbing Eris' power, while drawing on the others she's become proficient in—"

"No." Zeus' tone rang with finality. "We don't need our enemy knowing just how valuable a weapon she is just yet."

"I would appreciate it if you stopped referring to my sister as a weapon," Atlas said quietly. "The last time someone did that, she died."

Zeus sent him a level look. "We're all weapons in this war, Atlas. It just so happens she is one that the world has yet to fully understand.

Waiting until the opportune time to release her is of the utmost importance."

A headache began to build at the base of my skull. This was an argument that was becoming cyclical at this point, and I just didn't have it in me to join in.

Without bothering with a goodbye, I turned and left, then teleported myself home the moment I stepped outside.

NATHANIEL

4

Foolishly, when I returned from questioning Menoetius, I'd hoped to find my house quiet—and preferably empty of anyone who wasn't currently living there. As with most things lately, I had no such luck.

When I opened the front door, I found Apollo and Hermes on my couch, each holding a glass of wine—*my* wine—and Tessa and Yana were nowhere to be seen. I paused when I stepped inside, contemplating suggesting they both go enjoy their own supplies of alcohol, but I couldn't muster up enough energy for that much snark. Instead, I dropped down on the couch across from Apollo and leaned my head on the back of the sofa.

"Rough day?" Hermes asked.

"You could say that," I murmured, closing my eyes. "Where are Tessa and Yana?"

"Tessa took Yana to the dorms to get her belongings," Apollo replied tersely.

I arched a brow and lifted my head to look at him. "I'm surprised you let them go."

Hermes snorted, then topped off his glass from the bottle of wine that was sitting on the coffee table. "He didn't. They went."

Giving in, I took a glass off the cabinet behind the sofa and poured some for myself. "Yana should have her things here if she's going to be staying. She's been wearing Tessa's clothes the last two days."

"I offered to send someone for her, but she wouldn't have it," Apollo groused.

Hermes' lips wobbled. "Then she insulted his mother."

I gave Apollo a surprised look. "She insulted Leto, and she's still breathing?"

His lip curled in a sneer. "I am *trying* to be patient with all of these broken immortals. It's incredibly frustrating when they refuse my help."

"Not every problem can be fixed with healing magic, Apollo," Hermes said quietly.

"Clearly," Apollo muttered.

I scrubbed my hands over my face, suddenly feeling exhausted, then looked at him. "Considering what's happened, can you blame Yana for wanting to get her things herself?"

"Of course not. It doesn't change—"

"Just because she's an Ischyra doesn't mean you can control every aspect of her life," I said.

"Is she?" He raised his eyebrows in challenge. "She no longer has her powers. Can we still call her that? Is there even a reason to keep her on this damn mountain anymore?"

"You know what I mean," I said wearily. "She's still an immortal. One of us. We need to give her the same courtesy we would give each other. She's got exactly three living friends left, one of whom is locked in a cell and another who's missing. Cut her a break. And if you think she'll leave, if you think it's safe for her to leave, with everything that's going on, you're a fool."

"He's right, Apollo," Hermes said. "You need to bend on this one."

"That seems to be all I do these days," Apollo grumbled.

"How long have they been gone?" I asked.

"An hour or so," Hermes replied. "Tessa and I did some work on mindlinking, but I'll let her fill you in when she gets home. How are her shields coming?"

Hades and I had been working with Tessa each night, teaching her how to use her mental shields instinctually. She was a fast learner, and once she truly put her mind to it, it hadn't taken more than a couple of nights for her to manage blocking us out while she slept once she truly put her mind to it. As unfortunate as it was, the attack on Athens and the arena seemed to have given her motivation and confidence a much-needed jump-start.

"She kept Hades and me both out the last two nights, so she seems to have gotten that down," I answered. "We'll keep working with her for a bit longer, though."

"No dream walks, then?" Apollo asked.

"None."

He sighed. "And Menoetius?"

"More difficult than I'd hoped. I thought the magic that disabled his powers in the dungeon would at least weaken his mental walls, but they're more complex than I expected. I wanted to give Tessa more time to deal with Yana and Mary, but I'm going to need her help."

The door opened then, and Tessa and Yana walked in, each loaded down with luggage. With a huff, they dropped the bags just inside the door.

"What took you so long?" Apollo asked. "Did anyone see you?"

"We packed up all the recruits' things," Tessa told him. "And no, nobody saw us, so you can relax." She gave him a teasing smile, which he returned with a stony glare.

I gave them an amused look. "What's all that?"

"Mary and Anette's stuff," Tessa replied, walking over to the liquor cabinet and pouring wine for herself and Yana. "If either come back soon, we didn't want them to have to deal with going to the dorms to pack everything up." After handing off a glass to Yana, who didn't acknowledge anyone before sitting down in front of the fireplace, Tessa sat down next to me and tucked herself under my arm.

I kissed the top of her head. "I hear you were mind linking. How'd that go?"

She stared thoughtfully into her glass for a moment before responding. "Okay, I guess. I saw them all. Mary, Josh, Cronus, the missing Pleiades. They were in a stone cell with a slanted ceiling with a square cut into it that was letting in sunlight. Other than that, nothing identifiable."

"That's a good thing," I told her. "It might not have been much, but it's more than we had yesterday."

"I know. I'm sick of everything we try not working, though. There has to be *something* we can do."

"It confirms they're all alive, at least," Apollo said. "Did it seem as though they'd been draining Mary's power?"

Tessa shook her head. "No, and I was kicked out before I could find out anything more."

"Kicked out?" I frowned. "By Mary?"

"No, Josh." She traced her finger along the edge of her glass, her expression tense. "He just looked into her eyes and booted me. It was like he could see straight through her to me."

"Has Father learned anything more about Josh's origins?" Hermes asked me.

"Nothing new. We still have no clue who his parents are or what kind of power he has," I said, trying not to let my irritation at that fact show. "I think Hecate needs to question her witches again."

"She's questioned them three times," Apollo said. "None know anything about him."

"Everyone comes from somewhere," Yana muttered.

Apollo's jaw tensed at her tone. "Obviously, but we can only work with the information we have, which is minimal. Aside from the last four years in Renville, we can't get any trace on him."

Tessa pursed her lips. "It doesn't make sense. It shouldn't be this difficult to trace his magic. Scylla was able to see Josh when she examined the traces of his magic from Anette's mindlink. This shouldn't be any different."

"I'm starting to think he wanted to be seen," Hermes said with a sigh. "No witch could be as powerful as he seems, only to slip up exactly when we might see him."

"Precisely, so if one of you could come up with a brilliant idea, that would be most helpful," Apollo said.

"Has anyone checked his school records or his house in Renville?" Tessa asked. "I'm sure it's a long shot, but there might be something."

"Unlikely." Apollo stood. "But any connections in Renville are worth looking into, I suppose, so figure it out. I need to get back to the palace. I'll see you all in the morning."

Once Apollo left, Hermes stood and stretched his arms over his head, then yawned. "I should be going as well. I've got guardian duty tomorrow."

Immediately following the attack on the arena, Hestia and Hera had spent several days visiting each of the dead recruits' guardians personally to inform them of what had happened. On their return, both insisted on holding a funerary service, allowing the guardians their chance to say goodbye. After several arguments, we'd managed to convince Zeus that a funeral should be held, to which all guardians who'd lost their charge would be invited.

"What time will they start arriving?" Tessa asked quietly, slowly tracing her finger along my forearm as she carefully avoided meeting Hermes' eyes.

"Day after tomorrow, right before the services," he replied.

"Briefing first thing tomorrow," I reminded him. "This one's required."

He rolled his eyes. "So I've been told. Repeatedly."

I smirked. "Zeus isn't happy you've been skipping meetings?"

"I'm a very important person, you know." He puffed his chest out. "Battle strategy and allegiances are for you lot to deal with."

"Last time I checked, you were the only Elder in this room."

"He's got you there," Tessa remarked with a smile that didn't quite reach her eyes. "Goodnight, Hermes."

"Goodnight." He blew her a quick kiss, then disappeared.

Once he was gone, Yana tossed back the last of her wine. "I am going to bed," she announced.

"Will you be coming to the palace in the morning?" Tessa asked, watching her as she stood.

Yana set her glass down on the coffee table and didn't look at either of us as she began walking away. "I do not see a need, but if you think it is necessary, I will go."

"It might help to get out of the house," Tessa called after her.

"Uh huh."

Tessa and I watched as Yana walked down the hall toward the guest room we'd given her. When her door shut, Tessa groaned and slumped down in her seat. Of all the problems we'd encountered in recent days, I think she thought Yana's would be the easiest to address. It had become obvious, though, that wouldn't be the case.

"I wish there was *one* thing I could fix," she grumbled. "Just one."

I brushed my thumb down her temple. "No one can fix what's happened to her, love."

"I know." She rubbed her hands over her eyes then let them drop to her lap. "How did things go with Menoetius today?"

"Slowly and painfully." I propped my feet up on the coffee table and rested my head on the back of the couch. "Very slowly."

"You guys want my help?" she asked. "My Coercion isn't as powerful as yours, but—"

"It's powerful enough, so yes, Hades and I would be very appreciative of your help." I turned to look at her and looked over her face, taking in the tightness of her jaw and exhaustion that was clear in her eyes. "If you're up for it."

"The sooner we get into his head, the sooner we'll find Mary. At least, I hope that's the case." She sat up and looked at me. "And you don't need to be sitting in that dungeon all day, every day."

I gave a derisive snort. "Not according to Zeus."

She gave me a knowing look. "Even if your father didn't ask you to deal with Menoetius, you'd have offered to do it."

"I know." I laced my fingers through hers and brushed a thumb across her knuckles. "We'll go tomorrow after the briefing. Now tell me, what's your next plan for locating Mary? Did you and Hermes come up with any next steps?"

She chewed at her lower lip and shrugged. "Astral projection let me see her, but nothing around her. Mindlinking got me booted from her brain. Telepathy and dream walks aren't working, so I'm guessing whatever place they're keeping her is spelled against both of those things. Zeus doesn't seem to want to spare any actual trackers, and I've had next to no experience with that ability, so I'd probably end up wasting time if I tried, and Scylla hasn't had any luck tracing his magic anywhere past the Underworld."

"You tracked well enough when you were training with Athena and Ares," I reminded her.

"I had a solid starting point and a general idea of where they would be, plus I was only tracking them a few hundred feet at most. I have no idea where Mary would be, so no place to actually aim my tracking ability." She smiled appreciatively. "Thanks, though. I just think it makes more sense for me to focus on using the powers I'm stronger with for right now. If I'm going to keep training while all of this is going on, I want to stick with what I'm already decent at, you know?"

"I can appreciate that," I told her. "And let me handle my father. He's being stubborn about a lot of things these days, but there's no reason he can't have a tracker assigned to find Mary and the sisters, especially now that we know she and the Pleiades are being kept in the same place."

"Speaking of next steps... Now that we know they're together, I think it's time we go pay the others a visit down at Demeter's."

I nodded my agreement. "We'll talk with Demeter tomorrow, then. Atlas, too."

"Yeah." She shook her head. "Of all the ways to bond with your estranged daughters..."

"They'll have plenty of time to bond like normal gods and goddesses soon enough." I slid an arm around her shoulder and pulled her against me, thankful to finally have a few minutes alone with her. "Your family is going to almost triple in size once that happens," I said with a laugh.

"Then I guess you'd better get a bigger dining room table."

I smiled, hoping that what I said was true. The Pleiades had long been estranged from their father, and despite Atlas' absence, I didn't know how willing they'd be to give him a chance to incorporate himself into their lives. He'd be able to prove himself eventually, I had no doubt, but if they'd inherited any of his stubbornness, that was undoubtedly going to be a slow-going process. For his sake and that of his siblings, I hoped they'd be willing to try.

I suppose there was nothing like impending war to help bring a family together.

ACKNOWLEDGMENTS

To my husband for putting up with my incessant author talk, my oldest daughter for being my kindergarten marketing strategist, and my youngest daughter for just being her panda-loving self.

To every family member and friend with no interest in the YA paranormal genre who has taken the time to read my books. Your support means more than you can imagine.

To the BBs, for reasons I can't put into words. You guys rock, and it's been amazing getting to know you.

To the Bees for putting up with my constant vocabulary polls (smiles and waves at Antonia).

To my beta team, ARC readers, and my critique partner, Eric, who is NO LONGER the only person to actually like Mary's character.

To Brittany at TBR Editing & Design for my gorgeous covers.

To Jenifer Knox, my amazing editor. Your honesty and advice have helped make me a better writer.

To Nicole at Swamp Goddess for making my books look damn gorgeous.

To my fellow indie authors. I never expected to find such a supportive community when I began writing, and I couldn't be more thankful for you all.

Finally, to all of the readers who took a chance on Chaos and supported me throughout the writing process for Paradox. Your reviews, comments, and encouragement have turned this all into a fantastic journey.

ABOUT THE AUTHOR

Lucy grew up "down the shore" in New Jersey, where her love of the mythological was born when her middle school English teacher introduced her to the Odyssey. After high school, she received Bachelor's degrees in Psychology and English Literature before continuing on to her Master's degree in Library and Information Science. In her spare time, Lucy loves to read, cook, and go hiking with her husband and two daughters. Chaos is her debut novel.

Stay up to date! Hop over to www.lucyroyauthor.com to sign up for Lucy's newsletter, follow her on social media, and read up on news and other bookish things!

tiktok.com/@lucyroywrites
instagram.com/lucyroywrites
facebook.com/AuthorLucyRoy
x.com/LucyRoyAuthor
goodreads.com/LucyRoy
pinterest.com/authorlucyroy
bookbub.com/profile/lucy-roy

ALSO BY LUCY ROY

Tessa Avery Series

Chaos

Paradox

Entropy

Half-Blood Rising

The Valkyrie's Bond

The Valkyrie's Calling

The Valkyrie's Triumph

Stay up to date!

Instagram: @lucyroywrites

TikTok: @LucyRoyWrites

Lucy Roy's Facebook Page: https://www.facebook.com/AuthorLucyRoy/

Newsletter: http://bit.ly/lucyroynewsletter

Lucy Roy – A Reader Group: https://www.facebook.com/groups/LucyRoyReaders/

Twitter: @LucyRoyAuthor

www.ingramcontent.com/pod-product-compliance
Lightning Source LLC
Chambersburg PA
CBHW020354310726
48979CB00015B/2588/J

* 9 7 8 1 7 3 5 3 3 8 5 3 8 *